Hunter's
Heart
Ridge

Hunter's Heart Ridge

A MYSTERY

Sarah
Stewart
Taylor

MINOTAUR BOOKS
NEW YORK

First published in the United States by Minotaur Books, an imprint of St. Martin's Publishing Group

EU Representative: Macmillan Publishers Ireland Ltd, 1st Floor, The Liffey Trust Centre, 117–126 Sheriff Street Upper, Dublin 1, DO1 YC43

HUNTER'S HEART RIDGE. Copyright © 2025 by Sarah Stewart Taylor. All rights reserved. Printed in the United States of America. For information, address St. Martin's Publishing Group, 120 Broadway, New York, NY 10271.

www.minotaurbooks.com

Designed by Meryl Sussman Levavi

Map © Maggie Vicknair

Library of Congress Cataloging-in-Publication Data

Names: Taylor, Sarah Stewart, author.
Title: Hunter's Heart Ridge : a mystery / Sarah Stewart Taylor.
Description: First edition. | New York : Minotaur Books, 2025. |
    Series: A Franklin Warren and Alice Bellows mystery ; 2
Identifiers: LCCN 2025006031 | ISBN 9781250370730 (hardcover) |
    ISBN 9781250370747 (ebook)
Subjects: LCGFT: Detective and mystery fiction. | Novels.
Classification: LCC PS3620.A97 H86 2025 | DDC 813/.6—23/
    eng/20250311
LC record available at https://lccn.loc.gov/2025006031

Our books may be purchased in bulk for specialty retail/wholesale, literacy, corporate/premium, educational, and subscription box use. Please contact MacmillanSpecialMarkets@macmillan.com.

First Edition: 2025

10 9 8 7 6 5 4 3 2 1

For Esmond Harmsworth, for everything

Author's Note

Students of Vermont geography will know that you will not find the town of Bethany on any map of the Upper Connecticut River Valley of Vermont and New Hampshire. It exists, fictionally, between and among actual towns and villages, in the words of Tasha Tudor, "West of New Hampshire and East of Vermont."

A note about the spelling of "Vietnam": In 1965, some Vermont newspapers, including ones my characters would have read, were still using "Viet Nam," while *The New York Times*, other Vermont papers, and many national news sources had adopted "Vietnam" as accepted usage. I have chosen to use "Vietnam" to avoid reader confusion.

I have struggled with the use of the word "Negro" in writing this book. While it was in wide use in 1965 across many swaths of American society and was accepted usage in newspapers and in most scholarship and speech at the time, it is a word that has the potential to hurt and offend my readers and I do not use it lightly. I tried not using it in the spirit of not causing harm and determined that the resulting coyness, born of my own discomfort, was actually detrimental to a full understanding of Vermont and America during this period. The book *The Free Men,* by John Ehle, which is about the work of my father-in-law, John Dunne, and other activists during the civil rights movement in North Carolina, was helpful to me in researching the use of the word by Black and white activists in 1965 and in the years leading up to it.

Hunter's
Heart
Ridge

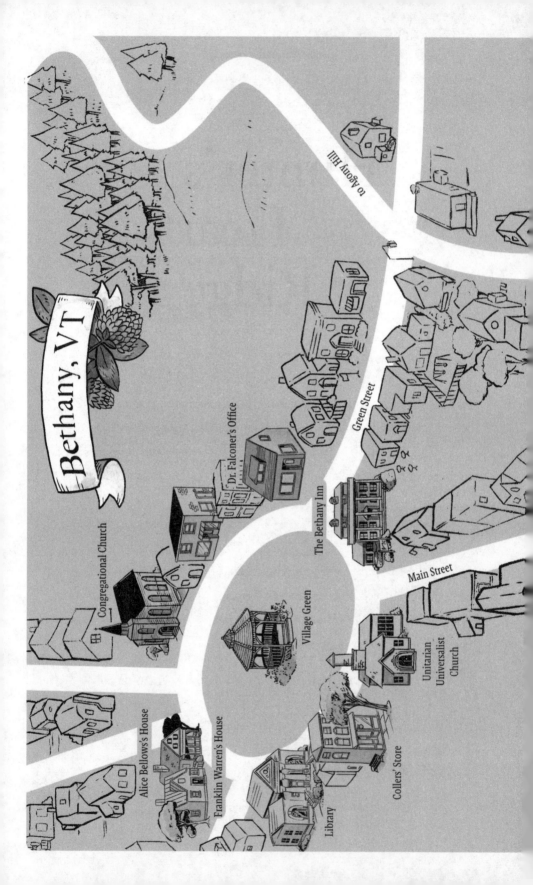

One

Most Sundays, Collers' Store on the green in Bethany, Vermont, was nearly deserted at ten thirty in the morning. The townspeople who were up and about at that hour were headed to church and didn't stop in for their papers and necessities until they had worshipped at their chosen venue, socialized for the requisite hour, and then determined it was time to be on the way. Though it was the day of rest, most residents of Bethany would have too much to do to lounge around all afternoon. Some would go home to farm chores. Some to kitchen duty preparing Sunday dinner. Shopkeepers like the Coller family would spend Sunday evening with the accounting and inventory books, getting ready for the week.

But at ten thirty in the morning on the second Sunday of Vermont's regular deer hunting season, Collers' was very busy—and decidedly more colorful than usual, thought Vermont State Police detective Franklin Warren. Standing around in small groups outside and purchasing beef jerky and donuts inside were an endless stream of men in red-and-black- or bright-green-and-black-checked hunting jackets, rifles stowed in their trucks. One street over from the green, at

Tyler's Texaco, the Fish and Game Department had set up a checking station to weigh and catalog the harvested deer. Those who had been successful that morning or the day before drove up in their trucks and unloaded the tagged deer, then loaded them back up again when they were done. While they waited, the lucky hunters told stories and exchanged vital statistics; there was a general air of festivity and good-natured ribbing and boasting.

Just a week ago, Warren had celebrated opening weekend of hunting season by joining a group of men from his new home at a deer camp about an hour out of town. The deer camp had been in the family of David Williamson for three generations now, and Williamson, the premier lawyer—one of four—in Bethany, had invited Warren along as soon as he heard he had some hunting experience. Warren had taken it as a gesture of goodwill toward a newly arrived resident and perhaps also as a means of getting in with the new state police detective stationed in town.

He had enjoyed himself much more than he thought he would, getting benignly drunk with the men and boys at night and spending last Sunday out in the woods with Williamson and his wife, who wouldn't stay at camp but liked to hunt, and Williamson's son and grandson, who had shot a spike horn. Sitting in the quiet woods and soaking in the primally satisfying sights of bare trees and trickling streams and distant hilltops had filled Warren up in some important way.

He had been consumed by his new job since arriving in Vermont three months ago, when he'd immediately been tossed into the middle of a confounding investigation. Since then, he'd been working twice as hard to make up for what he saw as his shortcomings in that business, though those shortcomings were known only to himself and a few other people in town. There had been some successes in the last month—a home robbery solved, a runaway teenager returned—but he didn't feel like he'd really been able to show Detective Lieutenant Tommy Johnson, his supervisor with the

Vermont State Police, what he could do. He didn't feel like he'd proven his worth. That kind of pressure was wearing; getting away from it all out in the woods last week had been just what he'd needed.

What he needed today was a pint of milk and the weekly newspaper.

"Busy, huh, Lizzie?" Warren asked as he stepped up to the counter and greeted Lizzie Coller, a small, frazzled-looking figure ringing up purchases on the imposing old cash register, the shelves and wall behind her a collage of interesting notices, advertisements, and products. He added a fresh donut from the huge glass jar on the counter to his purchases.

"Too busy," Lizzie said grumpily. Lizzie was always grumpy. "Dorothy had to make more donuts and she's supposed to be off her feet." Lizzie's sister Dorothy was about to have a baby, though no one in the Coller family had directly acknowledged this fact. Warren had the feeling that one day he would walk into the store and there would be a baby behind the counter next to Dorothy, and none of them would say a word about it.

Warren looked around the cluttered store, feeling a reassuring sense of familiarity. He'd lived in Bethany for three months now, and he realized with a start that if an out-of-towner asked him where to find the sugar or wrenches or ammunition, he'd be able to confidently direct them to the right section.

Finished paying, he tucked the paper sack under his arm and walked across the green, passing by a green Ford truck with a field-dressed buck lying in the bed. "Sorry, buddy," Warren said to the lolling head as he passed.

As he walked, he opened up the weekly edition of the *Bethany Register*, finding the social column, which informed him that Mr. and Mrs. Don Baldwin would be welcoming Mrs. Baldwin's parents and sister Tess's family from Springfield, Massachusetts, for the Thanksgiving holiday later this week. Mrs. Baldwin would be preparing a traditional roast turkey with stuffing and cranberry sauce. The Putnam family would be traveling to Burlington to celebrate the holiday with Mr. Putnam's sister's family. Warren skimmed the rest of the page and turned to the sports section and Fred in the Field, the regular sports-and-hunting column written by the paper's editor, Fred Fielder.

As you head out into the woods, Fielder admonished the deer hunters among his readership, *remember your good manners and make sure to take all safety precautions. You are part of an enduring tradition that is as much a part of Vermont as our maple trees and our rushing brooks and streams.*

Warren looked up from the paper as he approached his own house on the green. Sitting next to his Ford Galaxie in his driveway was a distinctively marked Vermont State Police cruiser.

And standing next to the open driver's side door was Trooper Walter "Pinky" Goodrich, Warren's assistant. Pinky's red hair against the green of his uniform reminded Warren of the bright leaves that had only recently fallen from the maple trees in the hills and valleys of his new home. When Pinky saw Warren approaching, he waved and started walking toward him.

Warren felt his heart speed up. It was Sunday. They were both supposed to be off duty.

Something was wrong.

"Sorry to bother you, Detective Warren," Pinky called. "But there's been a hunting accident at the Ridge Club. There's a man dead and he's . . . Well, I'll tell you everything on the way, but they want us to go out there right now."

Two

Once they were on the road in the cruiser, Warren said, "Okay, what have you got? Tell me about the notification first."

"Well," Pinky said, his eyes on the road. He was thinking hard, Warren could tell, trying to get it all in the right order. "Dispatch had a call from the Ridge Club that there had been a hunting accident. Victim dead from a gunshot wound in the woods. The regional medical examiner's already been out and called it."

"Tell me about the club first."

"Private hunting and fishing club." Warren didn't say anything, so Pinky kept going. "They've got a lot of members from Boston and Washington and so forth. Summer people. A few from around here too."

"Where's the club? Which town?" Warren asked. This was an important question. The answer to it would tell Warren who had jurisdiction.

"Hillyer," Pinky said. "You been over there yet? It's a pretty small place. Much smaller than Bethany. They don't even have a police department. So we got the call right away."

Warren felt a bit of relief at that. He was finding the Bethany police chief, Roy Longwell, difficult to work with, and he was glad to know that the state police might have clear title to this investigation. He had driven through Hillyer on one of his rambling drives as he was getting to know his new home. It had a small lake with a summer camp on it and, from what Warren could tell, some fairly expensive houses, older ones at the small crossroads that passed for a village center, and newer ones climbing up the hillsides near the ski mountain. There wasn't any industry to speak of, just some picturesque hill farms and proximity to the lake and the mountain, which Warren was betting made it popular with summer residents and winter sports enthusiasts.

"Do you know the name of the deceased?" Warren asked.

Pinky hesitated. There was something here. "Well," he said, "when the call came in, they told Tricia that Ambassador Moulton was dead."

"Ambassador? To where?" Warren said, turning to look at Pinky. This explained his demeanor. The dead man was a prominent person.

"I don't know."

"Has his family been notified? The State Department?"

"His wife died a few years ago, according to the other men at the club. He has one son, in California. Tricia was trying to find a number for him. We thought you'd want to talk to him. I don't know about whether anybody's called Washington."

They left town and drove west, toward the slopes of the Green Mountains and the remote valleys in the state's interior, passing through a couple of villages and town centers. Warren was starting to get a feel for these little Vermont communities. They seemed to be uniform distances apart, with the bigger farms on the outskirts and lining the river valleys or climbing a little ways up into the foothills. As they drove out of one village, Warren spotted a group of hunters up ahead on the road, rifles slung over their shoulders. Pinky slowed and they waved as the car passed.

"What kind of place is this club?" Warren asked after a bit.

Pinky stopped at a stop sign. "The Ridge Club? Well, as far as I know, it was founded by Cyrus Pillsbury back in, oh, maybe the 1880s or so. You know who Pillsbury was?"

"That big mansion just out of town, right?" Warren asked. "And the library. Wasn't he some kind of industrialist?"

"Yeah, that's right. He made his fortune in Worcester, Massachusetts, and built the place in Bethany as a summer home. He and some men in town who liked to fish founded the club. There was already a nice pond there, and they dammed up the brooks and made it bigger, stocked it with trout. They bought up a lot of the land around it and built a sort of lodge in, say, 1890 maybe. There's fishing and hunting and dinners. Like I said, a few men in town are members but it's mostly people from away." Pinky's family were moderately prosperous farmers in Bethany with many generations on their land, but Warren had noticed that he drew invisible lines between himself and the summer residents of Bethany. "I remember my dad telling me that presidents of the United States have come to fish and hunt at the Ridge Club."

"Really?" Since arriving in Vermont in August, Warren had been surprised at the contradictions his new home contained. On the one hand, it was a place that seemed to exist in the past, small towns that in many ways seemed more from the 1860s than the 1960s, inhabited by farmers who had never left their hometowns. But those little towns had raised titans of industry and crusading journalists, and there were celebrities and politicians and diplomats who made their summer homes here, state-of-the-art factories that manufactured machine tools and armaments that had been instrumental in the world wars, and famous writers and painters who came for the solitude and the summer air.

"Yup," Pinky said.

"Okay, tell me everything you know about the scene."

Pinky leaned forward to turn up the heat in the cruiser. "According to Tricia, there were five or six men staying at the club for the weekend, and they were all out hunting yesterday. This Ambassador Moulton had said he might turn in early, so they didn't worry too much when he wasn't at dinner. But when he wasn't up for breakfast, they looked in his room and the bed hadn't been slept in. This morning they sent Earl Canfield out to look for him." Anticipating the next question, Pinky said, "Earl's worked up there for years. He and his wife, Belle, live there. She does all the cooking and cleaning, and he takes care of the pond and he's, well, I guess he's not actually a gamekeeper, but he lets them know where to find the deer and the ducks. He's also the handyman around there, I guess you'd say. He paints the lodge when it needs it and does repairs. Belle's father did the job before him."

"And he found Ambassador Moulton when he went out?"

"No," Pinky said. "He looked for a bit but couldn't find him. The rest of the men went out to help, and I think one of them found him. They brought him back and someone said they'd better call us."

"You're sure it was a gunshot?" Warren asked.

"From what Tricia said, Earl Canfield thought he'd been shot, that there was blood. Coulda been some kind of accident, cleaning his gun or whatever. Tommy wants you to look and then maybe we call in the game warden if it looks like it was another hunter."

Chances were good that it was one of those possibilities, Warren knew. Vermont's deer season was only a week old and already there had been one death of a man who'd killed himself accidentally when he'd reached into the back seat of his car for his rifle and it had gone off. Warren had been at the scene with the state trooper who'd found him on Wednesday.

Then he realized what Pinky had said. "Wait—you said they brought him back?"

"Yeah," Pinky said, glancing over at Warren. "Too bad, huh?"

Warren felt his heart sink. The body had been carried back to the club, likely by multiple people who may have inadvertently destroyed evidence or left additional evidence. There was no way to record the temperature of the corpse, no way to glean anything from the position in which it was found. He watched the cold, gray-and-brown landscape roll by outside the windows of the cruiser and found himself hoping against hope that this ambassador really had shot himself while cleaning or reaching for his rifle.

If it was anything else, the investigation felt doomed to failure before it had even started.

¤ ¤ ¤

The road to the Ridge Club off the state highway was nondescript, marked only by a sign reading RIDGE ROAD. A few small farms and houses sat beside the narrow way, and then, as they climbed, a long drive appeared, with a modern house nestled into the hillside. It was low-slung and made mostly of glass.

"People in town call that 'the spaceship,'" Pinky told Warren as they passed. "I guess the architect is pretty famous, but that flat roof is going to give them some kind of trouble once it snows. I think it belongs to one of the men at the club. That's what my dad said anyway." Pinky's father was a great font of local knowledge. Sometimes Warren felt that Mr. Goodrich ought to be on the state police payroll.

Three miles up the road, a sign reading PRIVATE CLUB—MEMBERS ONLY marked the approach to the club. Pinky slowed and the cruiser's tires crunched on the gravel as he took the turn. They followed the narrow dirt road up and up, through skeletal hardwood trees intermixed with pine and hemlock, and after nearly two more miles, the road widened and forked, and they took the left fork. In the distance, Warren spotted the silver gleam of a large pond and a wood-shingled structure with a wide wraparound porch. He had been expecting something grander, he realized—something more like the Adirondack camp his mother's cousin owned and where Warren, his father, and his brother had gone every year in the late forties and early fifties. That complex comprised a large home and outbuildings on thousands of acres of land; Warren and his brother had loved the timbered mansion, filled with dark wood and plush carpets and mounted animal heads.

But the Ridge Club had a humble, timeless air about it. The lodge itself was a large Victorian farmhouse, the porch positioned so as to afford sweeping views of the pond and the forest beyond. There was a long extension to one side, a small cottage set back from the road on the other, a few outbuildings, and a horseshoe-shaped parking area. The pond created some openness in front, but the trees crowded in on the other three sides. Pinky pulled the cruiser up next to another one, one of the older cars driven by troopers out of the Bethany barracks. There were four other cars parked at the end of the drive, all with Massachusetts plates.

Out front, two men stood behind a uniformed state trooper, who nodded at Warren and Pinky. One of the men was perhaps fifty. The other, likely in his early twenties, had to be his son or some other close relation, so alike were their broad, slightly snub-nosed faces. They were both dressed in well-made outdoor clothing: dark-green woolen trousers and suspenders, wool sweaters. The younger man's hair was shaggy and dirty-blond where his relative's was neatly trimmed and shot through with silver. The older man took the lead and stepped forward.

"Jack Packingham, officers. This is my son, Skip. I'm the current president of the Ridge Club so I figured I should say hello and welcome you." His face clouded over. "This is a terrible day for the club. We've never had an unnatural death here, not in all the years we've been in existence. And that it should be Bill . . ." He looked exhausted and worried, and Warren wondered whether it was because his friend had died or because he was worried about the reputation of the club. Probably both.

Warren introduced himself and Pinky and he was about to ask the men to take him to Moulton's body when a man and woman came out through the front entrance as though they'd been waiting.

"Hi Earl, Belle," Pinky said, raising a hand to greet the couple. This was Earl Canfield, then, the handyman and caretaker. "This is Detective Warren," Pinky told them. "I told him you take care of everything around the place. Detective Warren, meet Earl and Belle Canfield."

Warren shook hands with Belle first and then Earl. Earl was a tall, stoic-looking character perhaps in his late forties or early fifties, dressed in work clothes and a wool hat. His face was tanned and weathered. Belle, a good bit younger, Warren thought, was wearing a thick woolen sweater over what looked like men's trousers. She wasn't the rounded, motherly figure he'd been expecting when he'd heard the club had a longtime cook and housekeeper; rather, she was tall and thin and her black hair was cut in a boyish short style that suited her narrow face.

"Who found Ambassador Moulton's body?" Warren asked the small group.

"I did," Jack Packingham said. "We did, that is. Skip and I. We were making a sweep of the woods out there on the ridge this morn-ing when I spotted Bill's jacket. We brought him back, though it was clear he was dead. Lot of blood from a wound on his chest. I suppose you'd prefer we'd left him, but it didn't seem right." Warren caught Earl Canfield shooting Jack Packingham a disgusted look. Warren shared the sentiment, and as though he could read Warren's mind, Jack said, "There's animals and so forth, and you don't know what the weather would do."

"I see," Warren said. "Where was he ambassador to?"

"Well, he wasn't the ambassador anymore. He'd been recalled to Washington since July. But he was in West Germany for the past few years. He was deputy chief of mission or something there, and then they made him acting ambassador for a bit, but someone else came in. I think he'd been in Greece before that, Czechoslovakia maybe. Few other places too." Warren felt a small bit of relief. At least he wasn't investigating the death of the current US ambassador to West Germany. He could only imagine what kind of bureaucratic nightmare that would be.

Warren said, "'Bill'? Was he William Moulton, then?"

Jack nodded.

"How long had he been a member of the club?"

Jack thought for a moment. "At least thirty years. His wife's father was a member, and Bill spent a lot of time here in the thirties and forties. But he'd been abroad for many years. Frankly, I was surprised when he said he wanted to come up for the weekend." He smiled sadly. "He wasn't much of a hunter. But I think he was fond of the place. We all are."

"Trooper Goodrich said that he hadn't been seen since last night?"

"That's right. He wasn't at dinner, but he'd said he was going to bed early, so no one thought too much of it." Jack's pale-blue eyes blinked rapidly, as though the sun had come out, though it hadn't. "We realized this morning that he hadn't slept in his room, and that's when panic started to set in. Earl went out at first light to look for him, but he couldn't find him and so he came back and we all suited up and went out. Skip and I took the eastern part of the property. As I told you, we saw his jacket and we . . . when we reached him, it was quite clear he was dead."

"How big is the property?" Warren asked him.

"Oh, about seven hundred acres or so."

Warren was surprised. That was a lot of forest. "One of the possibilities is that he was cleaning or loading his gun and that it discharged accidentally," he said. "Do you think it could have been that?"

There was a long silence as Jack and Earl eyed each other awkwardly, waiting for someone to say it. "They didn't tell you?" Jack asked finally.

"Tell me what?"

"We thought of that too. So I checked his rifle. There's still a round in the chamber." Jack waited a minute before finishing his thought. "It's hard to lever one in when you're dead, Detective Warren. Someone else fired the shot that killed him."

Three

need to look at the body and his rifle," Warren said to Pinky once the Packinghams had gone back inside. "But then I want to talk to everyone who was here at the time of his death. I'd like to keep them here until I can do that. Get a list together of everyone who was on site yesterday and this morning. Anything you can tell me will be helpful: ages, employment—that sort of thing." His stomach rumbled, and he turned to Belle Canfield. "Would it be possible to make some food and coffee for everyone? There will be a lot of waiting around, and it might help."

She nodded, smiling shyly. "We were about to serve lunch when you arrived. There's extra, Detective, for you and Pinky."

"Good, thank you. Trooper Goodrich, you should have something, and I'll eat later." He turned to Earl. "Can you take me to the body?"

The older man nodded and silently led the way across a small open area to a wood-shingled shed.

"We use this for storing chairs and fishing equipment," he said.

"When they brought him back, I thought it would be a good place to keep him safe. Cold, you know, but secure."

Trooper Rumson, one of the two state troopers who had been first on the scene, was stationed outside the shed, and he nodded to Warren. "I'm going to take a look," Warren said. "Trooper Goodrich is with them inside but make sure no one leaves until I've had a chance to speak with them all." Trooper Rumson nodded and Earl opened the door and stood to one side to let Warren go in.

The shed was neatly organized, with shelves and hooks along the walls. The body was on a table to one side, covered with a clean white bedsheet. Earl stood back and Warren approached, wanting to get as much information as he could before he touched Moulton's body. The state pathologist would autopsy him, but he might learn something from the man's external injuries or what he was wearing.

First, though, he said, "Mr. Packingham said Mr. Moulton wasn't an experienced hunter. Is that your feeling too?"

Earl hesitated and Warren had the sense that he wanted to be sure to get it right. Finally, Earl said, "He seemed . . . enthusiastic, but I wouldn't say he was the most experienced of the men." Earl's accent was different from his wife's and that of the other people Warren knew in Bethany. There was almost something Western about it, a twang that told Warren he wasn't from New England.

Warren kept his gaze on Earl's face. "So, he wasn't very skilled, but he liked it?"

"That's right." Earl's eyes narrowed slightly with something that Warren thought was humor. It made the weathered face and sharp angles seem friendlier all of a sudden, and Warren felt like he'd gotten a glimpse into the man beneath the stoic, competent caretaker persona.

"Would that be true for many of the men?" Warren asked him.

Earl's eyes crinkled at the corners. "You've got it. I think they like being out in the woods, you know. Busy men like that. It's a nice break from the city and their families. But well, the deer don't have a lot to be afraid of around here—I'll put it that way."

"What about you?" Warren asked him. "Are you an avid hunter?" He was curious about how familiar Earl Canfield was with the sport, how much of an authority he was on the men's level of skill.

"Well," Earl said slowly, "I know a bit, grew up hunting in Idaho, but the war fixed me. I did enough killing over in Europe. I don't hunt much anymore."

"Thank you, Mr. Canfield. I'll look at the body by myself," Warren told him. "Maybe you can help Trooper Goodrich get everyone organized inside." Warren thought that Earl Canfield was someone who needed a job to do. And though he was as much a person of interest as anyone else, deputizing him a bit might be a useful endeavor. Earl and his wife must know everything that went on at this club. Earl nodded at Warren's suggestion he assist inside and went out again.

Warren pulled the sheet back, put his hands in his pockets, and studied the body for a moment. Bill Moulton appeared to be a relatively fit man of above average height, perhaps in his late fifties or early sixties. His gray-and-black hair was still thick, and his shoulders and chest were broad beneath the wool jacket. There was a large bloodstain on the upper left-hand side of Moulton's chest, though it was hard to see because of the jacket's dark color. Warren leaned over to examine the source of the blood, just over the man's heart, and studied the bloom of congealed and hardened rusty brown on the wool. There was very little light in the shed, and it was difficult to see the entry wound because of the blood and the thick clothing, so he took the flashlight he always carried from his pocket and shone it on the wound. The surface of the jacket had been torn and pushed inward by the bullet entering the man's body, but he didn't think he saw any scorch marks, which meant that Moulton had been shot at long range, exactly what Warren would expect from an accidental shooting while hunting. There were no other injuries, at least none he could see.

Taking a handkerchief from his pocket and covering his hand with it, Warren then rolled the man onto his side and directed the beam of the flashlight across Moulton's back. There it was: a nice, neat exit wound on the dead man's right side. Where the bullet had pushed the fabric in as it entered Moulton's body, it had beveled it out as it exited. Over the years of his career, Warren had witnessed quite a few autopsies of gunshot victims. He remembered learning about temporary cavities, and tissue disruption, and abrasion rims. What it all boiled down to was that different kinds of projectiles made different kinds of holes in the human body. Sometimes bullets stayed in bodies, slowed down by bone or muscle mass. Sometimes they exited, as this one had done, through a hole that was larger in size than the entry site.

Which meant the spent casing was out there in the woods somewhere. With the right instruments and better light, there was more he might have been able to glean from the two wounds, but the body would shortly be going to someone who had many more of those instruments and much more knowledge at his disposal; better to focus on the people and the scene and leave the body to the pathologist.

Warren explored the pockets of the wool jacket and the man's wool trousers. The jacket held rifle cartridges and a Hershey's chocolate bar. The front pants pockets were empty, but the rear pockets yielded a few slips of paper that Warren removed and placed on another clean handkerchief that he spread out on an empty shelf. Two seemed to be receipts and the third had some notes on it. Warren struggled to read the scrawl but was able to decipher some of the items: *cherries, black; whole milk; cleaning solution.* A shopping list, then. Warren found a clean envelope in his pocket, put the papers securely inside and tucked it away.

The rifle—a new-looking Marlin 336—had been laid to one side of the table. Warren checked that, just as Jack had said, there was a round still in the chamber.

The round confirmed that Jack Packingham was right. Moulton hadn't shot himself—accidentally or otherwise—with this rifle.

Someone else had fired the bullet that killed him.

The question was, by accident or on purpose?

There wasn't much else the body could tell them until they could get his clothes off and subject him to the indignities of the state pathologist's hands and knives.

Outside the shed, the ambulance had arrived and Warren took the men inside and then watched as Moulton's body was loaded onto a stretcher and then into the back of the vehicle for the drive to Rutland, where the autopsy would take place. When it had gone, he showed the trooper which pieces of evidence he wanted taken back to the barracks and, looking out across the peaceful landscape, took a deep breath, and went to talk to the members of the club.

¤ ¤ ¤

The entrance to the lodge was at the top of a flight of stairs on the wide porch overlooking the pond and the hills beyond. The trooper posted at the entrance let him through the double doors, and inside, past a hallway lined with hooks and shelves for boots and outerwear and snowshoes, Warren hung up his coat and found Pinky and a group of people gathered in a large room just past the foyer of the main building. They must have just finished lunch because some of the people still balanced plates on their laps and there were trays of dishes on the side tables. A fire burned in a stone fireplace, and the space had a timeless gentility to it. Shiny mounted fish and the stuffed trophies of the heads of grazing animals decorated the walls on three sides, and everywhere there were framed black-and-white photographs of groups of men standing in front of the pond or the lodge. What had Pinky said? *I remember my dad telling me that presidents of the United States have come to fish and hunt at the Ridge Club.* Warren was betting that if he took a bit of time to study them, he might recognize some of the faces in the photographs. The furniture was understated and high-quality, the many Persian rugs worn but authentic. The fourth wall contained a large landscape painting—was it a Bierstadt?—and wide doors that opened into a dining room with round oak tables and views of the pond through a long row of windows.

Warren did a quick inventory. There were three other men in addition to Earl Canfield and the club's president and his son. Two of them were roughly the same age as Jack Packingham and one was a younger man like Skip Packingham. There were two women in addition to Belle Canfield: a tall, busty woman in an apron who was pouring coffee into cups on a side table, and a teenage girl, also in an apron, her brown hair in a high ponytail, who was standing next to her and stacking dirty dishes. A few remaining ham sandwiches sat on a plate on the table too, and Warren felt his stomach rumble again. It was now lunchtime, and he hadn't eaten since the hastily scarfed donut.

"Hello," he said to the room. "I'm Vermont State Police detective Franklin Warren, and as Trooper Goodrich has told you, I need to gather some initial information about what may have happened to Mr. Moulton. Trooper Goodrich and I will be taking statements from each of you in turn. We will likely need to talk to you again once we know more." He swept the faces, trying to ferret out nervousness or guilt, but all the faces looked similarly shocked.

"Obviously, the first thing I'd like to know is if there's anyone here who believes that he fired the shot that killed Mr. Moulton. It would have been an accidental thing, of course, not your fault, but we need to know if it's possible." He tried to make his face friendly, impassive, so that the responsible party would feel comfortable coming clean.

"We talked about that, Detective," Jack said, "but the truth is that none of us took a shot after the last time we saw Bill. The deer weren't showing themselves yesterday."

Warren looked around at the faces. Was this true? Again, all he saw was disbelief. "You hear any shots yesterday while you were in the woods?"

"Maybe," Jack said. "But they were pretty far away. You know how it is. Sound does funny things in the woods."

"What time was that?"

The club president looked around at the other men. "I don't know. Anyone else hear them?"

Earl said, "Someone was shooting on the other side of the road throughout the weekend. I don't think it was over here, though."

Warren nodded. He'd need to pin them down on that later. "Where are the rifles and ammunition you were all using yesterday?"

No one said anything. Finally, a mostly bald man smoking a pipe and lounging in a chair to one side of the room said, "There's a gun room on the other side of the hall with racks for rifles and shotguns and fishing rods and so forth. Our rifles are all in there, except for Bill's, I suppose. I'm only speaking for myself, but my ammunition is in the pocket of the jacket I was wearing yesterday." The man had very dark eyebrows that peaked in inverted Vs above his heavy eyeglasses. It gave him a villainous air.

Warren directed Jack to collect ammunition from all the hunters and stow it in the gun room with the rifles. Then he turned to Earl and said, "Can you help?" Earl nodded.

"Thanks," Warren said. "Excuse us for a second." He motioned to Pinky to follow him into the dining room and closed the door behind them. He chose a table with a view of the pond and settled into one of the hard wooden chairs.

"Here's the list," Pinky said, placing a sheet of lined paper and a pencil on the table. "Just the basics because we didn't have much time."

"Who've we got here?"

Pinky took the paper back and started to read from it. "The, uh, bald man is Herman Westwood, fifty-seven, from, uh, Lexington, Massachusetts. And then, well, Jack Packingham. You met him. He's fifty-five and he's from Boston. He's a lawyer, owns his own firm. His son, Skip, is twenty, also from Boston, a college student at Harvard. Skip brought a college friend along for the weekend, Seth Pellegrino, also twenty." He looked up, uncertain. "You want more than that?"

"That's good. Keep going like that."

"Um, well, Earl and Belle Canfield. As you know, they're the caretakers here. Earl is fifty and Belle is, uh, thirty-five. Delana Breedlove, she helps Belle in the kitchen, she's forty." Here Pinky hesitated for a moment and Warren saw a flush creep up his cheeks and across the bridge of his nose. "Jenny, her daughter, Jenny, she's eighteen. She helps out when there's a large party, making beds and cleaning." The flush increased. "And, uh, and the last one is Mr. Graham French—Colonel French I heard someone call him. He's, uh, fifty-seven, like Mr. Westwood. He lives in Winchester, Massachusetts."

Warren felt a little wave of hope. A Bostonian by ancestry and birth, he knew these places well. Perhaps it would be an advantage.

"Anything strike you, Pinky?" Warren had been teaching Pinky to pay attention to his first impressions, his instincts, his gut reactions—whatever it was you wanted to call the messages the human brain took in without processing them.

"Well, they're all on edge, but Packingham especially. I think he's worried about how it reflects on the club. On its reputation, he said. He kept saying that he hoped the newspapers wouldn't be interested."

Warren smiled. "I think he'll be disappointed on that front, but hopefully we can figure out what happened here before they get ahold of it."

"If we can believe them, it must have been some other hunter in the woods, right?" Pinky said. "Someone who took a shot and didn't realize it hit Moulton."

"Right. So, we need to know who else was out there in the woods yesterday. The game warden may be able to help. After I have a quick talk with each of them, we're going to walk out to where they found him."

"I'll call Clem—he's the game warden—later. He's probably out straight, this being the second weekend of the regular season."

"Okay, thank you, Pinky. Maybe you could find a map and then keep an eye on everyone while I talk to them one by one. Anyone hiding something, any two of them talking about covering up evidence—that kind of thing." Pinky handed him the paper and Warren placed it on the table in front of him, holding the tip of the pencil over the first line, which read *Herman Westwood*. "Send in my first victim, please."

Westwood came in slowly, as though he had all the time in the world, and rested his pipe in an ashtray on the table before he sat down across from Warren and offered his hand.

"Herman Westwood, Mr. Warren."

"Hello, Mr. Westwood," Warren said, studying the man's fleshy face and shiny head, only a thin ring of dark hair remaining on its perimeter. His green eyes were intent beneath his wayward eyebrows, partly obscured behind the thick-framed glasses. When he took Westwood's hand, Warren was enveloped by the smell of the pipe tobacco, a deliciously rich scent that reminded him of something he couldn't quite put his finger on.

"Could you confirm your address, date of birth, and occupation?" Warren held the pencil poised over the blank paper.

"I gave it to your colleague already."

"Yes, just confirming." Having witnesses repeat their vitals was a good warm-up, and it gave Warren a sense of his subject.

This subject was recalcitrant. "Is this all necessary? I thought Bill had an accident."

"Oh, it's very routine. Any unnatural death needs to be thoroughly investigated. You understand." Warren kept his voice casual, but he was on alert now. Herman Westwood didn't want to hand over the details.

"Oh, well, I live in Lexington, Massachusetts, at 512 Furlong Drive. I was born on the Fourth of July, 1908."

"And your occupation?"

"I'm a vice president at an engineering company."

"Which company?"

"Does it matter?" Westwood met his eyes, challenging him.

"It's routine," Warren repeated gently.

"Raytheon," Westwood said. "We're an engineering firm based in—"

Warren cut him off. "I know what Raytheon is. And when did you arrive, Mr. Westwood?"

"Friday evening. Earl drove up from Boston."

"Was Mr. Moulton here already?"

"Yes. I think he'd arrived in the late morning."

"How did he seem?"

Westwood picked up the pipe and turned it over in his hands. "Fine, I suppose. I hadn't seen him in quite a few years, but . . . he seemed as usual."

"How well did you know him, Mr. Westwood?"

Westwood picked up the pipe and sucked at it for a few seconds. The smoke made Warren want to sneeze. "We were at Harvard to-gether, friendly enough. And then I used to see him here—before he went abroad, that is. His wife's father was a member, and they had a house in Hillyer, not far from here, one of those cottages down at the bottom of the main road. But then they were living abroad, of course, and I believe the house was sold. I was delighted when I heard he'd be here this weekend, though a bit surprised, since it had been so long." Warren was interested in that. It was the same thing that Jack had said.

Warren studied Westwood for a moment. "You were surprised since he hadn't been here in so long?"

Westwood frowned. "I suppose I was a bit, but on the other hand, he knows the club well and is fond of it. He hasn't been back stateside very long and now that Marjorie's gone, I suppose he's at loose ends. And he's, well, he's had a tough go of it lately."

Westwood's use of the present tense didn't strike Warren as unusual. After all, it had only been a few hours since he had learned of his friend's death. "How so?"

"Well, he . . . I figured you knew. He was pushed out at the embassy, forced to retire from the foreign service after it had been his career his whole life. Political reasons, I think. He said that was why he wanted to come. To get out of Washington."

Warren nodded. He could see it, the lonely older man, retired against his will, widowed, calling up old friends to arrange a weekend in a place he loved.

"What time did you all head out yesterday morning?" Warren asked.

"Seven, I think," Westwood said. "I hunted with Colonel French— Graham French. He and I have known each other for quite a long time and we like to hunt together. But he . . . well, he got tired and came back while I stayed out. We all came back for lunch, though, and then I went out again alone in the afternoon. When we got back to the lodge, someone said Bill had gone to bed and . . . well, it wasn't until breakfast this morning that we realized he'd never come back at all."

Warren felt a flash of annoyance. Westwood had leapt ahead in the timeline. Warren would now have to be intentional about any holes in the man's story, and it would seem odd for him to go backward. "What did you do once you were back here yesterday evening?"

"Same as Friday. Dinner, drinks, cards. I turned in early, around nine, because we were going to go out in the morning. But then at breakfast, Graham said Bill hadn't been in his room at all and Earl was looking for him. Pretty soon, Earl came back saying he couldn't find Bill, so we all went out to search the woods. You know the rest. Jack and his boy found him."

Again, Warren had the sense that the man was skipping over a great deal of ground. But now wasn't the time to get into that. He needed to see the scene and he needed to know more about Moulton's death.

The next name on the list was Jack Packingham, but Warren decided to call them out of order. He got up and asked for Colonel Graham French, a thin man with military posture and close-cropped graying hair who came into the dining room somewhat warily. As French walked over to the table, Warren saw him stumble and then hesitate until he seemed to regain his balance.

"You're active military?" Warren asked when French sat down, carefully pulling the chair out and slowly lowering himself into the seat.

"No, retired. Two years now," French said shortly, his mouth set in a grim frown. "I teach history part-time at Tufts."

"I missed out, then," Warren said with a smile. "I was the class of fifty-five, and I was a history major."

"Oh." That seemed to startle the other man. "What do you need to know from me, Detective?" There was something tired about Graham French. His shoulders slumped and he seemed pale and thinner than he ought to be. He confirmed Herman Westwood's account of them hunting together yesterday morning and said he'd gone for a short walk around the pond by himself in the afternoon.

"Who noticed Mr. Moulton wasn't in his room?" Warren asked. Would French confirm Westwood's claim?

"I did." He looked away. "He'd, uh, asked me to wake him up. But it was obvious he hadn't slept in his bed."

"Did he seem okay to you on Friday night?" Warren asked. "Anything bothering him?"

French considered that for a long moment. "Well, he'd essentially been fired, forced to step down from his post. His wife died. I imagine *that* was bothering him." Something in French's voice put Warren on alert, and as if he could tell, French said, "He seemed . . . a bit adrift."

"Why was he forced out?"

"Oh, who knows the real reason?" French said. "There was a whisper campaign. He was deemed unsuitable and . . ." He shrugged. "He was out. That's how these things are done."

Warren sighed. He had so many questions, but he needed to get more information about Moulton and about the manner of his death. "Okay, that's all for now. Thank you, Colonel French." When French stood, he placed his hands on the table for a moment for balance, and his right hand shook as he lifted it. Quickly, he grabbed it with his other hand and held it as he walked out of the room. Warren watched him go, noting his halting gait. Graham French was not well, and Warren wondered suddenly if whatever was ailing him had affected his accuracy. Could he have fired the fatal shot by accident, his hands shaking as he tried to aim?

Warren decided to talk to the staff next. He already had Earl Canfield's account. He'd wait until the end for the Packinghams and the other young man.

Belle Canfield answered all of Warren's questions in a quiet, serious voice, as though she were a good student trying hard to please. Her dark eyes were wide, and she reminded Warren of a small child who wasn't used to speaking to adults. She didn't have much to offer. She'd been in the kitchen cooking most of the day yesterday. She hadn't heard any shots. Mr. Moulton had seemed fine to her, focused on the hunting and talking politics with the other men. Belle said she hadn't noticed anything out of the ordinary or seen anyone around the club who wasn't supposed to be there.

"How long have you been the cook and housekeeper here?" he asked her. He was wondering if she'd known Moulton before this weekend.

She smiled. "I started out helping my mother," she said. "And then I took over the job when she passed away. Fifteen years now, that'd be."

"Had you met Mr. Moulton before this weekend?"

She nodded. "He used to come here, but he hadn't been for a long while."

Warren studied her for a moment. Like the other people who had been at the club when the body was found, she still seemed to be struggling to take it in. Warren had seen lots of people in shock after witnessing death. It was the normal human reaction as the brain tried to integrate the new reality with the old one it was accustomed to. It was when someone didn't seem shocked that you wanted to pay attention.

Warren, wanting to lighten the mood, asked her, "What's for dinner tonight? I think I caught some delicious smells from the kitchen."

Belle blushed. "It's my turkey dinner. I always put it on for the men the week of Thanksgiving. Roast turkey, mashed potatoes and homemade gravy, cranberries, pickles, and my dinner rolls."

Warren said that sounded delicious and dismissed her, asking her to send in Delana Breedlove, the local woman who helped Belle in the kitchen. When she walked in, Warren found himself inconveniently conscious that she was, not to put too fine a point on it, a knockout, with dark hair and blue eyes that gave her a bit of an Elizabeth Taylor air. She was a different sort of personality than Belle Canfield—more fragile, Warren thought, and also more dramatic. She seemed shocked by the whole thing and kept asking whether it would be in the newspapers. From the breathless way she asked, Warren thought that perhaps she liked the idea. She had also been in the kitchen all morning and then washing linens and cleaning alone for most of the afternoon. She hadn't heard any shots yesterday. She had nothing to report that could shed any light on Moulton's death. When he asked her how long she'd worked at the Ridge Club, she said that she didn't actually work here. "Not like Belle and Earl. We just help out when there's a big weekend or a trout derby or something, Jenny and me. Or when Belle needs extra help. I've been doing it since I was Jenny's age. It's good money, and they always give you a Christmas ham or something." Warren thanked her and she left after wondering aloud again about whether the newspapers would be interested.

Her daughter, Jenny, came into the room a little timidly, but as soon as she opened her mouth, Warren had to fight to take control of the conversation.

"I can't believe it," she said, her brown eyes wide. "Ambassador Moulton. It's very sad. Do you think he was loading his gun when it went off? I know another man that happened to, but he only shot off part of his ear. Did you know he was an ambassador? Imagine that! I'd never met one before, which I guess makes sense. They'd be overseas, wouldn't they? Silly Jenny!" She laughed and picked up the pencil Warren had placed at the top of his writing paper. She turned it over between her fingers like a baton, and Warren suddenly felt it would be rude to ask for it back.

"Can you tell me how old you are, Jenny?" Warren asked.

"I was eighteen in April," she said. "My dad says it's been eighteen years of chaos. I'm going to visit my cousin Penny in New York City next year for my nineteenth birthday. Walter knows her. They were the same class in school, three years ahead of me."

"Walter?"

She pointed to the lounge. "Pinky. I don't call him Pinky, though, because I think it's tiresome when people keep on using your old childhood nicknames, don't you? For example, they used to call me Birdie, because we had a teacher who said I chattered like a bird, but I didn't like it so I told everyone not to call me that anymore and they didn't, mostly. But Walter never told people not to, even though I'm sure he doesn't like it. Some people have trouble saying what they mean, don't you think? And Walter is such a *strong* name." She sighed.

Warren had to resist the urge to smile. Jenny Breedlove was a breath of fresh air. But, he reminded himself, that didn't mean she wasn't hiding something.

"Okay, Jenny, so where were you yesterday?"

"Well, you know that my mother and I work here when they have a big event, right? That's not our actual job. What we do most of the time is we help my father at the hardware store. Did you know that my father owns the hardware store in Bethany?" Warren did not know this, though he had been into the cavernous shop off the green and he now remembered that the sign out front read BREEDLOVE'S HARDWARE. "Anyway, my mother and I have a bedroom by the kitchen for when we stay here."

"And Saturday? Where were you?"

"On Saturday? I was working all day. I helped Mrs. Canfield and my mother in the kitchen and then cleaned the rooms and helped serve dinner."

"When was the last time you saw Ambassador Moulton?"

"Well, I guess I saw him on Friday. He gave me a silver dollar after dinner! That was nice of him."

"But not on Saturday?"

"Well . . ." Jenny thought for a moment. "I served him breakfast. And then I saw him at lunch too. Do you think he was killed on Saturday?"

He thought for a moment about how to answer this and settled on, "That's something I'm hoping you can help with. Did you hear any gunshots, rifle shots, during the day on Saturday?"

She considered that. "I probably did. It's deer season, you know. But I don't remember hearing any specific shots, if you know what I mean. Then again, I had the radio playing while I was cleaning. They played 'Yesterday.' Do you like the Beatles? My cousin Frances saw them outside Carnegie Hall. She got a picture."

"I do like the Beatles. Lucky Frances," Warren said. "Now—"

"They played that song 'Turn! Turn! Turn!' by the Byrds too. I think that one's awfully good. You know it's from the Bible, don't you?"

"I do. Ecclesiastes. I believe it was written by Pete Seeger. Do you know his music?"

"Oh yes. He comes here sometimes, you know. His daughter goes to school in Woodstock. But I like the Byrds' version better. I'll have to ask Walter what he thinks."

Warren smiled. "Thank you, Miss Breedlove. Can you send Mr. Packingham in? The elder Mr. Packingham."

She frowned. "You don't have any more questions? Is this a *real* police investigation? Do you know what happened to him? Was he shot?"

"That's what we're trying to figure out." Warren smiled again, grateful for the moment of levity. "And I'll do my best to make it a real one. If you think of anything else, let me know?"

Jenny nodded and, looking a little confused, went out.

Jack Packingham was very anxious to assure Warren that the club took safety very seriously. "I'm betting that an inexperienced hunter was in the woods and took the shot," he said a bit too eagerly. Jack had hunted with Bill Moulton in the morning, with Earl along to guide them to the spots where he'd seen deer grazing, and then Moulton had gone off by himself in the afternoon. "He said he needed some time to think."

"What time was that?"

"One, I'd say. We'd just had lunch."

"Did he say what he needed to think about?"

"No, but I assume it was his, uh, employment situation. It was obviously weighing on his mind."

"Where were you after lunch?"

"I went out with Earl again. I like hunting with him."

"So you were together all afternoon?"

Jack confirmed that they had hunted together until dark. They hadn't seen any deer, and if he had heard some shots, they'd been pretty far away.

Skip Packingham was vague about what he'd done yesterday, but Warren got the sense that he'd told his father he was hunting but had actually spent the day lying around the lodge. When Warren pressed him to detail his movements, he confirmed that he hadn't gone outside at all. Warren studied him, trying to figure out what he was dealing with here. Skip seemed annoyed, his mouth set in a hard line and his fingers drumming impatiently on his knees. Warren had the feeling that it wouldn't be hard to provoke the boy, and he tried to confirm this by saying, "Seems strange you'd come all the way up here and then just sit around the lodge."

Skip scowled. "What's wrong with sitting and reading? Some people think hunting's cruel, you know."

Warren didn't respond. When he told Skip he could go, the boy looked surprised but slammed his chair back and stalked out of the room.

The final interview was with Seth Pellegrino, also a twenty-year-old sophomore at Harvard. Unlike his friend, Seth seemed calm and mildly bored by having to speak to a policeman. He was from California and said that he'd never been to Vermont before, which was why Skip had invited him to the Ridge Club for the weekend.

Seth said that he'd agreed to come along with Skip "for something to do" but that he wasn't himself a hunter, so he'd mostly stayed around the lodge reading during the day. He'd gone for a short walk, but he couldn't really remember when. He was vague on whether he'd heard any shots, and he couldn't say whether Moulton had seemed as usual since he'd never met him before. Warren was betting that the two college students had enjoyed the club's bar while all the adults were gone. There was something disconcertingly direct and confident about Seth Pellegrino. When Warren was his age, you felt you had to be respectful to anyone who was even a few years older than you were, but this young man seemed to think of Warren as an equal. Warren tried not to let it bother him.

Once Seth had gone, Warren sat for a moment and gazed out over the pond. It was gray and dead-looking now, but he could just about see it in the spring, a fine mist hanging over the surface of the water, brook trout jumping in the early morning. He looked down at his list. Jack Packingham, Skip Packingham, Herman Westwood, Colonel Graham French, Seth Pellegrino, the Canfields, and Delana and Jenny Breedlove. That was everyone who had been on the property at the time Moulton was shot. But was it? The woods were vast. Seven hundred acres, Jack had said. There could have been armies of hunters in those woods, and no one would have seen them.

They would just have time to look quickly at Moulton's room and then walk out to the scene of his death before it got dark. After that, he wasn't sure what they would do. He'd been invited to a dinner party tonight at the home of his next-door neighbor, Alice Bellows. Warren had fallen into the habit of stopping at Alice's for a drink at least once a week, and he'd attended a few of her dinner parties, which had featured both interesting amalgamations of guests and delicious food. It had occurred to him more than once that some might find it strange that his best friend in his new hometown was his fifty-five-year-old widowed neighbor, but he didn't care.

In any case, he realized, they might hear from the pathologist this evening. It was unlikely he'd make it to the party. He yawned and was just about to get up and go see if the map was ready when Pinky came in.

"I got a number for Ambassador Moulton's son," he said. "There's a phone in the hall if you want to call him."

Warren went to make the phone call, steeling himself for the task.

No matter how many times he'd done it, telling someone that their father or husband or aunt or friend was no longer among the living took a sliver of his humanity.

If he kept this up, he thought to himself as he made his way back toward the foyer of the clubhouse, he might not have much of a soul left.

Four

Planning a dinner party was a bit like planning a garden, Alice
Farnham Bellows thought to herself as she started trying to assign
names to the various places at her long dining room table. You had to
combine people in the right way in order to keep things interesting—it
was all about balance and contrast. People fell into very different *types*,
even beyond the usual categories of extrovert versus introvert or lit-
eral thinkers versus metaphorical thinkers. You had to know who people really *were* in order to combine them properly. In the garden, you
planted tall bloomers with lower ones, drifts of dull green with bright-
pink or red stunners, large clumps of perennials with showy annuals
sprinkled throughout. It was the same with people.

Alice's guests had been invited two weeks ago by telephone, and
all had responded in the affirmative to the invitation. The roast had
been ordered and picked up by Mildred, Alice's housekeeper, in
White River Junction this morning, and the chocolate-fudge Bundt
cake had been made and left to cool. Mildred, who did not usually
work on Sundays, would return after church to oversee the roast and
help Alice set the table. Alice herself had skipped church this morning

in order to peel potatoes for the *dauphinoise* and to trim the brussels sprouts. It had felt like a good day to stay inside, the November morning becoming increasingly bitter as Alice walked across the Bethany green for her papers and the candles she'd forgotten to buy last week and returned to stoke the fire in the kitchen woodstove. She'd had Billy, who helped her in the garden, lay fires in the dining room and living room fireplaces and bring in enough wood to keep them going during her party, but she didn't want to light them yet. So she brought her paper and pencil into the warm kitchen, drew a long rectangle on one of the pieces of paper, and started composing the party.

Alice herself would sit at one end of the table, and at the other, she would put her best friend Louise's husband, Theron. Theron, whom Alice and Louise had known since they were all children at the two-room Bethany Village Schoolhouse, was like a brother to Alice and he never minded playing host at her parties. Alice smiled at the prospect of seeing Louise tonight. She and Theron had been traveling a lot, visiting with their adult children, who had all settled in various far-flung places and were starting to have children of their own. Alice knew that this was the way of things when people became grandparents, but she couldn't help but resent all those babies and toddlers that had been keeping Louise from her weekly walks or teas with Alice. The party was in their honor, now that they were back in Bethany after their travels.

Louise herself would go in the center of the table on the fireplace side. Next to her on one side would be Alice's next-door neighbor, Detective Franklin Warren. Warren, as he was called by almost everyone who knew him, had moved to Bethany from Boston in August to take a job with the Vermont State Police. He and Alice had settled into a comfortable and neighborly friendship that Alice realized she'd come to value.

He also, by virtue of his job, *knew things*. Alice valued that as well.

On the other side of Louise would be Dr. Norman Falconer and next to Warren she'd put Dr. Falconer's wife, Rose. Their daughter, Barbara, a teacher in town, would go on the other side of the table, next to Theron. Barbara was engaged to a man who was due to be sent to Vietnam any day now. Her brother was completing his training too, and Alice knew that it all was weighing on the family and hoped that the party would give them a brief reprieve. Alice played with the seating assignments as though she were putting together a jigsaw puzzle, and finally, she had things just the way she wanted. She got out the fancy place cards from Garamelli's in Rutland and her nice pen, and she wrote the names in her best calligraphic writing on each card. When Mildred returned, they'd set the table and put out the cards.

Alice stood up and stretched her neck, which was stiff from the effort. It was one, time for a cup of tea, and then she would continue getting ready.

She had just filled the kettle when she heard a quiet tapping sound and looked up to see where it was coming from. Peering through the window over the sink yielded no explanation, but when she heard the tapping again and identified it as coming from the back door, she opened it to find her old friend Arthur Crannock standing there.

"Arthur!" Alice exclaimed. "Goodness! I didn't know you were in Vermont this weekend. Why didn't Wanda tell me?"

Arthur, an unassuming and still boyish man with thinning hair, mostly white now, and alert blue eyes, stepped into the kitchen, an apologetic smile on his face. "So sorry to startle you, my dear," he said. "I didn't see your housekeeper come in . . ."

"She's at church. She'll be here later, though. Tea?"

Arthur shook his head. "I've got to get back. Wanda's not with me this weekend. I had to come up to meet the painters at the house to go over a few things. She's helping Kristy get ready for the baby so she stayed in Brookline." Alice studied him carefully. With Arthur, there was always something happening beneath his words, and she was trying to figure out what it was. Was the trip actually related to his work as a spy? That's what Arthur was, after all, though his official job title was director of an organization that consulted with the State Department about international affairs. On the other hand, the house that he and his wife, Wanda, had bought in Woodstock *was* undergoing renovation. It probably did need to be painted.

That was the thing about spies, Alice thought. Sometimes they were doing exactly what they said they were doing. Her husband, Ernie, who had been a career diplomat and also, it had to be said, a spy like Arthur, had taught her that.

"Oh, how exciting about the baby. Are you ready to be a grand-father again, Arthur?"

He did not look ready. "I suppose. Wanda's about over the moon."

Alice searched his face. He had something to say. "What is it, Arthur?"

"Any word on our Russian friend?" he asked after an awkward moment of silence. "When we talked in September, you said that your source hadn't heard anything about any visitors to his cabin. Since I haven't been up here since then, I'm just wondering if that's still true?" He was nervous, Alice thought. He kept picking up the wooden spoon sitting on the counter and then putting it back down again.

Alice had known Arthur Crannock for many years. And for the last ten of them, since the death of Alice's husband, Ernie, she had not seen much of him, busy as he was with his various clandestine tasks around the world. Over the years, Alice had read the newspapers and wondered what role Arthur had played in whatever bubbling up of hostilities had happened that week. But then, in August, Arthur had reappeared, telling Alice that he and Wanda had bought a summer place in Woodstock, not far from Bethany, and that he had a little errand for her.

That was what Arthur had always called the jobs he gave Alice during the war. Back then, she was married to an OSS officer stationed in Cairo and other places, but she herself did not have any official role. And still, Arthur had often sent her on little errands. Now, a Russian dissident named Anatoly Kalachnikov had moved to Vermont to live in a small cottage at the end of a dirt road, and Arthur wanted to know what he was up to and who might be paying him visits. Alice had driven down a few times to have lunch with an old friend who lived near him in Reading, but she hadn't been able to collect any intelligence on the man.

"She's not my *source*," she said irritably. "She's my friend. But no, she hasn't said anything about Kalachnikov having any visitors. In fact, when I saw her a few weeks ago, she confessed to driving past his house because she hasn't seen or heard anything from him at all. He's kept himself quite to himself."

"Ah, well, thank you," Arthur said. "You'll let me know if that changes, won't you?"

"Yes, I will. Now, how long are you in town? I'm having a party tonight, just a small one. You remember my friends Louise and Theron?" He didn't seem to. "Well, anyway, they're back in town after visiting their children all over the country, and I've invited a few friends from town. You'd round us out, actually, Arthur!"

He smiled shyly. "I'd like that. I have some things to do tomorrow before heading back. I was dreading warmed-over soup in our not-quite-finished kitchen. Thank you, Alice."

"Six o'clock. Don't be late."

He nodded and his eyes wandered to the front of the house, his posture ramrod straight and his hands tensed at his sides. What was he doing? Checking for Mildred? Why? Alice felt a sudden flash of alarm. He knew that Mildred was not here. Had he been watching the house? The thought, once it flashed into her head, could not be chased out. *Is he here to do me harm?* She glanced down at the counter. The knife drawer was right there. She could move a few feet to the right and she'd be in front of it and could inch the drawer open. She had a nice long, thin filleting knife that would do the trick.

When he turned to go, she saw a pink scratch down the side of his face. "Arthur, you've hurt yourself," she said, moving toward him.

"I'm fine," he said too quickly, stepping back. "Scratched myself on a ladder in the house. Painters left it in a doorway. See you tonight." And he was gone in the way that Arthur was always gone— silently, easily, leaving you wondering if he'd been there at all.

Alice, sure he'd been lying about the scratch, watched through the back door until he'd disappeared.

Unsettled now, she turned and went back to her plan for the seating arrangements. Now that Arthur was coming, maybe she would mix things up a bit.

It was true that Alice liked planning her dinner parties as garden beds, but she also liked thinking of them as chemistry experiments. She could put people together to create interesting reactions.

Because now, the party had an ulterior motive. Alice wanted to know what Arthur was *really* doing in Bethany this weekend and where he'd gotten the scratch on his face. She took her seating plan into the study and started rearranging her guests to include Arthur. She put him to one side of her, so she could hear whatever conversation he had, and moved Franklin Warren to his other side. Then she looked at her plan and moved Barbara Falconer next to Arthur instead; he'd always had a weakness for a pretty face, though he kept it well hidden. Unlike some. Warren would go on Barbara's other side.

The sound of Louise and Theron's car in the drive made her stand up and go to put the kettle on. She had asked them to stop by early so they could catch up before the party.

It would be so good to see her old friends.

Five

Though he was prepared for a heart-wrenching notification, Warren found Bill Moulton's only child stunned but unsentimental at learning of his death. When Warren asked about the last time they'd spoken, the son couldn't remember and Warren started to get a picture of the relationship as a mostly distant one. Kevin Moulton was a professor in Berkeley, California, and he told Warren that he hadn't even known his father was going to Vermont. "I moved to California ten years ago, and I haven't seen him much since my mother died. Oh Christ, I guess I'll have to come back to deal with the Washington house and—"

"You'll have time," Warren said. "I assume you're his executor?"

"Yes," Kevin Moulton said. "I'm an only child. My God, what happened? You said 'a hunting accident.'"

"I'm sure you can understand that there will be an investigation and we don't want to say too much quite yet. We want to make sure we get it right," Warren said. "Can you tell me about his career? I understand that he was recently recalled to Washington."

"I don't know much about that. He'd been a diplomat all his life, all over the world. Sometimes we went with him; mostly we didn't. I had a letter from him in July, saying he'd been the subject of a smear campaign and that he was coming home and would like to visit me. I . . . put him off. I delayed writing back to him, but I would have done it." The tears came then, triggered as they often were, Warren had found, by guilt or regret. "I would have seen him, but . . . oh God!"

Warren expressed his certainty that *of course* he would have seen his father, and that his father knew that.

"Thank you. I . . . This has been quite a shock. I hope you understand. It's not that I didn't love him, but he . . . we didn't know each other well, if you see what I mean. But he wasn't cruel or anything like that." Warren expressed his sympathy again and said he'd be in touch.

Kevin Moulton thanked him again and said he'd try to book his plane tickets as soon as possible.

⌑ ⌑ ⌑

Bill Moulton's room was in the long, shingled addition to the side of the lodge. The first floor of the addition contained the kitchen and the staff bedroom that Jack Packingham said Delana and Jenny used sometimes when they were working weekends. The second floor had the members' accommodations. As he showed them the way, Jack explained that the addition had been built in 1953 as the membership of the club grew and the men wanted to stay for a few days during the fishing or hunting seasons. "The rooms are pretty rustic," Jack said. "But they do the job, and I think the members secretly enjoy feeling like they're back at Boy Scout camp. This is where Bill was."

He opened the door, and Warren and Pinky stepped into a small chamber with barely enough room for the single bed covered in a simple wool blanket, a small table and chair, and a coatrack and shelves on the opposite wall. The walls were decorated with high-quality prints of ducks and other game fowl. "Thank you. We won't disturb anything more than we have to. It shouldn't take long."

It didn't. Moulton had brought a leather suitcase, and inside, they found hunting clothes as well as two folded dress shirts. An overcoat and blazer hung on the coatrack. A pair of leather brogues was pushed beneath the table. Warren had already been through the pockets of the clothes Moulton was wearing and found his wallet, but when he put his hand into the pocket of the overcoat, he found a small notebook, which raised his hopes until he saw that it was empty except for some short grocery lists, similar to the one in his pants pocket. An empty tumbler sat on the small nightstand; Warren leaned over to sniff it and smelled gin, gone now but leaving behind the distinctive scent of juniper.

That was it. They closed the door firmly behind them and went back downstairs to look at the gun room.

Jack and Earl had collected ammunition from all of the club members while Warren was conducting his interviews. Pinky said he'd checked the rifles, and as far as he could tell, the men's accounts of their unlucky days of hunting accorded with the condition of the rifles and the amount of ammunition they said they'd brought.

"I marked everyone's," Pinky explained. "So once we find the brass that killed him, we can check it against what we've got here."

"Well done, Pinky," Warren told him. He looked around the large room, taking in the deer heads mounted up above the racks containing rifles and shotguns. Another wall contained racks with fishing poles and tackle, nets and waders.

On the far wall, groups of framed photographs showed men—and a few women—at the club through the years. Many of the photos featured the same composition and content, a group of fishermen and a few women in front of the pond, one of them holding a trophy, and a label below the matted photo reading RIDGE CLUB TROUT DERBY and the year. A lone, amateurish oil painting of the lodge struck an incongruent note, but when Warren leaned closer, he saw that it had been painted by someone named R. Packingham and assumed it was by Jack's father or grandfather.

There were a couple of old pictures of men with dead deer and bears, but most of the photos were of proud fishermen. As if he could tell what Warren was thinking, Pinky said, "The deer herd got down to almost nothing for a while there. You can see it in the photos. It's 'cause they'd cleared all the land for sheep. But they brought 'em back in the fifties, and now there's too many of them. You can barely turn around without seeing a deer."

"Is that . . ." Warren was looking at the faces of the men in one of the photos. "Is that Teddy Roosevelt?"

"I told you," Pinky said, smirking a little.

When he was done looking around, Warren called in Jack and Earl and asked them if there was a key for the gun room. There might be evidence here, and he wanted it secured until they knew what they might need to take away. Earl produced a large key ring and carefully detached a large bronze key from it. "Here you go," he said.

"And there aren't any others?" He was looking at Jack, and he thought he saw the man flinch a little as he said, "No, just that one."

"All right." Once they'd all exited the room, Warren locked the door behind them. "I'll need to hang on to this for the time being." Jack looked annoyed but nodded and said he understood. Warren tucked the key carefully into his trouser pocket for safekeeping.

The large hallway outside the gun room was lined with pegs for coats and outerwear, and up on the wall, pairs of snowshoes and other equipment hung above shelves and cubbies. The snowshoes were objects of beauty, made of richly colored and varnished wood, with rawhide webbing and leather straps that appeared to have been frequently cleaned and maintained. Warren remembered snowshoeing in the Berkshires with his father once. It had been a heady feeling, moving swiftly across the snow like a paddle-footed rabbit, nearly flying through the cold air.

He thought he'd like to feel that way again. "Belle's father, Nathan, made all of those," Earl told Warren when he saw him looking. "Nobody made better ones."

Pinky had found a map of the property, and back in the lounge, Warren told Jack that he wanted him to come along on the expedition. "I want to walk out to where you found the body, and I'd like you to come with us to show us the exact spot. And Mr. Canfield, I'd like you to come along as well. My sense is that you know the property better than anyone."

Earl, who had been tending the fire, made a sound that Warren took as an expression of humble acknowledgment.

"Of course, but, um, I do wonder if you could tell us what your plans are for us," Jack said. "It sounds terrible, but will we be allowed to continue hunting? Now that Bill . . . that the body's been taken away?"

"No, I understand. Not today," Warren said. "I'm sorry. Until I've had a chance to look for evidence, we can't risk anyone firing their own ammunition and confusing things."

"Of course," Jack said. "I wonder . . . Perhaps some of the men might like to go home, then."

Warren turned to face him and tried to look apologetic. "I'm so sorry. I really can't let you all go. I imagine it will just be for tonight, though. I need everyone to stay on hand so I can ask some questions once I've been out to the site, and then when I have some information from the pathologist, I may have more questions. I'm sure it won't take long. I so appreciate your cooperation. I know you all want to get to the bottom of this."

Of course, he had no legal standing to detain them. He hoped that by appealing to them as good citizens and gentlemen who, of course, would want to be as helpful to the police as possible, they would comply without any fuss.

It worked. "Yes, I suppose so, since we were planning on staying through Monday anyway," Jack said. "Right?" He looked around weakly at the rest of the group, who nodded and seemed to sink even more deeply into the couches, to stretch their feet out toward the warm fire.

"Well, for God's sake, if we're just going to be sitting around, I'd like to have a drink," Herman Westwood said loudly.

He got up and made himself a cocktail, and one by one, the rest of them went over to the bar. Warren thought about protesting but decided to pick his battles.

He felt a flash of envy. How he would like to settle in by a fire, pour himself a few fingers of scotch, and enjoy the day unspooling in front of him. Instead, he donned his warm jacket, found a hat in one of the pockets, made sure he still had his gloves there too, and went out into the cold day.

Warren, Pinky, Jack Packingham, and Earl Canfield got into the old truck sitting to one side of the drive, Earl at the wheel, and Pinky in the bed, while Warren and Jack crowded onto the bench seat.

The truck bumped along the club's drive and then took a turn at the fork in the road they'd passed earlier, jolting along a rough track that curved through deep forest and then skirted an open meadow that Warren imagined was a draw for the deer. They passed a small, dilapidated farmhouse that seemed abandoned, and then a few minutes after they'd entered deep forest again, Earl stopped and pulled the truck alongside a pile of felled trees and wood chips. "We'll walk from here," he said. "The men usually walk out from the lodge, but this is the most direct route."

The truck hadn't been warm, exactly, but Warren shivered as they stepped into the air outside. He and Earl and Pinky pulled their hats down over their ears and donned their gloves, then hunched their shoulders and followed Jack through the trees. Warren shivered and swore under his breath. "By God it's cold," he said. "It wasn't this cold this morning."

"Feels like snow," Pinky said. They trudged for a bit and then entered the thick woods via a narrow path.

"How did you know where to look for him?" Warren asked, turning back to address Jack.

Jack called up, "It was luck, really. We said we'd take the eastern border, even though we can't hunt on much of the land over here since it's too close to the road. But someone said they'd seen him walking this way. Can't remember who."

Warren glanced over at Pinky, who seemed to accept the explanation. They kept walking.

The land dipped and then rose again, and just as it had started to level out, a small clearing came into view. Warren could barely see the disturbed bed of leaves on the ground, the frozen pool of once-sticky blood, and the spot where the men had gathered to remove the body; their boots had created a small patch of bare ground.

"He must have been watching for deer in the clearing," Warren said when Jack stopped walking to show them the spot where they had found Moulton's body. No one disputed it. "Did you or your son take anything from the scene?" Warren asked Jack, watching the man's face carefully.

Jack stared at the spot of ground as though he was trying to remember. "Just his . . . the rifle. And a thermos . . . It was a shock, finding him like that, and the blood. But . . ." He furrowed his brow, making an effort to recall the experience. "I don't think anything else."

Pinky started taking pictures of the scene, and Warren watched for a minute to make sure he was doing it right, which he was. Warren asked Jack to show him which way the body had been lying, and as the man showed him, Warren removed his gloves and made a little drawing in his notebook, his hands almost immediately going numb in the cold air.

Warren and Pinky checked the ground carefully but didn't find the spent casing. There had been a frigid breeze when they got out of the truck, but now the air had gone very still, and until a bird called overhead, there was absolute silence. Warren got his bearings and marked the site of Moulton's death on the map.

"What's on the other side of the boundary here?" he asked Earl, pointing to the longest side of the property. The map didn't show what was on the other side of the Ridge Club's property line, just a sketchy illustration of trees and roads, but they were very close to the boundary.

"Private property mostly. Few houses."

"Who else might have been hunting yesterday?" Warren asked.

Earl scratched his chin, thinking. "Could have been anyone, really. I know a few men who used to hunt back there, but I don't think they do anymore. Anyone could have come in, though, parked along the road and then walked in."

Jack hesitated, then said, "We don't mind if the locals hunt back there. We ask them to check in and let us know, but they never really do."

Warren looked up at the sky. It was heading toward sundown now. But if he could figure out where the shot had come from, he might find some evidence of where the shooter had stood and fired. "I'd like to walk around a bit," he said. "What would be the outside range for him getting hit here? How far away could the hunter have been?"

Earl thought for a minute. "Well, most rifles, most hunters, I'd say a hundred and fifty yards, maybe two hundred. You're supposed to have the deer in sight, of course, so one hundred and fifty would be about right. Though . . ."

Warren finished for him. "If someone accidentally shot Moulton, it means they didn't have good ID on the deer."

"Yup," Earl said.

Pinky was a good tracker, and Warren asked him to look for any footprints or tracks leading to or away from the clearing while he and Earl and Jack waited at the scene. Pinky set off, his head down as he walked slowly away from them. A few minutes later, they heard him calling and made their way through the trees to where he stood. "I think I've got something," he said, pointing to a muddy spot on the ground. "Boot prints. You can barely see the chain tread. A few different ones. They lead to this spot and then lead away again. It was hard to make out the prints in the low light."

Warren looked back. Somewhere in the trees, he caught sudden movement. "What was that?" he asked too loudly.

"What?" Earl looked off into the woods too. "Bird probably."

And yet Warren couldn't help but feel that it was a man he'd glimpsed, dressed in green and moving quickly through the trees.

He looked down at the ground again and pointed to something in the mud. "More prints?" he asked.

"I think so," Pinky said. "Coming from the road." He glanced up at Earl and Jack and said, "I think they're different."

Warren took his meaning. These tracks could belong to Moulton or to another hunter who had been in the woods yesterday. Or perhaps these prints had nothing to do with the shooting.

In any case, Warren didn't want to talk through the scenarios now. He wanted more information about the cause of death before taking this any further so he told Pinky to take some photos of the prints so they might be able to match them and then said he was ready to head back.

"Tomorrow," Warren said, "we'll try to find out who else might have been hunting out here."

In the murky light, Warren peered down at the map, struggling to make out the words. "What's this?" he asked, pointing to a labeled feature at the back of the club's property. " 'Hunter's Heart Ridge'?"

"That's the ridge back that way," Jack said, gesturing to the bank of darkness behind them in the trees. "It's where the club gets its name. The story goes that there was a young man from Connecticut who came up looking for land. He was a hunter and trapper, and he fell in love with the daughter of a local farmer, but she wouldn't marry him and so he set up camp in the woods, just below the ridge, and he lived out there all by himself, hunting deer and rabbit for food, and he went, well, crazy during the long winter. Some of the men in town, including the girl's father, started to be worried about what he'd do. They tried talking to him, but he wouldn't let them get anywhere near the camp.

"Finally, they took a big group of men into the woods to confront him. They split up to try to come around the back of his campsite. After a few hours, one of the groups came upon a bloody heart, sitting there, just below the ridge. They assumed it was a deer heart, but when they got a bit farther into the woods, they found the body of one of the men." Warren knew where the story was going, but he felt the chill anyway when Jack said, "It was missing the heart. It had been cut out. They never found the hunter. Isn't that it, Earl?"

Earl made a sound that told Warren what he thought of the old legend.

But walking back to the truck in the twilight, Warren found that he kept checking over his shoulder, thinking he had again seen movement in the trees. He didn't relax until he and Pinky were on the state highway, heading back to Bethany.

☐ ☐ ☐

They were back across the town line by five, and as they drove past Agony Hill, Warren found himself imagining the little farm at the top of the hill, where in August he'd carried out an investigation into the death of a farmer named Hugh Weber in a suspicious barn fire. The man's widow, Sylvie, pregnant with her late husband's child, lived up there with their four boys, trying to keep the little farm going on her own.

Warren turned to look at the road sign as they passed, as though he might catch a glimpse of Sylvie Weber if he only looked hard enough.

How was she getting along? A lot of people had suggested that she sell the place after her husband died. She even had a little money now; she could afford one of the new Cape Cod–style houses in town, close enough for the boys to walk to school. But he'd heard she'd told anyone who asked that they were going to keep going on Agony Hill, that they all liked farming and wouldn't know what to do in a house in town. He'd heard from Pinky that she'd sold some of their cows, to make it more manageable for her and the boys, but had insisted on keeping the sheep and other livestock.

The uneasy guilt he'd carried since the day he'd closed the Weber case rose up in him anew. It had been his first case in his new job and he hadn't . . . well, he hadn't conducted himself with honor. He'd gotten away with it, though, which meant that this time he had to do everything by the book.

And he had to solve this shooting, whether it was accidental or intentional, and bring the shooter to justice.

"All right, Pinky," he said cheerfully, once his deputy had pulled into Warren's driveway on the Bethany green. "Get some sleep. It will be a long day, but we're going to lick this. Mark my words—we're going to lick this one!"

Pinky, looking bewildered by Warren's sudden burst of enthusiasm, said he'd do his best and drove off into the cold November night.

Six

Sylvie Weber threw grain to the turkeys and watched as they rushed over, stepping on each other and crowding into the corner of the pen. She threw some in the other direction, to spread them out, but they just hurried that way, leaving the other pile of grain untouched.

Turkeys were not very smart. She and the boys had tried feeding them in four different locations, hoping they would get into the habit of eating in smaller groups, the way chickens would, but instead they liked to attack one pile, and then move on to the next one as a group.

They'd raised twenty turkeys this year, one for their Thanksgiving dinner, four for the freezer, and the rest already sold for the holiday, which was coming up in only a few days now. The birds would eat for the last time tomorrow, so she gave them an extra scoop of grain and started planning where to do the slaughtering and how she'd get the turkeys all delivered before Thursday. At least it was cold enough that they wouldn't have to worry about refrigerating the birds.

A neighbor had given her boys the half-grown poults in October, in what Sylvie suspected was an act of charity, though he'd said something about hatching too many this year and that he'd be grateful if they could take them off his hands. In any case, the boys had had fun raising them, and they'd get some money from selling the birds. Sylvie was too pregnant now to do most of the work involved in raising the birds, but Scott, who was fifteen, could do just about everything, with assistance from Andy, who was thirteen, and Louis, who was six. Daniel, who was only three, tried to help, but mostly got in the way.

"How are they coming along?"

Sylvie looked up to find Isaac Rosen coming around the barn, where he was finishing up the repairs to the side that had burned in the fire this past summer. He was holding his toolbox, which meant he was done for the day. Sylvie sometimes thought that Isaac, who was from New York but had arrived in town last winter and whom she had met not long before the death of her husband in August, came to check on things at the farm because he was lonely. He had an apartment in town, but he had been on Agony Hill a lot, finishing the repairs at the hunting camp he had accidentally burned down last summer. As part of his penance and the owner's agreement not to press charges, he'd agreed to rebuild it, and he'd made steady progress through the fall. It was now enclosed, and Isaac had finished installing a woodstove and was almost finished putting the roof on. Also as part of his agreement with Detective Warren to make amends for the accident, Isaac had agreed to fix Sylvie's barn, and he'd been working away at it in his spare time. It had been slow going the last month since he'd gotten a job working with a man in Windsor who built houses and plowed snow in the winter. But when he'd been here last week, Isaac had told her he was just about done. He'd replaced the boards on the side of the barn that had been burned and now he'd buttoned everything up for the winter.

"Oh, hello, Isaac," she said. "They're getting fat, I'd say, though they're not very smart."

They watched the scrambling birds and then Isaac laughed and said, "That must be why we call a guy a turkey when he's not very bright."

She laughed too. "You must be right, Isaac."

"Well, I'm finished, Mrs. Weber," Isaac said. "That barn is . . . well, it's not good as new, but it's fixed, all right."

"Thank you, Isaac. You've done such a good job." They both let the moment of sadness about the reason for the barn repair settle around them and were quiet for a bit.

"It's been fun, Mrs. Weber. I learned a lot, you know. Been able to use it working with Mr. Bruce. I'm helping him build a new house in town. We got the foundation in and we'll try to finish the framing before it snows. When do you think it'll snow?"

She closed her eyes for a moment and inhaled deeply. "Might be soon, Isaac," she said. "The air smells like snow to me. But it sometimes does this time of year."

He sniffed the air, seeing if he could smell it too. "I'm going to go up to the camp and see if I can get the rest of the roof on before that snow falls. Take care, Mrs. Weber."

She said goodbye to him and watched him pull out of the driveway in the big truck with a plow on the front that belonged to Mr. Bruce, the builder from Windsor, and then went to wake Daniel from his nap. They chatted while he ate, and then he went to play with his cars—she knew this might only last twenty minutes or so—and she went to the living room to write. She'd moved Hugh's old desk from one wall to the other so that now it looked out toward the road and the fields beyond. The fields were brown and dead, with stalks of grass and weeds waving in the light breeze. The trees were like skeletons, all bony and jointed, the branches jutting off the limbs.

Skeletons. Bones. Feathers. The turkeys had gotten her thinking about swans, for some reason. How funny! Turkeys and swans weren't at all alike, but perhaps it was their necks that had put it into her mind.

That was it. Swans had lovely, curving snow-white necks, and turkeys had squat, red, warty ones. But both birds were somehow vulnerable because of their necks, she decided. To kill a turkey, you cut its throat and let it bleed out or chopped its head off with a hatchet. Did people kill swans that way? She wondered suddenly if you could eat a swan. Probably not. She had only seen a swan once in her life, when Hugh took her to a play somewhere down in the southern part of the state and they had had dinner at an inn with a pond out back. There had been swans on the pond, and she'd watched them swimming in slow circles until a table was ready and she and Hugh had gone inside.

In the collection of poems by William Butler Yeats that Mrs. Bellows had given her, Sylvie had read a poem called "Leda and the Swan." She'd remembered the name from a book of Greek mythology that Hugh had. She'd read the book once, even though many of the stories were so strange she wasn't sure what to think of them. Once Hugh told her that the ancient Greeks had written stories to explain the world, she thought she understood them better. But she remembered the story about the Spartan queen and how Zeus had fallen in love with her and become a swan to seduce her. When Sylvie had read the Yeats poem, she'd wondered what Leda thought about the whole thing, if she thought the swan was silly to try to seduce her or if she'd liked him, or if she was truly scared.

Swans. Turkeys.

Imagine a turkey trying to kiss you! That was funny. Sylvie laughed out loud and took a sheet of paper from the package she'd bought last week, settling it down next to the poem she'd written yesterday. She liked it, but she wanted to try it a different way, with the first line coming last and a different start to the second stanza. She'd leave it for a bit and try a new one about turkeys and swans.

The baby kicked once, then settled down, as though it knew she wanted to work. She picked up her pencil and started.

Seven

Jenny Breedlove stood at the window, watching Walter Goodrich and Mr. Warren get into the cruiser and slowly drive away, the back of the car visible through the bare trees until it turned the corner and disappeared.

She sighed. Walter looked so handsome in his uniform. She had always liked a uniform on a man, and when she'd looked up to find him coming through the door of the Ridge Club, she hadn't been able to control the laugh that bubbled out of her. That's how nervous and excited she was at the sight of Walter in his uniform! She'd said *Hello, Walter,* and he had blushed and said *Hello, Jenny.* If it had been anyone else blushing like that, she might have thought there was something in it, but because it was Walter, who always blushed, one couldn't be sure.

She'd hoped that it would be Walter who would ask her the questions they needed to ask about where everyone had been yesterday. But it had been Mr. Warren instead. She liked Mr. Warren, not because she knew him, which she didn't, but because he was giving Walter a chance to be a real detective. She had heard from her friend Cathy, who knew Walter's brother, that Walter was being trained by Mr. Warren on how to solve crimes and find clues and evidence.

But *was* Mr. Moulton's death a crime? When the men came back carrying his body that morning, they said there had been an accident. Mr. Packingham and his son had found him, and no one noticed Jenny watching from the window in the gun room as they carried him up the drive and into the pond shed. They'd left the front door wide open, and Jenny could hear them talking out on the porch while Earl went to call the police. *Not a word about dinner Friday night, right?* Mr. Westwood had said. Jenny didn't like Mr. Westwood. He always acted like she was interrupting when she came into a room, even though it was usually to give him something he'd asked for. Mr. French was all right. He was quiet and he at least said thank you, though Jenny never felt like he saw her as an actual person. Mr. Packingham remembered little things about her and her life and asked her about them when he saw her. She liked Mr. Packingham, even if her mother said he was cheap and that he'd left his wife for a younger woman.

Mr. Moulton had been jolly, and even though she'd never met him before, she thought he was probably the nicest of the men. And now he was dead.

She'd heard Mr. Westwood ask Mr. Packingham what had happened, whether he'd had a heart attack. And Mr. Packingham had said, *I don't think so. There's a bullet wound, looks like. And I don't think it was an accident—I checked his gun. He didn't fire it.*

Shouldn't that have waited for the police? Mr. Westwood had asked.

Mr. Packingham had lowered his voice so she could barely hear, and he'd said, *Better if we know what we're dealing with before the police get involved, don't you think? They don't need to know everything— just the essentials.*

Jenny couldn't figure out if she should say something to Walter about what she'd overheard. After all, they hadn't said anything that was actually . . . incriminating. But it seemed important. Maybe it would help him figure out what happened. Maybe it wouldn't.

And then, Jenny realized something. She liked detective stories, and she liked listening to people and figuring things out. Her father always said she had a good brain for finding things, a way of knowing where to look for lost rings or wallets and of sensing where the deer were when he took her hunting with him. *I need my lucky charm,* he'd say when Jenny's mother said that they had things to do and she couldn't go out with him. *I'm sorry, Delana, but I need my lucky charm.*

It was a bit like finding something for a customer in her father's hardware store, which was located off the green in Bethany and was the place where everyone in town went when they needed a tool or building supplies. When someone came in and asked Jenny for, say, a particular size of screw, or a ratchet or socket wrench, she would go to the same quiet place in her head and she would look around and somehow she would know where the item was; she would just know it. Her father had that skill too, and when she was able to find something someone needed, he would look at her with so much pride and love that Jenny felt warm inside. It was the same way she felt when someone said to him *Too bad you never had a son to take over the store for you, Harry,* and he would make a sound like air going out of a balloon as though that's all the person's opinion was worth, and he would say *Don't need one. Jenny's better than any man. She knows where everything is and she can do the books better'n me. She likes to talk too. Maybe too much sometimes, but that's better than not enough. People like a little conversation when they're in the store.*

Jenny *was* good at finding things, and she was here at the club and could listen and watch them and try to figure out if anyone was lying. That was how detectives caught murderers in the stories she read. If *she* could figure out what had happened to Mr. Moulton and tell Walter, that would be even better for him. Surely he'd get a promotion, and he'd be so grateful to Jenny that maybe he'd ask if she wanted to go to the Lyric Theater in White River Junction to see a movie.

She imagined sitting next to him, leaning against his shoulder, as the movie flickered on the screen. She could practically feel the warmth of his arm coming around her and how his shoulder would feel against her cheek.

Resolved, Jenny turned away from the window. Walter and Mr. Warren would have to go home tonight, but she would be right here at the club. She'd see what she could find. She'd get this whole thing solved for them, and then she'd present them with the solution, all wrapped up like a Christmas present.

Eight

Louise looked wonderful.

She'd had her hair cut shorter and had gotten very tan visiting Julia in Phoenix. Alice hugged her and looked at her and hugged her again and sat her and Theron down in the kitchen with tea while she worked on the potatoes. "It's so good to see you," she told Louise again, turning around to look at her oldest friend, who, despite the haircut, looked exactly the way she'd looked when Alice had attended her birthday party in September 1916 after they'd started school at the two-room schoolhouse off the green.

It was so amazing how people could change completely, and yet if you'd known them as children, they could look exactly the same. It was like your brain adjusted for the years and made a new face out of your memories. *Did it only do that with people you loved?* Alice wondered suddenly. No, because if someone had been cruel to you, you remembered that face as well. The brain remembered *harder* the things that happened when you were a child. In any case, it was good to see Louise.

After Louise and Theron had updated Alice on the growth and

activities of the children and grandchildren they had spent the summer and fall visiting, Louise asked who would be at the party.

"Well," Alice told her, "my next-door neighbor, the policeman. I told you about him. And the Falconers and then a last-minute addition—my old friend Arthur Crannock. He and his wife, Wanda, have bought a house in Woodstock, and he's up talking to painters. He was going to be on his own, so I asked him to come too."

"What an eclectic group! Oh, your parties are always so much fun, Alice."

Alice smiled, thinking about how she had once made herself anxious worrying about mixing people from different parts of her life. When she was first married and her parents and sister were still alive, Alice and Ernie had come back to Bethany for Thanksgiving and Christmas and for the summers. She had worried over visiting with her old friends, whom she had not seen much of since leaving for college and getting married. But Ernie had been charming, when he wanted to be anyway, and gradually, he and Alice and Louise and Theron had become a foursome on Alice and Ernie's visits home.

"Oh, there's Mildred," Alice said. "She'll be funny if you're in the kitchen. You two go home and get ready for the party."

But before they could leave, Mildred, wearing the black-and-white apron she wore when Alice was entertaining, came through into the kitchen, looking shaken. "Mrs. Bellows," she said, her eyes wide. "There's been a hunting accident out at the Ridge Club. A man named Bill Moulton's dead, shot in the woods."

¤ ¤ ¤

Once Louise and Theron had gone, Alice got most of the details out of Mildred. Bill Moulton, a name from Alice's past, and Ernie's too, had been found dead that morning. Mildred recounted all the details in her straightforward way. "He didn't come back the night before and so some of the men went out early to look, I suppose. He must have been cleaning his gun."

"Do you know that for sure, Mildred?" Alice asked. "Who told you he was cleaning his gun?" Mildred's news reports were generally reliable, but Alice had found that she sometimes had to ask for the source of her information.

"Well, Margaret heard about it from Jeff. I guess he was hunting with his boys this morning, and they ran into Clem." That would be Clem Duda, who was the game warden and would surely know something about this death.

Bill Moulton. Alice hadn't seen him in many years. She'd seen the news about him becoming deputy chief of mission to West Germany, of course, and she'd thought about how Ernie would have reacted to the news. He'd never liked Bill. Or, Alice amended, he'd *liked* him—you couldn't help but *like* Bill Moulton—but he hadn't *trusted* him and he'd believed him to be undisciplined, which to Ernie was about the worst thing you could be. In Ernie's business, putting your trust in someone who was undisciplined could get you killed.

Only a few months ago, she'd seen a small story in *The Washington Post* about Moulton being recalled and someone else getting the job. She'd wondered what he'd done.

She had her own ideas, knowing Bill.

"Well, he was a charming man. I'm sorry to hear of it," she said. "Mildred, can you set the table?"

"Yes, but, Mrs. Bellows, do you think this means that Mr. Warren won't come for dinner? Should I set one fewer place?"

"Let's wait and see, Mildred," Alice said. She excused herself to try to do something with the unfortunate roses and greenery she'd bought the day before. The flowers you could buy in Vermont in November were so disappointing. At least when she and Ernie lived in Washington, she'd been able to buy good flowers at Caruso's.

As they finished their preparations, Alice tried to get further details about the shooting, but none of Mildred's sources seemed to have known anything more. The roast was coming along nicely, and Mildred put the already-assembled potatoes into the oven. Alice had dressed and was straightening the cutlery on the table when she heard voices outside. In the hall, she checked her lipstick and straightened her Jean Muir shift and went to greet her guests.

The Falconers arrived first, then Louise and Theron, all spiffed up now. Alice asked Theron to fetch drinks for everyone and gratefully accepted the old-fashioned he brought her without asking.

Rose Falconer, normally cheerful and ever the competent and no-nonsense nurse, looked tired tonight. Alice touched her arm quickly to let her know she knew why. Over the past week, Alice had watched the news about the fighting in Vietnam between US forces and the North Vietnamese, in a river valley called the Ia Drang that Alice was sure Ernie, unlike most Americans, could have actually found on a map. The Falconers' son, Greg, and Barbara Falconer's fiancé, Tony Lindsey, had not shipped out yet, but it was only a matter of time.

Barbara seemed to be putting on a good face, however. She looked pretty and was practically glowing, her green dress setting off her blond hair and wide blue eyes. Ever since she was a little girl, Barbara Falconer had had the quality of lighting up any room she was in. It didn't mean that she was uncomplicated, but she had what Alice thought of as sunny energy. It felt welcome tonight.

Arthur arrived at exactly ten minutes past six, quietly entering the room and assessing the people in it before Alice had even had a chance to greet him. He was wearing a blue blazer and a green shirt that seemed to have been chosen to blend in with the colors of Alice's living room. Alice introduced him and was about to ask Mildred to take away Franklin Warren's place when there was a quiet knock and she opened the door to find him standing there in khaki slacks and a collared shirt and rust-colored sweater, holding a bottle of wine.

"Warren! I didn't expect you would make it," Alice exclaimed. "Mildred told me all about the accident up at the Ridge Club."

"I should hire Mildred," he said, smiling and stepping into the house. "There's not much more I can do tonight. And I had been so looking forward to this evening. I'm sorry to be late." He looked tired, Alice thought. But of course he would be. She had used the word "accident" on purpose, to see if he'd react, but he had not. Alice felt a flash of annoyance at his ability to give nothing away.

Theron had lit the fires for her in both the living room and dining room, and it made for a festive scene now that the one in the living room was roaring. How delightful a room full of good friends and a fire in the fireplace could be! She introduced Warren to the group and then took him over to the Falconers, to give him a moment to settle in with people he already knew.

"Hello, Warren," Barbara Falconer said. "What is your professional opinion on the snow we're supposed to get tomorrow? Do you get some sort of briefing? I'm giving the bigger kids a math test, and I suspect a lot of them are at home right now, praying that we get such a big storm we'll call a snow day."

"Oh, I wish I had foreknowledge of weather events," Warren said. "But I'm afraid it doesn't come with the job." Barbara laughed and he smiled, his face relaxing and letting go of the tension he'd been carrying. Alice left them to check in with Arthur, who was standing by himself in front of the fire and staring into the flames.

"Are you okay, Arthur?" Alice asked him.

Arthur took the poker off the hook on the hearth and prodded the logs. Burning embers shattered from one and rose up into the air. He didn't flinch. "Oh yes, just fine. Nice party, Alice. Thanks for asking me." His eyes darted over to the other guests, as though he was looking for someone. The scratch on his cheek was bright pink against his pale skin.

"Of course, now that you'll be spending more time here, you need to meet some people."

He replaced the poker. "Yes. I usually leave it to Wanda to arrange our social life, but I'm glad to be here tonight. Won't she be surprised when I tell her I've already made some friends?" He tried to muster a smile, but it didn't reach his eyes.

Rose and Louise came over to stand by the fire.

"Isn't the fire nice?" Louise said. "Mr. Crannock, I hear you're renovating a house in Woodstock."

"Yes," he said. "Attempting to, anyway." They chatted and complained about home renovation, and then Alice looked up and found Mildred standing in the doorway, letting Alice know that dinner was ready.

"Now," Alice announced to her guests. "Let's all go into the dining room. It's time to eat."

The crown roast and sprouts were delicious. The potatoes were good enough, if slightly undercooked, and Alice felt a sense of satisfaction as she looked up and down the long table and saw that everyone was enjoying the meal. Dr. Falconer was talking to Louise, who was telling him about a house near hers and Theron's that had been bought by a couple from Albany, New York. "They've got five children," she was saying. "They'll have to build on. But you know, it's the house where that man got shot last spring."

"Was that the man from Washington, DC?" Dr. Falconer asked. "They never found out who did it, did they?"

"Did they, Mr. Warren?" Louise asked, raising her voice to reach Warren, who was across the table. Alice's eyes shifted to Arthur. Sure enough, he had turned his head slightly so he could listen to the conversation.

"I believe that investigation is still ongoing," Warren said. Alice saw Arthur's head tilt again for a moment and then go back to whatever he was saying to Barbara.

"It's such a strange one," Louise went on. "That sort of thing never happens in Bethany. The people who bought the house asked me if it was true what they heard, that the man was in the foreign service and maybe was killed by a communist agent. Imagine!"

"I'm betting it was just a botched robbery," Theron said. "That house is set back from the road. If you didn't think anyone was home, you might just think that you could rob it without being seen." Alice saw Louise suppress a small smile. It was hard to imagine kindly Theron as a criminal.

"We were hearing about the accidental shooting out at the Ridge Club," Louise said then. "Norm, did you have to go out to it?" Dr. Falconer sometimes got called out by the state police to issue death certificates when the regional medical examiner wasn't available.

Norm Falconer looked up at Warren and said, "Not this time, for which I am very grateful, Warren. That would have been the thing that sent me over the edge today." He took a sip of his wine and said, "I suppose he was taken to Rutland?"

Alice watched Warren's face. He inclined his head but didn't say anything.

"You must have known Moulton, Alice," Rose Falconer said. "Didn't he used to summer here with his wife in the thirties and forties? I remember meeting them somewhere. He seemed the life of the party and she was, well, the opposite, poor woman."

"That's right," Alice said. "Her family was from Rutland and they had a house in Hillyer. Lovely little place. He was just starting in the foreign service then, and they had long leaves that they'd spend in Vermont. They didn't come back after, well, forty-six it would be."

She said it lightly, wondering if anyone else at the table remembered Bill Moulton and the summer of '46.

"What was he like?" Warren asked her. "I've heard a few different accounts of him from the men at the club."

Alice was aware that Arthur had stopped talking to Barbara and was completely focused on the conversation. "Well," she said carefully, "as Rose said, he was an incredibly charming man. He was a good diplomat. But he was . . ." She searched for the right words. "Messy, I suppose you'd say."

"What do you mean, Alice?" Louise asked. Louise knew Alice too well to let her get away with it. Alice decided she'd just come out with it. She was curious to see what Arthur would do.

"Well, he was a bit of a flirt and a bit of a drunk," Alice said. "I'll leave it at that."

Theron laughed out loud in his bighearted way. "Oh, Alice!"

Arthur smiled a tiny, tight smile.

"Would you agree, Arthur?" she asked him. "You knew him better than I did."

Warren looked past Barbara at Arthur, interested now. "*Did* you, Mr. Crannock?"

"We had some professional connections," Arthur said. "Alice's assessment is correct, I'd say. He was talented in his way. Knew a lot about Europe and the particular challenges. It's a real loss."

"What do you do, Mr. Crannock?" Warren's attention was fixed on him, and Alice could see Arthur's discomfort, though she doubted anyone else would.

"I work for a small organization down in Cambridge. We do research and analysis on international development and security issues, recommend policy and so forth. Nothing very interesting." He smiled and crossed one leg over the other, leaning elegantly back in his chair.

"It must have been interesting being the ambassador to West

Germany," Barbara Falconer said. "Was he there when the wall went up?"

"He would have been," Alice said. "Yes, I imagine it was quite a stressful time."

So why had he been sent home? That was the question. And there was one person at the table who likely knew the answer to it.

She glanced over at Arthur. He was talking to Barbara Falconer again, and Alice heard him asking her about the teaching of mathematics and which system she recommended. He said something about a Japanese method he'd heard about.

And then Norm Falconer, who had been listening quietly, spoke up. "I've just remembered. Moulton. Wasn't there something out at the Ridge Club? Do you remember, Alice? Wasn't it actually a stabbing? I had just arrived to take over your father's practice, so it would have been the . . . summer of forty-six." He raised his eyebrows.

Everyone turned to look at Alice, who wasn't sure how much she wanted to tell them. She settled on "I believe it was a drunken argument that got out of control. Another man stabbed Moulton with a steak knife or a fork or something at the dinner table. He was okay, though."

"How strange," Louise said. "It must have been some argument."

Alice was conscious that Warren had turned to watch her, and she said carefully, "Yes, it was strange."

"And now he's been shot . . ." Louise said. "Have you ever noticed how some people just seem to *attract* tragedy? It's a funny thing." She went into a long story about a neighbor of their daughter Julia in Arizona and how the neighbor had lost both her first and second husbands in car accidents.

Mildred cleared the table, helped by Norm Falconer, who, Alice suspected, was just bored of the story about the neighbor. Dessert was the rich fudge cake, which had come out perfectly, served with flaming cherries and brandy, and Alice smiled around her table as everyone clapped and Rose Falconer joked that David Williamson would be coming in with the fire department any minute if he saw the flames through the front windows.

"I love flaming cherries!" Rose Falconer said. "It's so festive."

"If we have another blackout, your dessert can serve as emergency lighting, Alice," Theron joked. They all laughed. The widespread blackout across the Northeast earlier in the month was still fresh in their minds and, for Alice, the impetus to squirrel flashlights and extra candles around the house in case it happened again.

"Oh, Theron," Louise said. "Don't be silly." She sighed and said, "Alice, your parties are always so much fun. I don't know how you do it."

One of those communal silences followed, a happy one, as everyone let their food settle and tried to assess how drunk they were and how tired.

"So *do* you think this thing out at the Ridge Club was just a hunting accident, Detective?" Theron asked Warren.

Warren murmured something about how they'd have to see. "It's likely," he said. "But the state pathologist will tell us more. Do any of you know the other members who were out at the club—Jack Packingham and Herman Westwood and Colonel Graham French? They all seem like good men. I feel badly that they've been detained while we clear it up." It had been elegantly done, Alice thought. He had thrown the names out there to see if anyone knew the men, without giving anything away about the investigation.

Alice looked over at Arthur again, and it struck her suddenly that he had been very, very quiet this evening, even more so than usual. Arthur was a skilled listener, of course. He had a way of blending into the background and carrying on a conversation in one quarter while taking in other conversations that were happening around the room. He was paying attention now, though.

"Jack's a lovely man. We've known him for years," Louise said. "He and Miriam came to Bethany for a long time, but I heard they were divorced. He must be very upset. Weren't he and Bill old friends?"

The conversation went on. Alice had been anxious that it might turn to the fighting in Vietnam. She had worried about the Falconers and how they would feel if it happened, but no one went near the subject, and by the time they'd finished dessert, everyone was pleasantly tipsy and sated. Alice had just offered brandies when Mildred disappeared, and Alice heard her speaking to someone in the hall. And then Mildred was back and was beckoning to Warren. She said something to him, and he followed her out into the hallway.

Whoever was at the door was for him.

Nine

When Pinky brought him home from the club that afternoon, Warren had told him to come and get him at the party if they got anything from the pathologist. So as soon as he saw Alice Bellows's housekeeper approaching him after dinner, Warren had known that they had results from the postmortem.

Warren stepped outside, glancing toward his own house just over the garden gate, one light left on in the kitchen. He pulled the door closed behind him so they would not be overheard. The chilled night air slapped his cheeks, and Pinky's breath hovered in a cloud of white mist in front of him.

"What is it, Pinky?" Warren asked, conscious that everyone inside the house was now wondering what had happened.

"Well, Dr. Miller did the autopsy. He knows how Moulton died." Pinky fumbled in his coat and came out with a sheet of folded paper. Warren tried to contain his impatience.

Once he had the paper open, Pinky started reading. "'Subject is a healthy fifty-seven-year-old man of—'"

"I can read that later," Warren interrupted him. "I just want to know about the cause and time of death."

"Okay, okay." Pinky turned the paper over and then looked up at Warren. "Dr. Miller said he died yesterday for certain. Rigor mortis was well set in, and though the cold makes it harder to pin it down, he feels confident that death occurred between nine A.M. and nine P.M. There was a barely digested sandwich among his stomach contents, so that might help too."

"That at least narrows it down," Warren said. "What about cause?"

"Well, he said he was confused right away. You saw blood on Moulton's jacket, right? There was an entry wound?" Warren nodded. "But Dr. Miller said there wasn't much blood at the exit site on Moulton's right shoulder. He thought we should be able to find the brass at the site . . ." He read from the paper. "When he looked at the damage to the, uh, heart muscle and surrounding tissue, he was really confused. He said the, uh, perforating injury looked *ragged* to him."

"So, what does he think for caliber?" Warren asked. Something knocked against the side of the house then, and they both jumped. Warren glanced in both directions to make sure no one had come outside.

"No, there wasn't . . ." Pinky shuffled the paper. "That's not . . . The thing is, when he started looking at the wound, he said it didn't look like what he'd expect it to look like." He met Warren's eyes, and in the light streaming through Alice's windows, Pinky looked very young. "He was shot, likely with a thirty-two-caliber bullet, but sometime after death. He doesn't think that's what killed him."

"What?" Warren practically shouted, and he made an effort to lower his voice to avoid being overheard. "What do you mean, Pinky?"

"That's right," Pinky said. "He wasn't killed by a bullet at all. Dr. Miller said . . ." He looked down at the paper again. "'Death was due to sharp force injury to the heart muscle by a pointed object. Damage to the upper thoracic cavity by gunshot was sometime postmortem.'"

"What the hell?" Warren took the paper from Pinky.

"A knife," Pinky said solemnly. "Someone stabbed Moulton in the heart with a knife and then shot him."

☒ ☒ ☒

It took Warren a moment to take it in.

"Is he sure?" he asked Pinky. "Is he absolutely sure?" Pinky nodded. "All right, give me a minute," he said. "I'm sure you can wait inside." He opened the door, and as he led Pinky in, he almost ran into Alice's friend Mr. Crannock.

"I'm so sorry," Warren said, dodging the older man.

"No, the clumsiness is all mine," Crannock said, smiling and bowing his head. "I was just getting something from my coat for Alice. Please, forgive me." He dipped his hand into the pocket of one of the overcoats on the rack in her entryway and pulled out a small card.

Warren explained that he'd have to go and said it had been nice to meet him. He'd liked Crannock, a gentle man who had asked Warren all about his impressions of Vermont. Earlier in the evening, they had traded Boston details and had a pleasant conversation, but the whole time, Warren had felt that the man was studying him, trying to read him, perhaps, and it occurred to Warren that Crannock must remember Warren's name from the newspapers.

And then Mildred had come to get him and said that Pinky was at the door.

Now, he found Alice back in the living room, to which the party had moved, and explained that he'd been called away. Her eyes lit up with interest, and he knew she wanted to ask what had happened, but she just said that she was sorry. "I had a good time," he told her. "Please make my apologies to your guests. I so enjoyed talking with them, and the food was delicious."

"Are you going so soon?" Barbara Falconer asked, turning to him from a conversation she'd been having with Louise and Theron. "It's so early."

"The case, I'm afraid," Warren told her, conscious of Mr. Crannock, now standing by the bar cart and fixing a drink. He wasn't obviously listening, but for some reason Warren again had the sense that he'd been keeping track of Warren's movements. Why did Mr. Crannock care about this case?

"Well, it's our loss." Barbara took his hand, and he felt a little flash of happiness. She looked beautiful, her skin luminous against her green dress and her eyes full of humor. In the three months since he'd moved to Bethany, Warren had come to consider Barbara Falconer a friend. She always lifted his spirits; she was a sunny, optimistic person by nature, and whenever he found himself in one of the low moods that had plagued him all his life and that had been more frequent since the tragedy of two years ago that had led him to quit his job in Boston and take one in Vermont, running into Barbara at Collers' Store or in the tavern at the Bethany Inn brought him out of it, if only for a minute or two. She was a little bit tipsy, Warren thought, and he told himself that that was why she held his hand a moment longer than necessary.

"Is there any chance this was an accident?" Warren asked Pinky once they were sitting at Warren's kitchen table next door and he was reading over Pinky's detailed notes from his conversation with the state pathologist. "Any chance at all?"

"It seems hard to imagine," Pinky said. "Most deer hunters would take a knife out with them for field dressing and maybe if there was a . . . fight of some kind, but if it was an accident, then—"

"Why didn't he tell us, whoever it was? And why finish him off with a rifle shot?" Warren asked. "We've got to question them all again tomorrow. Properly. Figure out exactly where they were on the map. Take statements about their whereabouts yesterday and early this morning. Find out if there was anyone else in those woods. And we need to know if anyone had reason to want him dead."

"Should we bring them down to the barracks?" Pinky asked.

Warren shook his head. "That crew will have the lawyers lining up. We need to keep it very casual. Let's go back there tomorrow morning. And listen, Pinky—we won't say anything about the knife, not yet. It's to our advantage that they believe we're still assuming it was an accidental shooting."

"You think one of them did it on purpose?" Pinky asked.

"I don't know what else to think," Warren said. "Taking the knife used to kill him away? Shooting him when he was already dead? Not saying anything? That's covering up evidence at the minimum and murder at the maximum. And it feels personal, right? If so, it's got to be someone who was staying at the club."

"Maybe," Pinky said. "You have any thoughts about which one of them it was?"

"Not really," Warren said. "You?"

"No . . ." Pinky hesitated, then said, "But Westwood, I think he was lying about where he was hunting."

"Why do you say that?"

"Because that time of day, deer are heading to clearings to graze. You wouldn't go into the deep woods then. It's not on the way back either. So, I wonder, why was he going that way?"

"That is interesting, Pinky," he said. "Now I'm wondering too. Okay, tomorrow we need to look for the knife at the club. We also need to find out who else might have been hunting in the woods."

Pinky stood up and put his coat back on. "I'll meet you there?" he asked. Warren nodded. Pinky was almost to the door when he turned around. "How was the dinner?"

"Nice. And I almost forgot to tell you." Warren recounted the story of the incident involving Moulton out at the Ridge Club in 1946. "You don't know anything about that, do you?"

Pinky reached up to stroke his chin, and then he smiled and said, "I would have been about two, so I don't remember it. Forty-six— now, that was just before the state police was formed, so it would have been someone local going out. Roy Longwell had just started with the Bethany department then. I can ask around in the morning."

"Thanks, Pinky. Get some sleep now."

Warren watched Pinky's headlights sweep across the side of his house as he pulled away. He thought about going back over to Alice Bellows's house and asking her some more about Moulton, but he was tired and her guests were still there, judging from the cars remaining in the drive.

Warren thought about his answer to Pinky's question. Had it been a good party? Now he wasn't entirely sure. He'd enjoyed talking to the Falconers, and the food had been delicious, the atmosphere convivial. But the whole time he had been there, he had the sense that there was some motive lurking just under the surface. Was it Alice Bellows's motive? Or someone else's?

During dinner, the conversation had turned to a fatal shooting at a house in Bethany last spring. The victim was a State Department employee from Washington, DC, who had bought a cottage in Bethany. Warren had been asked about the unsolved homicide when he'd arrived in town in August, and he had tried to get more information before being shut down by his boss and friend, Vermont State Police detective Tommy Johnson. Warren had been annoyed at Tommy's vague dismissals, but he'd realized that Tommy himself had been told to stay away from the case by someone much more important than a couple of Vermont detectives.

Someone in Washington, DC, most likely.

Warren had seen Alice's friend Arthur Crannock listening to the conversation about the shooting, and he couldn't shake the feeling that Crannock had been listening at the door when Warren was outside talking to Pinky.

Upstairs in bed, he tried to read but he was tired, and finally he put the book away and turned out the lights.

When he'd first moved into the 1830s house on the Bethany green this past summer, he'd felt the absence of his late wife, Maria, every night as a physical ache, as though someone had hacked off a limb and left him bleeding alone in his grief. In the months since, the grief had receded a bit, though it still sometimes hit him at strange moments. But he had stretched to fill the bed himself, and when he thought of Maria now, he could mostly recall good memories without falling apart.

Mostly.

Lying there, he wondered suddenly what Sylvie Weber was doing tonight. It was likely that she and her four boys were in bed, fast asleep already. They had to be up early to do chores and feed the animals. Back in the summer, in the weeks after he closed the investigation into her husband's death, he had found his mind too frequently turning to the long, upward slope of Agony Hill and to the small farmhouse. He had spent too many hours imagining himself pulling his car into the drive on a warm, dark night and finding her on the porch, waiting for him, her arms cool to the touch and her hair loose on her biscuit-tan shoulders . . .

Thank goodness that madness had passed. He was sure that some psychologist somewhere could tell him why he'd convinced himself he was in love with Sylvie Weber. It was impossible, of course, for so many reasons but top among them that a relationship with her was unethical because of the investigation into her husband's death and the fact that he could destroy her family if he ever revealed what he knew, that she could destroy him if she was the one doing the revealing. Any connection between them might alert Warren's colleagues that though the investigation into Hugh Weber's death had been closed, there were some things they didn't know.

And as if that weren't enough, she was a pregnant woman with four children, only recently widowed!

It had been ridiculous all around.

Warren adjusted his pillow and rolled around, trying to get comfortable. Luckily that was all over. He felt a normal sympathy for her, and he worried about her and the four boys and how they would manage up on Agony Hill. That was why he'd insisted they put a telephone in, something Sylvie's dead husband had rejected, along with other modern conveniences like an electric stove and a television. Yes, it was only natural that he should worry about a vulnerable widow, pregnant and with four children to care for. It was his duty as a policeman.

He thought of Barbara Falconer then and wondered idly what her fiancé was like. Alice had told him once that Tony Lindsey was an exceptionally charming young man. Warren had not been able to tell if she meant it as a compliment or not. Alice Bellows's comments often contained hidden layers and meanings.

Women! He shouldn't be thinking about these women at all. What he needed was to show Tommy Johnson that he could do the job. He needed to apply himself to this strange case. A knife in the heart and then a bullet! What a strange method of murder. Psychologically, it seemed to signal strong emotion, madness even. Or someone who wanted to be absolutely sure that Moulton was dead.

Or, Warren realized, it could indicate a desire to hide the manner of death.

The answer must be there at the club, or at least in the woods surrounding it.

He thought again of the sense he'd had that there was someone watching them in the woods. And then he remembered the story Jack Packingham had told them about where Hunter's Heart Ridge had gotten its name.

The poor, unfortunate local man, his heart removed with a knife.

Was it a coincidence? If it wasn't, he wasn't sure what the message was in the method of killing.

Warren felt a sense of purpose come over him. He had not distinguished himself on the Weber case.

But this was a new case, and he had the opportunity to redeem himself by solving it quickly and completely, wrapping it up so tightly that the state's attorney would barely have to lift a finger to prosecute it.

Warren was bone-tired. Today had been a long day, tomorrow would be even longer, and he was not awake very long before his brain was able to shut off and his body was able to rest.

Ten

A thin layer of frost had accumulated on the inside of Warren's bedroom windows in the night. Drinking his coffee at the kitchen table early the next morning, he tried to organize his thoughts. They needed to find out if anyone else had been in the woods on Saturday without alerting the club members to the new information about Moulton's cause of death. They needed to look for the knife that had been used to kill Moulton and see if they could locate the bullet that had been fired into Moulton's body. And they needed to start trying to figure out if anyone at the club—or anywhere else, for that matter—had had a motive for Moulton's death. Warren reviewed the list of persons of interest which, right now, included Skip Packingham, Seth Pellegrino, Colonel French, and Herman Westwood. Because Jack Packingham and Earl Canfield had been hunting together all afternoon and the women had all been at the lodge. Unless someone was lying.

He needed a more accurate timeline, and now that he had a map, he wanted to mark where everyone had been at the key points in the day. Maybe that would reveal something. Pinky's comment about

Westwood's claim about his location was interesting. Maybe there was something there.

Caffeinated and full of fried eggs and toast, he was washing his coffee cup at the sink when the phone rang, and he picked it up to find Tommy Johnson on the other end.

"How's it going, Frankie?" Tommy was the only person who still sometimes called Warren by his childhood nickname.

"You hear about the cause of death?"

"Yeah, weird, huh? Could it have been an accident, Moulton falling on a knife or something?"

"The knife wasn't at the scene, and his rifle hadn't been fired. But we're looking into whether any outsiders were hunting up at the club on Saturday. Pinky has the game warden asking around."

"Good. Clem should be able to help you. Keep me up-to-date, will you?"

"Of course," Warren said. He hesitated, then said, "One thing, Tommy. Moulton was a diplomat—pretty high level too. But something happened and he got sent home in July. No one seems to know exactly what, but it could be important."

"You think this had something to do with his job overseas?"

"I don't know, but it's a possibility. It's just . . . like you said, weird. It feels like overkill . . . a little cloak-and-dagger, if you see what I mean. No pun intended."

Tommy was silent, thinking. "Let's see what Clem finds. But I see your point. That makes it even more crucial we get this figured out, Frankie. I'll make some calls. Maybe we can find out more about why he got sent home. Sound good?"

Warren said it did, and they said goodbye.

He was just heading to his car when Alice Bellows came out of her side door with a trash bag.

"Can I take that for you?" he called to her.

"I can manage," she said, taking the bag to the side door of the garage between her house and his. He waited for her to reappear, and as she came around the corner and spotted him, she smiled a small, satisfied smile.

"I bet you know what I'm going to ask you," he said, rubbing his bare hands together to warm them. "That 'incident' at the Ridge Club nineteen years ago. What else do you know about it?"

She raised her eyebrows and gestured to the side door. "Do you have time for a cup of tea?"

Warren turned his wrist to look at his watch. "Ahh, I really don't. I'm sorry. Before I head out there again, I'd just like to know if it might have any bearing on Moulton's death. What happened?"

Something that Warren had come to appreciate about Alice Bellows was that she knew when to tell the long version of a story and when to tell the short version. She told it to him with as little fuss as possible now. "I was here that whole summer. Ernie was back and forth between London and Washington, and my mother was at the beginning of her final illness. I heard that something had happened out at the Ridge Club. At the store, someone said that there had been a stabbing. Well, that was something! There's always been a separation between the club and the surrounding towns, as you can imagine, and as I remember, there was a certain amount of schadenfreude about it all. My father was a member of the club, and he got the story from someone. You were a history major, Mr. Warren. What was happening in the spring and summer of 1946?"

Warren, who had been eleven years old that summer, had been more interested in his collection of cars and in Franny Gilman, who lived next door. He did not remember much of current events. But he *had* been a history major, and he searched the timeline in his head. "Well, it was that postwar period, I suppose. We were trying to figure out how to handle the Soviets."

"That's right," Alice told him. "At the club that summer were lots of men who were intimately involved with those decisions about how to handle them. I don't know for sure, but I suspect there was a lot of conversation about that or about other things. Feelings must have boiled over, and Bill Moulton, a young diplomat who spoke Russian fluently, was stabbed with a steak knife. I don't think anyone ever told the police who did it. They must have believed that the gentlemanly thing to do was not to reveal the name. It was not a very serious wound, and he was treated at the hospital. That's all I know."

"And he hadn't been back to the club since then," Warren said. "Which is interesting."

Alice just raised her eyebrows, and Warren, not sure exactly what this new information meant, thanked her. "If you needed to buy a, uh, tool of some kind, an *implement,* where would you go?" he asked her, remembering only as he was uttering the words not to say "knife."

She raised her eyebrows again but said, without having to think about it, "Breedlove's. The hardware store. You know where it is?"

"I do. Thank you."

Warren drove slowly around the green and parked right in front of Breedlove's Hardware. He was the first person in the door when the CLOSED sign was flipped over to read OPEN at eight thirty.

The business occupied a large storefront, the windows filled with displays of tools and household items, the inside of the store cluttered but organized. When Warren pushed through the door, a bell alerted the tall man behind the counter who Warren assumed was Delana Breedlove's husband and Jenny Breedlove's father. The man nodded at Warren but left him to browse on his own. Warren had been meaning to pick up a can of white paint to touch up a wall where he'd installed a shelf, so he found that and then walked the aisles until he came upon a display of knives and scissors. The store's selection was quite comprehensive, and Warren scanned the different varieties of blades that could have killed Moulton. There were ample possibilities: a utility knife with a two-inch blade. A kitchen knife with a bone handle and thin blade for filleting meat.

A hunting knife with a thicker blade that came to a slender point. A display of folding stiletto knives that reminded Warren of one his father had brought home from Italy after the war. Warren chose a kitchen knife since he needed one anyway and took it and the paint up to the counter.

"Five fifty-two," the presumed Mr. Breedlove said, methodically writing up the sale in a small notebook after he'd rung it up on the cash register. He was a nondescript-looking man with a quiet, competent air about him, though his Yankee reticence made Warren realize that Jenny must have gotten her talkativeness from her mother. It also made him wonder how this plain brown paper bag of a man had wooed Delana.

He thought about introducing himself to Mr. Breedlove and explaining what he was looking for, but he didn't want word about the cause of death to get out, so he just paid up for the items, took the forty-eight cents in change, and declined a bag, tucking the sheathed knife into his coat pocket and putting the paint into the trunk of his car.

¤ ¤ ¤

He arrived at the Ridge Club a little after ten. Pinky was waiting for him, and when the trooper on duty came out to meet them, Warren asked if he had anything to report.

"No, I don't think so. They're mostly awake now, and Belle Canfield made breakfast and coffee. Pretty good breakfast too." The man rubbed his belly thoughtfully, remembering. "The president, Packingham—he wanted to know how long they'd need to stay today, and I said I didn't think they'd be leaving anytime soon."

Warren told the trooper he could leave and went inside. He expected to find the men up in arms at being detained for the morning, but instead, the scene they came into was a peaceful one, everyone sitting around the fire and the smell of bacon and coffee and Herman

Westwood's pipe tobacco mixing pleasantly with the scent of wood-smoke.

And yet, out in those woods, someone had stabbed Bill Moulton in the heart and then shot him for good measure. It was quite likely it was one of the people in this room.

"Come have some breakfast," Jenny Breedlove told them. "There's plenty left, and it will just go to waste. Belle must have thought she was cooking for twice as many." She smiled and pushed them into the dining room, where Warren allowed that he'd already eaten but that maybe he'd have one pancake if it wasn't any trouble.

"Walter, you sit down right there, and I'll get you a plate. You too, Mr. Warren," Jenny told them, putting steaming cups of coffee in front of them and sliding the pitcher of cream down the table.

"Do you know what happened to Mr. Moulton yet?" she asked. "Because I was thinking about it last night, and I was thinking that maybe someone tied a string around the rifle to make it shoot and look like he did it himself. I read something like that in a story once. Did you find any strings by his body, Walter?"

Pinky blushed deeply. "Well, Jenny, I can't really talk to you about it," he murmured awkwardly as she went on, recounting the method of murder in the story. While she talked, Jenny put three pancakes, pillowy white in the centers and golden crisp at the edges, on each of their plates despite Warren's protestations, piled strips of bacon to the side, and then added pats of butter and maple syrup. The first bite was heaven. The second bite was better than heaven. He finished two of the pancakes before he began to feel uncomfortably full.

Belle Canfield was replenishing the bacon on the table, and when Warren told her the breakfast was delicious, she smiled shyly. "I'm glad you're enjoying it," she said. "That's our maple syrup, Earl's and mine."

"It's the best I've ever had," Warren told her. "Can I buy a gallon from you sometime?"

Belle grinned with pride, and Warren felt he'd seen something of her personality, the real one, not the one she showed her employers. "Of course, though we're just about out for the year. But sugaring season will be here soon enough."

He thought of something then. They'd found Moulton's thermos but no sandwich or other food with the body. "Mrs. Canfield? I wonder if you can help me with something. Do you remember what food Mr. Moulton took with him when he went out on Saturday?"

"I think I gave him a sandwich and some coffee," she said. "Some of the men took two sandwiches, but he only wanted one." Warren thanked her and felt a sense of pride in his police work. Moulton had eaten his sandwich and barely digested it, which put the time of his death as sometime after noon on Saturday. If the medical examiner was right, that gave them a much smaller window; assuming he'd eaten his lunch around noon, Moulton hadn't survived the afternoon.

Jenny Breedlove started telling Pinky all about another mystery story she'd read where the killer disguised himself as a minister. "Did you see *Psycho*?" she asked him. "They showed it at the drive-in last summer. It was awfully good. Pretty terrifying."

"Trooper Goodrich, we need to get to work," Warren said gently. He couldn't tell if Pinky was relieved to get away from the onslaught of conversation or disappointed, but Pinky told Jenny he'd see her later and followed Warren outside.

Pinky drove the cruiser out along the narrow road and pulled it in where they'd parked yesterday. Warren was pretty sure he'd be able to find the site again, but he was glad to see Pinky had marked it on the map and that he had a compass. They had dressed for the weather, and still they found themselves shivering for the first ten minutes of the hike out to the site.

The skies above the woods were growing increasingly cloudy and gray. The site looked much as it had yesterday. They spent nearly an hour carefully searching the ground around where the body had been found, but no knife or spent ammunition revealed itself.

"The knife's not here," Warren said. "And I don't think the brass is either."

"You think whoever killed him took them away."

"I do. And if it's one of them"—he gestured in the general direction of the club—"where is it? It must be in there somewhere, but I don't think I can quite justify searching their personal belongings. This is a very strange case, Pinky. I don't think I've ever had anything quite like it. A bunch of prominent men, the whole thing with the knife, and then the shooting? It's damned strange."

Pinky inclined his head in agreement.

Tracing a finger over the map, Warren stopped on the ridgeline. "Pinky, I was thinking, that story about the hunter and the man with his heart cut out . . . You don't think . . ."

Pinky's eyes went wide. "That it was some kind of ghost situation?"

Warren smiled. "No, I don't believe in ghosts, but I wonder if someone wanted us to think that."

"But then why didn't they leave the knife in him or . . . cut out his heart?" Pinky pointed out, looking a bit horrified at his own words. "If you were trying to copy the crime in the story, wouldn't you, uh, go all the way?"

Warren didn't answer. "Let's split up and walk around a little, in a radius from the scene of the crime, see if we can find anything else out here. Whoever stabbed him was up close to put the knife in, but he was shot from farther away. Bigger radius. Maybe we'll find evidence. Then we'll head back to talk to them."

Pinky nodded, then looked worried and said, "You think you can find your way back here all right?"

Warren laughed. "Do you think I should drop breadcrumbs like Hansel and Gretel?"

"No, I just . . ."

Warren knew what he was thinking. Warren wasn't used to being out in the woods. He had already gotten lost once this past summer. Pinky was imagining having to search for him.

"Don't worry, Pinky," he said. "I brought my old compass from my Boy Scout days. I'm going to head out this way toward the edge of the property, and then I'll turn around and meet you back here in an hour. Okay?"

"Sure," Pinky said.

They went off in opposite directions, Warren to the north and Pinky to the south. Now that he had a map of the property, he knew where he was in relation to the rest of the club and that he was heading toward the eastern boundary line. If someone had come in from outside, this was likely where they would have been. Warren kept his eyes trained on the ground, sweeping his gaze from left to right, staying alert to anything that seemed out of place. After a few minutes of walking, though, something else caught his attention.

The leaves were spotted with white specks that, upon closer examination, revealed themselves to be snowflakes. Warren turned his face up to the sky, and sure enough, it was snowing. The flakes were falling gently, though, barely accumulating, so he kept walking, enjoying the almost silent whisper of them hitting the ground.

He traced his progress on the map and, after another twenty minutes of walking, came to the edge of the property. On the other side of the line of trees was a wide field, corn stalks in rows into the distance. Warren walked along the boundary line, keeping his eyes on the ground, and he'd almost decided to turn around when he caught a flash of metal among the leaves. He bent over to inspect it.

It was a lipstick tube made of shiny metal meant to look like gold. Maria had had one similar to this one. He had a sudden memory of her leaning into the mirror in the bathroom, applying the lipstick when they were going out. The pain was no longer a punch but rather a strong, aching pull at his heart. He waited for it to pass, and then he picked it up and carefully, touching as little of it as he could, took off the cap and found a nearly new red lipstick. He put it into his pocket and marked its location on the map.

Back in the clearing, Warren only waited a few minutes before Pinky came loping along from the south.

"You find anything?" Warren asked him.

Pinky shook his head. "How about you?"

"Yeah. Look at this." He retrieved the tube and opened his palm to show it to Pinky. "It's still shiny, hardly any dirt on it. A woman was out this way sometime in the last couple of days and dropped it."

"Maybe," Pinky said dubiously.

Warren was sure it was important, though. "Let's go back and talk to everyone at the club again. I want to put everyone's locations and movements on Saturday and Saturday night on the map so I can see who might have been hunting near Moulton. If nothing else, they might have seen something. But we need to look around for knives. Based on the statements yesterday, the only people who have real alibis are Jack Packingham and Earl Canfield, though they alibied each other. The women too, I suppose, though that's a bit unclear. Especially with this now, we've got to pin those down."

"*If* it was someone at the club," Pinky pointed out. "It'd be nice if we could rule out someone from outside, wouldn't it?"

Warren knew he was right. "Yeah. The game warden's supposed to get back to us, but if he doesn't, how could we do that?"

"Well," Pinky said slowly, thinking, "there are a few houses down this road here." He straightened the map and pointed to the road they'd come in on. "I suppose I'd drive around and stop in at any house that's not too far from the perimeter. Ask if anyone was hunting or saw any cars headed this way. See if anyone's seen anything, look out for places someone might have parked. Probably good to do that before the snow falls. Any tire tracks that are there now will be covered up overnight, if this storm comes, anyways." He looked up at Warren. "Do you want to go do that right now?"

"What do you think about this snow?" Warren asked him, looking up at the sky. There were no more snowflakes flying, but the sky was still a thick gray.

"I'd say the bulk of it will come tonight," Pinky said. "But we'll probably want to get back to the barracks by four or so. Give us time to get home before the roads get bad."

"Okay," Warren told him. "It's one thirty now. Why don't we drive back and you can leave me at the club? Drive around and see what you can find and then meet me back there at, say, two thirty or three. That will give me enough time to interview everyone and update the map with their locations. I'll also look around and see if there are any knives in the gun room or in the lodge. I don't want to tell them how he died yet, though." They started walking, and when he heard Pinky's stomach rumble over the sound of their feet on the dead leaves, he said, "Are you actually hungry, Pinky? You just had pancakes!"

Pinky said, "My mother says I'm a bottomless pit. She always packs me lunch when I'm working a long shift. I got a couple of ham sandwiches and a thermos of soup in the cruiser." He patted his stomach. "Always best to be prepared, she says."

Warren smiled. "She sounds like a smart woman, your mother."

"Oh, she is," Pinky said, his face suffused with pride and emotion. "Good cook too."

Eleven

They had finished lunch back at the lodge, but Belle Canfield had left a plate of chicken-salad and tongue sandwiches on slightly stale bread for Warren and Pinky. Chewing the tough slices of tongue and bread, Warren, who had never liked chicken salad or tongue, thought a bit longingly of Pinky and his ham sandwiches. He was betting the bread they were made with was not the least bit stale. As he watched Belle Canfield arranging the plates and taking empty dishes back to the kitchen, he realized suddenly that she was having to stretch the food further than she'd intended. She'd likely have to run to the store if this went on any longer.

"Have there been any developments?" Jack Packingham said. "I ask only because it seems like there may be a storm coming, and if anyone needs to get on the road, well . . . sooner might be better than later." He was clearly anxious, his eyes darting to the windows, his hands fiddling with the hem of his sweater.

"I have a class tomorrow," Seth Pellegrino, dressed in worn Levi's and a new-looking blue ski sweater, said. "What am I supposed to tell my professor?" He didn't seem overly troubled, though. Warren thought that Seth, reclining on the couch with a glass of whisky and an extra chicken sandwich, was enjoying his foray into the life of a sporting man of leisure.

"I'd like to get on the road as soon as possible," Graham French said. "My wife worries when I drive in the dark."

"I'll do my best to make it very quick," Warren said. "Trooper Goodrich thinks the snow won't start in earnest until tonight, but I do need to speak to each of you again and to make sure we have the timeline of everyone's movements down. We'll do what we did yesterday, and you can leave as soon as I'm through. Unless . . . well, unless something comes up."

Warren looked around at the group. He saw them through new eyes now, a group of people who had information they wanted to keep from him. He saw them as suspects.

And all but one of them were also witnesses who had important information that could solve this case.

He just had to figure out how to get it.

"Colonel French, why don't you come in first? I'll try to be done with you as quickly as possible." He watched the man's face. Irritation sparked in his eyes, and then he got ahold of himself and said, "Yes, Detective."

"I'd like you to show me again on the map where you were Saturday," Warren said once they were back at what he'd come to think of as his interview table. He got out a sheet of paper on which he'd traced the rough outlines of the property. He'd traced ten maps from the original this morning. On this one, he wrote *French* at the top and handed it over with a pen. "Just write the approximate time and a line indicating your movements around the property, please."

Once again, irritation flashed in the man's eyes, but he took the writing implement and, his hand trembling, started marking it. "I hunted with Herman here and here . . ." He drew a wavering line along the western side of the pond. "Then, I was here alone for a couple of hours. Then I walked here and"—he drew a line around the pond—"here and back to the lodge. There you go."

"So you were alone for two hours in the afternoon?"

"Yes, but I didn't kill Bill by accident, if that's why you're asking." Warren noted to himself that Graham French hadn't said "shoot" and wondered if there was anything in it. "I didn't even take a shot. My damned hands don't work anymore, Detective. The doctors don't know why, but it's getting worse. My actual hunting days may be over, but I can still enjoy being in the woods."

Warren, feeling sorry for Graham now, was about to dismiss him when he thought of something. "You said Mr. Moulton had been pushed out of his post and that he seemed upset about it. Was he upset at anyone in particular? I'm wondering if there was any person he'd been, well, especially angry at, if you see what I mean?"

Graham said, "I didn't hear him name anyone. On Friday night, we were having a bit of a discussion about Vietnam. You've seen the news about the recent fighting, I'm sure." Warren nodded. "Anyway, we were going back and forth a bit and we came around to the Soviets and the wall and his dismissal came up. He blamed it on politics, said they'd gotten the wrong idea about him, but he never came right out and said why, though he was kind of muttering something about whisper campaigns and friends stabbing you in the back. I didn't have the sense it was a *specific* friend. And I knew how he felt." Graham pressed his lips together and sat back in his chair, his arms folded defensively in front of him.

Warren raised his eyebrows inquisitively and Graham went on.

"I was forced out. Even before my health started failing. I swore an oath to my country and part of that oath was to tell the truth, but no one liked what I had to say. I was in South Vietnam, Detective Warren, in an advisory capacity, and I told them what I saw, nothing more, nothing less. Next thing I knew, I was being pushed out. Thirty-five years with the army and now I'm teaching lazy undergraduates who can barely get out of bed about the Constitutional Convention."

"I'm sorry," Warren said. "Did Mr. Moulton agree with you about Vietnam?"

"In a way. Though he wouldn't say it. Bill was a diplomat, Detective. With him it was always the bigger picture and the conversations happening behind the scenes. Diplomats never say what they mean, do they?" The look of disgust returned. Diplomats, it seemed, were as bad as those who slept late.

"So who was on the other side of the discussion?"

"Herman, for one. He thinks we can win it. And Jack, I suppose. But Jack's understanding is . . . simplistic. His boy was spouting off a bunch of nonsense, thinking I was agreeing with him. Anyway, what I'm saying is that I knew how Bill felt. But I don't know exactly why he was sent away."

Warren was interested in this. "Did the discussion resolve itself?" he asked. He was wondering if bad feelings had lingered into the next day.

Graham frowned. "I suppose. I was fed up so I went to bed. Bill and Herman were really getting into it, and I found it tiresome. I saw the war on the ground, Detective Warren. I saw the villages and the houses and the godforsaken jungle that we know nothing about. We don't know what we're doing. We're lying to ourselves." The man's anger surprised Warren. But he didn't know what else to ask so he thanked him and told him he could start packing his things to go.

Jack Packingham came in next and marked his movements on the map on which Warren had written his name. He and Earl had hunted with Bill Moulton for a couple of hours, he told Warren, and then Moulton, surprising them, had said he wanted to go try one of his favorite places after lunch, do some thinking. Jack had taken that to mean that he wanted to be alone, so Jack and Earl had gone off and hunted together all afternoon.

"So you and Mr. Canfield were together from lunch onward?" Warren asked.

"Well, mostly. He'd set up a blind and I decided to use it. He said he'd go around the clearing and see if he could do any tracking on the other side."

Warren made a note of that. He was about to move on, when Jack said, "I know what you're thinking, that we were both alone, that it might have been one of us taking a shot and hitting Bill by accident, but I could kind of see Earl moving through the trees, Detective, and I assume he could see me. He wasn't out of my sight for more than a few minutes, and I heard no shots at that point."

"But you think you might have at other points in the day?"

"I'm sorry, I know it's important. But it's hard to remember. I might have heard a shot on Saturday or it may have been Sunday, but it was far away and it's hunting season so . . . I'd expect to hear shots in the woods, if you know what I mean."

"Thank you. That's very helpful." Warren jotted that down too. It *was* helpful, but now he was wondering if Jack was just a bit too eager to put Earl Canfield and himself beyond suspicion. "I hear there was a bit of an argument Friday night," he said casually. He wanted to see how Jack would describe it.

"Oh, that." Jack looked worried. Irritated too, Warren thought. "Vietnam. It's all anyone wants to talk about these days. I'm tired of it. If we're going to do it, we ought to do it. Deal with the Reds once and for all and be done with it. I understand Graham's position, but . . ." He shrugged. "Herman feels strongly, though, and the boys were siding with Graham, and then it got a bit . . . personal for my taste. But it was soon resolved. You know how men get when they drink."

Jack smiled, but the smile seemed thin to Warren, who asked, somewhat impulsively, "I know guns are stored in the gun room. Are there any weapons kept in other locations?"

Jack didn't seem surprised by the question. "Well, club rules are that rifles go in the gun room. We had an accident a few years back when a member was cleaning his gun in his room. No one hurt, thankfully, but for the plaster. So . . ." He shrugged.

"Would knives, bows, uh, machetes also be kept in the gun room?"

Jack looked a bit confused. "Some of the men have knives for dressing out deer, and I guess Earl keeps a couple for that purpose. But . . . why do you ask, Detective Warren?"

Warren didn't answer. "How long have you been hunting?" he asked.

"Most of my life. My father used to take my brother and me out when I was a boy. We started coming up here in the thirties. My mother's family was from Vermont. I started taking Skip as soon as he could hold a gun. It makes me happy that he likes coming up here too. The club is very important to me, Detective. I'd do anything for it."

"You a fisherman too?"

"Oh yes." Jack smiled. "That's really my first love."

"And the fishing equipment? Rods and lures and knives and things like that? That's all kept in the gun room too?" He looked down at his notes so his eyes wouldn't give anything away.

"Our members generally bring their own rods and lures and flies, but as you saw, we keep a few on hand in case of guests. There's a drawer with some tackle in it. I don't think anything was missing, though."

He was going to have to have Jack look to see if anything was missing from the gun room, but he wanted to know about 1946. Warren considered how to come at it. "I was told that Bill Moulton was involved in some sort of altercation here at the club back in 1946. That he had to seek medical attention." He didn't say *for a stab wound*. "Do you know anything about that?"

Jack cast his eyes down and slumped a little in his chair. "I figured someone would tell you about that. The thing is, Detective, that was just . . . well, honestly, it was the whisky talking. I hardly know what started it. It was silly."

"You were here?" Warren somehow hadn't considered that.

"Well, yes, I thought . . . All four of us were. Graham, Herman, Bill, and me. And quite a few other men, of course, too. My father was alive then, and he was here and—'"

Warren sat up and interrupted him. "The four of you were here when Mr. Moulton was stabbed nineteen years ago?"

"I thought you knew. I'd hardly call it *stabbed*. It was just a silly, unfortunate argument and Herman was holding a steak knife, I think, just a little steak knife, and really, it was like a *nick*."

"Mr. Westwood was the one who stabbed Mr. Moulton?"

"Again, *stabbed* would be a misleading way to des—"

Warren cut him off. "Can you tell me exactly what happened?"

Jack hesitated and said, "When men come to the Ridge Club, Detective, they have an expectation that any conversations they have will be confidential. As you know, there are presidents, judges, very important—"

"I don't want you to give away any state secrets. Just tell me what happened." Warren was angry now. He felt as though he were being manipulated.

Jack sighed. "As far as I remember—and as I said, it was a long time ago—we were sitting around the table having a lively discussion about Greece and the communists. Bill had been in Athens and he was talking about what he'd seen. I didn't know much about any of it. My father wasn't very political either, but Graham had strong opinions, and Herman was, well, I think he was having fun baiting Bill, arguing against whatever he said. There were a couple of other men there, guests, who actually worked for the administration in various ways and were all in on the idea that we had to strike back against the Reds by helping out anyone in their path. I've always believed that, Detective, and I think Bill did too. He let Herman get to him, though. They were sitting next to each other, both holding steak knives because they were eating. Suddenly, they were fighting and then Bill said, 'He got me,' or something like that. The knife was still in his shoulder. Herman was shocked. We were all shocked. It was . . . unbelievable. He was taken to the hospital and the police must have been notified, but Bill didn't want to press charges or anything like that. It was an accident, and Herman was horrified. He said he'd tripped. I know it seems like too much of a coincidence, but that's what it is."

Warren had many more questions he wanted to ask Jack, but he wanted to see what the other men who'd been there would say first and he needed to talk to the boys, so he told him to send in his son and ignored Jack's surprise at being released.

Skip Packingham seemed subdued today, his hair uncombed and his eyes lined with exhaustion. When Skip leaned over the table to pull out his chair, Warren got a whiff of stale sweat and stale alcohol. "Did you all hit the bottle a little hard last night?" Warren asked gently.

"What? Oh, yeah. It was so strange. No one wanted to talk about it, but what were we going to talk about? So we just kept drinking." He pushed his shaggy bangs out of his face. An angry red pimple had come up alongside his nose, and Warren found it hard not to look at it.

When Warren asked him to fill out the map with his movements on Saturday, the younger man sighed and said, "Like I told you, I just stayed here by the fire, reading a book. I don't actually like hunting all that much. Seems cruel to me. And it was too cold. But my dad likes hunting so I let him think I was going out."

"I see." Warren smiled. "I was the same at your age. Anyone here with you at the clubhouse?"

"People came and went. The ladies served lunch and I think all of the men came back and then went out again. Mr. Westwood sat and had a scotch with me after he ate, but then he said he was going back out. Mr. Canfield and my father went hunting again after lunch."

"And your friend Mr. Pellegrino?"

Skip's eyes darted away. "I don't know. He went out by himself and then he came back for lunch. I'm not sure what he was doing after that. Later in the afternoon I went looking for some sandwiches but I couldn't find anyone around. Maybe he went hunting again."

"So you were alone?"

"I guess."

Warren didn't like the hesitation in the young man's voice. There was something he wasn't saying. "Mr. Pellegrino didn't tell you where he was going? Aren't you the reason he's here? It seems odd he'd just go off on his own and not let you know."

Skip was peeling a bit of nail off and suddenly his hand jerked and a line of blood bloomed where he'd pulled off some of the skin with the nail. "Sorry." He took a napkin from the center of the table and pressed it to the wound.

Warren studied him. "This argument about Vietnam on Friday night. Tell me about it," he said.

Skip's eyes flashed. "Did my father tell you about that? Someone had brought a newspaper and we were talking about what's happening there right now. Colonel French was saying that we don't know what we're doing, and Mr. Westwood was disagreeing with him." He frowned. "My father too. Seth and I were trying to explain to them why we're antiwar. It's like he doesn't even realize we could get drafted! We don't want to fight people we've never met, who just want the same freedom we do! They were all drunk, and it turned into a debate. But . . ." He took a deep breath and Warren could see how upset he was, how much he was trying to control his emotions. "You can't imagine how it felt, Mr. Warren. All these old men, sitting around in a damned . . . hunting lodge, drunk and safe, deciding the fates of boys around the country and poor people across the world!"

"I can see how much it bothered you." Skip nodded. "Your father said that it got personal?"

Now, Skip looked confused. "I guess. Mr. Westwood said something about Mr. Moulton and . . . well, women. That he liked women too much. They'd been talking about old times and their old hunting exploits. I don't know what he meant, exactly. But it just . . . I'm sorry, I don't mean to get so mad about it. But this war, what they're doing, it's wrong. It's wrong, and they have to know how wrong it is!"

"Thank you for your honesty, Mr. Packingham." Warren closed the notebook and said, "You can go."

"You're . . . done?"

"Yes—for the moment anyway." Skip's face relaxed. He thought he'd gotten away with something. "Can you send in your friend, please?"

Seth Pellegrino, who seemed more together and less hungover than his host, came in a bit hesitantly, but his voice was assured when he answered Warren's question about where he'd been all afternoon. "I was in and out in the morning, but I got a bit bored so I went out for a walk and then came back for lunch and took a nap." His freshly washed and slicked-back hair and the new sweater gave him the look of a Sears catalog model. Warren didn't think he'd appreciate the comparison, though.

"Who did you see when you came back?"

"Um, well, no one, really. I came in and went straight upstairs to my room."

"Was anyone else on the second floor?"

Pellegrino's dark eyes blinked a few times. "How would I know? I didn't see or hear anyone, if that's what you're asking."

Warren thought he was lying. "What about downstairs? You didn't say hello to your friend Mr. Packingham? He was sitting by the fire reading all afternoon. You must have seen him when you came in."

The boy looked away. "Yeah? Oh, well, I was pretty tired, so I just went upstairs."

Warren studied him for a moment. "Can you show me on the map where you were walking on Saturday? Just mark your location with the approximate time."

Seth took the map and halfheartedly drew a looping circle that indicated the short walk he'd taken. When he handed it back, Warren thought he looked a bit smug.

"You're a Harvard student?" Warren asked.

"That's right."

"Where are you from?"

Seth blinked and said, "California."

"Where?"

"San Francisco. Well, San Mateo. Do you know it?"

"A little." Warren smiled. "It's nice here, isn't it?"

"Yeah, I suppose so." Seth started to say something else but stopped himself. Warren had the impression that Seth Pellegrino was a person with a great deal of self-control. This was interesting to him, because twenty-year-old boys were not generally known for this quality.

"I've been hearing a lot about the political discussion on Friday night. It sounds like it got a bit heated."

"You been in any discussion about this war lately that *hasn't* gotten heated?" Seth asked with a little smile. "Skip got pretty upset, but what his father was saying isn't anything we haven't heard before. It's what anyone who benefits from capitalism and the military industrial complex believes. He said that we have a responsibility to fight communism in Southeast Asia, that America can win because we're on the 'right side.' When you insist on seeing yourself as the good guy, Detective Warren, you are blind to what's really going on."

Though the boy's smug tone irked him, Warren had to admit that Seth had something there—in homicide investigation, drawing bright moral lines between yourself and the possibly guilty was a surefire way to miss the subtle motives that were usually the reason for the crime. He thanked him and called in the employees of the club, one by one, wanting to confirm the accounts of the men's whereabouts.

The women each came into the dining room and said they'd been in and around the club after lunch, Delana cleaning the bathrooms and common areas, Belle Canfield ironing in the kitchen and keeping an eye on the dinner, and Jenny cleaning bathrooms, making beds upstairs, and helping out where needed. They'd all been alone for stretches on Saturday afternoon, but their stories intersected in enough places—Belle going up to check on Jenny and bring clean linens, Delana seeing Belle cross the hallway downstairs, Jenny asking her mother what time she needed to start helping with dinner—that Warren didn't think there was anything there. Earl confirmed Jack Packingham's account. "Wasn't out of my sight for more than two minutes at a time," he said, as though he knew what Warren was thinking. None of them had much to say about the argument. "I wasn't really listening," Delana told him during her interview. "We were trying to get the dishes done. I guess we're all used to them talking politics after dinner and when they've been drinking." Jenny said the same thing, and Belle said she had been so busy she also hadn't really listened to the men's conversation. "I could tell they were talking about something," Belle said. "But we're not supposed to listen to what."

Warren needed to talk to Graham French about the 1946 argument, but he realized that Graham might already be on the road. But when he went into the lounge, the older man was sitting dejectedly by the fire and when Warren asked him why he hadn't departed, he said, "Too much snow. My wife won't have me driving in these conditions. I'm here for the night."

Warren looked at his watch and was surprised to see that it was nearly three o'clock. Outside the windows, the sky had become even murkier and grayer, and the snow had started to fall faster now.

"I'm so sorry about that. I'd like to talk with you again, though," Warren said. "Shouldn't take long." Graham looked surprised but got up and walked slowly into the dining room. Warren followed, watching the man's halting movements. Could he have mustered the strength to stab someone and then aim the rifle? He was still relatively fit. Would his years of military training have come back to him, even in his diminished condition?

Warren decided to jump right in. He started with "Tell me about 1946."

Graham's eyes went wide. "The . . . you mean the . . . when Herman . . ."

"Yes, the stabbing here at the club. You were here."

"Yes, I . . . just by chance, really. My parents were in Vermont and I was on leave. My wife and I decided to bring the children up to see my parents, and my father and I came to the dinner at the club. It was an annual thing—a fishing derby and the announcement of the winner and then a big dinner for all the men who were around. That was . . . well, there was a lot going on that year, and many of the men at the dinner were State Department or military, some academic types, and some businessmen and lawyers and judges and so forth. Many of the men had seen combat in Europe or the South Pacific, Detective. They had strong opinions about the Soviets. Things boiled over, Herman accidentally grazed Bill. But . . . he was fine. No harm done."

"When Jack and Skip found Bill's body, did anyone comment on how strange it was that the four of you were here together and that something had happened to Bill, that there was this . . . echo of the previous dispute?" Warren had to be careful. He didn't want to give away Moulton's actual cause of death, which made it even more of an echo.

Graham looked away, then back at Warren. "Yes, Jack did say something about it. He was in shock from finding the body, and he said something about how it made him feel a bit queer, thinking of the four of us here again and now Bill was dead. But it was obviously coincidence, Detective. Whoever shot Bill, well, it must have been an accident. Some local out hunting, right? I'm sure you'll find him."

Warren studied Graham's face. He seemed nervous, and was it Warren's imagination or was he relieved when Warren said he could go and that he should send in Herman Westwood?

Once Herman had come in—a bit reluctantly, Warren thought—Warren pushed over the last blank map and asked him to fill it in with his locations.

He took the pencil Warren offered. "I was out in the morning here, and then I walked back around eleven to take a phone call. Then there was lunch. I went back out again after lunch. I don't know where I was, really . . ." He studied the map and then halfheartedly drew a line from the clubhouse out and around the pond and then back.

"You're sure about that?"

"Not really. I was sort of just walking, and I kept the pond in sight so I wouldn't get lost."

"Did you see anyone?" Warren asked.

"I saw Earl and Jack at a distance, so I steered clear and found my own spot. Didn't see any deer, though, so I headed back when it started to get dark." He seemed restless, shifting around in his seat and glancing at the window.

Warren didn't like it, but he was conscious that he needed to move along. "Tell me about the argument you had with Mr. Moulton on Friday night," he said. "It sounds like it got heated."

"Heated?" Herman laughed. "That was nothing, Detective Warren. You should see some of the political debates we've had around that fireplace over the years. I would have liked to take Jack's boy out and give him a good hiding, disrespectful little shit, but I didn't. We were just talking politics."

"But it got personal between you and Mr. Moulton?"

"Who told you that?"

"I'd rather not say."

"We'd been drinking, Detective Warren." Herman's eyes narrowed. "I don't remember much of what we said, but it was all in good fun and all between old friends."

Warren waited, preparing his question. "Just like 1946, Mr. Westwood?"

Herman started and Warren thought that he was going to protest, but instead he leaned back in his chair and sighed. "I figured you'd dig that up."

Warren watched him. "Well? Did you and Bill Moulton have animosity between you left over from that earlier event?"

To Warren's surprise, he laughed out loud. "I'd forgotten all about it until Friday, Detective, and I suspect Bill had as well. It was . . . nothing! He could just as easily have gotten me with his knife when we started tussling. He said as much at the time. It was silly. We made up later that night after it happened and got good and drunk." He laughed again. "Good and drunker!"

"What about when you arrived here? Did you and Mr. Moulton acknowledge that the last time you'd seen each other you'd put him in the hospital?"

Herman nodded. "I think we did say something about it, in a light way, just, you know, let's not do that again."

Warren glanced toward the windows. He couldn't see beyond the falling snow. There was more there to uncover, but there wasn't time for it now.

He needed to be on his way.

But where was Pinky? They had brought two cars so Warren could get home on his own, but he was getting worried. He went out to the lounge to see if there was any sign of him, and he was just about to ask when he heard voices in the hall.

"Maybe that's your officer," Herman said, following him.

But a few moments later, a tall woman dressed in woolen pants and in stocking feet and a blue sweater came striding into the room. "Jack, darling," she called out. "I came to rescue you. Don't you know there's a big snowstorm coming?"

"Claire?" Jack Packingham jumped up and went over to the woman, who kissed him passionately and then smiled broadly at the rest of them.

"What's she doing here?" Skip asked.

The woman smiled and shrugged her shoulders. "Oops," she said. "I was supposed to stay hidden away in the house this weekend like a good little girl. But seriously, Jack darling, this storm is no joke. I could barely get up here on the road. I don't want to be stranded all alone at the house!"

Warren stepped forward and said, "I'm Detective Franklin Warren. And you are . . ."

"Claire Packingham, Detective. I'm sorry to barge in like this. I was supposed to stay sequestered, you see, but I didn't want to get trapped all by my lonesome."

She smiled flirtatiously and shook his hand. Looking at her carefully made-up face, Warren realized something.

Claire Packingham was wearing bright-red lipstick.

Warren was far from an expert on women's face paint, but he would have bet a lot of money that it was the same red as the tube he'd found in the woods.

Twelve

Alice and Mildred finished cleaning up from the party by ten that morning. They had a cup of tea and then Mildred, gesturing to the gray sky outside the window, said, "You still going to that poetry party? You'd better keep an eye on the storm."

Alice, who had been too busy to pay attention to the weather, looked up. "What storm?"

"Oh," said Mildred. "We're getting snow tonight. Might be a lot." Alice sighed. These early-season storms always made one feel unprepared. She loved a pretty layer of the white stuff as much as the next Vermonter, and years when it was late, she found herself impatient for the first flakes. But it always felt wrong when it snowed before Thanksgiving. She would have to get out her warmest coat and boots and make sure that Billy had a snow shovel to clear her walkway. Oh well—perhaps it wouldn't be very much after all. At least she'd already finished putting her gardens to bed. And as long as it didn't start until tonight, she'd be all right for her "poetry party," as Mildred had called it.

In actuality, it was a poetry reading at the college, put on by the English department. A few weeks ago, Alice had received an invitation to the event and asked her friend Sylvie Weber if she might like to go. Sylvie had demurred, saying she couldn't leave the boys, but Alice had assured her that they'd be fine for a couple of hours. "After the baby comes, you may not be able to do something like this for a while," she'd said. "So you should seize your chance now."

Sylvie had been noncommittal, but the next day she had called Alice on the new telephone that Detective Warren had insisted they have installed up on Agony Hill, and she had said, "Scott said he can watch the other boys, and I think, Mrs. Bellows, that I'd like to go and hear the poetry with you."

Sylvie must have been waiting just inside the door at the farmhouse up on Agony Hill when Alice pulled the Ford into the driveway later that day. The door opened and the younger woman came out, smiling, dressed in a shapeless wool sweater and skirt and an old wool overcoat that must have belonged to her late husband. It barely buttoned over her swollen belly, and Alice thought for a second about going back to her own house to get Sylvie something more suitable for a literary event, then thought better of it.

It would be poets, after all.

With poets, anything went.

"Hello, Sylvie. Isn't it cold?" she said as the younger woman awkwardly folded herself onto the bench seat.

"Yes, I think it's going to snow," Sylvie said. "The boys are hoping for a snow day tomorrow if the roads aren't cleared."

Alice reversed. "We'll see. How are they? Are they excited about the baby?"

"Andy and Louis are. Daniel doesn't really know about babies, and Scott seems embarrassed by the whole thing." Alice smiled. Scott was fifteen. He *would* be embarrassed by anything to do with babies. "But I told him that having babies is the most natural thing in the world. That's what Hugh used to say. I don't think it made him any less embarrassed."

Alice smiled. "I think you'll enjoy this gathering," she said to get Sylvie off the subject of her late husband and, if she was honest, the baby. Though she'd asked in the first place, Alice didn't like talking about babies. "My friend George Dill, who read your poems and loved them, as you know, has invited a well-known poet from Chicago to read. George thought we might like him."

Sylvie looked over and smiled shyly. "I have another poem he might like. I brought it to give him." She patted the pocket of the overcoat as Alice turned at the bottom of Agony Hill.

They drove most of the way in companionable silence, crossing the Connecticut River into New Hampshire, and as Alice parked on Main Street and she and Sylvie walked toward the college green, Sylvie laughed and said, "How funny to have a school just for men. Imagine only seeing other boys all the time."

Alice didn't say that from the stories Ernie had told her about his time at the college and more recent stories George had told her about his students, it didn't sound as if they only saw other boys.

The event was to take place in the reading room of the building where the English department had its offices, but first there was to be a wine-and-cheese reception in the poetry room, with readings by some of the students. Alice led Sylvie up the stairs and into the room, and George, who was already holding a wineglass and seemed in good spirits, greeted them.

Alice introduced them.

"How lovely to finally meet the mysterious poet of the hills," he said.

The room contained mostly students, good-looking young men, some, but not all, in blazers, and Alice thought about how five years ago, they would have had shorter hair, neater clothes, and different attitudes toward the adults in the room. Of course, things were always changing. Alice knew that. But over the past couple of years, it felt as though they had changed more quickly.

But maybe she was just getting old and someone had once thought that about her and her peers.

"I'm not very mysterious," Sylvie said to George. "But I brought you another poem." She took a folded and somewhat crumpled piece of paper out of her pocket and handed it to him.

George looked surprised, but he thanked Sylvie graciously and promised to read it the first chance he got. Then they all looked up to see a tall boy in a mustard-colored blazer and striped tie approaching them, and Alice smiled and said, "Calvin! How lovely to see you!"

"Hello, Mrs. Bellows," Calvin Carter said a bit shyly. "I thought that was you."

Alice had met Calvin when he arrived at the college last year as part of an initiative to bring talented Negro boys from Jackson, Birmingham, Savannah, and other places in the segregated South to private high schools and then to the college. She had agreed to serve on the board of the initiative, and Calvin and another boy had stayed at Alice's house for a weekend, and she'd had him for dinner a few times since then. Calvin was charming and interesting to talk to, and Alice had already invited him to come to her house for Thanksgiving. She was looking forward to hearing about his classes and his impressions of New Hampshire and the mostly white world he'd suddenly found himself in.

"Calvin, I'm so happy to see you. This is my friend Sylvie Weber. She's from Bethany too. Sylvie, this is Calvin Carter. He's a sophomore here at the college." Alice was suddenly seized with a fear about Sylvie's reaction. Would she act strangely around Calvin or refuse to shake his hand? Alice felt sick. It was likely that Sylvie, living as she had, had never met a non-white person in her life! She might react to Calvin with ignorance, and Alice didn't think she could bear it, to see hurt or even stoicism born of hard experience on Calvin's face.

When Calvin had stayed with her last summer, she had taken him on a walk around the green and left him for a few minutes to take photographs while she ran into Collers' Store. Coming out again, she'd seen Bethany's police chief, Roy Longwell, approaching Calvin, a look of determination on his face, and Alice had practically sprinted to Calvin's side to let Chief Longwell know that he was with her. She was not sure what would have happened if she hadn't made it in time. Remembering, her stomach went suddenly sour, her heart rate speeding in anxiety.

But Sylvie smiled warmly and shook Calvin's hand, and he said it was nice to meet her and asked if she knew the poet they were about to hear from. Sylvie said she didn't, and Calvin said he'd been told he had a lot of good and important things to say. Alice exhaled in relief.

"I think you'll both like him," George told them.

He asked Alice about her autumn and then said, "Oh, do you know who I saw the other week? Our old friend, Arthur Crannock! Did you know he's moved to the area?"

"Oh yes," Alice said. "I saw Arthur just last night." Like Arthur and Alice's late husband, Ernie, George had been in the OSS during the Second World War, but unlike them, he had given up the clandestine services as soon as the war was over. Instead, he'd gotten his PhD in English literature, started writing poetry, and settled into a teaching position at the college. Alice had seen him and his wife over the years and considered him an old friend, if not a particularly close one. She was grateful to him for showing such enthusiasm for Sylvie's poetry and worried a bit that she'd overstepped by giving him Sylvie's poems last winter. But he seemed very willing and the invitation to the reading had come from him.

"He was just the same," George said. "I was walking down North Main Street, lost in thought, and suddenly Arthur appeared in front of me. It was as though he'd come out of thin air! He said he was meeting with someone at the college, but I didn't hear who."

Alice was about to ask him when this had been when a young man in a bow tie came in and started ushering the guests into the reading room. Alice and Sylvie settled into folding chairs in the second row and waited while everyone got settled and George introduced the visiting poet, a man from Chicago who was wearing a hat and a black jacket and had a cigarette burning in an ashtray on the podium. Shuffling papers in front of him, he said, "I hope you don't mind the truth," looked up, leveling his gaze on his audience, and began to read.

The poems were short and powerful, with a staccato rhythm that reminded Alice of machine-gun fire, as she supposed it was meant to. The first poem seemed to be from the point of view of a woman in a Vietnamese village, lying in her bed and counting bombs. The second one was about American soldiers, their feet hurting, their bodies sore. The poem described their confusion and loneliness. And then the Chicago poet revealed the soldiers as Negro and speculated about the racist hatred they might experience once they returned home. Paired with the other poem, it painted a dark portrait of war—and of America and its attitude to its Negro citizens. He read some more, all on the war, and then finished with a poem about his son, imagining the boy as a soldier, dropping bombs on a Vietnamese village.

Alice felt the horror of war in all the poems, the absolute hopelessness of the innocent who couldn't escape death coming from every direction. The irony of dying for a country that did not consider you an equal citizen. She glanced over at Calvin, sitting on the other side of the room, and said a silent prayer for his safety, something she'd started doing recently whenever she encountered a young man who might be sent to war.

She remembered seeing American soldiers on leave in London, the haunted look in their eyes. Sometimes wars had to be fought, but anyone who made the decision to kill other human beings for scraps of land should be required to look into the eyes of someone whose family had been obliterated by fire from the sky, or a soldier missing a limb from a firefight. Listening to the poems, she realized how much tension she'd been carrying over the last week or two, ever since the first story about the fighting in Ia Drang.

When the poet was finished, he got a loud round of applause from the students, including Calvin—and a few of the professors—and quiet, somewhat solemn clapping from the others. A few sat silently, looking unhappy. It occurred to Alice that at least some of the older men in the room had seen action in Europe or the South Pacific. What must they be thinking? She turned slightly to look at George. He was clapping, his mouth set grimly, but Alice couldn't read his emotions. She found herself quite moved. Sylvie, when Alice turned to look at her, seemed spellbound. Her eyes shone, and she clapped slowly, overcome by the power of the words.

Suddenly, the poet pulled something from his pocket and held it up. It was a medal, a gold star on a ribbon with a dull silver star in the center. A Silver Star, Alice thought. Ernie had had one.

"I got this medal for bravery in battle," he said. "For staying alive over two days on a battlefield in Chosin, fighting the men my country told me were my enemies. Today, I give this medal back to my country in protest of the war in Vietnam. Today, I call for peace."

Calvin and the other students at the front of the room stood and applauded, and Alice found herself unsure what to do. She admired the man's stand, but she was not comfortable being part of the raucous demonstration. So she settled on polite applause. But the sick feeling in her stomach grew, a dark shame that spread through her body.

Everyone was starting to stand when George came up to the podium and cleared his throat. "Thank you, everyone. I beg your indulgence for one more moment. We have in our audience a young woman of significant and, dare I say, raw and authentic talent. I have had the pleasure of reading some of her work, and she has just given me a new poem that I would like to have her read to all of you—if she's willing, of course. Mrs. Weber?"

Alice didn't realize what was happening until George was holding a hand out in their direction and Sylvie was whispering, "What should I do?"

"Exactly what you want, dear," Alice whispered, patting her knee. Sylvie stood and walked to the podium, where she was greeted by polite applause. Her belly hidden behind the podium, she looked very young and very small. But she took the folded paper from George, smiled shyly, and began to read in a surprisingly assured voice:

His red neck swoons, or sighs, my knife arcs above his trembling breast
Like Zeus he tries to rise, dragon wings churning the air
Black blood shivers loose

It was a poem about slaughtering turkeys, Alice realized. The poem's narrator, cutting off a turkey's head with a knife, was wondering if the bird was actually a man. Sylvie was responding on some level to "Leda and the Swan"—Alice had lent her a copy of Yeats's poems last year—but the poem was from the point of view of a young woman who seemed to be experiencing the act of sex as an empowering experience rather than the rape of mythology and Yeats's poem. Alice was fascinated. Sylvie's other poems had been lovely, experimental, domestic, powerful in their way.

This was something different.

She got enthusiastic applause, and then Alice watched while she was surrounded and congratulated, and once the audience began to drift from the room, Sylvie found Alice and said, "We should be getting home to the boys, I think."

"Of course." Something on her face made Alice ask, "Are you okay?"

"Just tired."

Calvin came over to congratulate Sylvie, and Alice told him she was looking forward to seeing him at Thanksgiving. His face clouded over for a moment and he said, "Mrs. Bellows, I'll let you know later this week, but I might be going down to Birmingham for a demonstration. A friend of mine is organizing it and I'd . . . well, I'd like to be there."

"Of course, Calvin," she said. "I'll miss you, but it's just fine either way. But . . . you'll be careful, won't you?"

"Yes, I will." He smiled and went off to talk to the poet. Alice tried to push down the anxiety that now bloomed in her chest.

They made their goodbyes and as she was leaving, she found George and asked him the question that had been bothering her during the reading. "When was this?" she asked somewhat abruptly. "That you saw Arthur?" Arthur had told her he hadn't been up since September.

George, preoccupied by the departing crowd, said, "Oh, probably a week or so ago. Nice to see him. He was looking awfully well."

A week ago. Alice was certain now that Arthur had said he hadn't been to Woodstock since September. She could picture his face as he'd told her. He'd lied.

Outside, the snow had already started.

"Sylvie, I hope you didn't mind being put on the spot. I didn't know George was going to do that," Alice said, once they were back in the car, holding their hands over the Ford's heater vents.

"It's fine," Sylvie said. "I liked reading. Poems should be read, shouldn't they?"

"They should, and that was a triumph."

"Oh, well, I'm glad they liked it. I liked his work, the man from Chicago." She frowned and said, "One of my brothers was in Korea. My sister says he's never been right since then." She put a hand on her belly and breathed in sharply. "Sorry; I just had a funny pain. Must be the baby moving around."

Outside the car windows, the snow was coming down very slowly and very softly. It was lovely and relaxing, and yet, Alice felt uneasy.

It was Calvin, she realized. A part of her wanted to go back and find him and say, "Don't go, Calvin! Let others demonstrate! You've been given a chance. Please!" But of course, it wasn't her decision to make. She felt ashamed of herself and her polite clapping again, and she looked over at Sylvie, who was gazing out the window at the darkening landscape flashing past. They crossed the Connecticut and drove alongside it and then away from it back to Bethany, the familiar landmarks and sights obscured by the dancing snowflakes.

Alice pulled into the Webers' driveway. Sylvie opened the door and the light came on. "Are you really all right, Sylvie? You look a bit pale."

"Well, I started feeling a few little pains a couple of hours ago." She put a hand on her belly. "They're not anything serious, though— probably just the usual getting-ready sorts of pains. Dr. Falconer said I wasn't due until December."

"Would you like me to take you down to the hospital?"

Sylvie started to get out. "Oh no, I'm fine. I don't think I'm very close. I don't think it'll happen today at all. I just need to rest."

Alice thought she sounded quite confident. But still, Alice hesitated. "Why don't I come in for a bit? I've brought the boys some roast and potatoes and dessert left over from my party last night. It's packed up in the trunk, and I think they'll like it." Sylvie agreed and Alice fetched the food and followed her into the large cozy kitchen, with its big cookstove and table and the new black rotary phone on a shelf.

The oldest Weber boy, Scott, was sitting at the table, grappling with a stack of papers covered in mathematics problems, his pencil poised but unmoving above the work. His tan Labrador puppy, Bounder, nearly six months old now, with huge paws and ears that seemed too big for his body, was fast asleep at his feet, his nose twitching as he dreamed. The youngest boy, Daniel, was sitting on the floor, playing with some little cars and trucks. He had made himself a road out of spare ends of rope and twine, all the pieces braided together and the cars and trucks traveling up and down the road, accompanied by exclamations, words of caution, and then loud crashing sounds when they collided. Alice greeted them and put the food and the dessert on the counter.

"Now," she said. "What's all of that, Scott? Homework?"

He looked up and nodded. "I can't make it come out right, Mrs. Bellows," he said, shaking his head. He was a big, broad-faced giant of a boy, an inch taller than the last time she'd seen him; his eyes were still haunted by grief.

Alice hesitated. She needed to be on her way, but he looked so despondent that she couldn't help saying, "Well, I was very good at mathematics back in the old days. Let me have a look and I'll see if I can help you." She read the problems that he was working on and, the methods coming back to her, helped him see how to solve them. Alice frowned, watching Sylvie stop for a moment and lean on the counter by the sink where she'd been filling the tea kettle. "Sylvie, you go and have a rest," Alice said. "I'll stay a little while and start dinner for them."

"Are you sure?" Sylvie asked. "Don't you need to get home before the snow really starts?"

"The Falcon will get me home," Alice said. "I don't think we'll get much more than an inch."

She worked with Scott on his math and when she looked up, she was surprised to see that an hour had passed. The snow was still falling outside the windows, faster now, and she was just about to finish heating the food and then go check on Sylvie and be on her way when the side door opened and the two middle boys, Andy and Louis, came in, bringing the gray smell of the outdoors with them. There were snowflakes decorating their hair, and their cheeks were pink with the cold. Alice was about to say something cheerful about the snow when she saw the look on Andy's face. "What's the matter, Andy?"

"They're gone! The turkeys are all gone!" he said. "We went to try to get 'em in under the barn and they weren't there at all. I think something got 'em."

Alice felt her heart sink. These boys had had so much loss this year. "How many were there?" she asked.

"Twenty," Louis said sadly. "And we was going to use the money to get a television. Ma said we could." His round face and snub nose were turned up to her.

"'Were,'" Alice corrected. "Did you see feathers out there?" She suddenly remembered coming up on the carcass of a turkey at her grandparents' farm. Something had killed it and taken its head. There had been white feathers all over the ground.

"No," Andy said a little hopefully. "But we looked all around and we didn't see 'em anywhere. Maybe someone took them."

"But who would take them?" Alice looked out the window and felt a bit of alarm start to creep over her. "How much snow is on the ground out there?"

"A lot," Louis said. "We counted to ten and our footsteps were already covered. Where's our ma?"

They went to stand by the big cookstove, thawing in its radiating warmth.

"She's just having a rest," Alice said. She glanced at the window. The snow *was* coming down awfully fast. She decided she'd better get on the road.

"What's that?" Louis asked, pointing at the dish with the leftover cherries and fudge cake.

"That is some fancy dessert I've brought you," Alice said. "You're supposed to light it on fire when you serve it, but I don't have any extra brandy. I think you'll still enjoy it, though."

She took the cloth off the bowl so they could see it.

"I'd really like it to be on fire," said Louis solemnly.

"Another time, Louis. Besides, you ought to have a proper dinner first," Alice told him. "I've brought you some roast and potatoes."

"I am pretty hungry," Louis said. "Do you think we could—" Before he could finish getting the sentence out, they heard Sylvie's voice from the living room.

There was something desperate in her tone, and Alice leapt up and ran toward her voice.

She was on the couch, pale and clutching her belly, when Alice came in. "Sylvie, are you all right?" Alice asked. "Is the baby coming?"

Sylvie looked up, and Alice could see that her forehead was set against the discomfort and slick with sweat. "I don't think it's time," Sylvie said. "I have had a few labor pains, but they're not very close together." Her face went white, and she clutched her belly again and doubled over for a long moment. "It's a different kind of pain. But it can't be labor, not yet. Must be something I ate. Could you get me some water and maybe I could lie down upstairs and sleep? I think that will help." Alice nodded and went through into the kitchen to get the water. She looked out the kitchen windows and saw that the storm had now arrived in earnest. The snow was falling so fast and so thickly that she could not see the car.

Alice brought the water into the living room. "Sylvie, dear," she said. "I'm going to call Dr. Falconer. Even if you're not in labor, I think we better have him take a look at you. Is that all right?" Sylvie started to protest and then was seized with another bout of pain.

Alice, taking it as assent, went into the kitchen to use the phone.

She picked it up but heard only dead air from the receiver. "Hello, hello," she said. Though her own phone was now direct dial, some parts of town were still on party lines. Nothing happened. "Boys?" she asked them. "The phone—has it been working?"

"Yes, Mrs. Bellows," Scott said. "We used it yesterday to call down to Collers' to see if they had any bacon of ours left or if they wanted more."

"Well, it's not working now," Alice said. She lowered her voice and spoke to Scott. "I think your mother might need to see a doctor."

"Is the baby coming?" Scott asked. "She said if it started coming, I might need to drive her to the hospital."

"I don't know," Alice told him. "But I'd like the doctor to take a look at her, just to be sure." She tried to make it sound breezy, but she could see she had worried him. "Maybe you could try the phone again. I'll go check on her. We ought to convince her to lie down, I think."

Back in the living room, she found Sylvie looking slightly more relaxed and felt hope surge in her chest. Maybe it really was just indigestion. "Sylvie," she said, "the phone's not working. Could I help you lie down upstairs and we'll see if that makes you feel better?"

"I think I'm all right now, Mrs. Bellows," Sylvie said. "I really think that if I could sleep for a little bit or just rest that I'll be well again." She did look a bit better, and Alice called for Andy to come and help his mother walk upstairs. Alice followed them into a small bedroom at the far end of the landing. The double bed was covered in a colorful quilt that matched the faded floral wallpaper. The room had the feeling of Alice's childhood, with graceful, old furniture and a pleasant mess about, clothes draped over a chair, papers and books stacked up on the bedside table.

Alice got Sylvie settled in the bed and pulled the quilt up over her legs. "You just rest there for a minute," she said. "I'll go see if Scott was able to get the telephone to work." She followed Andy back downstairs and gave him a firm smile when he looked up at her warily, as if to ask what was going to happen. "Scott, any luck?" she called out. He was still holding the telephone receiver but he shook his head.

"It's dead," he said. "The wind is blowing really hard now. It may have knocked the lines down."

"Okay," she said. "I think I'll need to drive down to get the doctor. Could you boys go out and clean off my car?"

Andy nodded and put his wet coat back on. While they were outside, Alice tipped the leftover roast and potatoes into a pot and added some wood to the old cookstove. She'd heat the meal up for them and see if they had any bread, and then she'd go check on Sylvie again.

The kitchen was lovely and warm, and again, Alice felt pulled back to her own long-ago childhood. She had lived in town with her parents and sister, in the house on the green where her father had had his surgery and where she lived now. But her mother's parents had a farm out on the western side of town, on Granby Hill Road, and she had spent every summer of her life until she left for college in Boston living out at the farm. There was nothing like a cookstove to warm up a room. In the old days, there would often be some cold days in May and June, and she remembered sitting by the stove in the mornings, her bare feet stretched out toward it while she chatted with her grandmother and helped to shell peas or knead bread dough.

She got some more water and was about to take it upstairs when she heard Sylvie's voice, loud and urgent on the top floor: "Mrs. Bellows!"

Alice started to go up the stairs, but just then the back door flew open and Bounder came flying in, covered with a dusting of snowflakes, Scott behind him saying, "Mrs. Bellows. It's already pretty deep out there. Your car's snowed in and so is our truck. I don't think we can go anywhere at all."

Thirteen

I t was a bit awkward, you see," Claire Packingham told Warren once he'd shown her the lipstick tube and she'd confirmed that it was hers and that she'd dropped it in the woods on Saturday. He'd asked her to come sit down in the dining room and explain herself. "Jack didn't want Skip to know I was up for the weekend. He'd asked Skip to come along for the hunting, and Skip hadn't been interested at all. Honestly, Detective, don't get me started on how he treats his father, who's never been anything but generous to him. But Jack is a pushover. Anyway, Skip didn't want to go, so we made plans for me to come up and stay at the house for the weekend while Jack was hunting. Then he would join me and we could do some hunting on our own. I love to shoot—I was raised in Montana; my daddy has a ranch there—and he said I could come up and hunt with them one of the days. It would have been fine, but at the very last minute, Skip announced he wanted to come and bring a friend of his from Harvard. So, we decided I'd just stay at the house, and once Skip was gone, Jack would join me and we'd have a few days checking up on the construction and whatnot. You must have seen our house,

Detective. It's the one with all the windows down the road a way. The architect is an absolute genius."

Warren felt he was being manipulated, and it made him angry. "I don't understand why he didn't tell me that you were here on Saturday," he said. "There's been a death, Mrs. Packingham. I'm trying to conduct an investigation!"

"I know, Detective. I'm a lawyer. I know how it looks. But the truth is that Jack didn't know I was here at the club." She put on an exaggerated look of embarrassment, her eyes wide and childlike. "He thought I was all tucked up down at the house. I shouldn't have done it, I suppose, but I wanted to get out for some hunting, and this is the best place. I figured if I stuck to the edges of the property, way up in the woods, I wouldn't see anyone. I know, it was very naughty of me."

Warren studied her. She was a beautiful woman, her dark-blond hair grazing her shoulders and her greenish-brown eyes large and made to appear even larger with the application of black kohl to the rims. The red lipstick brought out the green in her eyes, and the bright-blue sweater contrasted with the bright spots on her cheeks, pink from the cold. She appeared to be much younger than Jack, and when Warren asked her for her birth date, she grinned and said, "I'll save you the trouble, Detective. I'm thirty-five. Yes, I'm much younger than Jack, and yes, he and I started seeing each other before he and Miriam were officially divorced. Yes, I feel a bit guilty about it, and yes, Skip and his siblings blame me for the divorce. They've been *horrid* to me." She smiled.

"Thank you," Warren said a bit uncertainly. He wasn't quite sure what to do with Claire Packingham. "Did you see anyone when you were here? Did you hear any shots?"

"I didn't hear any shots," she said. "But I did hear a car."

"On the road?"

"Well, it came up on the main road, but then it stopped not far from where I was hunting. I didn't want anyone to see my car, so I'd parked pretty far up the road and hiked into the property on that side.

The car went by slowly and it sounded like it shut off. I waited for a bit but I didn't see anyone and by the time I left there wasn't any car." She reached for the pack of cigarettes she'd placed in front of her on the table and shook one out, lighting it in a graceful series of motions and replacing the lighter in her purse.

Warren asked a few more questions and then let her go. The snow had been falling steadily and he decided that he would have to go as soon as Pinky got back. He stood up and went over to the window. Where was Pinky, anyway? He'd been gone an awfully long time.

Out in the lounge again, he saw Jack Packingham nervously meet Claire's eyes. Skip was now scowling in a corner, a drink already on the table in front of him.

"I'll need to call the barracks and see if Trooper Goodrich went back there instead of coming here," he told them.

"There's a phone in the hall," Jack told him, glancing between his wife and son. "You're welcome to use it." Warren didn't envy Jack the mess he now appeared to be dealing with.

Claire said, "I tried to call and all I got was dead air. That's why I came to get you, darling."

"I'll just try it," Warren said. In the hall, he picked up the receiver and put it to his ear. The line was indeed dead. He depressed the cradle and tried again. Of course, the wind and heavy snows would have knocked down the phone lines.

Where was Pinky? Warren went to the windows and looked out at the storm, trying and failing to spot something that would tell him his assistant had returned.

Back in the lounge, a fire roared in the fireplace and leftover sandwiches sat on plates on a side table. Half-finished drinks littered the tables, and Herman Westwood was smoking his pipe alone. "Are you going, Detective?" he asked. Warren said he was and asked where everyone else had gone.

"Well, I think the arrival of Mrs. Packingham has caused a bit of an issue for Jack. That boy of his went flouncing up to his room, and Jack and Claire went to talk. He doesn't seem very happy with her for barging in." He smiled a conspiratorial smile. "I, on the other hand, am glad for a bit of feminine charm around here. I wonder how old Jack landed such a trophy."

Warren was trying to figure out what to do about Pinky when Earl Canfield came in. His hair was damp with snowflakes that were melting every second he stood there in the warm lounge.

"If you're going to go today, you'd better get on the road. They won't have cleared the main roads, and I did my best with the top of our drive, but it's falling faster than I can plow."

"Thank you, Earl," Warren said. "I thought Trooper Goodrich was going to come back here before leaving, but maybe he saw how bad the roads were and decided to go straight home. I tried to call the barracks, but the phone wasn't working."

"I'd say that's just what he did," Earl said. "Pinky's got a good head on his shoulders. The phones are probably out of order. This is heavy, wet stuff that sits on the lines and brings them down."

"Okay, thanks. I'll be going, then," Warren said. "I'll be back to-morrow, but now that I've got statements from everyone, I think the men can get on the road as soon as they're clear in the morning." Earl didn't say anything, and Warren thought that the expression that came across his face was a dubious one. Perhaps the storm was worse than Warren thought.

The front yard of the lodge had been transformed into whirling white. Warren could not even see where his car was, much less figure out a path to get to it. He stood there for a moment, contemplating, and then plunged into the storm. After a few minutes of walking in the already ankle-deep snow, his hands up in front of his face to protect it from stinging crystals that spiraled into his tender skin, he ran into something solid. It was the Galaxie. His instincts had been good.

He opened the door with some difficulty, clearing the snow

beneath it with his foot, and got in. It was only slightly warmer inside the car, and he sat for a moment, worry sneaking up his spine, before saying out loud, "Okay, then," and turning the key in the ignition. The Ford started right up. No problem there. But it was when he shifted and put his foot on the accelerator that the problems started. It moved forward only a few inches before coming to rest in a cradle of snow. Warren tried again, pushing much harder on the accelerator this time. The car moved, and he felt his hopes rise. Maybe he'd be able to get out. He crept forward in first gear, the tires crunching on snow.

He could not recognize much of the road, so he navigated from his memory of where he had parked. The windshield wipers flailed desperately, and a large dark object appeared ahead. It was the pine tree at the side of the drive. Good. He knew where he was now. He steered to the left of it and kept going slowly down the drive, trying to remember how long it had taken to get there on Saturday. Surely, not more than five minutes, maybe ten, which meant that at this almost imperceptible speed, it would take him nearly a half hour to get to the main road. The main road must be better, he thought. Once he got there, it would be clearer. He would be home by dinnertime. He kept driving. The snow was strangely mesmerizing. He felt that he was in a sort of fugue state, everything focused on the stretch of white ahead of him.

Nine minutes went by. Ten. He was about to tell himself that he was almost halfway there, when he hit something hard and the car came to a stop.

Warren pulled his hat down over his ears and got out of the car. He must have hit a tree. It was hard to see anything but once he was outside, he could see that it was not one tree he'd hit but several. He had driven into the deeper snow and trees at the side of the drive, and the car wasn't damaged but was now stuck in a small grove of evergreens. He got behind the wheel and tried to reverse, but the car was now completely trapped, the tires spinning on the wet snow. Warren sat there for a minute and then opened the car door again and stepped out into the storm.

Fourteen

Years before, when she wasn't paid to work at the Ridge Club but only came along with her mother to do little jobs or play in the woods while her mother worked, Jenny had discovered the strange acoustics in the kitchen at the lodge.

She was fetching some bleach for her mother in the pantry once when she suddenly heard two men talking, just as if they were right there in the pantry with her. After a bit, she'd realized that they were on the other side of the wall, in the dining room, and that the register up on the pantry ceiling, which was meant to let out the heat from the kitchen, funneled conversations from the back of the dining room right into the little space. She had wondered if anyone else knew about it, but no one had ever said anything, and so Jenny had gotten in the habit of going into the pantry and listening sometimes. Mostly, she heard men talking about fish or deer or baseball or politics. But sometimes she heard more interesting tidbits, like one man telling another that he had lost all his money in the stock market or another man telling a story about going to a hotel with his secretary.

She had known she shouldn't listen to the conversation about the hotel, but she hadn't been able to help herself. Jenny had heard a lot of interesting things over the years.

That afternoon, she had been peeling potatoes in the pantry next to the kitchen when Colonel French and Mr. Warren's voices had drifted through the register and down to Jenny's ears.

Jenny had slowed her peeling, removing the rough brown skin in a single ribbon from the potato in her hand before shifting its position, the peeler poised over the next section of skin but not touching it. She could peel potatoes fast when she wanted to, but that afternoon she had not peeled very fast because she had not wanted to be done.

She had wanted to listen.

Listening to the men telling Mr. Warren what they'd been doing, Jenny was surprised to hear a lot of lying. Seth Pellegrino, for example. He told Mr. Warren he had taken a nap, but Jenny, who had made up his bed while he was at breakfast that morning, had gone in to leave him a clean towel and she was absolutely sure that his bed hadn't been slept in or even lain on. Everything, even the little creases she liked to make on the club members' pillows, was exactly the way she'd left it. She didn't think he'd been in his room at all.

And Mr. Packingham said he hadn't touched anything when he brought the body back, but Jenny knew that wasn't true from the conversation she'd overheard. There had been other lies too—Mr. Westwood saying he had gone out hunting again right after lunch when Jenny had seen him go out without his rifle, and Mrs. Packingham saying she had only been hunting on club property on Saturday when Jenny had seen her walking near the pond on Friday morning. She had seen Mrs. Packingham when she went out for a walk after breakfast and thought she was just a hunter from New York or something who had gotten lost, but then when Mrs. Packingham came right through the door today saying she wanted to see her husband and she wasn't going to get stranded in the storm, Jenny recognized her as the woman she'd seen on Friday, lurking near the pond and smoking a cigarette, then flicking the last of it onto the surface of the water before disappearing back into the woods. Jenny had been so mad she'd wanted to follow her and tell her that there were frogs and birds and fish living in the pond and how would *she* like it if someone threw a cigarette in *her* house?

Jenny had listened to Belle and her mother answer Mr. Warren's questions, and then Jenny's mother had poked her head in and said, "He wants to talk to you now. Are you still peeling those potatoes?"

"There's a lot," Jenny said, indicating the large bag on the floor.

"Well, go into the dining room and then come back and finish up." Her mother had sounded tired and short-tempered, but when Jenny walked by her, she put a hand on Jenny's shoulder, looking at Jenny as though she wanted reassurance that she was okay.

Jenny had not said anything, though. She had felt funny then, thinking about everything she'd heard through the register in the wall and realizing that she'd gotten herself into a bit of a dilemma.

She could tell Walter everything, and he would probably be grateful. The information about all the lies might be very helpful, and Mr. Warren might be very happy when Walter told him.

But then, she had seen suddenly, everyone would know about her listening, and they might stop talking in the dining room. And there was a lot more she needed to learn. In a way, all the things she'd heard had only made her think of more questions.

So she'd decided that she wouldn't say anything just yet. She'd keep listening and try to find out who was lying because they had something to hide and who was lying because they were just trying to keep some little part of themselves a secret.

She would know more before she said anything. Saying something would get people in trouble.

As she'd walked past to go into the dining room, Jenny had quickly glanced back at her mother's face for a moment. Her mother looked tired. And more than that, she looked scared.

And that gave Jenny a very bad feeling inside, a sort of nauseous worry that settled in her stomach like the hard knot you got when you were sick.

Because one of the people who'd lied was Jenny's mother.

Fifteen

Alice flew up the stairs and into the bedroom. Sylvie was now on the floor, crouched with her hands and face on the edge of the bed.

"Sylvie! Are you okay?"

"I think it *is* the baby," Sylvie panted. "I'm sorry. It feels better sitting like this, though. I'm just going to stay like this for a minute until it stops." But then she gasped and arched her back.

Alice turned around to find the boys in the hallway, now looking alarmed. "Go back downstairs," she said to them. "Try the phone again and get me some old sheets and towels, please." Then seeing their faces, she said nervously, "It will be all right. Don't worry."

"Should I walk down to the Churches'?" Scott asked.

"No," Alice said. "Their phone won't be working either, and it's too far to walk to town. Besides, I don't think Dr. Falconer's car could make it up the hill. Now, go back downstairs and do as I said. Leave us alone for a little bit. It's okay, boys." She turned back to Sylvie, who had relaxed again.

"I'm okay," Sylvie said. "That one's done." She sat back on her haunches and looked up at Alice. "I really didn't think this was it. It felt different, but now it feels the way it did with the boys."

Alice studied her. "Do you feel a heaviness down below, where the baby's going to come out? Do you feel like the head is right there?"

"I'm not sure, but I think so," Sylvie said weakly.

"What was it like the other times?" Alice asked her. "Were they easy births or difficult ones?"

Sylvie smiled a little. "Easy ones," she said. "Even with Scott. Hugh said I was lucky, and it was because we didn't go to a hospital, because we did it right here and I didn't experience any stress. He may have been right. Scott came right out and so did the other boys. There was pain, but not for very long."

Alice felt a small sliver of relief slip in under the worry. "You think you can get back up on the bed?"

"Yes, but I don't want you to have to . . . help me."

"Sylvie, please don't worry about that. I've seen it before. I know what it looks like. I know what happens." Alice looked away, the words catching in her throat. "You're not to be embarrassed in the slightest."

Sylvie got up on the bed and took off her underthings. Alice took the quilt off the bed and found a thin cotton blanket draped over a chair that she put on Sylvie's lap. It wasn't long before Sylvie called out again and started moaning. Alice could see the waves of a contraction come over Sylvie's body, the way it moved the baby toward the light.

What a mystery life was!

Scott brought towels and old bed linens and handed them to Alice, his face scared and sheepish, and she got them under Sylvie on the bed and covered her with another sheet. "Scott, boil some water and find some scissors, will you?" she asked him. He nodded. He'd of course watched many births of animals, and he'd cut many cords. "She's going to be okay," Alice told him. "She's done it before, you know."

Time moved in fits and starts. One contraction had hardly ended before the next one began.

Alice felt a kind of calm come over her. They were going to have to do this, she and Sylvie. There was no one else to help, except for the boys. They were just going to have to do it and hope that it was another easy birth.

After a little bit, Alice said, "The pains are very close together, Sylvie. I think that means the baby's almost here. Do you feel like you can push?"

"I don't know," Sylvie said breathlessly. "It feels different somehow. Should I try?"

Alice hesitated. "No. Wait until you feel like you have to, like there's no other choice. You remember the feeling?"

Sylvie nodded. When the next contraction came, Alice put a hand on her head. She felt hot and feverish, and a thin layer of sweat came off on Alice's hand. "Sylvie," Alice said. "I'm just going to take a look." Alice moved the blanket aside. She could not see the baby's head. What she saw instead made her gasp. At first, she thought it was a foot, and she felt adrenaline pulse through her body, but it was not a foot. It was a hand. That was not quite as bad, she thought, because it meant that the baby was head down, but it would make things very difficult because the baby's shoulder would come at the same time as its head.

Sylvie gasped as another contraction started.

"Sylvie," Alice said. "The baby is coming, but I can only see a hand and arm. I think the head and shoulders are behind it. I might have Scott go on skis to town to see if he can come back with the doctor. Do you have a pair of skis anywhere that he could use?"

Sylvie weakly put up a hand. "No," she said. "No, don't send him. It's too far. I can do it. It'll be the shoulder that will be the problem. You'll have to pull because it will get stuck otherwise." Alice nodded. Sylvie said, "No matter what I do, you have to get it out." Alice thought about the strength it must have taken to say this. Sylvie had delivered countless lambs and calves, had delivered four babies herself. She knew it would be very painful.

"Okay," Alice said. "I'm sorry. For the pain, Sylvie." Sylvie nodded. "I need to go get some soap and things to get my hands very clean. I'll be right back. I'll keep the boys downstairs."

Sylvie nodded. "Please," she said.

Alice ran downstairs. In her head, she echoed Sylvie's words. *Please, please, please.*

Sixteen

The snow was swirling even faster, if that was possible, and Warren, his shoulders hunched down into the collar of his jacket to protect his face from the stinging needles of ice, spun around 180 degrees. He couldn't tell what was woods and what was the road, but if he walked toward the open spaces back the way he'd come, he would reach the lodge soon enough, wouldn't he?

As he started to walk, he realized his error. He had driven off the road, so he didn't know which direction he had been facing when he exited the vehicle. For all he knew, he could be walking back toward the main road and away from the club. Trudging through the wet snow was difficult, and before long, he was breathing hard and could feel a thin layer of sweat gathering under his clothes. *Keep going, keep going*, he chanted to himself. Ten minutes of walking brought him to what seemed to be part of the road; he could just make out lines of dark trees on either side. He crossed his fingers inside his gloves and turned to the right, working off the map in his head and trying to walk in as straight a line as possible.

Suddenly, he remembered getting lost in the woods up on Agony

Hill not long after he arrived in Bethany. When he'd finally emerged, Sylvie Weber had been waiting there. He had felt silly for the level of panic he'd felt, but she had understood what it had been like, thinking that perhaps he was lost to the world. He remembered her face, soft and understanding in the golden summer light. What had she said to him? *You can always follow the brook, though. Just walk along and you'll either come out at the river or the road.* Was that true here as well? It was hard to know, but he did seem to be walking down, and if his memory served, there had been a slight decline as they approached the lodge and the fishing pond. He kept going, Sylvie's face swimming up in front of him. She must be close to having her baby now. He would have to ask Mrs. Bellows if she had heard anything. He had thought about stopping by to check on her a few times recently, but he'd already stopped by at the end of October, around Halloween, to see how Scott and his new puppy were getting along. All was well there. They seemed to be fast friends, and the rowdy yellow Lab seemed to have calmed a bit, though Sylvie had told him that he was chewing everything he could find.

He was terribly afraid of making her feel indebted, of her some-how seeing on his face the thoughts he'd had that night outside the house, the late-summer chill creeping across the fields and gardens, the wild vision he'd had of taking her in his arms. After all, she owed him a great debt, and the last thing he wanted was for her to feel it. So he would stay away, but he would ask Alice Bellows if there was any news.

Thinking about Sylvie had been a distraction for a moment, but soon the cold in his legs and feet brought him back to the present. He had been walking for twenty minutes now, and he didn't know if he was any closer to the lodge and safety.

He trudged on into the blinding white of the storm. Perhaps this was what death was like, white nothingness on and on and on . . .

Despite the pain in his feet, it wasn't unpleasant, exactly. There was something comforting about the oblivion of the storm.

Just when he'd started to give up hope, something large and dark rose before him, and he realized it was Earl Canfield's truck. He had done it. He was back.

He kept walking, and then the dark shape of the lodge appeared out of the storm, and he stumbled up onto the porch and through the door into the entryway, where he stood for moment, catching his breath and letting the warmth of the inside seep into his cheeks and chest. When he took off his outer clothes to hang them on the hooks, he left a pile of melting snow on the floor, and he slipped out of his boots and walked around it carefully so his socks wouldn't get wetter than they already were. As he made his way through the foyer, he heard someone shouting in the lounge.

"I told you to leave it." Warren recognized Jack Packingham's voice.

"Are you bored of the subject?" came a second male voice, Skip's, Warren thought.

"Oh, come on. Can't we all be friends?" a female voice he recognized as Claire Packingham's said. Another voice, also male, said something Warren couldn't quite catch. He stepped into the lounge and found all of the men, plus Claire, sitting around the fire, whisky tumblers still in front of them. There was a charged, angry atmosphere in the room, worse than when he'd left. It surrounded him, and his eyes went to the floor where a smashed glass was half on and half off the carpet.

"Detective Warren, you look as though you had an encounter with an abominable snowman!" Jack said. They all turned to look at him.

"He is the abominable snowman!" Claire said. "You poor thing. Come in and get warm."

Jack's face was red. Skip was leaning forward on the couch, Seth next to him, and the other men were watching the Packinghams.

"Are you all right?" Herman Westwood asked Warren after a moment.

"Got my car stuck and I had to walk back," Warren said. "The storm has really come in. I couldn't see a thing, and I drove my car off the road into the trees. I got a bit turned around, but I made it back on foot."

"Thank goodness you're all right," Jack said, though Warren didn't think he was very pleased about having a policeman back in the mix.

"So we're all here for the night. Isn't that cozy?" Claire said.

"Trooper Goodrich was driving around the perimeter of the property," Warren said. "I'm worried he may have gotten stranded too. Should we go out and look for him?"

"It wouldn't do to get more of us lost," Earl said. "If we knew exactly where he was . . ."

No one said anything. Warren knew Earl was right.

Finally, Graham French said, "Let's get you warmed up first, Detective Warren. Can I get you a drink?"

"Yes, please. Scotch. Neat. I've got to steady my nerves. But just a small one."

The drink Graham handed him was not a small one, and Warren did not protest. He took a long swig and felt it warm him from within.

Then he went to try the phone again, but it was still dead.

He was stuck here until the storm was over and the roads could be cleared.

And Pinky was somewhere out there, perhaps safe and warm at home, perhaps wandering lost in the blizzard.

Warren hovered for a moment outside the lounge on his way back, hoping to overhear something that would explain the tension, but there was only silence, and finally he strode in and said, "Phones are down. I guess I'm here for the night if that's okay with all of you. Would there be a room I could use?"

"Of course," Jack said. "We've got rooms all over the place. I'll ask Belle to make one up. I think she went to check on their woodstove, but it's the cottage just across the way there, so she should be back soon."

"They're going to make one up for me as well," Claire said. "Since there aren't any double beds anywhere."

Skip scowled, and Jack just looked embarrassed and said, "Claire," very quietly.

"Thank you," Warren told Jack. "Since I'm stuck here and on the clock, could I ask you and Mr. Canfield to come into the gun room with me? I wanted to check to make sure nothing's missing."

Warren led them down the hallway to the gun room, where he took the key from his pocket and opened the door.

"Look carefully, check the drawers, the racks, really take your time to be sure," Warren said. "I just want to make certain."

Earl nodded and started opening drawers and counting items. Jack tipped his head back and scanned all the racks and shelves along the walls.

"Everything there?" Warren asked after a minute.

"I think so," Earl said. "Looks good to me."

Jack was staring at a spot on the wall.

"Mr. Packingham?"

"My father's Winchester," he said finally. "I keep it here and use it sometimes, but I don't see— Oh, there it is." Earl had pointed to a spot on the wall, and Jack reached up to touch the rifle and said, "Everything seems to be here, Detective. But of course, I can't know for sure. There are a lot of rifles here and it's not like we have an inventory."

Back in the lounge, Warren sat down close to the fire to warm up his frozen toes. "Would you like another drink?" Herman asked, pointing to the empty glass in Warren's hand. Warren's impulse was to refuse. He was on the job, after all, but he'd just been through a fairly harrowing experience, and another drink would calm his still-jangling nerves. Perhaps he was rationalizing, but it also occurred to him that relaxing with the club members over a drink or two, rather than formally questioning them, might be a better way of gathering information about what had happened in 1946 and whether leftover tension had caused problems over the past couple of days.

"Really, just a small one this time," Warren said. He accepted the tumbler and sat down next to Skip on the couch. The warmth from the fire and the spirits started to seep into his bones. He could feel his body relaxing, his brain settling into a pleasant dullness.

Once he had thawed a bit, he found a dry coat in the hall and went to the porch to look at the veil of tumbling snow. He couldn't see anything beyond the roofline now. If Pinky was still in the woods, he was surely lost, his bearings gone in the whiteout. Had he been able to shelter in his car or one of the houses along the road? Maybe he'd made his way to one of those houses where he was asking about who'd been hunting on Saturday. Maybe he'd realized that the storm was intensifying and was sheltering with the homeowners right now.

But then Warren had a terrible thought. What if Pinky had found the person who shot Moulton? What if that person didn't want anyone to know what had happened?

He turned when he heard the door open, and then Jenny was there, wrapped in a wool blanket and wearing a pair of boots much too big for her feet. "Do you think Walter is okay?" she asked him. "Do you think he made it back home before the roads got real bad?"

"I'm sure he did, Jenny," he said, trying to sound reassuring.

"But when you started trying to drive home an hour ago, Mrs. Packingham said the roads were covered in snow already. If Walter was driving around the other side of the club property, at the end of Ridge Road, it would have taken him a half hour to even get back to the main road. He would have had to start a while ago. Wasn't he supposed to come here first? If he didn't make it here, then he probably didn't make it out of the woods."

Warren wasn't sure what to say. She was right. The fact that Pinky hadn't made it back to the club was not a good sign. He would have had to go past the club to get to the main road. "Trooper Goodrich is an experienced outdoorsman, Jenny. He's always well prepared, and I know for a fact that he had some soup and some of his mother's ham sandwiches in the car, so I think he'll be okay." He smiled at the girl, but he was worried now too.

"But what if someone . . ." She trailed off, reaching out to push a little pile of snow off the porch railing. Her breath formed a little cloud in front of her when she exhaled.

"What if someone what?" Warren prompted her.

She waited a moment, thinking. "Nothing. I just hope he's safe is all."

"Me too, Jenny," he said.

They stood there for a few more minutes, watching the snow fall, and then they went inside.

Seventeen

Jenny was worried.

She had been worried about Walter ever since Detective Warren came back inside, saying that he'd gotten his car stuck in the snow. When she went out on the porch, she'd been hoping that Detective Warren would say something to make her feel better. But she'd been able to see immediately that he was worried too. She'd realized that that was why he'd come out onto the porch.

He was looking for Walter.

She went back to the kitchen to finish cleaning up, and she was wiping down the range when Belle came into the kitchen and said, "Jenny, can you make up rooms for Mr. Warren and Mrs. Packingham?"

"Sure," Jenny said. "I'll do the one next to Mr. Packingham for her, and then Mr. Warren can have the one at the end of the hallway." She hesitated before saying, "I can make up the one next to it in case Trooper Goodrich comes back and needs a room too."

Belle studied her for a moment, and Jenny thought that she was seeing how worried Jenny was about Walter. "I'll have to go make sure we have enough linens," she said finally. "I guess I can do some laundry if I need to."

"I saw at least three more sets in the linen closet upstairs," Jenny told her. "Don't worry. You have enough to do. Is there enough food for the extra people?"

Belle sighed. "I can stretch it, but it may not be as fancy as they're used to." She went off, walking slowly, her shoulders rounded, and Jenny wanted to run after her and hug her and say it would be okay, but instead she went upstairs and started making up the extra rooms. Belle looked so tired and sad. Jenny resolved to do extra to try to take some of the burden off her. She had always liked Belle, who wasn't kind to Jenny the way some older women were, telling her she was pretty and asking her if she had a boyfriend. Belle was really, truly kind, giving Jenny little treats and asking her questions that showed she liked Jenny as a real person, not just because she was Delana's daughter or because she worked at the club.

The rooms were small, but Jenny liked their sense of self-containment. Her own room at home over the hardware store was cluttered and messy, pictures covering the walls and her things on every surface. Her mother made her tidy up every once in a while, but mostly her parents let her be. These rooms, though, were empty and clean. They made you feel like you could be anyone you wanted.

The Ridge Club's bed linens were pretty old. Belle had once said that Mr. Packingham's father had bought them all from a store in Boston when they built the extension. She had told Jenny she'd mentioned to Mr. Packingham that they might need new ones, and he'd said, "We just bought those! They should be good for another twenty years at least." Belle had grumbled about how men didn't understand these things, but she'd gone through and taken out the worst of the sheets. Looking through the linen closet in the hall, Jenny found three clean sets and started making up the beds.

The most worn set she gave to Mrs. Packingham. She didn't like

Mrs. Packingham much, from the little she'd seen of her. The way she'd just marched right in and said all that stuff about Skip. Jenny wasn't sure she liked Skip much either—he always treated her like she was a piece of furniture rather than an actual person, unlike his friend, who had tried to get Jenny involved in a long conversation about migrant farm workers in California or something—but she thought it must have been awful to have your father go off with a younger woman and then make you spend time with her. And of course, she now knew that none of them could be trusted, that they had lied to Mr. Warren. She would have to watch them carefully.

When she was tucking in Claire Packingham's top sheet, she tucked it in extra tight. There was nothing that Jenny hated more than sheets tucked in too tight. You felt like one of those Egyptian mummies, and you always got too hot in the middle of the night.

After she'd made up Detective Warren's room, she went across the hall to the other room, the one she'd make up for Walter, just in case he needed it tonight. She'd saved the best sheets for him, and she made the bed precisely, exactly the same amount of fabric tucked in on each side and the top sheet tucked in, but not too snug, the blanket perfectly smooth with no wrinkles in it at all. When she was done, she went to the window.

Somewhere out there were the deep woods and Hunter's Heart Ridge, where Walter might be lost.

Belle had told her the story once, when they were hanging sheets out to dry after the trout derby. Jenny could just about remember the words she'd used, so large an impression the story had made on her.

There was a young man who came up from Connecticut, I think it was. This is before Vermont was Vermont, and he was surveying the land and he got to know a man who lived up there and was trying to farm the land. The farmer had a daughter and the man fell in love with her, but she didn't love him back and he started to go mad from the heartbreak. Some people thought he'd gone back to Connecticut because they didn't see him for a long time, but then there started to be sightings of him in the woods. The people who lived nearby would find deer hanging in the trees and see smoke from fires. He shot at a few of the farmers who lived in Hillyer, and finally they decided that something had to be done about him. So a group of men went into the woods to try to find him. They looked all day and finally, right at dusk, they came upon a fresh and bloody heart, placed carefully on a rock. There was a knife in it, and they assumed the young man had killed a deer and cut out the heart and left it there. But then they followed the trail of blood and they found the body of one of the men in their party, with the heart cut out. They never found the hunter, no matter how hard they looked, but when I was a girl, I would sometimes see a figure in the woods, darting between the trees. He was dressed in green, so he blended in. Others saw him too. Maybe it's a ghost. Maybe it's not.

Jenny watched the snow swirling outside the windows, shutting her eyes and saying a silent prayer for Walter's safety. *Please, God, I know I'm not always perfect and I don't always act right, but please, God, bring him back safe.* She smoothed the blanket on his bed again before going out of the room and heading downstairs to get cleaned up for dinner. If Walter came back tonight, she hoped he'd feel how much care she'd taken with the room.

She hoped he'd feel her love.

Eighteen

Dinner at the Ridge Club was a surprisingly formal affair under the circumstances. Belle Canfield had had Jenny make up rooms for Warren and Claire Packingham, and Warren arranged himself the best he could, using the washcloth and new toothbrush Jenny had put on top of the towel on his bed. While Warren had to make do with what he'd been wearing all day, the other men came down in shirts with ties and blazers and nice trousers. It was obviously a ritual.

Claire had clearly suspected she might have to stay at the club and packed accordingly; she had changed into a green cocktail dress and fancy shoes and looked ready for a magazine cover shoot. Warren saw the other men noticing, casting furtive and appreciative glances at her long legs and backside, draped in the dress's silky fabric. It made him nervous, the men's leering energy and Claire's clear penchant for drama.

Belle and Delana came in with plates of shredded turkey on white bread with gravy and mashed potatoes. It was a humble dinner that Warren assumed had been constructed from leftovers, but the men dug in and ate heartily. For dessert there was fresh apple pie, the crust crispy and the filling just the right amount of softness and firmness.

"Mrs. Canfield, I believe your apple pie is the best I've ever had," Claire said. "I wish I could make a pie nearly as good. Jack will tell you, I'm hopeless in the kitchen. Aren't I, darling?"

"Yes, but I don't care," Jack said. "I can hire someone to make pie."

Skip Packingham said something under his breath, and Jack smiled and said, "I'm going to pretend I didn't hear that, Skip."

Claire raised her wineglass in her stepson's direction. "Skip, you'll have to stop hating me one day. And when you do, you'll discover that I'm actually a nice person and that I love your father."

Skip scowled and Warren, hoping to avoid another conflagration, jumped in and asked the men, "Had Ambassador Moulton always been in the foreign service? I've been trying to get a sense of his career, but of course, I've been busy out here and haven't been able to call down to Washington, DC."

"Graham, you were in his class at Harvard, weren't you?" Jack asked Graham French.

"That's right," Graham said. "Class of thirty, same as me. After the war, he joined the foreign service. I forget all the places he was posted. Greece, Colombia, Czechoslovakia, all over the map. He always had good stories, didn't he?" Herman and Jack agreed that he had.

"And when did he become a member of the club?" Warren asked.

"Well," Jack said, "he and Marjorie got married in thirty-one, so it must have been then. Her father was a member, an old friend of my father's, and they spent those summers in Hillyer. I think Marjorie liked getting Kevin out of the city, and Bill really did enjoy the company at the club. He spent a lot of time here for those summers they were here."

"It didn't sound like he and his son were very close," Warren said.

"The poor kid was raised by nannies and headmasters," Jack said.

He turned to his son. "Whatever you say about me as a father, I never sent you away."

"That's true," Skip said sarcastically. "You never sent me away. Hard to do that when you've left your family for a girl half your age."

Jack took a long, furious drink of his wine. "Don't talk about Claire like that," he said angrily. "She's your stepmother."

"No, Jack, I'm flattered," Claire said. "Half your age? That would make me twenty-seven! Skip, I'm deeply grateful." The sarcasm oozed from every word. She batted her eyelashes at him in mock flirtation, and everyone at the table looked away in embarrassment.

"Skip." Jack glared at him. "Show some respect."

Skip started to say something and then stopped, pressing his lips together and slumping in his chair.

"Why don't we go into the lounge?" Herman suggested. "Cool things down a little." Warren happened to be looking at him when he said it, and he caught a little glitter of excitement in the man's eyes.

"I think that's a good idea," Graham said. "Let's have another drink." He stood slowly, reaching behind him to push the chair away. He pushed too hard, though, and it clattered to the floor. Warren jumped. Jack stooped to pick up the chair and put a hand on Graham's arm.

Warren said he would help clear the table, and against Belle Canfield's protests, he gathered up a stack of dessert plates and brought them into the surprisingly small kitchen. "I'm going to help wash some of those pots," he said. "You can't stop me. I added to your count and the least I can do is help you clean up."

"Put an apron on so you don't wreck your clothes," Delana said. "Jenny, hand him one, will you?"

"I've got the spare because I can't find the nice one, but you can have it, Detective Warren," Jenny said, flashing him a smile. "My clothes are old anyway." She handed it over, and Warren thanked her and put it on.

Warren started scrubbing the pots in the sink. There was a relaxed conviviality in the kitchen, away from the men, and Warren thought about how he'd loved sneaking into his grandmother's kitchen as a small boy. He would sit under the table and listen to the housekeeper and her daughter and the maid chatting away while they cleaned and cooked.

As he worked on the pots, Warren looked around the kitchen, his eyes settling on a block of wood on the counter, some of the horizontal slits cut into it occupied by knives of various sizes and some of them empty. That was interesting. He thought about how to ask the women if one was missing without giving away Bill Moulton's cause of death, but he couldn't come up with anything.

"I should make some cookies or something," Belle said, almost to herself. "Since we're all waiting."

"They like the molasses ones," Delana said. "With the raisins." She walked behind Belle, turning her body to pass without bumping into her, replacing a pot on a rack on the wall and then turning to pass behind Belle again. It struck Warren that they had performed this dance many, many times over the years. It was the kind of working relationship he felt he was building with Pinky. Pinky! Where was he? Warren felt his anxiety over his assistant return. The temperature was dropping outside.

Belle started taking ingredients from the pantry, asking Jenny to turn on the oven and fetch her a wooden spoon. Delana took a clean dish cloth from a drawer and began drying the pile of clean ladles, spoons, and knives next to the sink. By the time she was done putting the knives away, the knife block was full again. So much for that line of thinking.

Unless the knife had been cleaned and replaced.

Despite everything that was on his mind, he found the quiet conversation and the warm water on his hands soothing, and he was sorry when he was done, and he took off the apron and hung it on the wall and went back to the lounge.

The fire was roaring now, and the table lamps cast a cozy glow over the lounge. Warren watched as the men went up one by one to refill their glasses. The older men poured liberally, as did Skip Packingham. Only Seth Pellegrino went easy, splashing a finger of scotch into a glass and filling it the rest of the way with soda. Warren followed his lead for his own drink.

"Has this happened before?" Warren asked after a long moment. "Members getting snowed in here?"

Jack said, "My father and I got snowed in once years ago. We'd come up for some deer hunting and there was an early storm, just like this one." Earl had come into the room to tend to the fireplace, and Jack called out, "Earl, do you remember that? You'd just taken over for Nathan. What year was that we got stranded? You were living out at Nathan's place then, weren't you? You had to come on snowshoes to help us shovel out."

"Fifty," Earl called back. "That was a big storm."

"Come and sit down, Earl," Jack called out. "We're all snowed in. Why don't you join us?"

Earl looked uncomfortable. "Thank you, but I'm needed in the kitchen. There's a lot of cleaning up to do. I don't want to leave it all to the women."

"Why don't they join us too?" Seth Pellegrino suggested in a voice loud enough to carry all around the room. "No reason we should be segregated by sex. It's 1965, after all." He grinned provocatively.

"I like the way you think, Seth," Claire announced, turning to address the other men. "It's ridiculous the way you Easterners have everything all separate, like you're still living in England or something, and the women get sent out of the room after dinner. Where I grew up, women were there for everything. You can't imagine how strange it was when I started law school!"

Jack looked annoyed at Seth taking over the role of host, but he didn't have any choice now but to say, "Sure, why not? We're snowed in and we won't be going anywhere anytime soon. The cleaning can wait. Earl, why don't you and the ladies come in and sit by the fire and have a drink?"

"Well, if you're sure," Earl said uncomfortably. He went through to the kitchen and came back with the women following him, Belle holding a tray and Delana and Jenny looking confused and timid.

"I brought some of the pie in case anyone's still hungry," Belle said quietly, placing plates and the pie on a side table. "And there are molasses cookies in the oven."

"I love those molasses cookies," Jack said. "You always remember, Belle. Your mother made them too."

"It's her recipe," Belle said with a warmth Warren hadn't seen before. Her rapport with the men was familiar to him in some way, and he realized suddenly that he was thinking of Pauline, his mother's housekeeper, who had lived with Warren's family, cooked for them, cared for them, and washed their clothes from the time he was a baby until she died when he was in college. What was it about wealthy men and their housekeepers? These men had grown up in the same world Warren had, with household help at every stage of their lives. Had they recreated the conditions of their childhoods at the club? He wondered suddenly if their devotion to the club was more about being cared for by a neutral maternal figure than it was about hunting or fishing.

"I'll have some pie," Herman said, standing up.

"Sit down," Seth Pellegrino told the women. "I'll make your drinks. What would you like?" Belle and Delana said they'd have a glass of sherry, and Jenny said she'd just have ginger ale.

"Oh, don't you want a drink?" Seth asked her. "You're not going anywhere tonight, and it will warm you up."

"Well . . ." Jenny said uncomfortably. "No, thank you. I don't like alcohol. It's bitter. And besides, I'm not twenty-one."

"Neither am I," Seth said with a wink in Jenny's direction. "But don't tell the cops that."

"We'll keep it between us," Warren said, winking back at Seth, though he now felt irritated at the young man.

Jack leaned back on the couch, projecting his voice across the room. "Belle, we were just talking about Nathan. He was an old character, wasn't he? I was remembering the last time I got snowed in out here. He and Mary took good care of us."

Belle smiled, and again, Warren saw her housekeeper persona fall away. "He loved a good snowstorm during deer season," she said. "He always said that it gave the woods back to the experts."

"That's right," Jack said. "I remember quite a few deerskins tacked up on the side of your old house. He told me that you had to be patient in the snow, because the deer weren't on the move, but that if you found them, you had an advantage. He was a good tracker, wasn't he?"

"He loved hunting," Graham said. "Earl, did he make you pass a test before you could marry Belle?"

Everyone laughed and Earl said, "Just about. Before he hired me, he took me out for an overnight in the woods. Told me all kinds of stories, to see if I'd scare easy, I think." He shared a private grin with Belle, who shook her head and smiled at some favorite memory.

"What kinds of stories?" Claire Packingham asked. "Did he tell you the one about the hunter who carved up some poor man's heart? Jack told me that one. I love it!"

"Oh yes," Earl said.

"You used to tell me that one when I was little," Skip reminded Jack. "It terrified me." He said it in a light tone of voice, though, and when Jack laughed, Skip did too.

"Do people really see the hunter in the woods sometimes?" Skip asked.

"Belle has," Jenny blurted out. "Right, Belle?"

Belle nodded. "I have," she said matter-of-factly. "A good few times over the years."

Seth made a noise that indicated he thought it was nonsense. "Surely it was just a local man, out hunting or walking," he said. "Why would you think it was a ghost?"

"I didn't say it was a ghost," Belle said. "It's a man."

"You mean he's just a very old man who lives in the woods? That's ridiculous." Seth looked around the room for support, but no one came to his aid.

"Nathan always said there were things we don't understand out in the deep woods," Jack said. "I'll go along with that." That seemed to settle it somehow, and Seth let the subject go.

There was a comfortable silence, and then Herman took a long gulp of his drink and said, "Well, Mr. Warren. Have you figured out what happened to Bill? Did he do himself in or did one of us do it?"

"Herman!" Jack chided him. "What a thing to say."

"We're all wondering," Herman said. "But I suppose you'll say the investigation is ongoing and you can't tell us anything, won't you, Detective? That's what policemen always say."

Warren smiled and shrugged. "You'd be right, Mr. Westwood."

"How did you become a policeman anyway?" Graham asked Warren. "You went to Tufts. You seem like a smart sort of man. You could have done anything."

Now Warren felt a hot anger building in his chest. It was almost word for word what his parents had said to him and what many of their friends had communicated without words over the years, ever since Warren had expressed his desire to join the Boston Police Department after he graduated from Tufts. His answer had always been that he knew he could do anything and that this was what he wanted to do, and it was the answer that he gave Westwood, who nodded but didn't look convinced.

"I think it's awfully important that good people want to be policemen," Jenny said. "After all, they're responsible for keeping the peace, and you can't do that unless you're a very *good* person, can you?"

"Is there such a thing as a 'good' policeman?" Skip asked. "I don't know you can say that after what we've seen in Alabama. Maybe you think some of those men were 'good' men, but they were part of a police force that did terrible things."

"I didn't mean those men," Jenny said, flustered now. "They shouldn't have hit the marchers."

"But they did," Skip told her. "They had to. It was their job."

"Surely you're not arguing that every single police officer in the world is corrupt?" Jack asked his son.

Skip leaned back in his chair. "They might not be on their own, but the job corrupts them," he said. "We've seen that clearly. Isn't that right, Seth?" He glanced at his friend for reassurance.

Warren hoped that no one asked him what he thought about this premise. The truth was that he'd seen corruption firsthand. He didn't think Skip was 100 percent right, but he wasn't 100 percent wrong either. Suddenly, he thought of Pinky and felt anxiety race through his body. Relaxing by the fire, he'd gotten distracted by the conversation and forgotten about Pinky.

"That's right," Seth said. "It's the system, you see, not the individual man. Because—"

"I suppose you'd say the same about soldiers," Herman said before Seth had a chance to finish, leaning forward to stare right at Skip. "I suppose you're one of these who says boys shouldn't have to fight if they don't want to."

"I do say that," Skip said. "I don't want to go to war. I don't want to fight people I have no issue with who are just trying to survive."

"Oh God, this again," Jack said. "You'd think Friday night would have been enough for you. You were out of order then and you're out of order now."

"Out of order?"

"When we were asked to go and fight Hitler, we didn't say we had no issue with the German people. We heeded the call!" Jack said. "That's what your generation doesn't understand."

"We understand better than you think," Skip said. "You have to accept that your way of looking at the world is finished. You're a bunch of old men, sitting around and watching things burn while you talk and talk about patriotism."

"Jesus Christ!" Herman said.

"What *do* you think, Mr. Westwood?" Seth asked. "You said you think we can win this war. You're making the bombs that will keep this war going. You've got the profit motive."

"I think you know nothing," Herman said. "Our technology allows for better war outcomes, for more precise targeting. That's the whole point of it!"

"What kind of technology?" Seth asked calmly. Warren saw in his eyes a bit of the gleam of a cat with a mouse, and he watched as Herman started to rise to the bait and then thought better of it.

"Nothing I want to tell you about." He got up and went over to the bar and swore under his breath. "And I think we're out of scotch."

"I'll go and get another bottle," Delana said, putting her drink down on the coffee table.

"No, I'll do it," Jenny told her. "You and Belle hate the cellar. I'll go." She stood up and gave her mother a smile. "You stay here and rest."

"Thank you, sweetheart," Delana told her.

"You make the Hawk missiles, don't you?" Seth asked Herman. "Are they using those in Vietnam?"

Herman turned to look at Seth, and Warren was sure he was going to clock him, but instead he grinned and held his empty glass in the air. "Son, I don't know why you've got a bee in your bonnet, but I'm on vacation. You can go fuck yourself!"

"Herm," Graham said. "There's no need to be vulgar. Is there a television anywhere? It's almost six o'clock. Let's turn it on and see if there's anything about the storm."

Earl said, "There's one in the kitchen. It's not getting a signal. There's a radio, though." He got up and switched on the radio sitting on a table against one wall, turning the dial until the static resolved and a man's voice came in in the middle of a sentence.

... to Vietnam, where South Vietnamese forces held back a communist attack forty miles northwest of Saigon. US military sources say US casualties were light. North Vietnamese forces sustained heavy losses. In a second week of fighting in the Ia Drang Valley, North Vietnamese sniper fire was infrequent yesterday.

In New England, an early-season snowstorm has caused widespread power outages and road closures. Motorists are advised to stay off the roads until further notice, and listeners should set aside water and provisions as the outages may continue.

In Ohio, an alert zookeeper . . .

Graham got up slowly and went over to fiddle with the dial, lighting on a few stations but moving on again and saying "Shhh" when the men started talking again.

"What are you looking for?" Skip asked him.

"More news," he said shortly. He kept fiddling, finally leaving it on big-band music.

"Sounds like we're making good progress," Jack said.

"I read in the paper that the war could take ten years," Skip said. "How many people are going to die in ten years?"

"Didn't we do this on Friday night?" Herman asked. "Besides, that's ridiculous. Fearmongering. It's nothing like ten years."

Graham looked up. "You know my opinion on this, Herman," he said.

"Damned pacifists," Herman muttered. "Don't they see if we just do this thing and do it once and for all, we'll stop 'em in their tracks?"

"Do you really believe that, Mr. Westwood?" Seth asked. "How many troops do you think it will take to do it once and for all?"

"Well." Herman checked to see if he was in earnest. "They say a hundred thousand will make a real difference. With the right equipment."

"Bullshit," Graham said in a low voice. "This isn't the kind of thing you can—"

Jenny, wearing a pretty green coat with big black buttons on the front, entered the room again. She was carrying two bottles of scotch, and she put them on the bar table. Herman went over to replenish his glass. "Thank you, young lady," he said.

Jenny started to take her coat off. "Oh, it was no— Ow! What was . . ." Her hand had gone into her pocket, and as they all watched, she pulled it out again. "Why is this in here?"

She was holding a long, slender-tipped knife.

Nineteen

Where did that come from?" Warren practically shouted, jumping up and crossing the room to her. Jenny looked startled and just stood there, frozen, holding the knife out in front of her.

"I . . . It's not mine. It was in the pocket of my coat. I put it on because the cellar's cold." She looked genuinely confused to Warren's eyes.

"Are you okay? Did it cut you?" Warren asked.

"No, it just poked me."

Warren took a napkin from the table and held it out. "Put it right here, Jenny," he said. "Try to touch it as little as possible, okay?"

"What's going on?" Jack asked. "Why are you taking the knife?"

Warren didn't say anything, and Herman said, "It must be an important piece of evidence, Jack."

"But it's not like Bill was killed with— Oh." Jack's eyes went wide, and he stopped talking.

Warren looked around the room. He could feel his covert investigation sliding away as his suspects realized the implications of the discovery. Earl was staring at the knife with an expression of horror, and so were Belle and Delana.

"Someone killed Bill with a knife?" Graham French asked. "I'll be damned."

"Oh my God," Delana said. "But . . . why was it in Jenny's pocket?"

"Someone must have put it in there, hoping she wouldn't find it for a while," Warren said. "Does anyone recognize this knife?"

After a long silence, Jack said, "I've seen it around the kitchen. I think I've used it for cutting up deer." He looked to Belle and Delana for confirmation, and they nodded.

"Have you seen it recently?" Warren asked them.

Delana said, "I don't think so," but didn't sound sure.

"Mrs. Canfield?"

Belle shook her head.

Jenny carefully placed the knife on the napkin Warren was holding out and took off the coat to hand to him. "Is it a clue?" she asked. "Is it an important clue?"

Warren said he'd be right back and took the knife and Jenny's coat through to the gun room, where he used the key in his pocket to open the door. He placed the pieces of evidence on a high shelf and looked around the room. It was just the way he'd left it when he'd been in here before with Earl and Jack. He locked the door carefully and tried the knob to make sure it was secure.

Herman Westwood strode up to him once he was back in the lounge. "What does this all mean? Are you saying that Bill was stabbed with a knife?" He seemed to be in a state of high excitement, his face set in fear.

"Now, Jenny," Warren asked her, ignoring Herman. "Where exactly was the jacket hanging? Can you show me?"

She nodded and motioned for him to follow her into the hall. The hooks were along the wall just outside the gun room, the same ones where all the club members' coats were hanging, everyone's boots lined up beneath. "I had it on that hook right there," she said. "That's where my mother and I always hang our coats, down at the end there, so they're not in the way of the members' things."

Warren looked from the front door to the closed gun room door and back to the row of hooks along the wall. It would have been easy for someone to slip the knife into the pocket of Jenny's coat without being seen by anyone. "When was the last time you wore it, Jenny?"

She thought for a moment. "I don't think I put it back on after I got here Friday after lunch. I . . . It's my warm one, you see. I borrow one from the hook if I have to go outside when I . . ." Something seemed to occur to her then, and her face froze.

"Jenny?" She was staring at the hook where the jacket had been.

"Oh . . . I guess, uh, Friday afternoon."

"You're sure there's nothing else?"

"No. I was just trying to remember."

"Thank you."

So the knife could have been put in her pocket any time after Bill Moulton was killed. How nice it would have been if she'd narrowed the window a bit.

Back in the lounge, everyone was sitting around in stunned silence. Claire said, "Detective Warren, do you mean to say that Bill Moulton was killed with a knife and not a rifle?"

Warren hesitated before realizing he didn't have a choice. "We think that's a possibility," he said.

"My God, is there a madman with a knife stalking us?" Herman asked. At first Warren thought he was being sarcastic, but then he realized that the man was actually scared. "Are we safe here?"

"Don't be ridiculous, Herman," Graham said. "It must have been some sort of a hunting accident. Right, Detective Warren?"

"An accidental stabbing?" Skip asked.

There was a long silence. "And why was the knife in her pocket?" Seth asked.

"It might not be the same knife," Graham pointed out. He was right, Warren thought. Perhaps someone was trying to confuse him.

"Does anyone know anything about how it got there?" he demanded of them. "If you know anything, anything at all, it's very important that you tell me." The faces stared back at him. No one said anything.

There was a long silence and then Jenny said, "I swear I didn't put it there. You don't think that I . . ."

"No one thinks that, Jenny," her mother said, going over to comfort her.

"That's right, Jenny," Warren said. He tried to remember what had been happening just before she went down into the cellar. Who had been there? Who had left the room? Damn! He shouldn't have had the whisky! His memory was hazy and blurred.

Still, no one said anything.

Jack had been very quiet, and suddenly he said, "Let's let our detective do his job. I know this has been unsettling, but we're all stuck here together, and we might as well find something to occupy us. Who'd like another drink? I'd love a game of rummy, if anyone's interested."

"I am, darling," Claire said. "Skip, Seth, do you want to play with us?"

"Not if you're playing," Skip said.

"Skip." Jack's voice had a note of warning in it.

Claire laughed. "It's okay, Jack. We all know Skip hates me. We'll play gin rummy."

She settled down at the table by the fire and Jack joined her. Now Warren was watching everyone in the room, trying to read their faces. Who seemed uncomfortable? Who was too quiet? Claire expertly shuffled the cards and dealt while everyone else found a place to sit and watched the game unfold.

"You know, Mr. Warren," Herman said, "I could swear I've met you before. You look so familiar."

Warren felt a little buzz of anxiety. When he'd realized the men were all from the Boston area, he'd wondered if any of them would remember seeing his picture in the papers. "I've been told I have one of those faces," he said lightly.

"No, I could swear it's more than that." But Herman didn't seem to remember anything more, and he sat back in his chair with his drink.

The room was silent for a bit but for the sounds of the card game. Warren shifted his gaze, trying to read each person's mood. "By the way," Skip said. "What you said before, Claire? I don't hate you. I don't think enough of you to hate you. You just disgust me."

Claire ignored him, keeping her gaze on her hand. But Jack shot his son an irritated look.

Graham, clearly uncomfortable, cleared his throat. "Now, young man," he said. "Let's keep things civil."

"Oh, I'm being very civil." Skip glanced meaningfully at Claire, who continued to ignore him.

Seth was sitting next to Skip on the couch and, clearly trying to alleviate some of the tension, said, "Can I get you another drink, Skip?" He didn't wait for Skip to say anything before refilling the young man's glass.

"I could swear I know you from somewhere," Herman said again to Warren. "Were you in the paper for some case you were working on? This Boston Strangler thing—was that your case?"

Herman had the attitude that people always had when they'd seen the stories about Maria's death and the aftermath but couldn't quite remember the details. Warren had encountered a few of them, and it was part of the reason he'd left Boston once he'd been cleared. He hated the looks he got, hated the way he was reminded of Maria's death and the suspicion that fell on him in the months after it.

Usually, he tried to steer people away from it. He had an out too, because he *had* worked on one of the Boston Strangler cases, back when the killer was called the Mad Strangler. But now, for reasons he didn't quite understand, he decided to just tell them. "I used to be a homicide investigator in Boston. My wife was murdered in our apartment—I was the one to find her—and I was accused," he said, trying to keep his voice neutral. "I was cleared eventually, but it was in the papers a lot, and my picture was in a lot of the stories."

A prickly silence fell over the room for a few seconds.

"My God, that's right," Herman said finally. "I remember now. You almost went to prison. It was big news—accused by your colleagues? You quit, didn't you, and went out West or something? I thought you'd moved out there."

Warren shrugged. "I thought about it. I loved Montana, did some fly-fishing and some hiking and got my head on straight again. I realized I wanted to be back on the East Coast. And now, here I am."

Jenny stood up and came over to him. She touched his arm gently and said, "How awful. I'm so sorry for your loss, Mr. Warren. Did they ever find out who killed your wife?"

"Jenny," Delana warned her.

"No, it's all right. I appreciate that, Jenny. No, they never did. The case is still open in Boston." She touched his arm again before going back to sit on the couch. "Now," Warren said, feeling emboldened, like he'd gotten some power back by being forthright with them. "You know all my secrets. Maybe you can tell me some of yours. What was the source of the tension at that Friday-night dinner?"

Jack sighed. "We told you. There was a fight about politics. It got heated. Nothing that hasn't happened here a thousand times before."

Suddenly, Warren was angry with them all. There was a murderer at the Ridge Club, and they were protecting the club's reputation.

"Then what really happened at that dinner in 1946? What did Moulton say to make you so mad you put a knife into him, Mr. Westwood? Don't tell me it was an accident. Don't tell me you tripped."

Herman's eyes turned to Warren. "Bill was just . . . maddening.

He seemed so jolly and fun, but he had a nasty streak," Herman said. "He liked to get you going and press your buttons. He—"

A panicked gasp came from the other side of the room.

They all looked over at Delana, who was standing now and pointing at the window. "There's someone out there," she said in a high, trembling voice. "I just saw something move on the other side of the window."

"What?" Graham French went slowly to the window and cupped his hands around his face, looking out at the storm. "I don't see anyone."

Delana pointed. "I saw something move. I know I did."

Warren went to the window too. "I think it was that tree branch," he said, pointing to the overhanging limb of a maple tree next to the porch. "It's bowing under the weight of the snow. See?" He beckoned to Delana to come over. She pressed her forehead against the window and peered through the glass.

"I guess," she said after a long moment. "I'm sorry. I thought I saw someone." The room was vibrating with apprehension now, everyone looking toward the windows and instinctively drawing closer to the fireplace.

Warren told her it was okay and went back to the couch. It took him a moment to remember what he'd been talking about with Herman.

"What were you saying about Mr. Moulton? You said he liked to press buttons. What did he say to press *your* buttons?" Warren asked. He sensed that this was the crux of the thing, right here, and it occurred to him suddenly that Delana's cry of alarm had almost prevented him from getting the answer.

Herman thought for a moment and then lifted his shoulders as though he was looking for a bit of dignity and said, "I won't repeat the specifics because of the company." He raised his eyebrows in Jenny and Delana's direction. "But he made a comment about my wife.

Something very out of order. I saw white, Detective. I swear to you I didn't know what I was doing. He wasn't mad later, because he knew he'd been in the wrong."

No one said anything. Earl got up to add another log to the fire. Everyone was still glancing nervously toward the windows. Earl looked deeply uncomfortable, and Warren wondered how many times he'd witnessed private interpersonal drama. It would be part of the job at a place like this. And it would be part of the job to keep quiet about it. What had Earl been asked to keep quiet about over the years?

"Well, he was an old lech," Claire said finally. "I only met him once, over the summer. Jack and I were in New York, and we ran into him. He asked us to go for a drink, and as soon as Jack went to the john, he put his hands right on me and started slurring about how lucky Jack was and what he'd like to do. I shut it down pretty fast, and I told Jack about it, but Herman's right. He wasn't a nice man."

"Did you confront him?" Warren asked Jack. This was interesting. What had Jack thought when Bill Moulton had asked to come up to the Ridge Club? Had he still been angry? Had he seen a chance for revenge?

"No, there was no need." Jack seemed uncomfortable, though, and Warren was now alert to his body language. Jack got up to refresh his drink and stood moodily looking into the fire.

"Personally, I wouldn't believe a word she says," Skip said, nodding toward Claire and going to stand near the fire but keeping a comfortable distance between himself and his father.

"Skip," Graham warned.

"Did you know," Skip asked, "that *he* started seeing her when my mother was in the hospital having an operation? Claire worked for him and he started taking her to lunch, and then—"

"Show some respect!" Jack shouted. He strode across the room and the slap came so fast that not even Skip seemed to anticipate it.

Delana screamed.

Skip's hand went to his face, and he looked absolutely shocked that his father had hit him, the surprise mirrored on Jack's face. Seth jumped up and came over to put a hand on Skip's arm, ready to stop him if he tried to retaliate. "Everyone, sit down!" Warren told them. "Right now!" He felt that he was losing control of them, of the situation.

After a few awkward moments, they complied. Graham and Herman started up a card game, and Skip and Seth went to play backgammon. Jack looked miserable, but Claire seemed delighted by the whole thing, casting glances at Skip and then at her husband and laying out a game of solitaire on the table.

Jenny went over to check on her mother, who was ashen faced. Warren joined them.

"Are you all right?" he asked Delana.

Weakly, she nodded her head. "I'm fine," Delana said, looking into the fire. "But . . . it's like a movie, isn't it? Or an Agatha Christie novel. Everyone snowed in and then the knife showing up."

Belle Canfield had some knitting, and she and Earl sat down, Earl sipping his scotch and Belle focusing on her needles and yarn. Warren wanted to apologize to them, but of course, it wasn't his fault.

The radio was playing big-band music, and for a little bit, they just listened . . .

And then the top of the hour came and the news was on again. *"Officials continue to deal with an early-season snowstorm and warn travelers to stay off the roads until crews can plow."*

"We haven't had one of these in a long time," Earl said. "Such an early storm. It—"

Suddenly, the room was plunged into darkness, the only light now coming from the fireplace, and the radio went silent. Someone emitted a gasp, he wasn't sure who, and then Jack's voice came: "I guess that was inevitable. The snow has brought the power lines down."

Twenty

'll get some candles," Earl said. In the low light from the fire, Warren looked around at the assembled faces. Was everyone here? He had the sudden thought that someone had killed the lights on purpose. But that was ridiculous! The snow was piling up on the tree limbs outside. Of course the lines had come down.

"There are flashlights in the kitchen," Belle said. "I'll get them."

"I've got one upstairs," Jack said. "I always keep a flashlight by my bed. I'll go and—"

"Everyone, remain where you are," Warren said. He suddenly felt very strongly that he needed to keep track of them. The knife told him that in their midst was someone with a secret, someone who had killed Bill Moulton and then tried to turn suspicion onto an innocent girl. *But how do you know she's innocent, Warren?* Their situation had finally hit him in the moments after the lights went out, and he no longer trusted anyone; he wanted to make sure nothing happened in the darkness. "No one move from their seat! Mr. Canfield, please go get the flashlights and candles if you can find them. The rest of us will stay here."

"There are flashlights in the kitchen and oil lamps in the dining room," Belle said quietly. "Earl, bring some more matches." Warren was suddenly grateful for the couple's calm competence.

While Earl was gone, Warren kept an eye on the rest of them. *Who was it? Which one of them?*

Herman Westwood? He was angry—and arrogant—and he apparently had reason to kill Moulton. He had almost done it once before.

Jack Packingham? Moulton had made overtures to Jack's wife. How had that felt, when Claire had informed him? His old friend. It must have felt like a huge betrayal.

Of course, he needed to consider the staff too. Earl Canfield? He hadn't been here in '46, but perhaps there had been a slight over the weekend that no one knew about. Belle Canfield? Could Moulton have treated her with a lack of respect, demanding something once too often?

And what about the Breedloves? Could Delana or Jenny have had some unknown reason to kill Moulton and then stage the whole thing with the knife?

He realized he'd forgotten Graham French. Broken, beaten-down Graham French. What possible reason could he have to want Moulton dead? There was his work, of course. Military men and foreign service officers had all kinds of connections and cross purposes, especially now. The possibilities for offense and betrayal were endless. And what about Skip and Seth?

Earl came back with the flashlights and handed one to Warren, who immediately switched it on and shone it around the room, counting the occupants to make sure everyone was there. Earl and Belle ferried oil lamps back to the lounge and set them up on the tables around the sides of the room.

Once they'd lit them, the room was filled with soft, orange light that revealed a crescent of worried faces.

"Okay, now, we'll just—" Warren was starting to say when suddenly Delana Breedlove screamed, a high-pitched, bloodcurdling scream that filled the room and sent adrenaline racing through his veins.

"What the hell—" someone said. And then, like a monster out of a winter legend, a giant glowing figure appeared in the doorway, its white head and shoulders grotesquely shaped and twisted, moving out of the darkness with its hands outstretched. It was reaching for them, making unintelligible sounds as the light from the oil lamps seemed to swirl and Warren looked down and saw his service weapon in his hands, heard his voice say, "Stop where you are!"

It was Jenny who saw the monster for what it was.

"Walter!" she screamed, running to the snow-covered figure. "It's Walter! Oh, Walter, you're all right after all!"

⌘ ⌘ ⌘

Warren's first reaction was relief. Pinky was alive. His second was embarrassment. His deputy had returned to the club and come into a scene of chaos. Warren had no control over the situation. He could have killed Pinky in his panic! Ashamed, he shifted into crisis mode and he found his flashlight and waved it around to get their attention, shouting, "Everyone sit down! Trooper Goodrich, come by the fire and take off your things. Are you hurt? Are you okay?"

Pinky's voice was strong when he answered. "I'm okay, just a bit frozen. I may need help unzipping my parka, though. My hands are very cold." Belle and Jack helped him take off his hat and gloves and then the outer jacket and the heavy wool pants he'd put on over his regular pants.

"Thank goodness I had these in the car," he said, gesturing to the trousers, now in a wet heap on the floor. "I'm soaked through, but they kept me warm at least. My God, I'm glad to see you all."

"We thought you were dead, Walter," Jenny said dramatically.

Warren handed Pinky a glass of whisky and told him to have a sip and to sit down by the fire to get warm. "I was hoping you'd made it home before the snow really started," Warren said. "I tried to call the barracks, but the phones were down. I would have gone after you, but we didn't know where you were or whether you were even out there."

Pinky took a long sip, grimacing as the alcohol made its way down his esophagus and into his stomach. He stretched his legs out toward the fire, and in the candlelight from the table, Warren could see utter relief on his face. He'd made it. He'd survived. "I figured the phones were down," he said. "It's good you didn't come after me. I'd been stopping at houses along the end of the road when the snow started piling up. I stayed too long at one, and when I came out, it was getting bad. I figured I'd have a better chance of making it back here than getting all the way to the main road, so I turned onto Ridge Road and made it about halfway back when the cruiser spun into a snowbank. I wasn't sure what to do. I didn't have snowshoes or skis, and I was worried about getting stuck, so at first I hunkered down in the car. I figured I could just wait it out. But after a couple of hours, it was still coming, and I was worried I'd be buried. You hear of people running out of oxygen that way."

"Here, Walter," Jenny said. "Belle made these cookies, and I've brought you a few. To get your strength back." Pinky thanked her and gratefully bit into one of the molasses treats.

"Anyway, I decided I needed to try to walk back here," he said. "But I didn't realize how turned around I'd get. I couldn't see a thing in the whiteout. I must have wandered for two hours, getting colder and colder as the snow got deeper and deeper. Finally, I saw a building, but it was that abandoned house on the other side of the road. At least I knew where I was then."

"That must have been Nathan's old place," Jack said. "Belle's father's house."

"That's right," Pinky said. "I hope you don't mind, Belle. I went inside, but the stovepipe was busted, and anyway, there wasn't any wood to burn. I thought I might get warmed up, but a window upstairs must have been stuck open. It wasn't much better than the outside. It was dumb, but I was thinking about this fire right here, and I thought I could make it back, so I just started walking. Finally, I saw the lights and I thought I was home free. But then the power must have gone out. Luckily, I was close enough that I found my way." He looked up, his eyes settling, Warren thought, on Jenny, who was holding the plate of cookies. "I'm awfully glad to be back here."

"That must have been you I saw through the window," Delana told him, casting Warren a judgmental look. "I knew I'd seen someone."

"We didn't realize it was you," Claire said. "Everyone was all up in arms about the knife."

"What do you mean?" Pinky asked. "What knife?"

Warren explained about the knife. He could tell that Pinky had lots of questions, but Warren said, "We'll talk later," and Pinky, who now had steam rising off his socks as they dried by the hot fire, nodded.

"Detective Warren, is it okay if Jenny and I go to bed?" Delana asked. "We're going to need to be up early to make breakfast, and it's been a long day."

Warren wasn't sure what to say. Was it okay to let them go? "Does the door lock on the inside?" he asked her.

"Yes," Delana said. "But you don't think . . ."

"Lock it just to be safe," Warren told her, trying to keep it light. "Probably nothing to worry about, but I'd appreciate it if you'd indulge a worried policeman."

"Of course. Good night, everyone," Delana said.

Jenny, who seemed subdued now, followed her out of the room, her flashlight beam making strange shapes and shadows on the wall.

The rest of them settled in around the fire, dragging chairs in and gathering in a circle with their drinks. They sat in silence for a long time, watching the snow fall outside the windows, the firelight and the light from the oil lamps changing the features of the faces around the half circle until Warren wasn't sure who was who. Despite the events of the night, there was something soothing about the darkness and the fire and the storm outside. He dozed off for a bit and was startled when Claire knocked against his leg when she got up and added a log to the fire.

"Do you really think we're in danger, Detective Warren?" she asked him when she sat down again. "Why did you tell Delana and Jenny to lock their door?"

"Always good to err on the side of safety, Mrs. Packingham."

"I don't understand about the knife," Graham said. "Why would someone stab Bill and then shoot him too?"

"Is that what happened?" Jack asked. "How odd. I don't see why . . . *Is* that what happened, Detective Warren?"

"He won't tell you anything, Jack," Claire said. "Policemen never do." Warren watched her light a cigarette and lean back in her chair, inhaling with pleasure and blowing a lazy smoke ring that was caught in the flickering light as it drifted across the room and disappeared.

"But when do you think he was killed?" Jack asked Warren. "You don't think he was killed just before I found him? That he was out all night alive?"

Warren considered what he should say and settled on, "No, we think he was killed on Saturday."

"Well then, why . . ." he trailed off.

"Why what?" Warren asked him.

"I don't know. It seems so strange. The whole thing," Jack said.

"He obviously thinks one of us killed Bill," Herman said. "Which of us do you think it is, Detective Warren?"

Warren took a sip of his scotch. "You tell me. Who had reason to want him killed?"

"Are you serious?" Seth asked. "You're really asking them that?"

Graham laughed bitterly. "After that fight on Friday night, I'd say that Bill might have wanted to kill us."

"Why do you say that?" Warren asked. "What happened on Friday night? You've all been talking around it. You'd better tell me."

Herman hesitated, and then he said, "We were talking about why he got fired. He said something about his ethics and patriotism being called into question and that it was all hogwash. I said that maybe his womanizing had finally caught up with him."

"And?"

"He was furious, and he tried to pretend like he didn't know what I was talking about. My God, everyone here knows what he was! I didn't want to say it before, but . . . you wouldn't believe the things he got up to, Mr. Warren."

"Herman," Jack warned.

"Sorry," he said.

The fire popped and crackled, and Earl stood up to tend to it. When he'd added a big log, he picked up a flashlight and turned to Jack and Warren. "Will you be all right for the rest of the evening? Belle and I would like to get back to our place before the snow is much worse. I'll have to shovel a path over there, and well . . . I'm not as young as I used to be. You can let us know if you need anything, and you can always wake up Delana."

"Yes, Earl, of course," Jack said. "We'll all go up to bed soon. Thank you for everything. I'm sorry it's created so much work for you and Belle. We'll be out of your hair as soon as the roads clear out and Mr. Warren says we can go."

"Not to worry," Earl said, though Warren detected an undercurrent of annoyance.

"It's fine with me," Warren said. "We know where to find you."

Belle reminded them that there was extra food in the kitchen and they all listened to the couple's footsteps disappear down the hall.

Warren, knowing that someone would suggest they all go up to bed before too long, took a chance and asked, "Mr. Westwood, what did you mean that you all knew 'what he was'?"

Herman lowered his voice a bit and said, "He couldn't leave women alone. It got him into trouble. After I suggested on Friday night that maybe that's why he'd been sacked, he flew into a rage."

"He got very angry," Graham said. "Delana and Jenny had come in, and we didn't want them to hear, so we tried to smooth it over, but Bill told Herman to shut his mouth and said that if he didn't, he was going to make him."

"What do you mean?" Warren asked, keeping his voice low, though he knew the women were far away.

"What do you think, Detective? Bill and Delana. I didn't want to ruin the reputation of a good woman who by all accounts has—"

"Herman!" Jack said.

But Herman went on, barely lowering his voice. "I said something about him revisiting the scene of one of his crimes, and I'll tell you, he didn't like that too much. He asked me what I meant, and I told him. I think he was genuinely shocked." He laughed bitterly. "You could see him doing the math right at the table. He was terrible about women, though Delana didn't seem to mind at the time, if you know what I—"

"Stop it," Jack hissed at him. "Stop it right now!"

Warren couldn't help himself. "You mean Delana? That Delana?" He gestured in the direction of the kitchen. "And by math . . . you mean . . . Jenny?" His voice was almost a whisper.

"Oh yes. She and—"

"I won't have it. Stop gossiping," Jack broke in. "I think we should all go to bed." His voice was tight and angry. Everyone else was shocked into silence.

Warren assented, if a bit regretfully. "I'll lock the front door behind us, and Trooper Goodrich and I will be upstairs in case there are any issues. Hopefully we can all get some sleep and the power will be back on by the morning."

No one protested. They all took flashlights and once they'd all gone upstairs, Warren and Pinky went through to the foyer and looked out the front door into the storm. Warren could see two dark figures ahead in the swirl of white: Earl and Belle, shoveling a path to their cottage. He turned the dead bolt lock on the big front door, and pointing the flashlight at the row of hooks on the wall, he said, "What do you think about that knife, Pinky? How did it get in Jenny's pocket?"

"I'd say the killer came in and wanted to get rid of it as soon as possible. The coat was right there, and he must have known Jenny wouldn't wear it for a while."

"You don't think he was trying to place blame on her?"

Pinky's voice was incredulous. "Why would he do that? Jenny's just a girl. She's got nothing to do with all of this."

"You heard what Herman said."

"That's just nasty gossip," Pinky said. "Jenny's dad is a good man. He owns the hardware store!"

The wind made the exterior wall creak, and they both jumped. It was beginning to be very cold in the lodge away from the big fire, and Warren could feel his extremities starting to go numb.

"I want to take a look at that knife," he said. "And then we can talk some more in my room." They made their way through the dark hallway and he unlocked the door to the gun room, letting Pinky go ahead of him inside before shutting the door behind them again. Warren took the knife down, unwrapped it, and shone the light on it so he and Pinky could examine it.

It was a filleting knife, similar to one that Warren had for preparing fish or chicken cutlets. The tip was very thin, only half an inch or less, and Warren saw how they'd gotten it wrong. Going in, a knife like that would have made a small wound, more similar to the entry wound of a .32-caliber bullet than a broader knife like the ones used to field dress deer.

Using the napkin to turn it over, Warren said, "There's some reddish stains on the other side. I think he was killed with this."

"So whoever killed him brought it back and hid it in Jenny's jacket pocket to try to frame her?"

Warren thought for a moment. "To frame her or because it was convenient. Or . . ."

"Or what?"

"Or, what if it was Delana? What if she put the knife there, thinking she'd be able to retrieve it later?"

"Mrs. Breedlove?" Pinky sounded outraged. "How can you think that it was her?"

"You heard what Mr. Westwood said," Warren said gently. "Maybe she was angry at him, and seeing him again . . ." But as he said it, he realized where the theory was flawed. She had been in the lodge all afternoon.

"He was shot too," Pinky pointed out. "Whoever it was would have had to have hidden the gun as well as the knife."

Warren looked up at the guns on the wall. "Jack Packingham told me that he couldn't be sure a gun wasn't missing. He was looking for that one and didn't see it at first." He pointed to the antique rifle mounted proudly on the wall. "Maybe there is one missing and no one noticed. Anyway, let's lock up and go to our rooms. We can talk some more there." He hesitated, and then he said, "I'm glad you're okay, Pinky."

"Well, I am too," Pinky said. "I had a few bad moments out there, but all's well that ends well, I guess."

They locked the gun room door and made their way back through the dark hallway, their flashlights casting long shadows on the walls.

When he was a boy, Warren and his brother had loved to scare themselves by creeping around their house at night in the dark and looking over their shoulders before telling each other they'd seen a ghost or a man with a hatchet. As he and Pinky went silently through the hall and up the stairs to the bedrooms in the addition, he looked over his shoulder once and could have sworn he'd seen a shadow move.

Twenty-one

Jenny waited until she heard Mr. Warren and Walter's footsteps going upstairs before she came out of her hiding place in the dining room. She wasn't sure what she would have done if they'd found her; there was no way to explain why she had waited until her mother's breathing slowed and evened in sleep, then pushed the covers of her bed back and tiptoed quietly through the dark kitchen and into the dining room, where she tucked herself behind the door to listen to the conversation in the lounge.

She had heard them talking about the knife, and then she had heard Mr. Westwood say *He obviously thinks one of us killed Bill. Which of us do you think it is, Detective Warren?* and then she couldn't hear what they were saying for a bit because of the wind, and then she heard Mr. Westwood's voice saying *He was terrible about women, though Delana didn't seem to mind . . .* and Jenny had almost stood up and run out of the room when she'd heard her mother's name and understood that Mr. Westwood was saying there had been something between her mother and Mr. Moulton. She couldn't hear the rest of what they had to say, and finally she heard them say it was time to go to bed, and the lights went out one by one or were carried from the room, and then she heard their footsteps on the stairs. She was about to creep back to bed when she heard Mr. Warren and Walter talking, and then she had to wait nearly ten minutes until she heard their footsteps on the stairs before she could return to her bed, huddling under the blankets and shivering for a long time until she warmed up.

The night still seemed like a bad dream. She'd gone down into the basement to get the extra whisky, holding her breath when she went over to the racks where they kept the spirits to avoid breathing in the dark, mousy smell of the cellar. Back upstairs, she'd been taking off her coat when she'd felt a little prick of discomfort just under her ribs and put a hand into the pocket of her coat, feeling something hard and unfamiliar. Confused, she'd pulled out the knife.

It was funny how one's brain slowed down at a time like that. It had taken her a couple of seconds to even recognize the object for what it was.

A knife.

She had known immediately that it was important from the way Mr. Warren jumped up to take it from her.

Mr. Moulton stabbed! Think of it!

The more she tried to understand it, though, the less sense it had made.

Because she had seen the knife on Saturday. When lunch was done and the men had gone out into the woods, her mother had started slicing the leftover pork roast from Friday's dinner off the bone. Jenny had seen her, and after Jenny had cleaned the downstairs lavatory, she'd come into the kitchen to find the knife lying on the counter next to the serving dish, her mother's apron discarded next to it. Where had she gone? Jenny had gone looking for her and found only empty rooms, empty hallways. Later, there had been no sign of the knife or the apron in the kitchen, only the board and the chopped meat.

But when Mr. Warren asked, her mother had said that she didn't think she'd seen the knife recently.

Jenny hugged herself, finally warm again. Thank goodness Walter was okay. It must have been awful for him, stuck out in the snow, not knowing if he was going to make it back to the lodge. Had he thought about Jenny at all? Had he hoped he could get back to her?

She drifted off to sleep thinking the happy thought that maybe it was the idea of seeing her again that had given him the will to live, that had brought him back to the club and to safety.

Twenty-two

The Ridge Club was quiet, the guests already in their rooms and done using the two bathrooms on the floor. Pinky was sitting on the chair in Warren's room. Warren was sitting on the bed.

He thought of something. "Hey, Pinky, you ever find out anything driving around before you got stranded?"

"Well, I can't be sure, of course, but I don't think anyone else was out hunting in those woods on Saturday. Butch Hilton's the only hunter still living out here, so I stopped at Butch's place. That's where I stayed too long. But he's down at the nursing home now. His daughter lives in his house, and she didn't know of anyone." In the eerie light from the flashlight, Pinky's grin looked almost demonic. "There are a couple of old farmhouses out along the road, not far from the property line, pretty short walk. One of them's empty, and the other seems to be under construction. I don't think anyone was hunting here."

"And now we have the knife in the pocket of that coat. Doesn't seem like it was someone from outside, does it?"

"Nope." Pinky's voice sounded tired.

"Pinky, you know that Jenny Breedlove is carrying a torch for you, don't you?"

"What?"

Warren was glad that they were in half darkness. He figured Pinky's blushing would reach new heights of crimson bashfulness. "You're too smart not to see it," Warren said gently. "Do you have feelings for her too?"

Pinky sputtered a bit and then said, "She's like a little sister. I've known her my whole life. I mean, she's, well, Jenny's . . . Jenny. My mother always said she was like a sunflower."

Warren found himself confused. Did Pinky think of her as a sunflower? Was this a good thing? "*Do* you have feelings for her, Pinky?"

Pinky hesitated, and then he said, "In books they say it feels like getting hit by lightning. Like, you look at a girl and you feel an electric shock. I never felt like that with Jenny, so maybe I don't."

Warren smiled. "I don't think it always feels like that."

"What was it like with your . . . your wife?"

Warren hesitated and then said, "It was lightning for me. With Maria. But I've heard people say it can happen lots of different ways. Sometimes it's lightning, and sometimes it's . . . well, a gentle summer rainstorm, if you see what I mean."

"I don't know." Pinky sounded even more confused. "Why is it like rain?"

"Never mind. In any case, I think Jenny's hiding something. See if you can find out what it is, okay?" Warren hesitated, then asked, "Do you think there's anything to that story about Moulton and Mrs. Breedlove, Pinky?"

Pinky sighed. "I didn't like that at all. Poor Jenny. She's got nothing to do with any of it, and if she heard that kind of gossip, I don't know what it'd do to her."

"Could it be motive for murder?" Warren asked. "Could Delana have been so angry with him that she . . ."

"Stuck a knife in him, then shot him?"

Warren saw what he meant. That didn't feel like Delana. He thought of the tall, quiet man who had rung up his knife and paint at the hardware store. "Maybe? Or Mr. Breedlove? Or . . . maybe someone else, who was offended by Moulton's womanizing? Or maybe someone we don't even know, someone who has nothing to do with any of this."

"There's . . ." Pinky started to say.

"What?"

"There's that story Mr. Packingham told us about the hunter cutting out that man's heart . . ."

"Are you suggesting Moulton was killed by the ghost of the lovesick hunter?"

"Well, not quite like that, but . . . when I was in the woods, I had the feeling a couple times that someone was watching me. You don't think . . . ?"

Warren sighed. "If only it were that easy, Pinky. I'm exhausted, and I can only imagine how tired you are with what you've been through. Let's get some sleep and attack this again in the morning. Hopefully the power will be back on and we can do a real search for evidence."

They said good night, and he waited until Pinky had closed the door to his own room across the hall to close his door and make sure his service weapon was on the small table next to the bed.

Warren stripped down to his boxer shorts and got into the narrow bed. Someone had added a couple of blankets, and he was quite comfortable as he dozed off to the sound of snowflakes gently slapping the roof, thinking of white—white snow, white smoke, white fog, blank stretches of it that he wanted to burrow into. The lodge settled in under the snow, the eaves creaking and the floorboards groaning. The sounds floated and disappeared, and then Warren slept.

He woke sometime later to a sound that breached the expanse of nothingness. His eyes opened to darkness, and he lay there staring at the ceiling. It took a moment to come back. He was at the Ridge Club.

They were trapped by the snow. There had been a power outage. It must be the strange surroundings that had woken him.

But no, he had heard something. The sound was what had roused him from his sleep. Warren sat up, trying to remember, trying to access the sound from his dreams. What had it been? Footsteps? A door opening?

No, he realized, reaching for the flashlight next to the bed and then his gun.

A shot.

Twenty-three

Time folded in on itself, minutes taking hours and hours slipping into nothingness. Sylvie panted, listening to the sounds of the house for a moment, trying to get centered before the next pains came. Between the sets of agony, she could hear the boys talking in quiet voices downstairs and then one of the cows bellowing in the barn. The snow *slap-slapped* softly on the roof. She was only dimly aware of Alice at her side, murmuring encouragement.

"You can do it, Sylvie. It's almost over. You'll feel that pressure, that awful pressure, like there just isn't room and you're being ripped open. It will be worse because of the baby's arm. You'll want to get it out of there." Sylvie tried to refocus her ricocheting attention on the words. Alice was right. That horrid *pressure* was what told you that you were almost there. She remembered that the first time it had happened to her, with Scott, she had been embarrassed, thinking that she had to go to the bathroom, but Hugh said it was just the baby, making its way into the world.

A rush of longing for Hugh swept over her. He had not been a good husband in a lot of ways, but during her labors, he had known what to say and made her feel that she was in good hands. He had stayed with her. *Please, Hugh,* she said inside her head. *Please make this okay; please make this turn out well.* The next pain came, and she could feel something shift. There was terrible burning, which she knew meant that the baby was right there, almost on the outside. This was worse than it had ever been before, and she realized, remembering lambs she'd delivered, that it was worse because the head and the shoulder were going to have to come out at the same time. She tried to go to the white space in her head, but the pain, which was red, erased all the white. *White, wide whiteness, pink and red, fire.*

"Sylvie." Mrs. Bellows's voice came through the haze. "Sylvie, you can do this. I can see the baby's little arm. I'm going to help bring it out, okay? It's going to hurt, though."

Sylvie didn't have it in her to respond, but she felt insistent, awful tugging, a turning inside out, which must've been Mrs. Bellows pulling the baby, and then . . . and then the pain was not quite so bad, and she had a bit of space in her head, and she thought, for some reason, of Franklin Warren.

Franklin Warren. She saw his face. In a way, he had saved her life, and Scott's too, and he came into her head as though he were a kind of saint or an idol, something to focus on and steady herself with. She focused on his face, and she gathered all her will to push, even though it hurt, even though the pushing made it much worse.

"His wife died," she murmured to Mrs. Bellows, hardly knowing what she was saying. "His wife died and their baby. I think he was broken open, like . . ." Another wave of pain came over her. "I can't," she whimpered. "I can't. I need to stop." It felt as though she were being torn from the very center of her body. "Stop, just stop! For God's sake, stop!" She wasn't sure if she was speaking English or the French of her childhood.

"You have to, Sylvie," Mrs. Bellows said. "The baby's shoulder is right here, I think. I don't want to pull too hard, but it needs to come out. I'm worried it's been stuck too long, Sylvie."

Sylvie knew what that meant.

Somewhere down in the red pain place, she found another space where there was not red, not white, but a calm *blue*, and she breathed it in, suddenly resolved, and then she pushed.

Sylvie heard screaming and realized it was her own voice. She screamed and screamed, screaming for all she had lost and for Franklin Warren and his dead wife and baby, and then just pain, pain, pain, pain, pain, pain, and then, thank Jesus, thank Jesus, thank Jesus, the slippery, sliding entrance that was familiar to her, the first thing about all of this that was familiar to her, the feeling of relief, relief, relief, relief, sweet relief that the burning was over.

And then time folded again.

"It's breathing." Mrs. Bellows's voice came as if from a great distance. "Sylvie, oh, Sylvie, it's a girl. It's a little girl. She's perfect. She's breathing, and it's a little girl."

Twenty-four

I t was midnight now. The baby was sleeping. Alice had cut the cord and waited for Sylvie to nurse her and deliver the afterbirth, and then she'd brought it and the bloody sheets and towels out into the hall and found fresh sheets and blankets and diapers. She had brought Sylvie some water, and the baby had nursed again, her small, red face pushed up against Sylvie's breast, and then fallen asleep in Sylvie's arms. In the candlelight, they were glowing and lovely, like a Madonna and child in a Renaissance painting. Alice felt a quick stab of discomfort as she watched them, and it became so strong that she had to turn away. Gathering up a towel and cloths she'd missed so Sylvie couldn't see her face, she murmured something to Sylvie about checking on the boys.

Downstairs, she put the soiled linens in the mudroom and stood there for a moment with her hands on the cold stone of the old wash sink, trying to pull herself together. When she felt calmer, she found the boys hushed and sitting around the kitchen table. Alice realized that they must have heard the terrible sounds of their mother in labor, and she put on a broad smile to reassure them.

"Now," she said. "Why the glum faces? You have a sister!"

No one said anything.

Louis looked up, his eyes wide. "Is *Maman* dead?" he asked. His little face was so woebegone that Alice reached out to touch his head.

She laughed. "No, Louis, no. She's not dead at all. It's just that having a baby is awfully hard. Have you ever yelled out when you fell and hurt your knee?" He nodded solemnly. "Well, your mother felt like that. For a little bit, it really, really hurt. But now she's fit as a fiddle. And you have a sister. Can you believe it?"

The boys still looked a bit shell-shocked, so she said, "I promise you, she's fine. I'm letting her rest, but I'll take you up and show you in a bit. Are you hungry? I'm hungry. What can we make?"

Little Daniel shouted, "A cake, a cake—let's make birthday cake!"

"Well," Alice said. "Let's see if you have the ingredients."

There were eggs and butter and milk in the refrigerator, and Andy showed her where the flour and sugar were. She put the butter near the stove and let it soften, and then she showed them how to beat together the sugar and butter until it was creamy and yellow, then beat in the eggs and, finally, the flour and baking powder and some vanilla and milk.

Louis wanted to smell the vanilla extract. "I love that smell," he said, closing his eyes and inhaling deeply, and Alice remembered doing the same when her grandmother was baking. She had tried drinking it once and discovered that though it smelled delicious, it tasted bitter and alcoholic.

She let the boys help pour the cake batter into a pan by candlelight and asked Scott to stoke the big cookstove.

"Aren't you glad now that you don't have an electric stove?" she said as she slid the pan into the oven. "If you did, it wouldn't work and we wouldn't be able to make a cake. I have an electric one now, but I miss the one like this I had when I was a little girl. It's so much nicer, isn't it? I remember staying with my grandparents and reading by the stove while my grandmother sang. She had a beautiful voice, and she would sing hymns while she cooked and cleaned."

"What's 'hims'?" Louis asked.

"Songs you sing in church," she explained. "Like 'Nearer My God to Thee,' or I'm sure you've heard 'Angels We Have Heard on High' and 'Silent Night' at Christmastime?"

"Oh yes," Andy said. "We like to listen to those on the radio."

"Well, my grandmother would sing songs like that. Anyway, I'm very glad you have a woodstove so we can make this cake. We'll be able to smell it in a few minutes."

The boys looked pleased. They must have heard many comments at school about their old-fashioned way of living. But then Andy said, "Do you have a television, Mrs. Bellows?"

"Yes, I do. I don't watch it very often. Well, I like to watch the news."

"We never had one, because Hugh said it would rot our brains, but Ma said we could get one with our turkey money. But the turkeys are gone, Mrs. Bellows. So we may not be able to get one at all." He shook his head sadly. Alice remembered that Hugh Weber had liked the boys to call him by his first name, just one of the dead man's strange ideas.

"Maybe the turkeys will come back," she said. "Maybe they just found a safe place to hide out during the snowstorm." But she knew this was unlikely. It was more probable that a family of foxes had found them and made a very large meal of it. There was no good in lying to these children. They knew the realities of farm life. Sometimes you worked and worked to raise an animal, and it died of disease or was killed by a predator. Sometimes you weeded a garden all summer, and just when your first tomato was ripe and juicy, a woodchuck came along and ate it.

Sometimes, your father died.

"Did you know they make color televisions now?" Louis said. "You can see everything!"

"Can we see the baby?" Andy asked, once the smell of the cake had started to waft around the darkened kitchen, lit here and there by candlelight.

"Yes, of course," Alice said. "They've had a good rest now. I wonder what her name is."

"I want to name her Julie," said Louis.

Scott and Andy laughed, and Andy explained, "We had a cow named Julie, and he wants to name the baby after her."

Alice smiled. "Well, Julie is a nice name, but we'll see what your mother thinks. It will be her choice."

They tiptoed up the stairs in a silent procession. Sylvie had dozed off, and so had the baby, but she heard their footsteps and opened her eyes and put out an arm for the boys to come to her. They gathered around hesitantly, afraid to hurt her, and she said, "Come meet your little sister."

"What are you going to name her?" asked Louis. "Julie?"

"Well," Sylvie said, smiling at him, "I think we already have a Julie. I always liked the name Margot. What do you think about that? Margot? It's spelled with a 't' at the end, though, so you can't start calling her 'Maggot.' Promise?" The boys laughed, and Daniel said in his baby-ish voice, "Maggot! Little wormy!"

Scott smiled shyly. "I like it," he said. "Margot."

Sylvie looked up at him, and Alice caught something heavy pass between them. They had secrets, these two, but maybe they could put those secrets aside. Alice said a small, interior prayer. "I always liked the name Margot," she told Sylvie.

"I think he would like it," Andy said softly, putting out a fingertip to touch the little face. "I think Hugh would like it."

They all watched Margot. She was a beautiful baby, Alice thought, forcing herself to look. Her thin hair was very black and her eyes very blue, just like her mother's. Her little nose reminded Alice of a strawberry. Her tiny tongue came out between her lips, and she twisted this way and that.

"I think she's hungry," Sylvie said. "Are you all okay?"

"We are," Alice said. "Actually, we're making a cake. It was Daniel's idea. We'll bring you a slice when it's done. It's a birthday cake for Margot, but she'll have to wait till she's a little older to eat it."

Louis shouted, "I'll have her piece!"

Downstairs, the kitchen was softly yellow. Alice and the boys sat at the table until the cake was ready, watching the snowflakes wheel and spiral and dance outside the windows.

Twenty-five

Warren dressed quickly and went out into the hallway. The lodge had cooled in the night, and he shivered in the frosty air.

Pinky was already coming out of his room. "What was that?" he asked sleepily.

"I think it was a shot." Warren's flashlight guided him to the end of the hall where Skip had come out of his room in his pajamas. Seth came out of his own room while they stood there.

"What's going on?" Herman Westwood opened his door and came out, already dressed in his regular clothes but hastily buttoning his shirt. Graham French came out too, in pajamas and a robe, and then Claire, also in a robe, her hair covered in a scarf.

"Was that a shot?' she asked. "It sounded like a shot."

Warren shone his flashlight over the terrified faces lined up along the hall. "Can everyone say their name?" he called to them. "I want to make sure everyone's here."

The voices came out of the darkness:

"Seth."

"Skip."

"Claire."

"Graham."

"Herman Westwood," Herman said grumpily.

"Trooper Goodrich."

Silence.

"Jack?" Claire said. "Where's Jack?"

"Is everyone accounted for?" Warren asked the assembled group. "Delana and Jenny are downstairs. Mr. Packingham?"

Claire shone her flashlight around at the faces. Warren put a hand up when the strong beam reached him.

"No, Jack's not here," Claire said, panic in her voice. "Where is he? Jack? Jack?"

"Dad?" Skip called out. Warren heard real fear in his voice.

"Which is his room?" Pinky asked. Claire pointed to the first room on the corridor, and Skip rushed over and looked in. "He's not in here," he said.

Warren came up behind him and looked into the room, shining his light on the bed. No one was there. "Did he go somewhere?" Warren asked Claire.

He could hear that she was crying now. "No, no! I don't know. I just . . . woke up. I don't know."

Warren tried to remember what he'd heard. Had it been just outside his door or downstairs? "Where did the shot come from?"

"I don't know. Downstairs maybe?" one of the men said.

"Everyone, come downstairs to the lounge," Warren told them. "We need to find Mr. Packingham. But I want to make sure you're all safe in the meantime."

Pinky went to the stairs and shone his light to show people the way. They trooped down, slowly, and once they were at the bottom, Warren told them to wait while he checked the lounge. When he was sure that Jack wasn't there, he brought them in and asked them to wait there while he and Pinky searched the lodge.

"Where's Jack?" Claire was still crying. "Where is he?"

"Mrs. Packingham, I need you to calm down and stay here. Trooper Goodrich and I are going to look for Mr. Packingham."

"Don't leave us," Herman said. "There was a shot. What if there's someone here with a gun?"

"It'll just be a minute," Warren said. "Just sit tight."

"What's going on?" Delana asked as she and Jenny came through into the lounge from their bedroom by the kitchen. Jenny was wearing a man's flannel dressing gown over her nightclothes.

"We thought we heard a shot," Jenny said.

"Is everyone okay?" Delana asked.

"Come in here and sit with the rest of the group," Warren told them. "Mr. Packingham wasn't in his room. Trooper Goodrich and I are going to go and try to find him."

"Be careful, Walter," Jenny called after them as they left the room. "There might be a madman on the loose."

Warren checked the phone again as they made their way through the hall and found only the same dead air. Then, slowly, methodically, they searched the lodge. First, they shone their flashlights into the dining room, sweeping them across the floor and the tables and chairs, then went through the side door into the kitchen. They checked it carefully, looking into the pantry and all the closets, and then carefully swept Delana and Jenny's room.

"We need to make sure he's not upstairs," Warren whispered to Pinky.

They looked in each of the bedrooms and the upstairs bathrooms and then came back downstairs to the front hallway, where they checked the front door, which was still locked. From the lounge they could hear the low murmur of voices.

"Check the lavatory," Warren told Pinky. "I'll look in that little equipment room. Then we should wake Earl and Belle and make sure they're okay and that he's not there." Pinky nodded and went off to the bathroom next to the lounge.

Warren carefully opened the equipment room next to the gun room. It held vacuums and mops, and he carefully shone the light around the small space. No one there.

Pinky had come back from checking the lavatory, and he nodded toward the closed door of the gun room and said, "Should we look in there?"

"I've still got the key in my pocket, but we should make sure," Warren said. Pinky shone his light on the door. It was closed but when he tried the handle, it turned and the door opened a crack. Warren put a hand on his holster. Pinky pushed the door in with his foot, his gun up in case someone was inside.

But Jack Packingham, lying on the floor of the gun room in a pool of blood, was all alone.

Dead and alone.

¤ ¤ ¤

"My God," Pinky said in a low voice. "Another one."

"Close the door behind us, Pinky. We need to take a look before they find out he's dead. We don't have much time, though. His wife's going to want to know where he is. Do you see a weapon anywhere?"

"Well . . ." Pinky's flashlight swept across the walls. "There's a lot of weapons in the room, but . . ." He turned to close the door and then shone the light on the floor all around the body. "Nothing within reach. I guess he didn't do it himself."

"Dammit!" Warren said. He could feel Pinky's disapproval. "Sorry, Pinky. It's just that it feels like someone's playing with us. You know what I mean?"

"Why did he come down here?" Pinky asked. "Was he meeting someone? And how did he get in?"

"If he was meeting someone, it was likely someone in the house or someone he let into the house," Warren said. "The front door was locked. We just checked it. And I thought I had the only key to the gun room, but obviously not."

Pinky knelt down and shone his light on Jack's hand. "Looks like he had one too." The key, the twin of the one in Warren's pocket, was one of three on a brass ring still clutched in the dead man's hand.

"Why did he lie to me, Pinky?" They both knew it was a rhetorical question. Warren knelt on the floor by the body and shone his light on the blood on Jack Packingham's chest. "I can't see well enough. I can't tell anything about the entry wound. You have any thoughts about what kind of gunshot that was that we heard?"

"That's the thing," Pinky said. "It woke me up, and I knew it was a gunshot, a rifle shot, but I didn't really *hear* it, if you know what I mean."

"I do. It's the same here." Warren studied the position of the body. Jack must have been standing just inside the door when he was shot. He would have stepped back—or been shoved back by force depending on the caliber of the projectile—and fallen. But something about the way he was lying there didn't seem right. It was more like he'd crumpled where he'd stood.

The gun room was full of shadows. Warren shone his light around to make sure there wasn't anything he was missing.

"I don't like this. Whoever shot him is likely to be still in this house and likely still armed. We've got to go wake up Earl and Belle. And I need to make sure no one else has come onto the property tonight."

In the flashlight beam, Pinky's eyes were wide. "You don't think there's someone . . . else . . . here, do you?"

"We searched pretty thoroughly, Pinky. But there's the basement and there must be attics. The first thing is to break the news to the others, though. Let's secure the room as best we can."

As they left the room, Warren did one last sweep of the walls. The faces in the photographs of fishermen and hunters over the years stared out at him. He had the strange feeling that he was leaving Jack's body with ghosts. Jack Packingham had loved this club. In a way, he'd dedicated his life to it. And it had come to this. It seemed oddly fitting.

"What time did he get out of bed?" Warren asked Claire, once they'd broken the news of Jack's death to her and to Skip.

Graham had gotten them all brandies. Delana was sitting on the couch trying to comfort Claire. Skip was sitting in one of the chairs with his head in his hands.

"I don't know, I don't know." Claire was sobbing. "We said good night, and he went into his room. I had my own. They only have twin beds, and I can't stand sharing a twin bed. I must have fallen asleep. Oh God, what happened? Jack! Jack!"

Delana was stroking Claire's hair and offering her sips from the glass of brandy. Claire, still taking in the news, had managed to answer a few of his questions. The rest of the company had been stunned into silence.

"Did anyone else get out of bed at all?" he asked. "For anything? To use the bathroom or for any other reason?"

He couldn't read their faces in the low light, and it made him nervous. What was he missing?

"I used the john," Herman said. "About midnight."

"And you didn't hear anything or see anyone else?"

"No, I don't think so. I was half-asleep, but I didn't see anyone out in the hallway."

"Anyone else?" Warren asked.

No one said anything.

Warren checked his watch. It was two A.M. now. It was November, heading toward the shortest day of the year. It wouldn't be light for another five hours at least. He felt panic begin to rise in his throat. They were trapped here with a killer, and Warren had no idea which of them it was.

"We've got to go wake up Earl and Belle. Pinky, can you do it?" Warren asked.

"Yes," Pinky said. "It's not far to their cottage. Earl shoveled a path when they went, so I think I can do it with boots and a flashlight."

Warren nodded. "Okay. Ask them to come over here. We need to keep everyone together."

"I'll go with you," Jenny said. "You shouldn't go alone. I'll go get dressed."

Pinky nodded, and if he was blushing, Warren couldn't tell in the low light. He thought about telling her to stay in case something had happened to the couple but decided she knew the property as well as anyone, and it wasn't the worst thing for them to go together. Pinky was armed, and he'd know to go in first to make sure there wasn't anything she shouldn't see inside. Jenny was back in just a few minutes and she and Pinky went out of the room, their flashlight beams bobbing along the hall.

"Are you going to call the police?" Seth asked.

Warren waited to see if anyone was going to remind him about the phone lines and the roads. Finally he said, "I am the police."

"Oh, right; sorry. My God. We're just . . . stuck here, aren't we? Until they can clear the roads?"

"Well, we need to stay here until we can get some help, but Trooper Goodrich and I will keep you safe."

"You didn't keep Jack safe!" Graham said. "What is going on here, Detective Warren? Was it an accident? Did he commit suicide?" He looked utterly drained, his face ghostly in the sparse light.

Warren hesitated. Normally he'd want to keep the details private. But someone had shot Jack Packingham, and he needed to gather some information very quickly. He made the gamble. "There's no weapon with the body," he said. "Someone else killed him."

It took a few seconds for it to sink in. Warren knew exactly when the implications of what he said made their way through their sleepy brains; a low current of horror ricocheted around the room.

"You mean . . ." Seth said.

"It's one of us?" Graham asked.

"Oh my God!" Herman shouted. "Someone's going to kill us all."

Delana's voice came high and anxious. "Who would kill Jack?"

"Calm down," Warren said loudly. "Stay where you are! We're going to sit right here where we can see everyone. Seth, can you add another log to the fire? Let's keep warm and wait for Trooper Goodrich to come back."

Claire, on the couch, was still crying but quietly now, and Delana continued to comfort her. Warren felt sorry for Skip, who was still sitting there with his head in his hands. Seth added wood to the fire and the flames shot up, consuming the new logs. The warmth spread out toward the couches, and they were all silent, staring at the flames. The dancing colors were mesmerizing. Warren had the sense of time melting and elongating as they all stared at the fire. If only they could actually lose themselves there. If only they could go back to the moment before the shot was fired.

His reverie was broken by the sound of voices in the hall and flashlight beams crossing on the floor and then approaching the lounge. Jenny and Belle came in, then Pinky and Earl, and Warren got up to go talk to them.

"My God," Belle was saying. "Jack. Is everyone else all right?" She was crying, Jenny's arm around her shoulders.

"Yes," Warren told her. "Did you hear the shot?"

Earl shook his head. "I don't think so. We were sleeping pretty soundly, and our place is quite well insulated. It was those two banging on the door that woke us up." He looked back at Warren, his eyes glittering in the beam of light reflected against the wall. He looked tired and stricken, and Warren realized he must be worried about his and Belle's jobs, in addition to the shock of the situation. Earl and Belle depended on the club for their livelihood and the roof over their heads. What would happen to them? What would happen to the club?

"Earl," Warren said. "I need you to come and look at the gun room with me and tell me if anything's missing. Is that all right with you?" The older man nodded, and Warren told Pinky to stay in the lounge with everyone else. "Keep everyone here, where you can see them. Pay attention."

Pinky nodded, and Warren felt grateful that they had built their working relationship to the point that Pinky knew exactly what he meant. *Who is showing too much or too little emotion? Who seems nervous or wants to leave the room?*

Warren's flashlight swept the hall. It was eerie now, the light making strange and menacing shadows on the walls. He opened the door to the gun room carefully, so as not to disturb anything. It was just as they'd left it. Jack Packingham was lying on his back, his hands up and over his head, the dark stain on his chest, the blood running down and freezing in geometric shapes as it coagulated.

Other than a quick intake of breath, Earl didn't show any reaction to the body. He shone his own light up on the gun racks and seemed to count the shotguns and rifles as he moved it across the wall.

"Jack's Winchester," he said. "It was there earlier and now it's not."

He was right. Warren remembered Jack looking for the Winchester before and the exact place it had been. It wasn't there anymore.

"Anything else?" Warren asked.

Earl shone the light around the room. "Nope."

"Earl, he said he didn't have another key, but there's one in his hand. Did you know he was lying?"

Earl hesitated, then said, "I thought he might be. That was his father's ring of keys, one for every door in the club, and I think Jack liked the idea he could always get in here if he wanted to. He must have hung on to it."

Once out in the hall, Warren locked the door of the gun room behind them and told Earl to go back to the lounge. He waited for a moment until he was sure he was gone and then stood in the quiet hallway for a moment. He trusted Pinky to keep them all together, and this was his one chance to search the club alone.

He took his shoes off and crept quietly up the stairs with his flashlight. The rifle had to be somewhere in the lodge and somewhere there had to be a piece of evidence that would lead him to the killer.

The first door led to Jack's room, so he started there, looking behind the bed, behind the nightstand, in the drawer of the nightstand, and then in the dresser against the wall on the other side of the room. Finally, he went through Jack's coat pockets and his suitcase. Nothing of interest.

Next door was the room where Claire Packingham had spent the night. She only had one small overnight bag, but her things were what he would have expected: expensive lacy underwear and makeup and face lotion that must have cost a fortune. There was a leather purse tucked under the bed, and secreted deep in an inside pocket of the purse, obscured by a tissue, was a business card, a simple cream-colored rectangle of card stock that read CHRISTOPHER WASHBURN, ATTORNEY-AT-LAW.

He slipped into the room next door and knew immediately that it was Skip's from the new red woolen jacket, which he'd seen Skip wearing yesterday. A quick look at the wallet on the nightstand confirmed it. Warren got to work, lightly searching the room. He quickly looked through the suitcase pushed against one wall. There wasn't anything of interest, just a pile of clothes on the floor and some leather boots.

But in the pocket of a canvas jacket hanging in the small closet he found something interesting:

Two marijuana cigarettes.

Warren replaced them and thought to himself that Skip was lucky that they were in the middle of a murder investigation. Marijuana was the least of Warren's worries.

The next room was Graham French's, and it felt as orderly and neat as Warren would have expected from a military man. There were no clothes strewn about in this room, and when Warren carefully opened the drawers in the small bureau, he saw that Graham had unpacked, neatly folding his clothes into the drawers.

Because the room was so spartan, Warren had the sense that something was being hidden from him, so he carefully unzipped the suitcase, which was mostly empty. He looked around, even lifting up the mattress on the twin bed and shining the flashlight beneath it, but there was nothing there.

The next two rooms were Pinky's and then Warren's on the other side of the hallway, and next to Warren's was Herman Westwood's. Warren opened the door and slipped inside. He had a sense of anticipation, an instinct that he'd find something here. Was it just because he didn't like Herman, because he thought he was hiding something?

The room was somewhere between Skip Packingham's and Graham French's in terms of neatness. There were a few clothes strewn around here and there and a tan Burberry overcoat draped on the chair. Warren looked around and finally, saying a silent prayer, opened the suitcase. There were some more clothes inside, and he felt the pockets to see if there was a weapon in any of them.

In a zippered compartment inside the suitcase was a leather document case. Holding his flashlight beam on it with one hand and using the other to slip it out of the pocket, Warren felt both discouragement and interest when he discovered it was locked with a small combination lock. There was no way in. But Herman Westwood had brought documents with him that he wanted to keep locked up. Why?

Warren replaced everything and went out into the hallway.

There were two rooms left. Bill Moulton's and Seth Pellegrino's.

Warren had been gone for fifteen minutes already and he didn't want to be gone too much longer, so he made the decision to search Seth's. He'd already searched Moulton's and hadn't found anything of interest there.

Like Skip's room, Seth's room was messy, clothes on the floor, two books and a notebook piled on the nightstand. Warren leafed through them. The notebook was blank; the books were a paperback by Len Deighton and *Shadow and Act* by Ralph Ellison.

In the closet, Warren found a small, worn-looking green canvas briefcase. He carefully unzipped it and found that it was full of small journals and loose notes. He hesitated. This was incredibly dangerous. It would be hard to put everything back just as he had found it, but now that he was presented with all of this, he couldn't not look at it. He brought the briefcase over to the bed and took everything out, keeping it in a stack so that he might be able to put it back in the right order.

The first few pieces of paper seemed to be notes on Bill Moulton. Someone had written *William Moulton. State Department Employee. CIA? Dismissed from embassy in Bonn. Why?*

Why indeed? Warren kept reading. In addition to the details on Moulton, the papers contained notes on Herman Westwood and Graham French. The notetaker had written *Raytheon Corp* on a piece of paper and included newspaper clippings about Raytheon's development of missile technology.

And then, on a new sheet of paper, he'd written *Colonel Graham French!!!!! Vietnam advisor. Fired for reporting futility of war effort!!!!! Approach and offer anonymity!!!*

What the hell was going on here? It was obvious that Pellegrino had wangled an invitation to the hunt club from his friend Skip with the purpose of learning more about the men. But why?

Could Pellegrino be CIA or . . . working for another intelligence service? Moulton had left his job very suddenly. If he had been a spy or put himself in a compromising position with his tomcatting, then perhaps someone had paid Pellegrino to find out more or to even make an approach for a foreign government.

Moulton would have needed money after his career ended. Had he been vulnerable to Soviet intelligence?

Warren shook his head. He had spies on the brain again. What he needed was to focus on the fact that they were stranded and Jack Packingham was dead. He replaced Seth's belongings as best he could and went back to Jack's room for one last check, lingering at the window for a moment. Jack had seemed troubled when they were discussing the knife. He had asked Warren a question about when Moulton was killed. Why? What had he seen that made him ask Warren this question? What had made him go down to the gun room after everyone was asleep?

Warren had found some interesting things, but what he had not found was a weapon.

And if the murderer was indeed someone who was at the club, he had not figured out how that person had managed to get back to bed and emerge from their bedroom only moments after Jack was killed. He would see it. He just needed time to find out who had a motive to kill Moulton and Packingham.

Thanks to Seth Pellegrino's hard work, he now had some ideas.

Twenty-six

Warren decided not to try to search the basement and attic alone, instead opting to secure the latch across the basement door on his way back to the lounge. Everyone was still sitting around the coffee table, their faces illuminated by the firelight and the oil lamps. He felt a sudden pitching in his stomach. One of these people was likely the killer. That person was at this very moment in danger of being discovered. Someone might have seen something or heard something. The killer would be watching and listening to see if they were at risk. Whoever had killed Moulton had very likely had their own reasons. Those reasons might be difficult to uncover. Could this same person have killed Jack Packingham because Jack had figured out who had killed Moulton? Warren needed to figure out who that was without putting all these people in danger.

"Trooper Goodrich," Warren said quietly. Pinky got up and came over, and Warren stepped into the hallway, then gestured to the staircase where they would be far enough away to talk without being overheard. "Everything okay in there?" he asked.

"Yeah, I guess. Mr. Packingham's son is pretty upset. His friend was trying to calm him down, but Skip was getting a bit hot. He wants to know what happened. So does Mrs. Packingham. She was crying, and he asked her what she was crying for since she hardly knew him. He really doesn't like her."

"Well, his father's dead," Warren said. "It's probably to be expected that he'd be upset."

"You find anything?" Pinky asked.

"No—no obvious weapon anywhere, but Mr. Packingham's Winchester is missing. I need to talk to Skip in private. If I go and light some candles in the dining room, can you send him in in a few minutes?"

"Sure." He hesitated, though. "I think you might be right about Jenny."

"Yeah?"

"When we were walking over to Earl and Belle's, I told her that if she knew anything at all, she should tell us because this was a very dangerous situation. She went all quiet, which for her is . . ."

"Unusual?" Warren asked.

"Yes."

"Earl and Belle were in bed when you got there, right? Is there any way they could have been over here and then gotten back to their place before you arrived?"

Pinky made a sort of *Hmm* sound, and then he said, "I don't see how. They were in their, uh, sleeping clothes. Also, there were no new footprints. Jenny and I had to walk through a few inches of snow on top of the path that Earl had shoveled so . . ."

Warren saw what he meant. "Anything else?" he asked.

"No . . . just, I think there's some tension between Mr. French and Mr. Westwood. They almost threw punches a few minutes ago."

"Over what?"

"Well, Mr. French picked up a drink and finished it off, and it seems it was actually Mr. Westwood's, but I don't think that's what it was, if you know what I mean."

"Yeah. Anything else?"

"Seth—Skip Packingham's friend? He was nervous the whole time you were gone."

"He had good reason." He told Pinky about the notes. "I need to talk to them. Okay, give me a few minutes and then send them in—Skip first."

In the dining room, Warren found a candelabra and lit the five candles in it; it made the room feel festive until Skip came in and Warren remembered why he was there.

"Do you know who killed my father?" Skip demanded. He sat down in the chair across the table from Warren, and Warren could see his eyes were wet with tears. "I need to call my mother and my brother and sister. I don't know what to tell them . . . I . . ." He was just a boy, Warren realized. A boy who had lost his father.

"I know how upsetting this is. Of course you want to call your family, but the phone lines are still down. We'll make sure you can talk to them just as soon as the lines are operational."

"So, you don't . . . you're sure he didn't kill himself?"

"Quite sure." Warren knew he shouldn't be quite so declarative, but the boy was suffering.

"Oh, thank God. I'm sorry, I know it sounds awful, but I'm so relieved. I . . . we had that argument, and I thought he . . ." He sobbed and put his head down on the table. Warren let him cry for a moment and then watched as he became embarrassed and worked to push the feelings down. He did not want Warren to see him this vulnerable, and Warren felt a little shiver of fear, knowing the lengths men would go to not to feel vulnerable.

"I'm sure he knew you loved him," Warren said, though, of course, he was not at all sure of this. "Did he say anything to you about being afraid of someone here? Did he mention anything like that to you?"

"No," Skip said. "He loved this place. I think he loved it more than anything else. Even her." His voice grew bitter. "Have you looked at her? She probably killed him! She wanted his money! You know, when they got married, my mother said Claire was marrying him for his money. That she'd picked him out and planned the whole thing."

"Do you have any reason to believe that, Skip? That's a very serious accusation."

He hesitated and said, "Well, not exactly, but she made him build that huge house, the one that looks like a spaceship. Now that he's dead, it's all hers, as well as their house in Boston and his stake in the law firm. My brother told me. She organized all of that."

Suddenly, Warren knew where he'd seen the name of the lawyer on the card in Claire Packingham's purse. It was the same lawyer his brother had used when he'd gotten divorced the last time. Christopher Washburn was a divorce lawyer.

Skip was looking at him expectantly.

"I want to ask you something else, something about your friend Seth."

Skip looked wary and, Warren thought, a bit guilty, though it was hard to tell with the shadows cast on his face from the flickering light.

"Why did he want to come along on the hunting weekend?" Warren asked.

"Well, I . . . I guess for the same reason that anyone . . . It's pretty up here. It's a nice break from college."

"Is that the only reason?" Warren prompted.

"What do you mean?"

"You tell me."

"Well . . ." He wasn't quite there. Warren would have to dribble out a bit of what he knew, though he didn't want to reveal where he'd gotten it.

"Your friend was seen looking into the lives of some of the men here at the club," he said. He made it sound serious, but really, it could mean just about anything. "I know why he's really here."

There was a bit of a standoff, Skip sitting there in silence and War-ren letting it get thicker and thicker until Skip blurted out, "He only wants to reveal the truth about the war. The men here, well, they're the ones who are keeping it going. He'd been working on a story for the paper, and he came across Colonel French's name. He remem-bered that I'd said my dad knew him and went hunting with him. He knew that Colonel French was one of these advisors that they sent over to try to train the South Vietnamese, and he'd seen his name somewhere. He thought he might talk."

The paper.

Warren realized what must have happened and said, "He's a re-porter for *The Harvard Crimson*. So he asked if you could get him an invitation?"

Skip hesitated. "Yes."

"I assume you didn't tell your father about this?"

"No." Skip's voice broke. "He was so happy when I said I wanted to come up for the weekend and bring a friend. He loved this place, and he was always trying to get me to come up. Especially since he married Claire. It was like he thought that a weekend of shooting poor, defenseless animals in the woods would erase what he did to us, to my mother, to our family!"

"Mr. Pellegrino wanted to write about Colonel French?"

"Well, he thought there might be a story in it. He thought it might be a good way to stop the war."

"So you invited him along to spy on your father's friends?"

Skip scowled. "I gave him access to a corrupt world of wealth and privilege. It was the least I could do."

Warren sighed and said, "Thank you, Skip. One last thing and then you can send Seth in to see me. You said no one else was around when you were in the lounge Saturday afternoon, is that right?"

Skip nodded. "That's right. But you won't tell Seth it was me who told you about why we wanted to come to the club, will you? You can say that you figured it out on your own?"

Warren almost felt sorry for the boy. He was clearly a bit in thrall to his friend. He had offered him the one thing he had to offer. "Yes, of course."

"Thank you." Skip trudged out of the room, his shoulders dropped in defeat.

Seth came in just as warily, as though he already knew what Warren was going to say. But still, Warren had to nudge and lead before the boy admitted that yes, he'd arranged to come hunting with Skip because he was interested in the members of the Ridge Club in his capacity as a reporter for *The Harvard Crimson*.

"I assume that none of your subjects knew about the real reason you were here?"

"No. I don't think so. I'm a pretty good actor." He didn't sound ashamed at all; rather, he was a bit smug.

"So, what did you find out?"

"Detective Warren, I'm a journalist. I can't reveal my sources or the results of my investigation to you."

"Even when a murder's been committed? Two murders?"

"Even then." He met Warren's eyes defiantly, and Warren found he admired the boy's courage. It would come in handy in his career.

"You were interested in Colonel Graham French?" Warren came right out with it, hoping Seth wouldn't ask how he knew.

"Well . . ." He hesitated. "Look, someone—an alumnus who helps us out from time to time—had mentioned his name to me, said he was one of these *advisors* we hear about and that he'd gotten into trouble for something he said. Well, that sounded promising. I figured he might want to talk to me. I didn't even know Moulton was going to be here, though when I met him, I remembered the story about him getting fired coming across the wire. And then when I got here, it turned out Herman Westwood was here too. Honestly, it was Mr. Westwood I was most interested in. He's a warmonger, Mr. Warren. His company is making bombs and weapons, and he's in bed with the Department of Defense. It's to their advantage, see, that we get into war with the North Vietnamese because they stand to make a lot of money. Uncovering the hidden connections and relationships between the war machine and other parts of the government might stop it."

He said the words with such earnestness and passion that Warren felt oddly unsettled. What would Seth Pellegrino have done to follow his story?

"So on Saturday afternoon, you went upstairs to search all their rooms while Skip kept watch downstairs?" Seth nodded. "And no one saw you? No one else was up there?"

"No," Seth said, looking smug. "It was quiet."

"You know," Warren said, "it's a nasty thing you've done. Taking these men's hospitality, spying on them, lying to them."

The boy shrugged. "In this case, I'm perfectly comfortable with what I've done. If I can stop the bloodshed of innocents by exposing these men for what they are, why wouldn't I do that? All of this, all of these men, they thrive on secrecy, Mr. Warren. Sunlight is the only way. It must be exposed." He seemed to be about to say something else and then stopped, settling instead on, "Isn't that your job as a detective? Finding the truth, exposing lies?"

Warren had started to say that the difference was that everyone knew who he was and what his job was, but Seth cut in.

"I have to tell you something, Detective. I couldn't tell you before, because you would have known I was in Mr. Westwood's room on Saturday. Like I said, Skip and I stayed back when the men went out hunting after lunch and he stood guard in the hallway while I searched all the rooms. But when I was in Mr. Westwood's room,

I looked out the window, and I saw someone in the woods by the pond, like he was waiting for someone. He was wearing brown, so he blended in with the trees. But it wasn't any of the people here at the club." He gestured toward the lounge. "It was someone I didn't recognize. Some other man."

Twenty-seven

Seth tried to describe the man, but Warren got almost nothing useful from his efforts. "Medium height, with shoulders a little stooped over. His face was just . . . normal. He was older. But he definitely wasn't one of the men here."

"Was he carrying anything? A rifle or . . . any kind of a weapon?"

"I don't think so," Seth said. "But he could have had something in his pocket."

Like a knife.

Warren thanked him, and they sat there in silence for a moment, watching the snow fall outside the window. "I guess you've got a pretty good story now," he said. "Forget *The Harvard Crimson; The Boston Globe* will want this one. 'Top Diplomat and Boston Lawyer Slaughtered at Elite Hunt Club.'"

"I don't take pleasure in their deaths," Seth said. "It's Skip's father."

"So, what do you know about why Moulton was dismissed?" Warren asked him. "You said you saw it come over the wire." When Seth didn't answer, Warren said, "Come on—he's dead. Any story you write about him now is going to be about his death. Every single reporter will have the story within twenty-four hours of us getting out of here."

"Well," Seth said, "the wire story said that the State Department was investigating him for ethical lapses. It made it sound like it was money or something. He's a Harvard alum, so we were interested, a little. My editor said I should ask around. We have some contacts at the State Department who answer questions for us sometimes. They know everything going on. But no one knew anything about Moulton. It was *radio silence*."

"And . . ." Warren prompted him. Seth was obviously trying to convey something, but Warren wasn't picking up on it.

"And what they said was that when things are quiet like that? When no one knows anything? It's because the CIA is involved. They said it felt like CIA."

Warren wasn't sure what to ask next, so he told Seth he could go. He walked the boy back to the lounge and went over to pour himself a cup of the coffee that Belle had brought in. He needed to stay alert. But there was a low hum of anxiety in the room.

"Listen up, everyone," Warren said to them. "Mr. Pellegrino saw a man on the property on Saturday, the day Mr. Moulton was killed. He didn't recognize him. I need to know—and this is very important now: Did any of you see a strange man on Saturday or at any other time?"

"What do you mean, a strange man?" Claire asked. "Was there someone else here? Did he kill Bill and Jack?"

Graham French stood up and said incredulously, "Are we just going to sit here and wait for whoever killed Bill and Jack to kill us too?"

"Who is it?" Delana asked.

Warren ignored her. "Earl, you and Jack were out all afternoon. You didn't see anyone, did you?"

Earl shook his head. "I would have told you if I had. We didn't see anyone."

Jenny had been very quiet, and Warren said, "Jenny, what about you?"

She seemed to wrestle with herself for a moment, and then she blurted out, "I didn't see any man, but I saw her." She was pointing to Claire Packingham. Her voice was very quiet. "She was walking around the pond on Friday."

Claire looked up, her eyes glittering with tears. "I told you I came over here to go hunting," she said shortly.

"You didn't say you were here on Friday," Warren pointed out. "What were you doing?"

"I was . . . I was curious. I've only been here a few times. I wanted to see what it was like with everyone here. Jack told me not to, but I thought it would be fun to just . . . get a sense of the place during hunting season."

"Why didn't you tell me?" Warren asked her. He was tired of these people lying to him! Didn't they realize he was conducting an investigation?

"You didn't ask," she said shortly.

Frustrated, Warren turned to Belle and then back to Delana. "When I spoke to Seth and Skip, they said there was no one around the club on Saturday afternoon. No one downstairs. No one upstairs. But you both told me you were in the kitchen or ironing or cleaning. Is there anything else you want to tell me?"

Belle spoke first. "I'm sorry, Mr. Warren. I went over to our place for a little rest. I fell asleep and stayed longer than I meant to. Mr. Packingham was very particular about me being around when there were guests, in case they needed something, and I didn't . . . I didn't want him to be upset at me. I'm sorry."

Warren nodded. "And you, Mrs. Breedlove?"

Delana hesitated. "It sounds so silly now. I saw Belle going over to her place through the window in the upstairs bathroom, and I decided to go and have a piece of pie before she came back. I figured I could have a slice and some coffee and no one would know. Or maybe they'd think one of the men helped themselves. I got myself a plate and Belle wasn't back yet, and so I put on my coat and I sat out on the porch for a little while to enjoy it and I . . . that's where I was. I didn't see anyone who wasn't supposed to be here."

"Thank you," Warren said. "I wish you had told me the truth from the beginning, but I appreciate your honesty now."

"This is ridiculous," Graham said. "I'm going to get my rifle from the gun room. If there's someone out there, I'm going to be armed if he tries anything. You can't stop me."

"Me too," Herman said, standing up. "You can't keep us here like sitting ducks, Detective."

Warren said, "Nobody's going to do that. Trooper Goodrich and I are armed. We will protect you."

The men kept moving, though, and finally Pinky stood up and held his service weapon up in the air and said, "No one is going anywhere! You heard Detective Warren. Stay here!"

"Thank you, Trooper Goodrich," Warren said, once everyone had sat down again. "Mr. Pellegrino has something to tell you all." Seth started to protest and Warren broke in. "Tell them why you're really here. Who was it who said that sunlight is the only way?"

Seth hesitated, then said, "I'm a reporter for *The Harvard Crimson*. I asked Skip to get me an invitation so I could meet you all, see if I could get a story or stories out of it."

Of all the reactions Warren had been expecting, he hadn't been expecting Herman Westwood to burst into laughter. "You were spying on us? You were . . . *undercover* this whole time?"

"I wouldn't say . . . *undercover*. No one asked me what I was doing here."

Claire stood up and went over to Skip. She brandished her glass and, with tears glittering in her eyes, said, "You hated your father that much? You had to betray him, here, in the place he loved the most?"

"Me? What about you? You took everything from him! His family, his home! And then you got bored. He told me, you know? He told me you'd gotten bored with him and wanted a divorce. He knew. He had someone following you, Claire. This weekend was supposed to be a break, to get his head straight. But you insisted on coming along and ruining everything. You probably killed him!"

"Shut up, Skip!" she screamed, going back to sit on the couch again.

"I can't believe this," Herman said. Warren saw now that he was very drunk. "I can't believe this son of a bitch was spying on us. Skip, how can you live with yourself?"

"Leave him alone, Mr. Westwood," Seth said quietly with a level of control that Warren found surprising. "I convinced him to invite me, and I still think it's worth it to expose the rotten core at the heart of this war."

Herman laughed. Slurring his words, he shouted, "Well, you're even dumber than I thought you were, Mr. Pellegrino, because we, this place, Mr. Pellegrino? We're yesterday's story. A bunch of washed-up has-beens. You want to know who's running the show? Look to the *young men in suits*. They're the ones, Mr. Pellegrino. Not us. We're a bunch of old men looking out at the ashes of the world we saved." Herman laughed again, an unhinged, cackling laugh that made Warren nervous. In the jumpy light from the fire, his face was shadowed and sinister.

Seth couldn't help himself. "What do you mean, Mr. Westwood? Who are the young men in suits?"

"They visit me. I don't know who they are! They're running things, Mr. Pellegrino. They're the ones you want!" There was an embarrassed silence in the room. "I know how I sound. They say this will be a modern war, neat and quick! All the bureaucrats! As if war is ever anything but men scrabbling at each other's throats!" He got up and went over to pour himself another drink.

Warren followed him and tried to discreetly move the bottle out of reach. "Mr. Westwood, let's lay off the—"

"Don't tell me what to do!" Herman shouted at Warren, sloshing the yellow liquid over the edge of the glass and onto the surface of the bar. "Someone's been looking through my things! Maybe it was him!" He pointed at Seth. "Maybe it was someone else!"

"Just stop it!" Claire said. "Everyone, just stop it!"

Now Skip was crying, very quietly, his shoulders shaking almost imperceptibly. Delana went over to sit next to him. She didn't make a big production of comforting him, but she put a hand on his shoulder and sat with him, a reassuring hand on his arm.

"We're going to wait for the light," Warren said. "We're just going to sit right here and wait for the light."

"There are sandwiches," Belle said quietly. "And a pot of coffee. Why doesn't everyone help themselves?"

They did. The food seemed to calm them for a bit—even Claire, who was now crying softly again, Belle patting her shoulder and trying to console her. Skip slumped on the couch, staring into the darkness beyond the circle of people around the fire.

It was now three A.M.

"What are we going to do, Mr. Warren?" Delana asked.

"We're going to sit here and we're going to stay warm and wait for the snow to stop and the morning to come so that we can go for help," Warren said. "Why doesn't someone tell a story or something?"

"What, like a ghost story?" Jenny asked.

Warren smiled. "I don't think that's a good idea. How about a story from your life?"

Graham cleared his throat. "All right, then. This reminds me of a night when my battalion was stuck down in a forest near Nancy, in the northeast of France. We were going at daybreak, and we had to wait through the night. We knew what was coming, but we just sat there and waited for the earth to turn. That's all it was, waiting for the earth to turn around again so morning would come."

"What was it like, being in a war?" Seth asked suddenly. "Were you scared all the time?"

"Most of the time," Graham said. "At first. And then it becomes second nature, being scared. Fear is good. It keeps you from doing stupid things."

"What happened the next morning?" Seth asked him. "What were you waiting for?"

"The Germans were on the other side of the river, and we needed to push them back a half a mile or so to allow for another division to come in and establish a supply route. We thought there were about a hundred of them, but it turned out to be more like two hundred. We still pushed 'em back, though. Lost forty-two men doing it."

"How'd you push them back?" Seth asked. He had the reporter's ability to make his questions seem conversational, as though he were just being polite in asking. It put people at ease and made them talk. Warren almost thought about warning Graham, but he was curious too. His own father's stories about World War II were incomplete, focusing more on the men he'd fought with than on what exactly they'd done. At some point, he'd realized that was because there was trauma associated with the memories.

"Well," Graham said, "that is actually a pretty interesting story. Once we realized we were outnumbered, we had to get creative, so we set up some bonfires around their perimeter. Sowed a little confusion. The smoke made them think we were moving to their west, but we came in from the east. We got about sixty of 'em right away, and then it was a fair fight."

"Very good," Herman Westwood said.

"Was it worth it?" Seth Pellegrino asked.

French was quiet for a long time. And then he said, "How can you ask a question like that? Jesus!"

"It's a real question," Seth said. "Men died. Was it worth it?"

"Yes, it was worth it. We beat Hitler! We saved the world! My God."

There was a long silence. Seth, thankfully, left it alone.

"Earl, you were over there, weren't you?" Herman asked. "I remember you saying you sowed some confusion over there yourself."

"Yes, I was," Earl said.

"Which branch?" Warren asked.

"Army."

"Devil's Brigade, right?" Graham asked.

"What's the Devil's Brigade?" Seth was leaning forward, listening intently.

"First Special Service Force," Graham said. "American and Canadian unit. We all have a lot to thank you for, Earl."

Earl murmured something about doing his duty. He was embarrassed by the attention, though, and Warren remembered what he'd said about hunting deer. *I did enough killing over in Europe.*

"Where were you?" Warren asked him.

He sighed. "France, Italy, wherever they needed me."

"You left, though?" Seth asked him. "You didn't stay in after the war?"

"I'd had enough," Earl said. "Some people are suited for the lifestyle. Some aren't. I went back to Idaho, where I'm from. But I was bored there, and I remembered a man I'd served with who said he was from Vermont. He always made it sound nice, so in forty-nine, I decided to see what it was like. I knocked around a bit and then started working for Nathan. He was the caretaker here, and Belle's mother was the cook. And here I am." In the low light, Warren saw him look over at Belle and smile.

There was a long silence, and finally Seth said, "What about you, Mr. Westwood?"

"I wanted to serve, of course," Herman said. "But I had flat feet. I got my engineering degree instead, and I've contributed in that way." His voice was defensive, and Warren held his breath, waiting to see how Seth would respond.

"What about Mr. Moulton?" Pinky asked. "Did he serve in World War II?"

Warren sent him a silent thank-you. This was a good way to find out more about Moulton.

"Bill was OSS," Graham said. "Who knows what he got up to?"

"That's, like, the intelligence wing of the army, right?" Pinky asked. "Before there was a CIA?"

"That's right. A lot of the things that went right in that war were down to the intelligence men. Well, D-Day . . . there's a whole history there that no one knows. I could—" He seemed to catch himself then and stopped talking.

"Bill knew where all the bodies were buried, didn't he?" Herman said.

Warren thought of Alice Bellows's husband. She had seemed to know quite a lot about Bill Moulton, and he realized suddenly that her husband's connections must be how.

More than that, though, he knew that he'd found a motive for Moulton's death. Moulton must have known all kinds of secrets about people who had been spies or were hiding things. Someone didn't want him to tell what he knew. Jack Packingham might be dead because he found out what it was.

He was looking around the circle of faces when Claire screamed suddenly and called out, "There's someone out there! I just saw someone moving outside the window." She was pointing to the windows behind them, the ones that looked out on the pond, and Warren and Pinky jumped up to investigate.

But before they could get there, a window pane shattered.

Twenty-eight

Warren ran over to the window. The snow was now blowing through the broken pane, drifting on the windowsill. He couldn't see anything beyond.

"Someone help me," he called out. "Get a tablecloth or something to cover it up." Seth Pellegrino pulled a cloth from one of the tables, but Earl Canfield was faster, and he took a large wooden plaque from the wall and placed it over the window, blocking the broken pane, then tucked the tablecloth in around it. The temperature in the room dropped suddenly, the outside air seeping in around the edges.

"What was that?" Herman asked. "Who's out there?"

Warren pressed his face to one of the intact panes and peered out into the night, then searched the floor below the window, now littered with glass, for a rock or other projectile. "I can't see anything," he said. "Maybe it was the wind?"

"If it was the wind, they'd all be broken," Herman said. "This is intolerable. I want out of here right now. I'm going to get my gun. If you can't protect us, we need to protect ourselves."

"Me too," Graham French said. "Two men are dead and something's going on here. There's someone out there. Who is it, Mr. Warren?"

Warren felt he was losing control again.

"I'm going to go see what that was," he said quickly. "Trooper Goodrich is armed and he's going to stay here. The best thing you can all do is stay together and stay calm. It will be light soon. Trooper Goodrich, can I talk to you for a second?"

"Don't leave us," Delana Breedlove said. She sounded terrified.

"It's okay. They'll be right back, Delana," Belle told her. "Earl's here and the detectives will be back."

"I'll be back in three minutes," Pinky said. "Don't worry."

"Walter won't let anything happen to us," Jenny told her mother.

They went out into the hall outside the gun room. "I need to see if there are any footprints or any sign of someone on the property," Warren said. "It's probably futile at this point, but I need to at least look before it's all covered by the snow. Can you make sure no one leaves the room? And don't leave anyone alone. If someone goes to the bathroom, have someone else go with them and keep an eye on things, okay? I'm not going to go far, but if I'm not back in an hour, then come after me."

"Who do you think Mr. Pellegrino saw on Saturday?" Pinky asked.

"I don't know. He didn't recognize the person. So someone else was around when Moulton was killed."

"If he's telling the truth about not recognizing him," Pinky said.

"I think he was."

"What do you think broke that window?"

"I don't know, Pinky. I'll keep an eye on my watch. An hour, okay? If I'm not back, you'll have to come after me."

⌥ ⌥ ⌥

Outside, the flashlight emitted a strong light onto the field of white. The snow was still falling, but it had slowed and Warren could now see the outlines of trees; he could at least get his bearings outside. But quickly he saw his mistake. The snow was so deep that he'd likely fall and get stuck. So he tucked the flashlight into his coat pocket and took the metal snow shovel that Earl had brought back and began to shovel a path ahead of him as he trudged through the heavy snow. It took a huge amount of effort, though, and his heart was beating fast and hard after only ten minutes of it. It only now occurred to him that he should have taken a pair of snowshoes from the hallway, but there was no point in going back.

He slowly made his way around the lodge, stopping every few feet to catch his breath. He told himself that at least no one would be able to surprise him out here; no one could approach him in this deep snow without making noise that would alert him. He was armed and had the shovel for protection too. But in the darkness, he felt vulnerable and too conspicuous.

The trees were bowing to the ground under their burden.

He kept going, bending to scoop up a rectangle of snow in front of him, twisting to deposit it to the side, stooping to do it again.

Finally, he stopped and took the flashlight from his pocket. Ahead of him was an expanse of open ground dotted with areas of darker snow, and it took Warren a moment to understand what he was seeing: a path through the snow, made by a person trying and failing to completely lift each foot as they went so that the trail looked almost like that made by a person on skis.

He shone the light out into the darkness, trying to see the prints better. They were covered over by a few inches of snow, which meant they had been made a couple of hours ago, around the time Jack Packingham had been killed. Warren, abandoning the shovel for a moment in the snow, walked closer, plowing through with great effort, to see where they'd come from and stopped, confused.

What the hell?

They didn't originate from the lodge or from any of the structures belonging to the club. Instead, they seemed to come out of the forest, loop around, and then disappear back into the woods. He considered following them into the trees for just a moment and then realized how stupid that would be. He needed to wait for light—and backup.

He'd made it to the other side of the dining room now, and he shone his flashlight on the broken window and immediately saw the culprit: a large, heavy tree branch from the big maple tree next to the lodge. It was still lying beneath the window. The movement of it bowing suddenly to the ground under the weight of the snow was the movement that Claire had seen, and the torquing of the branch as it fell had caused it to swing into the window, shattering the pane, and then fall back to the ground.

He could try to signal to them through the window that everything was okay, but he didn't want to scare them further, and he had thought of something while he was walking.

Earl and Belle lived in the cottage off to the side of the driveway, by the pond. While he had searched the rooms of everyone staying at the club, he hadn't searched theirs yet. Now that Jack was dead, Warren had to consider that either he or Earl had been lying about where they were on Saturday afternoon. Jack had been very quick to say that he and Earl had been in sight of each other the whole time they were in the woods.

They had known each other a long time. Earl owed his livelihood to Jack and the club. Who knew what secrets they shared or what bonds had been forged over the years? What if they'd been lying?

What if an important piece of evidence was hidden at the Canfields' cottage?

Or what if *someone* was hiding there?

His arms were aching now from the effort of shoveling, but he was able to go back along the path he'd made toward the driveway, and then he set off, checking the time on his wristwatch by the light of the flashlight. He found the path that Pinky, Jenny, and the Canfields had walked after the discovery of Jack's body, and though there was an-other inch of snow there now, it was much easier walking than in the deep snow. When he reached the little cottage, he stepped up onto the porch and stopped for a moment to get his breath. It had been hard work shoveling and walking through the snow, and his heart was pounding with the effort. Standing at the front door, Warren could see that it had good views of the clubhouse and the pond, probably a necessity for Earl's position. He'd been assuming that the house had always been there, but now that he was closer to it, it seemed recently built, with newer windows and a simple construction that felt more 1950s than 1880s to Warren.

He leaned the shovel against a chair, took off his gloves, and paused to get his service revolver out before opening the door. Holding his gun in one hand, he used his other hand to shine his flashlight around once he'd entered the house. He could see the shapes of chairs and couches to one side of the room, and when he swept the light over the other end, he found a kitchen, complete with electric stove and new electric refrigerator. A woodstove was still radiating heat against one wall. He searched the living room area first, opening drawers and cupboards. Everything was neat and organized. There was no televi-sion here—Warren supposed that Earl and Belle watched over at the club when there was something they wanted to see—and on one wall was a simple portrait of Earl and Belle dressed in formal clothing and standing with an older couple. The older man looked enough like Belle for Warren to be certain it was her father. The orchid corsage on the front of Belle's simple pale dress revealed it as their wedding photo. Another framed photo of a group of men in uniform seemed to be the only other object in pride of place. Warren thought that was interesting. It told him that Earl's two most important roles were as Belle's husband and a man who had served his country. Despite his demurral at the chance to speak about his experiences in the war, Earl was proud enough of his time in uniform to keep this photograph and to hang it in plain sight. Warren's own father had a photo of himself in uniform with five good friends from his platoon. Only three of them—including Tommy Johnson—had made it home, and the photo sat on his father's dressing table at home, always clean and dust-free.

The kitchen didn't offer up anything in his search either. A large pantry was filled with neat rows of gleaming canned goods: beans, tomatoes, pickles, jams. He checked the knives in a block on the counter, but they all seemed to be in their places. Then he followed the short hallway, which led to three rooms—two bedrooms and a bathroom. One bedroom was clearly occupied but very neat. This was Earl and Belle's; the bedcovers had been hurriedly pulled up when Pinky and Jenny had roused them from sleep.

Here too, Warren's search yielded nothing out of the ordinary. He quickly searched the two drawers in the small bathroom, and then he stepped into the other bedroom, which was nearly completely empty.

There was nothing here. Not the missing rifle. Not a bloody rag used to clean the knife. In the dining room, Warren saw copies of some of the trout derby photographs from the lodge hanging on the wall. Most had Belle and her father in them, which was likely why they were here. Nathan Reese had been a short but powerfully built man, with a serious expression above his gray beard in most of the photos. They were all similar in composition: a large group of men and a few women, all standing in front of the pond, the winner holding a fish and a trophy. Printed below the mat were the years in which they'd been taken. Was there a 1946 photo among them? Warren scanned the years and found it. He didn't recognize the man holding a large fish and the trophy, but he was able to pick out younger versions of Herman Westwood, Graham French, Jack Packingham, and Bill Moulton. Belle Canfield, much younger, stood to one side with her father.

And then he recognized someone else.

A slight man, standing in the second row on the left, between two larger men who partially obscured him.

The expression on his face was neutral, as though he were trying not to stand out.

If you weren't looking carefully, you might have missed him.

But Warren didn't miss him: Arthur Crannock, Alice's friend, whom Warren had met only two nights before.

Arthur Crannock had been at the Ridge Club in 1946.

The last time Bill Moulton had been here.

And he was here, in Bethany, now.

It couldn't be a coincidence.

Warren was sure of it.

He went back outside again and started across the driveway, still carrying the shovel. The snow seemed to have really slowed now. Perhaps the storm was passing.

Warren trudged along the path, thinking about what he'd learned.

Everyone had been in their rooms when the shots were fired. Earl and Belle had been tucked up in their beds. The front door of the lodge was locked. These things were incontrovertible.

How had Jack Packingham been killed?

And what did it mean that Arthur Crannock had been here in 1946?

He thought about what he'd said to Pinky that he felt there was someone stage-managing all of them. It was as though all these things—the prints in the snow, the superfluous bullet in Bill Moulton's chest, the extra key in Jack Packingham's hand—had been inserted into the case just to confuse him. He felt a wave of anger. This was his chance to prove himself in Bethany. He wasn't going to let whoever it was stop him from doing that.

Warren picked up his pace, his boots crunching on the top layer of snow, which was starting to freeze.

He was almost to the lodge when he heard the shot.

Twenty-nine

Everything was awful, Jenny thought. Really, truly awful.

Mr. Packingham was dead. The rest of them were trapped at the lodge with no power and no way of getting out of the woods. Everyone was angry at everyone else, and they had started turning on each other, their suspicion and fear getting the better of them. Mr. Warren had gone out into the snow to find out if there was a maniac stalking them, and probably something terrible would happen to him.

She still didn't know why her mother had lied about the knife and about where she'd been on Saturday.

And it was really cold.

But despite all of that, Jenny could feel a warm little kernel of happiness in her chest.

Life was funny, wasn't it? Something awful could happen, and then the next moment, something wonderful could happen.

The wonderful thing was that she was stranded here with Walter.

After Jenny and her mother had been awakened by the shot and heard the voices out in the lounge and found out about Mr. Packingham, she had volunteered to go with Walter to wake up Earl and Belle.

They had gone out into the night, trudging along in the snow that had fallen since Earl had shoveled a path to the cottage. It wasn't that far—only a hundred yards on the other side of the drive—but there was enough snow that it was slow going and Jenny had slipped and almost fallen at one point, and Walter had reached out for her and caught her by the arm. When she stood up again, they were touching and standing very close, and Walter had said, "Are you okay, Jenny? Be careful; it's slippery."

She had looked up into his eyes, which she could just barely see because it was so dark, but she had felt a kind of electricity between them, and for a moment, she almost thought he was going to kiss her. *Time stood still.* Jenny had read that in a book once, and she hadn't really understood what it meant. But now she did. Time had stood still. And then Walter said, "We better get to Earl and Belle's," and Jenny had nodded and they had kept walking. When they got to the house, Walter said very quietly, "Jenny, if you know anything or saw anything, you should tell Mr. Warren, you know." Jenny was too shocked to do anything but nod silently, and then Walter had knocked on Earl and Belle's door and then knocked again, and then they'd heard footsteps inside and the door had opened and it was Earl, dressed in his pajamas—which had been funny to Jenny because Earl was not the kind of person you expected to see in *pajamas*—and after Walter told him what happened, he called to Belle and she came out too, in a bathrobe, and then they got dressed while Jenny and Walter waited for them. While they waited, Walter turned off his flashlight because he said it was better to save the batteries.

And then—and this was the most exciting part of all—they sat down on the couch in the dark to wait, and there was a whole long couch, but Walter sat right next to her, with their thighs touching each other. He didn't move at all, though, and while they sat there in absolute silence, Jenny could feel the heat of his leg next to hers. She almost turned to him and said *Oh, Walter,* like people did in the movies, but at that exact moment, Earl came out of the bedroom and said, "Let's take some extra flashlights just in case we need them," and Walter had stood up and said, "Good idea," and Jenny's *Oh, Walter* stayed in her head.

At the moment the window broke, Jenny had been sitting by the fire and thinking about how Walter hadn't had to sit right next to her on the couch but that he had anyway, and she was wondering about what it all meant. And then there was a huge crash and Walter, who had gotten up to see who was out there, jumped in front of Jenny, like he was trying to protect her.

Jenny smiled, remembering.

But then she remembered all the awful things, and she remembered that her mother had lied about the knife, and that was what got Jenny thinking about everything.

She stared into the fire and turned it all over in her mind, and then she was thinking about Walter and how he'd said that if she knew anything, it would be really helpful to them if she would tell Mr. Warren.

Did she know anything? She wasn't sure. A lot of people weren't being honest with Walter and Mr. Warren—Jenny included. It was the knife that had made her realize something about what happened on Saturday. She tried to remember. She tried to get it all straight. Lunch. The strange man. Mr. Moulton. A gunshot. It was like she was doing a jigsaw puzzle and all the seemingly unconnected things were pieces she had to put together.

Jenny stared at the fire for a long time and, finally, she thought she knew what happened.

And now she knew how to prove it. She would tell them she had to go use the bathroom. That would buy her a bit of time at least.

The wind was blowing outside the windows of the lodge. Everyone was tense and scared. The shutters creaked and moaned. Jenny jumped as something banged against the outside of the house.

"What was that?" Seth asked, turning to the window.

"Nothing," Mr. Westwood said. "Stop trying to scare us."

"He's not trying to scare us," Skip said. "I heard it too."

Jenny started to say that she was going to go and use the bathroom and that she'd take a flashlight.

And then Mrs. Packingham was pulling something from the pocket of her robe.

Thirty

By the time Warren made it back inside the lodge, there was utter confusion in the foyer just outside the lounge. Everyone was crowded together, and Warren could hear Pinky saying, "Give it to me. Give it to me right now!" and Earl's voice saying, "Mrs. Packingham, you need to give that to him," and the beams of everyone's flashlights were crossing and flashing in a sickening whirl.

"I'm getting my gun too!" someone shouted, and Warren recognized Herman's voice.

"It's me. I'm back," Warren called into the darkness. "What's happening? What was that shot? Was anyone hit? Trooper Goodrich?"

"I don't think anyone was hit," Pinky called out to him. "But dammit, I can't see anything. Mrs. Packingham, stay where you are!"

"Claire, give it to him right now," Graham French was shouting.

"Give Trooper Goodrich the gun!" Warren roared.

"Okay, here it is."

He couldn't see her hand it over, but he heard Pinky say, "Got it," and he shone his light in Pinky's direction so he could secure it.

Earl, taking charge, called out, "Get back in the lounge! Sit in the chairs so the officers can see who's who!" and everyone started moving back toward the lounge. It was a few moments before everyone was seated again.

"What happened?" Warren asked Pinky, who was pointing his flashlight at the people sitting in the lounge.

"We heard something outside and she"—he pointed the flashlight beam at Claire Packingham—"pulled out a .38 Special! She'd been keeping it hidden in her pocket all this time. I went to get it from her and the gun went off. It's a wonder no one was shot."

Warren gave Pinky the key to the gun room and told him to go lock up Claire's weapon.

"Mrs. Packingham, I don't have to tell you how dangerous that was. What were you thinking?" Warren asked Claire, shining the flashlight up at her face. She looked terrible. Her eyes were sunken and bloodshot from crying, and she looked years older.

"I thought there was someone out there! They killed Jack and I thought they might kill me too. I swear I heard something out there. Someone was watching us!"

"It was probably me," Warren told her. "It was a tree branch that hit the window. There's no one there. Everything's okay. We just need to stay calm and wait until morning comes. Okay? Can we have some coffee here and just all sit here and wait? It's five o'clock now. The sun should be rising in two hours or so. The snow is slowing. Please just hang on."

But Skip had stood up and was gesturing toward his stepmother. "You had a gun this whole time? You probably killed him! Have you looked at her? That would be awfully convenient, wouldn't it? You'd get all his money—all the money that was supposed to be ours."

"I didn't kill anyone," Claire was shouting. "You hated him. You're the one who wanted him dead! This place is full of guns. *You* probably shot him! You wanted to punish him because he loved me!"

"He didn't love you!" Skip screamed. "He knew you were talking to a divorce lawyer! The lawyer called him as soon as you left the office. He told me last week!"

The room went completely silent. Claire slumped in her chair.

"Stop this," Warren told them. "This isn't going to help things." But now his mind was racing with possibilities. Had Claire, alone in her twin bed, asked her husband to meet her in the gun room for a tryst? Had she convinced him to open the door and then shot him before somehow racing back to her room?

"Do you really think there's someone out there?" Delana asked in a tearful voice. "Is there someone just . . . trying to kill us all?"

"I didn't see any sign of another person," Warren lied, thinking of the footprints in the snow. "But I can't be sure." Pinky had come back now and he loomed in the doorway as though he was reminding them to stay where they were.

"Then who killed Jack?" Claire asked. "If there's no one out there, it means it was one of you!" she said. "I was right to bring a gun. If the police can't keep us safe, we have to do it ourselves. Poor Jack was murdered by someone in this room, and whoever it is is just waiting for us to let our guards down."

"Did you hear something?" Delana said suddenly. "I think I heard someone walking upstairs."

"Oh God!" Claire moaned. "They're coming for us!"

Everyone started to get up and crowd together, shoving and pushing each other.

"Stop!" Warren shouted. "Stop it right now!"

He could hear them all breathing, could feel the fear in the air. That kind of fear was dangerous. Each of them was like a cornered animal. They would do anything they had to do to survive.

Suddenly, Pinky's voice came out of the half darkness. "Where's Jenny?" he asked. "Jenny, are you here?"

Silence.

"Jenny?" Delana called out. "Jenny, where are you? Oh my God, where's Jenny? Maybe that was her upstairs." They were all quiet for a moment, listening for sounds from upstairs, but none came.

Pinky's light swept the room. "She's not here." Warren could hear the panic in his voice.

"Stay there," Warren said more harshly than he'd intended. "I'm going to go look for her. Keep everyone in this room."

He ran through the lounge and the dining room, shining the flashlight across the floor and behind the chairs and tables. Then he checked the kitchen and the bathroom and bedroom behind it. Taking the back staircase upstairs, he checked each room carefully, looking under the beds and behind the doors. "Jenny?" he called out. "Jenny, are you up here?"

She wasn't there.

"Where is she? Where's Jenny?" Delana screamed when she saw him coming down the stairs. "Did something happen to her?"

"Hang on. I just want to make sure she's not in the gun room," Warren told her. He got the key from Pinky and went through to the hallway and then, very much afraid now of what he might find, unlocked the door.

He was relieved to see that Jack Packingham's body was just where they'd left it. It seemed suddenly entirely within the realm of possibility that it could have disappeared or that a different body could be lying on the floor. Warren leaned over and shone the light on the corpse. Something had started percolating in his brain while looking at the trout derby photograph in the Canfields' living room, and he inspected the wound on Jack's chest, trying to see if he could be right. But the light wasn't strong enough, and he didn't have the right tools.

He didn't have time for this. He needed to find Jenny.

Warren shone the light on one side of the room at a time, examining the walls, the guns, the equipment on the wall, and then he went out and locked the door again, and went back into the hallway, shining his light around at the clothes and hats and gloves and the snowshoes hanging on the walls. He stopped. There was a blank space on the wall between two sets of snowshoes.

A pair was missing.

Back in the lounge, he told them what he'd found. "It looks like she took a pair of snowshoes," he said. "Does anyone have any idea at all where she might have gone?"

No one said anything.

"She loves the woods," Delana said finally. "She loves walking in the woods and . . . maybe . . . she's out there?"

"Why would she go out into the woods?" Herman asked. "We're in the middle of a snowstorm! We're being stalked by a homicidal maniac. She's not an idiot."

"Maybe she was upset," Delana said nervously. "She likes to get out in the woods and think. She goes to that old house. Belle's father's house."

"But why would she go now? It's dark and cold and snowing," Warren said.

Pinky started to say something, then stopped, then started again. "She . . . maybe . . . she was . . ."

"Yes?" Warren prompted him.

"I told her it would help us if she told you what she knew, if she helped us with the case. Maybe she went out to look for, well, evidence."

"Does she do a lot of snowshoeing?" Warren asked Delana. "Is she experienced on them?"

"I . . . I don't know," Delana said.

Earl cleared his throat and said, "She takes them out from time to time. I showed her how to put them on, and I gave her some boots to use. She's good on them, but . . . it's cold and the snow is deep. There's no crust on it yet, so she may sink down, and I don't know if she'll be able to get out of it if she falls."

"I'm going to have to go after her," Warren said. "Earl, will you come with me?" Earl nodded and said he'd go and get snowshoes ready for them.

"I'll come with you," Pinky said. "I couldn't forgive myself if something happened to her. And . . . with all due respect, Detective Warren, I know the woods better than you do. I should do it. I'll go with Earl, and you stay here."

Warren considered that. Pinky was right. But he had the sense that the reason Jenny had run away was very important to figuring out who had killed Bill Moulton and Jack Packingham. Jenny must have gone out there because she thought she had solved the case. She was the key to everything.

He needed to do it himself.

And one of them needed to stay at the lodge.

"I need you to stay here," he said. "I need you to protect them." Pinky's face clouded in the dim light, but he nodded and Warren, handing the key back to him, said, "Keep an eye on them. Don't let anyone near the gun room."

He went up to his room to get an extra sweater, and he was coming down the stairs, the light bouncing against the walls, when he heard a small sound, a throat being cleared in the darkness, and said, "Who's there?" His flashlight swept the bottom of the staircase, and he saw Delana standing there.

"Mrs. Breedlove?"

"I'm sorry. I told Trooper Goodrich that I wanted to talk to you. In private. He said it was okay."

"Yes? Is it about Jenny?" He pointed to the carpeted third stair and they sat down, Warren at one end up against the railing and Delana at the other.

"I'm sorry, Detective Warren," she said. "I just . . . I'm so worried about Jenny and . . . I didn't want to say anything, but on Friday night I heard the men talking about . . . well, now I wonder if Jenny did too and maybe that's why she's run off."

Warren kept his flashlight pointed down, away from her face. "I'm sorry. The men talking? What were they talking about on Friday, Delana?"

"About, well . . ." She was crying now, and her voice got very quiet as she said, "Me and Mr. . . . Mr. Moulton."

"I see," he said gently. "Tell me. Just what I need to know so we don't waste time. I need to look for Jenny."

She nodded. "There's not that much to tell. It was in 1946," she said. "That summer. The year when Mr. Moulton was last here and he and Mr. Westwood got into the terrible fight. I was helping out at the club. Mrs. Reese—that's Belle's mother—she used to use some of the local girls to serve when they had big events at the club. He was at the club a lot, and he was very nice to me. And . . . one thing led to another. He didn't force me, if that's what you're thinking. But . . ."

Warren waited. He didn't want to ask the delicate question, and he thought she'd go ahead if he just kept listening.

"He told me he loved me and we could get married, that his wife didn't love him, that she never had," she said. "It was stupid of me, but I really believed him. I thought he'd take me away and we'd live in the city and have a big house. I didn't know anything, and he was so handsome and he made me laugh."

"Did anyone know?" Warren asked.

"I didn't think so," Delana said. "I would meet him out by the road, not far from Belle's old house, and we would walk in the woods . . . I don't regret it, Mr. Warren. It was . . . it taught me about how to love someone, I think. I was sad when he and his wife went back to Washington and when I figured out that . . . but I never regretted it."

Warren waited for her to say *And I had Jenny, and I never regretted that.*

But she didn't.

He didn't want to ask, but he had to. He swiveled the flashlight so he could see her face. "And Jenny," he said very quietly. "Was Jenny . . . his?"

Delana's eyes went wide, and she burst into tears.

"It's okay," he said. "I'm not judging you. I won't tell anyone unless I absolutely have to. I won't tell Jenny if she doesn't already know. I just need to understand."

Delana sighed. "I met Harry, my husband, in the fall and well, do you know, I think that bit of confidence I had from Bill, Mr. Moulton, I think it made me a bit bolder than I would have been. Harry never would have gotten around to asking for a date, but I made the first move and we were married within two months. He's so shy. It was . . . in those days, we were still thinking of the war. You didn't wait around. I realized I was pregnant the day we got back from our honeymoon. I guess I knew . . . if I was honest with myself. And it was clear to me when Jenny was born two months early . . . Well, not really early. But that's what we thought. If the doctor knew, he didn't say anything. It was so easy to pretend. I hadn't thought about it in years. That's the truth. Jenny and her dad, they're just alike. They're such a pair. I think I fooled myself into thinking that it never happened."

"Did you overhear the men's conversation on Friday night?"

In the low light, he could see her shake her head. "No. I knew they were having an argument about something, but I didn't know what it was. I didn't hear, but Belle must have heard them because she got this look on her face, and she said for Jenny to go get more potatoes, even though she had a full platter. I guess I wasn't paying attention, but Belle must not have wanted Jenny to hear what they were saying. I think she was protecting her. And then the next day, Bill, Mr. Moulton, found me in the kitchen right after lunch. I was cutting up the leftover pork. I didn't know where Belle was but I guess she was having a rest, and Jenny was still cleaning the bathroom."

"What did he say?"

"He said that he'd realized something when the men were talking the night before, and he asked me if Jenny was his. I was so worried about someone hearing us, but I whispered that I thought so, but I was married and I never wanted my husband to know, and I pleaded with him not to say anything. He said he wouldn't, and he asked if there was anything he could do for me. He asked if Jenny and I were okay for money, and I said we were. He said she looked like his son, and that once the men said it, he realized it had to be true. Before he left, he said she was a nice girl and that, in his way, he was proud that she was his, but that he would never tell, that he would take the secret to his grave."

"And then?"

"And then nothing. He left. I was so upset. My husband . . . I put the knife down and took off my apron and I went outside for a while to think. When I came back, the knife and my apron were gone. It's the knife that was in Jenny's pocket, but I didn't tell you, because I didn't want you to think I killed him. I didn't want you to find out about us. I didn't think Jenny was around when I was talking to Mr. Moulton, but . . . maybe she heard our conversation or maybe she heard the men talking the night before. I don't know. Maybe . . . she did something." She sobbed. "Maybe that's why she ran away."

Warren fixed his eyes on her. A picture was coming into view in his mind. The knife. An unknown person stealing into the kitchen and taking it from the counter. "Delana," he said. "This is important. Who was around when this happened? Who was in the dining room?"

She thought for a moment and said, "They all were here for lunch. Mr. Westwood, Mr. French, Skip, Seth, and Mr. Packingham. But then most of them went back out again. I'm not sure when . . . Do you . . . *Do* you think Jenny heard us?" She sounded terrified. The revelation of this long-held secret would be devastating for Delana and the Breedlove family, Warren knew. It could destroy the marriage, the close relationship between Jenny and her mother and Jenny and her father, Delana's employment at the club, the reputation of the hardware store. He could hear how desperate she was. That kind of desperation led people to take drastic actions to make sure their secrets weren't revealed.

Who else at the Ridge Club had secrets they wanted to keep?

"I don't know. Thank you, Delana," he said. "Don't worry. I'll do everything I can to find her." He didn't say the rest of what he was thinking. *Before whoever is out there finds her first.*

Thirty-one

The idea had come to her while she watched the fire, but Jenny hadn't come up with the whole plan until Seth started shouting about hearing something outside, and Jenny had gone to the doorway of the lounge, just to see if anyone noticed her stepping away. No one did. Everyone was very focused on him and then on the shot and Mrs. Packingham and then Detective Warren coming in. In all the confusion, Jenny had slipped into the supply closet when the rest of them came out into the hall. She waited there behind the door and listened to Detective Warren telling Mrs. Packingham to give Walter the gun and everyone to go back to the lounge.

There were all kinds of jackets and boots and gloves on the hooks and shelves in the hallway, and she felt around for what she needed and got dressed quietly, listening to the voices in the other room. Carefully, going by feel, she had reached up to take down one of the pairs of snowshoes on the wall that Belle's father, Nathan, had made.

Then she listened again to make sure nobody was coming, and slipped out the door into the cold darkness. She put on the snowshoes, just the way Earl had shown her, and stepped off the porch into the deep snow. She had taken a flashlight, but she found that the sky had turned that strange yellow-black it always turned just before the sun rose, so she tucked the flashlight into a jacket pocket and found she could see well enough to make her way down the steps and set off around the pond and into the woods. She was light enough that the broad snowshoes actually kept her fairly high on the snow cover, and she made good progress, putting the lodge and the club buildings quickly behind her.

Once she was into the deepest part of the woods, though, it grew dark again. Jenny stopped and took off her gloves and then took the flashlight out of her pocket and switched it on. Then she replaced her gloves and tried to stick the flashlight under her right arm since it was awkward holding it in her gloved hand.

But she only made it a few steps before the flashlight fell, disappearing immediately into the deep snow.

Jenny scrabbled for it, but the gloves made it impossible to feel it underneath the snow, and she knew it would be a disaster to take them off. Her father had taught her that once your hands or feet got cold and wet, there was no warming up until you were inside again. But she was worried that if she kept going, she would get lost in the darkness of the woods. And now that she'd gone down on her knees to look for the flashlight, the snowshoes had gotten stuck beneath her and she couldn't get them free.

Jenny sighed. She hadn't thought this through at all. Her father had a big sign over the counter at the hardware store that said MEASURE TWICE AND CUT ONCE. Jenny remembered realizing that though it applied to woodworking, it applied to other things as well. Her mother sometimes accused her of "barreling ahead," and she'd started trying to "measure twice" before doing anything.

She'd definitely barreled ahead. And now she was stuck.

"Oh, for Pete's sake!" She sat there for a long time, nearly an hour, feeling sorry for herself and getting colder and colder. She had been very stupid about this whole thing. Why hadn't she told them what she was thinking as soon as she'd realized about the knife and the apron?

But she needed to know for sure before she admitted to herself what it meant, and before she said anything to Walter or Mr. Warren.

If she ever got up off the ground.

The snow was seeping through her pants, the cold making her skin burn. This wasn't good. Jenny knew that. She didn't know if anyone had even noticed she was gone. It might be hours before someone came looking for her. Did Walter know she'd left? Would he come after her? She imagined looking up to find him running through the snow.

Jenny, he would call out. *Are you okay?*

Oh, Walter, she'd call back. *You've saved my life*.

But when she looked up, there was no Walter running toward her to save her life.

But there was something else.

The sky was even lighter now, and she realized that it was nearly morning. She could actually see in the forest now, make out the details of the bark on the trees above the snow. This gave her a burst of energy, and she twisted her body, trying to rise and ignoring the numbness in her legs. When he was teaching her to use the snowshoes, Earl had told her that if she fell down, she should roll to the side to get back up without taking them off. She tried it, turning to one side and lining the snowshoes up so they were parallel to each other. Then she tried rocking herself to the other side and getting them up above the snow.

It took a couple of tries, but she was able to do it.

Finally, she was standing and she could walk.

She wasn't sure where she was, but she found the source of the light in the sky. That was east. If she walked in that direction, she should come out of the forest pretty close to the road. Belle's father's old house wouldn't be far.

The house was her destination.

Jenny had first discovered the old house when she was ten. It was before she had started helping her mother and Belle, and her mother would sometimes bring her along and let her play at the lodge or in the woods.

One day, she came out of the woods, and walking along the road, she saw a house that had grass and flowers all grown up around it and no car in front. It reminded her a bit of a house in a fairy tale, out in the middle of the woods, nothing around it, and when she looked in the windows, it looked abandoned, with none of the things inside, like pots or pans or shoes, that told her a family lived there. So she sat on the porch and pretended that *she* lived there, that she was a fairy princess who had been banished to the woods by an evil witch. She lived all alone, with no one but the animals for company, and one day a handsome prince was going to come and rescue her. After that, she went back to the little house whenever she could, and at some point, she had asked Belle about it and Belle said it was the house she lived in when she was a little girl.

Jenny liked that. It was so strange to think of Belle as a little girl. She seemed like one of those people who had always been the age she was, but Jenny's mother reminded her that Belle was younger than she, Delana, was. *She's still a young woman, really,* Delana told Jenny, and Jenny had asked why she didn't have a baby then, and Jenny's mother had gotten sad and said that some people just didn't have babies, and Jenny thought maybe she was thinking about the fact that Jenny never had a brother or a sister. Once she had heard her mother crying in the middle of the night and her father saying *It's okay, Delana. We have Jenny. Jenny's enough for me. And I have you. You and Jenny are all I want.* She hadn't known exactly why her mother was crying until she was older and read in a book a girl at school was passing around about the monthly curse and how it all related to babies. Then she understood that her mother's monthly curse must have come, and that meant she wasn't having a baby, and that must be why she was crying.

Jenny looked up and saw that she was almost to Belle's house.

But she saw something else too.

Snowshoe prints in the clearing.

Someone else was out here.

Thirty-two

Alice sat in the dark kitchen, watching the snow fall. She'd sent the boys off to bed and checked on Sylvie and the baby, who were sleeping peacefully.

It was three thirty A.M. She knew there were books in the other room. She could have gone to get something to read by candlelight while she kept her vigil, but she didn't want to read. She wanted to think.

She wondered suddenly where Warren had gone the other night when he'd left. He'd obviously gotten some news about Bill Moulton's death, and she was very curious about what it was. It seemed likely to be something from the autopsy, she thought. Mildred had initially reported that she'd heard it was an accidental shooting, but when she'd come back the next day, she'd heard that the police seemed to be looking at the men at the club.

Bill Moulton. The first time Alice met him had been in . . . Mexico City, she thought. Ernie was an undersecretary there, and Bill had arrived to work at the embassy. They hadn't overlapped for very long, and Ernie hadn't trusted him at all. The next time she'd seen him was in Washington, at a party. They'd made small talk, and he'd been very, very drunk and very, very affectionate with a woman who was not Marjorie Moulton.

Those had been such strange years in Alice's life. She was often alone, and alone she explored the city, the quiet streets of George-town, the restaurants near the White House or on Fourteenth Street. Ernie was increasingly overseas for reasons he couldn't explain to her, culminating in that last trip to West Berlin in October 1955, the one he hadn't come home from.

Bill Moulton. Why had the conversation about him at her dinner party so unsettled her? It was because she knew things, of course. Once, buying wine at a shop on New York Avenue, she had seen Bill Moulton stumble out of a seedy hotel at ten in the morning. He hadn't seen her, and she had been able to witness the look of shame and excite-ment that crossed his face as he stepped out into the bright sunshine. She had mentioned it to Ernie, who had made quiet note of it. She had never heard anything more but knew somehow that Moulton would have been given a warning. Someone in his position could be forgiven extramarital dalliances. But he could not be forgiven sloppiness.

And of course, there was the summer of 1946, which Bill and Mar-jorie had spent in Bethany. Alice was with her parents for the summer and Ernie had been visiting. They had gone up to the Ridge Club one night to have dinner with the Moultons and a large group of guests. It was not the night of the stabbing incident. Alice had heard about that later.

She had not liked Bill any better. He had flirted outrageously with the wife of a guest and barely noticed Marjorie. Alice had seen things that night that had bothered her deeply.

But she had pushed her discomfort down. Why? Ernie had been preoccupied by something or other that summer, she remembered. She herself had been preoccupied with her mother's illness. It had been easier to forget.

For so long after Ernie died, Alice had shoved her memories of those years down somewhere where she couldn't find them. It was a matter of safety, she felt. The things she knew could get her killed, and not remembering was the safest course of action.

But now she was remembering Ernie's voice on the phone from Bonn, telling her he'd landed and made it to the hotel. He hadn't told her about his plans to visit West Berlin.

Guess who I saw? he'd said. *Bill Moulton. And Arthur's here too. It's a bit of an old home day.*

And then, three days later, the men at her door. A heart attack, they said, because it was always a heart attack. They were very sorry. They would handle all the arrangements. They had the decency to keep the visit short, to not spin out the lies. They'd sent a woman, some secretary she supposed, to make tea and make sure Alice ate.

Alice wondered suddenly who it was who had gotten Ernie killed. Had it been someone undisciplined, someone who had had one too many drinks and let something slip? Someone who had not checked carefully enough for a tail? Someone like Bill Moulton? Whoever it was who had killed Ernie in that shabby hotel room in West Berlin on October 9, 1955, must have had to do it because of the undisciplined action of one of Ernie's sources or Arthur's.

Alice shook her head. This was not the time to be thinking of all of this.

She bustled around the kitchen, doing dishes, wiping down the surfaces as best she could in the candlelight, trying to push down the other memories, the earlier ones. But finally, she sat in the chair next to the woodstove, and something about the darkness, the late night, the lack of sleep, the adrenaline that was still moving through her body, made her start to cry. It was like her usual defenses were down, and now the memories that she'd kept at bay for twenty years came rushing in.

She remembered the sterile rooms looking out over the destroyed

London streets. The nuns who had barely looked at her the whole time she'd been there, except for one of them, a young woman with a soft Welsh accent who had been kind to Alice and explained how everything would go, how the baby would make its way into the world.

The baby's face, pink and wrinkled and golden. Alice had held her only once. It was wartime, they said. It all had to be done very quickly.

Wartime. Everything was different in wartime. In wartime, you did what you had to do.

Alice sat there in Sylvie Weber's quiet house for nearly an hour, and then she stood up, tired of the indulgence of memory. She finished cleaning and then sat down, and she must have dozed off at some point because she woke with a start when the dog woofed upstairs in Scott's room. At falling snow, probably. She listened and all was silent.

And then, for reasons she didn't really understand, she felt anxiety creep up her spine.

Carefully holding the lit candle, she crept up the stairs and into Sylvie's room. Sylvie was still sleeping, but the baby was starting to stir, her little lips and tongue working. Alice picked her up and held her against her chest. But the baby was hungry. She didn't settle.

"Sylvie?" Alice touched her forehead. It was warm and moist, and Alice felt a little surge of worry rise up in her chest. "Sylvie?" she said again. "The baby's hungry." She held her candle over the bed.

Sylvie stirred and when she opened her eyes, the alarm in Alice's chest rose a little. Sylvie's eyes in the candlelight were glassy and unfocused.

"Are you okay?" Alice asked her.

She tried to sit up. "Yes. Just tired. I'll . . ." She reached for Margot, but Alice had to help her bring the baby to her breast.

"Sylvie, do you think there's something . . . wrong? Are you okay?"

"No. I'm just tired."

That was normal, wasn't it? Alice thought. Giving birth was tiring, and she had been through a terrible ordeal. Once the baby had eaten, they both fell asleep again, and Alice tiptoed downstairs.

She checked the big grandfather clock in the hall. It was five A.M. Still at least a couple of hours of darkness before the sun would start to come up.

The yellow Lab padded down the stairs and whined softly for her to scratch his head. It made Alice feel better to have him next to her. She watched the snow swirling outside the windows and said, "You stay here with me, Bounder. We'll keep watch while they sleep."

The dog whined again and laid his head alongside her knee.

Thirty-three

A t first, Alice thought she was imagining the thin line of light on the horizon. She got up from the chair in the kitchen where she'd been sitting and looked out the window toward the east. The snow had stopped in the last hour, and as the sky grew lighter, a winter wonderland revealed itself outside the windows. White snow, thick and heavy as meringue, clung to every tree branch, pulling them down in graceful-looking arcs she knew were actually doing great damage to the trees.

Alice loved the snow. Usually, the first snowfall was cause for celebration. She loved walking on the green and watching children throw snowballs and make snowmen and snowwomen in front of the school. But this storm was early, and it had trapped them at exactly the moment they needed not to be trapped, and Alice felt the little buzz of anxiety return. Was Sylvie just tired as she'd said? As soon as the phones were back, Alice would call Dr. Falconer and ask him to come up and have a look at Sylvie and the baby.

She added wood to the cookstove and put on water for tea. She hadn't slept more than an hour in her chair and she needed caffeine.

Scott came down while she was pouring herself a cup and cooking eggs for the boys and for Sylvie. The sky outside was now pale gray. She handed him a plate just as they heard the sounds of the baby crying upstairs. "Here," she said to him. "Why don't you take her some water and the eggs, and I'll be up in a minute."

But he'd barely been gone before he was at the top of the stairs saying, "Mrs. Bellows?" and she felt that tug of anxiety again as she flew up to the second floor and into Sylvie's room.

"Sylvie?" Alice felt her forehead and now it was clammy and cold, and she could see that Sylvie was having trouble focusing her eyes on her.

"Alice?" she said. "I'm not . . . I can't get the . . . I think I might be bleeding."

Alice looked up at Scott, and she knew he could see that something was very, very wrong. His mother's face was pale, her eyes vacant. "Go outside," she said quietly. "See if there's any way we can get the truck out. We need to get her to the hospital." He nodded and went out and she heard him clattering down the stairs, calling for Andy and Louis to come and help him.

"The baby," Sylvie said weakly. "She needs to eat." She gestured for the baby, and Alice picked her up again and brought her to Sylvie's breast. The baby suckled vigorously, and Alice wedged a blanket under her head to prop her against the breast.

"I'm just going to look," Alice said as she pulled the top sheet away from Sylvie's body. She didn't even have to lift Sylvie's nightgown to see how much blood there was. It was soaking the sheets beneath her. "Sylvie," Alice said, to make sure she understood. "We need to take you to the hospital. I don't know how we're going to do it. But we need to get you there."

Sylvie nodded weakly.

"I'll be right back," Alice said. "I'm going to put the baby back in her basket so she'll be safe." She took the baby and laid her down in the basket she'd found downstairs and lined with blankets and helped Sylvie fix her nightgown.

She came into the kitchen just as Scott came back inside. "The snow's too deep," he said. "But I think I can get down to the Churches' on skis."

"But the phones won't be working," Alice said.

"No, but Mr. Church has a plow. He might be able to come up and plow, and we could drive behind him to take her to the hospital."

It was a good idea, but it was at least four miles to the Churches'. "She wouldn't want you to," Alice said. "You could get stuck . . ."

Scott was already putting on his hat and gloves. "I can do it," he said. "I'll bring him back."

Bounder stood at the back door, looking expectantly out at the snow. "Take him with you," Alice said.

"No," Scott said. "He's not trained yet. He might get lost in the snow. I'll be okay." He bundled up and went out into the brilliant morning. It was now almost eight o'clock.

Alice put food on the table for the younger boys. They were quiet, worried about Sylvie and now about Scott too. Alice asked them to go out and shovel the snow off her car so it would be ready when Scott returned and went back up to Sylvie.

"I'm here, Sylvie," she said. Sunlight now poured into the room. Margot was fussing, and so she picked her up and held her, the baby calming against Alice's body.

She felt the small, warm weight of her, floppy and helpless. Alice didn't like holding babies and she avoided it when she could, but this baby needed to be held, and she let the small body relax into her arms, Margot's fuzzy head soft against Alice's cheek.

"I thought . . ." Sylvie said, her voice barely a whisper. "I thought you didn't have babies. That you didn't have children."

Alice's hand froze on the baby's back.

"You knew what it was like," Sylvie said dreamily. "You knew what it felt like. You can't know that if you haven't had a baby."

Alice stood very still, the baby's small hands pressing on her collarbone, the small lips puckering now, the instinct to feed strong and primal. She could hear the sounds of the house. The boys talking downstairs, a cow bellowing in the barn. Snow slid off the roof onto the ground with a soft *thwap*.

There was a dense silence in the room.

"Did your baby die?" Sylvie asked. No one else would have asked this question. Alice considered how she could answer and knew there was no way.

So she said nothing. She held the baby tight to her chest, feeling her warmth, willing Sylvie to stop talking. She did not want to explain, she did not want to even think how to explain about that sterile room in London, about how she'd cried, looking out the window at a damaged building.

The baby had felt impossibly light that one time she'd held her, Alice's hands on her soft back before she handed her over; through the window, she'd seen the waiting car. She had stayed another three days before checking into a small inn in the countryside, giving a fake name and telling the innkeeper she'd been visiting her husband, who was on leave.

"I'm sorry if that's what it was," Sylvie said softly. "I'm so sorry."

Alice felt tears fill her eyes. She didn't know how to explain what it had felt like to walk the Sussex beach alone, her body slowly forgetting, as much as it could, what had happened to it. She didn't know how to explain that she had flown alone back to Washington a month later, watching the green fields of England grow smaller below the plane. She'd written to Ernie, telling him that she had to have an operation and would stay in Washington for a couple of months. He'd been somewhere he couldn't tell her the name of and hadn't even gotten the letter until after V-E Day. And then the war had ended, and everything was different.

So she put the baby back and said, "Scott will get help, Sylvie. You're going to be okay. I promise."

Thirty-four

Warren and Earl found Jenny's tracks immediately. She'd taken a route around the pond and into the woods, and they followed along, Earl up ahead and Warren keeping up with him, but not without some significant cardiovascular effort. It was easier walking in the snowshoes than it had been shoveling a path, but it was still a lot of work lifting each foot and placing it on top of the snow, balancing his body so that he didn't sink straight down, and then lifting the other one and placing it carefully. Earl was practically running, his snowshoes skimming the surface of the snow. There was something graceful about the way he moved; you could see his long years of experience using snowshoes, and Warren was glad he had brought him along. If Jenny was in trouble, Earl might be able to get to her in time.

As they went, Warren tried to put it all together. Moulton must have arranged with Arthur Crannock to meet up in the woods. It was the perfect rendezvous spot, far from Washington, no chance they could be followed, no chance they would be seen by anyone other than the men at the club.

Crannock had been to the club. He knew the spot, knew where to go. They had chosen a place at the edge of the Ridge Club's property where they wouldn't be seen. Either the meeting had gone wrong or the point of it all along had been to kill Moulton, maybe because he knew too much and, untethered from the foreign service for the first time in his life, was now a danger to the United States.

Or, Warren realized, because Moulton was a danger to Crannock personally.

Whatever had transpired between them, Warren had the feeling that it was related to the grocery lists he'd found on Moulton's body and in his room. In retrospect, the grocery lists seemed strange. Why would he have them at the club? Did he really do his own grocery shopping? Could they be some kind of code?

So where had Crannock waited before meeting with Moulton? Claire Packingham said she'd heard a vehicle, so he must have driven up to the property and walked to a prearranged location.

Warren imagined Moulton in his room the night before, assembling the list, copying parts of the code from the paper in his room onto a different piece of paper to carry with him the next day.

But on the other hand, Warren realized, what if Moulton had planned to meet *someone else* to give them information? A Soviet agent perhaps? Perhaps he hadn't even known that Crannock was in Bethany. What if Crannock had killed him so that other meeting couldn't take place?

In that case, it was very, very likely that the other person he was meeting was someone at the club. Graham French, bitter, with a lot of knowledge valuable to the Soviets, knowledge that the CIA would not want out in the world? Herman Westwood, privy to top-secret information about US weapons systems? Herman was a drunk, Warren thought. Perhaps he had been indiscreet. He had brought documents with him that he cared enough about to keep locked in a document case. Could they have been plans he was going to share with someone at the club?

Jack Packingham? A lawyer connected to many people in high places. Warren could only guess at what he knew. But why had he been killed? It must have been because he'd seen something on Saturday or knew something and was about to reveal what he knew. He'd been hunting with Moulton in the morning. Maybe he'd found out about Moulton's meeting.

But how had Arthur Crannock come to understand that Jack was a danger to him?

Unless he'd seen Jack on Saturday. Or . . .

Up ahead, Earl waved and Warren saw that Jenny's tracks had stopped and turned back in the direction of the club. They had now done a giant loop out through the forest, passing by the spot where Moulton was killed. Warren tried to push down the frustration he was feeling. What should have taken them twenty minutes had taken an hour. What had Jenny been up to?

They followed for another fifteen or twenty minutes and then reached the road, though Warren could only tell it was the road from the way the trees lined up. They trailed her snowshoe prints along the edges, and trudging behind Earl, Warren had the sudden thought that maybe he was being foolish to trust the man. After all, Earl could have been the person Moulton had come to meet. Last night, Graham French had talked about Earl's service. Earl hadn't wanted to talk about it, but he had been a member of the Special Service Force. Warren's father had once mentioned the elite unit to him. There'd been a story about someone he knew carrying out what had effectively been an assassination during wartime. He wished he could remember the exact details, but he thought his father's acquaintance had slit the throat of a German officer in a busy bar. He'd done it so quickly and quietly that no one had known until the bar closed and the dead man didn't get up from his seat in a dark corner.

Could Earl have stuck a knife in Bill Moulton and then killed Jack

Packingham because Jack had realized it was Earl? But why would Jack have lied for him?

And Earl and Belle had been asleep when Jack was killed. There was no way either of them could have walked over to the lodge, shot Jack, and made it back home and into bed without leaving tracks on the snowy path. Pinky had been absolutely certain of that. Still, Warren patted his jacket where he'd put his service weapon. Earl wasn't armed, so if he did have an ulterior motive in getting Warren out here, Warren thought he'd be able to handle himself.

They kept going and then Earl pointed, and up ahead, Warren could see the ramshackle place they'd passed by on Sunday.

An orange glow peeked up and over the edge of the horizon, and a few minutes later, the world transformed into something magical and glorious, the early-morning sun sending diamonds of light in every direction. Warren felt a strange moment of pleasure at merely being alive in such a world until he remembered why he was out here.

There was an innocent girl in these woods, in danger from an unknown threat.

Suddenly, Earl stopped and Warren hurried to catch up. As he got closer, he saw why.

The prints of Jenny's snowshoes led right up to the house, and the shoes now sat on the porch. He felt a wave of relief come over him. She was here. She was alive.

They were almost to the house when he heard a rifle shot. The sound bounced against the ridge and echoed across the expanse of snow and forest as though the shooter were right in front of Warren. Horrified, he watched as Earl crumpled and remained still on the snow, his legs bent at an unnatural angle.

"Earl!" he called out, leaping into action and trying to cross the fifty yards between them. "Hang on, Earl! I'm coming!"

And then there was another shot, and Warren felt the sting of a bullet grazing his arm.

Thirty-five

When she heard the sounds of a truck outside, Alice assumed it was Ed Church. "Scott must have made it to the Churches'," she told Sylvie. But once she'd thrown on her coat and boots and run outside, it was Isaac Rosen she saw, getting down out of the cab of a large truck fitted with a snowplow and waving to her, his bright-red hat and scarf a cheery note against the overwhelming white. The younger boys had finished uncovering her car and the sight of the plow truck filled her with hope; if Isaac could plow a path down to the main road, it was likely already cleared and Alice would be able to drive Sylvie and Margot to the hospital.

"I saw Scott on the road, Mrs. Bellows," Isaac called out to her. "He told me about Mrs. Weber. I got stuck at the camp last night. I went to try to finish up that roof before the storm and when I came out, I couldn't move the damn truck. I was afraid of running it into a tree so I decided to just stay at the camp. Once the snow stopped, I thought I'd come down and make sure they were all right here, but I saw Scott on skis, and he told me what happened. Follow me to the bottom of the hill and then the roads should be cleared from there."

His cheeks were pink, his boots caked with snow.

"Oh, Isaac," Alice said. "I could just about hug you. Help me get Sylvie into the car and we'll get going."

☒ ☒ ☒

Alice drove slowly behind the plow truck down Agony Hill, Sylvie lying on the back seat and the baby on the floor in a basket.

"It's going to be okay, Sylvie," Alice said. "It's going to be okay."

In the rearview mirror, she saw Sylvie nod weakly. The baby cried out, then settled.

Isaac plowed the road ahead of them, a single channel appearing out of the deep snow. There were still a couple of inches on the road, but the Falcon handled well, as long as she crawled along.

When they reached the bottom of the road, Alice felt her heart lift; the road crews had been through, and the main road was clear. They'd be able to make it to the hospital. Isaac pulled over and waved as she drove past. He'd said he'd go up to check on the boys and stay with them until there was news. Alice drove as fast as she could, talking to Sylvie and telling her everything would be okay. But as they pulled into town, Sylvie stopped replying, and when Alice said, "Sylvie, are you okay?" the silence in the back of the car made her press her foot on the accelerator and drive faster, which still wasn't very fast.

She pulled up in front of the hospital and jumped out to run inside and tell them to come and help her, and the nurses came to get Sylvie and the baby from the car. Dr. Falconer had made it to the hospital, and they brought them right in. Alice explained everything to Dr. Falconer, and then she sat in one of the hard chairs in the waiting room, feeling the stress and tension of the night descend over her like a heavy blanket.

Sylvie had to be okay; she had to be. Those boys. They couldn't lose their mother, their only surviving parent now, just when they were starting to live again, just when the little family had achieved some kind of equilibrium.

She thought about what Sylvie had asked her. *Did your baby die?*

For twenty years, Alice supposed she had pretended that the baby *had* died. Most of the time, anyway. It was easier and safer that way. Otherwise, the other memories came too. Those were the memories that she could not allow to come to the surface, the memories she could not allow to have their way.

She'd started to suspect she was pregnant at Christmas. Ernie had been traveling for months, and when he returned, he seemed distant, occupied by something. He had good reason, of course. The world hung in the balance, this battle or that threatening to topple all the progress he'd worked for. One failed mission could be the thing that lost it for them.

Their Algerian housemaid had unpacked his bags for him, and as she gathered the laundry, she had put aside a woman's chemise and said, "Mrs., your gown is in here."

But of course, it was not Alice's gown. She took it, so the housemaid wouldn't know, and then sat with it for a few moments, raising the fine silk fabric to her nose and smelling the unfamiliar perfume. It had felt, she thought later, like the universe was giving her a gift. She had been consumed with guilt, and now, with proof of Ernie's own infidelity, she did not need to let it trouble her.

But her problem remained. So, in February of 1945, she got a boat to London.

She shook her head. She could not think about all of this now. *She could not.*

When would they know about Sylvie? When would someone come out to tell her?

And then, her mind drifting to her next door neighbor, she wondered if there had been any new developments in the Bill Moulton murder.

Funny her mind had gone right to that word.

Why *murder*? It could quite easily have been an accidental shooting. They happened during hunting season, especially as more and more inexperienced hunters came up to Vermont to try their hand at the sport. Another thing that would likely get worse with the interstates, Alice thought.

But she felt quite certain it had been a murder.

Assuming it was murder, one had to ask why.

Alice had once heard it said that there were only three reasons for homicide: greed, passion, and power. But Alice knew that there were more. Madness, for one. But more importantly, concealment. This was the one that she suspected men like Arthur Crannock had become familiar with in their work. Sometimes, human beings killed other human beings because they didn't want them to reveal something.

She found herself wondering yet again which had been the motive for Ernie's execution. In her first years of widowhood, Alice had been content to accept the official story. Truthfully, she'd been afraid not to. She knew that pointing out the obvious discrepancies and inconsistencies in what they told her would put her on the radar of whoever was responsible.

At the time, she'd wanted nothing more than to settle Ernie's affairs, pack up and sell their Washington house, and move back to her hometown, using some of the money from Ernie's pension to modernize the house on the Bethany green and to expand the gardens they'd built together. For ten years, she'd been content to let it lie.

Until Arthur Crannock had appeared among her plantings one hot and humid day this past summer. He and Wanda had bought a house in Woodstock, he'd told her. They remembered how fondly she and Ernie had described the area. He just wanted to give her notice, in case they ran into each other, he'd said. What he hadn't said was that of course Arthur knew the area already. He had visited Alice and Ernie in the summer of 1946. Had he been there the night of the famous incident at the Ridge Club? Alice couldn't remember now.

Since Arthur had appeared that day, telling her he wanted her to do something for him, to keep an eye on this Russian who had settled in a town not too far from Bethany, Alice had found that the past kept barreling back into her present. Seeing Arthur reminded her of that whole period of her life, when she and Ernie were living abroad during World War II and after, and Arthur would give her small jobs to do, because she was good at them, but also to keep her busy, she supposed. She had followed foreign diplomats and journalists, sat in cafés and beauty parlors and dress shops to listen to the conversations between wives and mistresses and nannies of men whom Arthur and his organization were interested in for one reason or another.

And last night, of course, had brought back those other memories she thought she'd buried long, long ago. It was no good thinking of that again. Those memories could bring her nothing but pain.

If she was honest, Arthur's assignment had brought back good memories too. It had been fun to get up to her old tricks, hiding and spying, trying to find back channels for information.

It reminded her of the old days, when she and Ernie would go on vacation and he would disappear for a few hours to try to get a glimpse of someone or to have a meeting. Sometimes she helped, watching for someone in a place where only women could go unremarked.

Who had gotten Ernie killed? Finally, after ten years, she felt a burning need to know. Which of the motives had it been? Power? Or concealment?

Or perhaps greed or passion?

Alice looked up as someone came through the door from the emergency room into the waiting area. Maybe there was news about Sylvie. She stood up, but it was a doctor she didn't recognize, and he was there to talk to a family waiting on the other side of the room.

She sat down again to wait.

Thirty-six

Another shot zoomed past Warren's ear, and he dropped to the ground to avoid it, plunging into the deep snow and feeling his knees twist and buckle as his feet strained against the straps of the snowshoes. The bullet that had hit his bicep had only grazed him, he thought, ripping the fabric of his coat and taking off the top layer of skin. He felt a stinging pain, but not the kind of full-body shock that resulted from a serious gunshot wound. There were a few drops of blood on the snow beneath him, but not an alarming amount, and when he tried to move his arm, he was pleased to discover he was able to reach into the coat pocket for his service weapon. He took off his gloves and got the revolver settled into his right hand.

"Police," he called out, raising his head just a little to try to see where the unknown gunman was shooting from. "I'm armed. Don't shoot!" Up ahead, Earl was still unmoving on the ground. Warren needed to get to him and administer aid, but he knew that if he got up and crossed the open field, the gunman would pick him off, and then all of Earl's chances of survival would be gone. Protocol told him to treat Earl first, but only if it was safe to do so. If he was in danger, he knew he should attempt to remove the threat before administering aid. But in this case, he couldn't see the shooter.

"Police!" he called again, hoping it might elicit something that could tell him where the gunman was.

The only answer was another rifle shot. It echoed across the field, the sound bouncing off the ridge in one direction and the trees in the other, muddying the sound and making it reverberate indistinctly.

Where was it coming from? If he could figure that out, he could make a plan. But he wouldn't be able to do that on the ground. He was a sitting duck. He needed to get out of the open and into the cover of the trees.

He was about forty yards from the trees, he estimated, and if he ran, he should be able to clear the distance in under a minute. That was without the deep snow cover, though. And though they'd twisted and he wasn't sure the snowshoes were still secure, they were still attached to his feet. He'd either have to straighten them out or take them off.

Quickly, he made his decision and used his increasingly wet and cold fingers to undo the straps. Then he got up on his knees and stood.

For the moment, everything was silent.

Warren took off running, if his frantic, exhausting waddling in the deep snow could even be called that, toward the trees.

He was almost to a large pine when the shot came flying past him. Again, the sound bounced and refracted and dissipated. Warren summoned an extra burst of energy from somewhere and sprinted through the deep snow into the cover of the trees. Now he couldn't be seen in the open field, and he could put the trees between himself and whoever was firing the shots. Breathing hard, his heart pounding from the effort and the rush of adrenaline that he knew was keeping him from feeling the pain of the gunshot wound to his arm, Warren leaned against the trunk of the pine tree to catch his breath.

Another shot came, this one far wide of him, he thought, the echo a bit farther away.

The echo.

The gunshot echoing.

Suddenly, he realized something. What had everyone said when they came out into the hallway after being awakened by the shot? *I think it was a shot.* They'd assumed it was in the house, but they'd all been asleep.

What if there hadn't been a gunshot at all?

Or—he tried to get the thoughts straight in his head—what if there had been a gunshot but it hadn't been inside the lodge? What if it had been outside and the echo of it against the ridge was what made everyone assume it had been inside?

Why had they all assumed Jack Packingham had been shot?

Because of the gunshot. Because Jack had been found dead just after they heard the gunshot. It had made sense to assume that's how he'd died. But in the darkness, in the chaos, without being able to really examine the crime scene, Warren knew he'd missed something. There'd been no smell of gunpowder.

And there'd been no firearm with the body. They assumed it had been taken away by whoever had killed Jack, but what if . . . Warren was trying to get it all straight when another shot was fired into the trees.

He stayed behind the pine and kept turning it over.

What if there hadn't been a firearm there because . . . because there never had been one?

What if Jack hadn't been shot at all?

In the darkness of the gun room, Warren inspecting it with only the light from his flashlight, the wound on Jack's chest could have been a gunshot. But now Warren couldn't believe he hadn't seen it, especially with what had happened to Bill Moulton. Jack Packingham could have been stabbed, just like Moulton, and then whoever had killed him had fired the shot from outside the lodge to make them all think he'd been shot.

And, Warren realized suddenly, to make them think he'd been killed just then, at the moment when everyone came out of their bedrooms, clearly having been asleep and now beyond reproach.

When, in fact, Jack had been killed earlier.

Someone had met him downstairs, killed him with a knife, and come back upstairs.

And then a few hours later, once everyone was asleep, how hard would it have been to lean out a second-floor bedroom window, fire a rifle toward the ridge, and then drop the rifle into the deep snow outside the lodge's extension, close the window, get back in bed, and come out into the hall with everyone else?

Not hard at all, Warren knew.

But again, he came back to the question of why Jack had been killed. He must have seen something or realized something. It seemed impossible that his killer could have gotten him into the gun room against his will, so he must have gone in there on his own, and he must have gone in there because there was something in the gun room he was curious about, something he'd seen and hadn't understood.

Warren looked out from behind the tree. He scanned the field and the tree line. He could still see Earl's prone form lying on the snow. If Earl was badly injured and bleeding, he didn't have much time. And was Jenny safe in the house? Warren knew he needed to act. He stepped out and again scanned the edges of the field. It all looked the same, the blindingly white field of snow and then the darker areas in the trees.

But then he saw something move, very slightly, and he caught a flash of light, and squinting his eyes, he realized it was sunlight on the barrel of a rifle.

The person holding it was wearing greenish outerwear and blended into the trees, but Warren watched, and sure enough, it seemed to be a person of medium height, holding a rifle up at their shoulder.

Warren waited. If he could move through the trees without being seen, he might be able to circle around and disarm the shooter. Then he could tend to Earl and make sure that Jenny was safe.

He started slowly moving through the deep snow, dragging his legs one at a time, gaining only a few inches with each step. If he could travel in the slightly less-deep snow at the edge of the clearing, he thought he might be able to get there faster.

But then he risked being spotted.

He kept going, his arm throbbing now that the initial shock had worn off. When he glanced down at the snow, he saw a drop of blood, and then another.

Suddenly, his attention was snapped back to the tree line. Something moved again.

Warren got his gun up. With a handgun, it was going to be nearly impossible to take the shooter down at long range.

But the figure was moving toward Earl.

Warren kept his weapon up and aimed.

Whoever it was wasn't going for Earl, though.

The shooter was moving quickly toward the house.

And Jenny.

Thirty-seven

Finally, Dr. Falconer came out.

"She'll be okay," he said. "We stopped the bleeding." Alice could see the stark relief on his face, and she knew that, like her, he'd been thinking about the boys and the new baby and what would happen to them if their mother died. He reported that Margot was healthy and being cared for in the nursery and that Sylvie was resting now.

"Oh, Norm, I'm so relieved. You can't imagine how worried I was." Alice felt all the stress and worry of the night flow out of her. With it came a few tears.

"Alice, you saved both of their lives, you know. I doubt she could have delivered the baby herself with that compound presentation—that's what we call it when the hand prolapses like that. It's funny. For most of human history, women have been doing this mostly alone. Nine times out of ten, the doctor is a useless addition to the birthing room, but this was the one time she needed one. You were an excellent stand-in. You can go and see her now. I'm going to have Rose drive up and check on the boys and see if they need anything so you can get some sleep. You deserve it."

In the ladies' room, Alice took a moment to compose herself, pressing a wet towel to her face and applying her lipstick carefully in the mirror. She studied her own face for a moment, trying to find the traces of last night, of the events of so long ago.

It was just her old familiar face, however. Alice had never been considered a beauty, either as a young woman or as an older one. Ernie had called her his "funny valentine," and she had always assumed the nickname intended to convey that he loved her but did not find her objectively beautiful. She hadn't cared much about it for most of her life. She had been loved and adored by those who mattered to her—desired too, though she did not want to let herself think of that. She learned to dress well and wear her hair in a style that suited her face, and she thought that now, at the age of fifty-five, she'd settled into handsomeness.

She wondered suddenly, with an accompanying stab of pain, what the baby had grown up to look like. She—Alice forced herself to think of her with the pronoun—*she* would be a young woman now. Perhaps she had a family. Perhaps, perhaps, perhaps. *Stop*, Alice told herself, reapplying her lipstick and turning away from her reflection in the mirror.

Sylvie looked small—and yes, beautiful—in the big white bed, her face still very pale and her hands thin on the sheets.

"Mrs. Bellows, I don't know what I would have done if you hadn't been there," she said quietly. "Dr. Falconer said I would have died— and the baby too." She didn't say thank you, but Alice understood that the expression of gratitude was implicit. She had noticed this about Sylvie. She hadn't learned to make mindless expressions of gratitude or socially appropriate small talk. To some people, it made her seem odd and ungracious, but Alice knew that it was just her way.

"I think you can call me Alice, after what we've been through together," Alice said gently. Tears rushed to her eyes before she knew what was happening, and she leaned over the foot of the bed and fussed with the blankets so Sylvie wouldn't see. "I'll be back tomorrow, but get some rest tonight, all right? And if Daniel is too much for Scott and the other boys, I could take him on a little outing tomorrow."

She turned to look at Sylvie once before she left the room, and the younger woman had an expression of interest and concern on her face. As she often did with Sylvie, Alice felt that the younger woman was somehow seeing through her.

She didn't like it.

Alice drove home through a winter wonderland. The sun was high in a bluebird sky now, and every surface sparkled, the tiny crystals of snow catching the light. The trees were heavily weighed down with it, and it had drifted and mounded in the fields, where the wind had made little hills and valleys.

It was already warming up, though. The snow might not last the week. It wouldn't be until after Thanksgiving or perhaps the first of December that it would snow again and the snowbanks would settle in for good.

Winter wasn't here quite yet.

She had already driven through the village and out along the Woodstock Road before she realized what she was doing.

Arthur and Wanda's house was right in the center of the Woodstock green, a lovely white Greek Revival with a passing resemblance to Alice's own house. It was covered in scaffolding, and construction equipment littered the driveway. The house was completely dark, and there was no car out front, but Alice tucked a small paperback cookbook sitting on the back seat of the car into her pocket and went to the front door anyway and knocked. There was no answer.

So she went around the house to the back door, tried the handle, and found it locked.

She turned to go, but something made her walk instead toward the small garden behind the house, which was quite concealed from passersby. Arthur had said that Wanda had plans to clean it up and put flowers and vegetables back here. It didn't look like they had done anything in that direction, though of course, it was all under the snow and they might be waiting until the construction was done. Alice made her way across the yard, feeling the wet snow seeping through the fabric of her pants and into her short boots, insufficient to keep her dry.

Why was Arthur here?

The question seemed suddenly urgent to her. He said they wanted a summer place, but Alice's instinct told her there was more to it than that.

So, what? Was he here to keep an eye on the Russian? Ostensibly, he had Alice to do that. But maybe he didn't trust her.

He was running Alice now, as much as it shamed her to admit it. Would he find other locals to run, little spies he could delegate to?

Or was it related to the man who had been shot in his home last year? Alice suspected that Arthur's presence in Bethany had something to do with that. Perhaps the dead man had been there to keep an eye on Kalachnikov and had been killed by a Soviet agent. Perhaps Arthur was here to root out the Soviet agent or his connections.

If he had been meeting with Bill Moulton, which Alice suspected, what had happened that had thrown Arthur so completely?

Because Arthur, who never seemed thrown, had been thrown the other night. Alice was sure of it. She wanted to know why.

She went back to the door at the back of the house and felt along the top of the doorframe. No key. It was too much to expect Arthur to allow such a lapse in security. All the windows next to the back door were locked when she tried them. But the ladder leaning up against the scaffolding reached the second floor, and, Alice thought, who would think to lock those windows?

Feeling ridiculous, she plowed through the snow to the ladder and planted a booted foot on the bottom rung, realizing she'd left prints in the snow. Oh well. In for a penny, in for a pound. It wasn't hard to climb up. She was still quite strong—she had her gardening to thank for that, she thought—and she had been right about the window. It wasn't locked, and it was large enough that she was able to step into the room without too much trouble, shutting the window behind her in case someone happened to walk around the back of the house.

Snow fell from her clothes onto the floor, melting in the still-warm house.

She started her search in the room she found herself in, but it was mostly empty, clearly a guest room in progress. The bedroom next door was significantly larger and she assumed it was Arthur and Wanda's—the walls had already been covered in a yellow floral paper, and the bedclothes and vases and art bore the signs of Wanda's sense of style, feminine but also modern. Very expensive. Alice went through the drawers in each of the night tables, but her search only yielded a couple of receipts and a bottle of hand lotion in Wanda's drawer and a pair of toenail clippers on Arthur's side. She checked the third bedroom, which was full of sealed boxes, and the bathroom. Then she went downstairs.

The first floor was still under construction, drop cloths and buckets of paint in the living room and exposed walls ready for new plaster. She drifted around, enjoying the feeling of seeing behind Arthur's carefully controlled presentation of self. A shopping bag on the floor in the hallway had a box of Alka-Seltzer in it. A pair of scuffed shoes sat to one side of the closet.

She went into the kitchen.

"Hello, Alice."

The voice came from somewhere behind her, and she spun around, her heart pounding, her brain scrambling for words. "Oh! Oh, Arthur, my goodness. You surprised me. I . . . I stopped by to drop off the cookbook I told Wanda I'd give her, and you were out. The back door was open, so I just came in to leave it here. My goodness. You startled me. I'm sorry. I'd thought you'd gone back to Boston." She was speaking too fast, babbling incoherently, so she took the cookbook out of her pocket, placed it on the counter and forced herself to smile at Arthur. Had he checked the back door before inserting his key? Had he seen her footprints by the scaffolding? If he had, he would know she was lying.

"I'm driving back tomorrow. The snow knocked down some of the construction materials, and I wanted to make sure the roof's all right before I leave." He was standing very still, watching her with eyes that suddenly reminded her of a snake's, cold and appraising.

"Oh yes, of course. Well, I should get back. Tell Wanda this is the one she wants. It's really excellent."

"I will." He kept very still, and Alice could hear her heart beating in her head. She was suddenly conscious of her breathing, her arms, her legs. She wondered if she was too tired to run, to fight.

They stared at each other.

"Alice," Arthur said. "Why are you really here?"

He had moved between her and the door so smoothly and carefully that she didn't realize he'd done it until he was already there.

She forced herself to breathe before saying, "Arthur, you know me so well. I wanted to ask you if you had anything to do with all this business at the Ridge Club."

"What do you mean?" He kept his face impassive and leaned back against the counter.

"You know what I mean. I think you were out there talking to Bill Moulton. A man like him, dismissed in disgrace from the embassy. I can guess why—some sort of trouble with someone's wife or mistress, someone important, I'd say—but a man like that, just think of what he knows. Having him out there just walking around, angry at his former employers? Well, it wouldn't do, would it?"

For just a moment, she thought she'd miscalculated. But then Arthur laughed and said, "I swear, Alice, if you'd been a man, you'd be running the whole place now. Nothing gets by you, does it?"

She smiled, still uncertain. "Well?"

He sighed. "Yes, I had made arrangements to meet up with him. He had lots of names for me: possible moles, double agents, leaks— well . . . all kinds of things. He'd written them down in some kind of code, he said, and he would give them to me. But he was angry about being dismissed, so I needed to handle him carefully. And I wasn't entirely sure he hadn't been turned during his time in Bonn. I was worried we'd be followed if I met him in Washington, so we came up with this idea to meet out at the club. I'd been out there once or twice, just after the war. You might remember. I knew the property and knew we could meet up without being followed."

"I thought it was something like that," Alice said.

"There was an old, abandoned house, and I went out there to wait; then at the appointed time, I went over to the meeting place." He raised a hand to his face. "Scratched the heck out of my face walking through the woods there."

After a moment, Alice said, "And?"

"Well, that was the strange thing. I heard someone coming. I figured it was Moulton but then I heard a woman's voice. She was kind of talking to herself, but I couldn't make out what she was saying. I took off to avoid being seen." Arthur raised his eyebrows. "Not the ideal scenario for tradecraft. I figured there was very little chance of making contact with Moulton without being seen by whomever it was, so I decided I'd better get out of there."

"And?"

"I had second thoughts. I thought maybe I could wait and salvage the thing. I waited thirty minutes, then went back. And Moulton was dead. Someone had stabbed him, and the knife was still in his chest. Well. You can imagine. That wouldn't have done. That wouldn't have done at all. I got out of there as quickly as I could."

Alice studied him. She could not tell if he was lying or not. That was the thing about Arthur. It was entirely possible that he had killed

Bill Moulton and was making up the story. But if he was telling the truth, then by listening to him, she had put her life in danger. She knew too much now. If Arthur stopped finding her useful for his own purposes, then there was no reason to let her live.

It would be very easy, she knew. A car accident. Poison that made it look like she'd had a heart attack. He had lots of options.

"Believe me if you want, Alice," he said quietly, as though he could read her mind. "But I need to go. I've got something I have to do. I just came back because I forgot something."

He wanted her to go, but she didn't move.

"Arthur?" She said it in almost a whisper. "Who killed Ernie? Why was Ernie killed, Arthur?"

Arthur studied her for a moment. "Nothing good can come of asking that question, Alice. Because if it gets around that you're asking that question, people may start asking other questions. Like about that trip you took to London in the late winter of 1945, while Ernie was in the field."

Alice felt it like a slap. She thought she'd been so clever. But of course Arthur had known. Arthur knew everything.

She didn't say anything. What was there to say? After a long moment, Arthur said, "Best to force an interaction with our Russian friend, I think, Alice. You'll think of something. But this whole thing . . . it's got me wondering. I'd like to move it along. You'll let me know, won't you?"

Alice, shaking now, nodded and went out into the snow. She didn't breathe normally until she was in the car, driving away from her old friend.

Thirty-eight

Warren ran, his legs churning through the deep snow, his arm throbbing now as his heart pumped blood through his body. He watched as the shooter reached the porch of the house and deftly removed their snowshoes before opening the door and disappearing inside.

The glare of the sun on the snow was so bright that he was nearly blinded as he tried to keep a line of sight to the house. Was that someone in the window? Had he caught a glimpse of Jenny? Of the shooter? He couldn't tell.

Who was it? He didn't know. But something had started to click into place in his unconscious mind, and as he ran, he found himself thinking of rifles.

The pathologist's report. *Death was due to sharp force injury to the heart muscle by a pointed object. Damage to the upper thoracic cavity by gunshot was sometime postmortem.*

Sometime postmortem.

Why had Jack Packingham gone to the gun room? Perhaps he had seen something there or . . .

Suddenly, Warren remembered Jack saying *My father's Winchester. I keep it here and use it sometimes*. He'd looked for it and hadn't been able to find it and then Earl had pointed it out. But there had been something there, a moment of hesitation on Jack's part. Had it been in a different place? Had Jack realized something about the rifle?

Another shot rang out, and Warren couldn't tell where it was coming from. He tried to place it, but it echoed against the ridge, and it could have been coming from any direction.

Any direction.

Suddenly, the wound on Jack Packingham's chest made sense.

If, in fact, the gunshot they'd all heard last night had been fired outside the lodge and echoed against the ridge so that none of them could tell where it was coming from, then why?

Why would someone have gone to so much trouble to make him think Jack Packingham died just before two A.M.?

Because the person who had killed Jack had an alibi for the time of the death.

Who had an alibi?

The person who hadn't been in the lodge.

The person who shoveled a neat path to his own house, sent his wife over, then stayed behind, hiding in the gun room until Jack came downstairs to see if his realization was correct.

The person who knew how to kill a man quietly and silently with a knife because he had done it in the war. And once Jack was dead, the person who had a key to the front door and locked the door behind him before he went back to his own house, where he'd waited until it was time to walk to the edge of the woods and fire a rifle to wake them all up.

Earl Canfield.

Warren watched in horror as Earl, apparently unhurt, got up and started running for the house.

Thirty-nine

It wasn't until she'd taken off the snowshoes and entered the old house, her flashlight beam bouncing on the walls, that Jenny realized how absolutely, completely, and utterly stupid she'd been.

She should have told Walter all about it, about recognizing the knife when she pulled it from her pocket.

Walter could have gone to the house and looked around for her. That would have been safer. Or they could have gone together.

But she'd been stupid and careless, and she'd barreled ahead again, and now she just needed to find what she was looking for and get back to the lodge. Maybe no one would even notice she'd been gone.

And then she could say *Oh, Walter, I've got something to show you,* and she would take it out and hand it to him. Maybe she would even do it in front of everyone, the way the detective did in mystery novels. She would show the piece of evidence, and then she would tell them about Saturday and about how it was pulling the knife out of her pocket that had made her realize.

What a strange feeling that had been! It had reminded her of the time that she had put on another girl's jacket by mistake at school and put her hand in the pocket to take out her gloves and pulled out a sandwich instead!

It was cold inside, so she kept her coat and hat and gloves on and wandered around, looking at the things that Nathan and his wife, Belle's mother, had hung on the walls, opening drawers and cupboards, looking under stacks of papers and old clothes. There were old magazine pages torn out and taped on the wall and a few framed pictures. In one corner of the living room, there were stacks of old newspapers that had become homes for mice. Jenny opened the door to the basement and looked at the old calendars hung on the wall going down the stairs. There was a calendar cover she especially liked, an art deco painting of a beautiful woman in a red dress. And then, in the darkness at the bottom of the flight of steps, she saw something that wasn't supposed to be there, or rather, she thought, had only been there since Saturday and that was what made it wrong.

She descended the stairs and she was at the bottom when she heard a gunshot—a rifle shot, she was pretty sure—and then another, and though she couldn't tell what direction they were coming from, she was pretty sure that they were getting closer to the house.

She made her decision. Stepping off the bottom stair into almost-darkness, she picked up the white apron that had been thrown down the stairs and stood to the side, ready to retreat deeper into the cellar if she needed to.

She heard the front door open, and then she heard a voice say, "Jenny?"

She held her breath, but the footsteps came toward the cellar door and stopped, and then she heard them descending the staircase.

She didn't know what to do.

The beam of a flashlight moved across the cellar wall and stopped on her.

"Are you okay?" Belle asked.

Jenny nodded.

"Did you see the knife in the kitchen?" she asked. "Did you realize about the apron? Is that why you're here?"

Jenny, terrified, nodded again. Belle's light swept down to the white apron Jenny had picked up and was now holding in her arms. The white apron stained with dark brown.

Belle sighed. "It's okay, Jenny," she said. "I'm not going to hurt you."

And then they heard more footsteps upstairs and a distant voice, though Jenny couldn't tell what it was saying.

Belle lifted the rifle and turned toward the stairs. "Stay here, Jenny," she said. "Whatever you do, don't come up those stairs."

It wasn't until she had disappeared into the darkness at the top and shut the door behind her that Jenny heard three gunshots, evenly spaced and very loud, a message, Jenny thought.

Or a call for help.

Forty

"Earl, stop! I'll shoot!" Warren called as he neared the house.

The older man didn't stop moving, though, and by the time Warren got within range, he had taken off his snowshoes and bolted into the house, slamming the door behind him.

Warren moved as fast as he could, stopping to fire three distress shots into the air before reloading and holding the handgun out in front of him and coming through the door.

It was like stepping back in time. The room he had come into was papered with peeling floral wallpaper and filled with antique furniture, worn velvet chairs, and a couch that sagged in the middle.

Earl had already collapsed into one of the old chairs, looking exhausted, breathing hard, snow crusting his pants and coat. He looked up at Warren and said, with the wry smile that Warren liked so much, "I'm too old for this nonsense."

Belle Canfield stood in front of a closed door behind Earl, the Winchester trained on Warren, who had his gun up too. He was almost positive he could take her down, even with his arm beginning to go numb, but Earl was between them, and he didn't know where Jenny was.

"Belle, I'm not going to shoot you," he said in a low voice. "I'm not going to hurt you. I just need to know where Jenny is, and I need to know what happened."

She nodded toward the door behind her. "She's in the basement. She's fine," she said. "I'd never hurt her." She let the rifle droop a little, and slowly, still keeping it on Warren, she went to sit next to Earl.

"Does Trooper Goodrich know you're gone?" Warren asked her.

"I don't know," she said. "I told him I had to go get some bacon from the kitchen."

"He'll be here once he realizes," Warren said, though he didn't, in fact, know if this was true. Had Pinky heard his three shots and taken them for a distress signal? "But we might have time. Help me understand what happened. Help me understand why you killed Bill Moulton."

She nodded. "I didn't mean to," she said. "I barely knew I was doing it. I wasn't in my right mind."

"Belle," Earl said very quietly. "Be careful."

She turned to look up at him and then shook her head. "I'm tired," she said.

"Was it because of the fight on Friday night at dinner?" She looked over at Warren quickly and nodded. "Because of what the other men said about Delana?"

There was a long silence.

"I didn't know," she said. "I didn't know what he'd done to her. All this time." Her face was awash in pain, her cheeks pink from the cold air.

"You didn't know about Bill Moulton and Delana and . . . Jenny?" He kept his voice low.

"That's right," she said. Earl was still sitting there silently, but Warren had the sense that he knew what was coming. He seemed resigned, the snow slowly falling from his clothes onto the threadbare carpet beneath him.

"You stabbed him because he had a relationship with Delana?"

"No, you idiot," Earl said. "That's not why."

"Earl," Belle said gently.

Something in her face when she looked back at Warren made him see it. "Because *you* had a relationship with Mr. Moulton?"

He thought of the pictures from the 1946 trout derby. Arthur Crannock had been there. But so had Belle Canfield. A sixteen-year-old Belle Canfield.

"Relationship!" Earl said. "She was a child. He took advantage."

"So, you were angry when you found out that he'd had a relationship with Delana too?"

Belle stared at him. "It wasn't that he had a relationship with her. It was that Jenny was . . ." She glanced at the closed door to the cellar and lowered her voice almost to a whisper. "His child! All this time! I didn't know. He told *me* getting rid of it was the only way. There was no choice. He drove me down to Boston and made me go in to see this doctor who . . . The doctor gave me gas, and when I woke up, it was gone. Bill . . . Mr. Moulton said it was better. He said I had to or he would tell everyone!"

Warren waited. He didn't realize he'd been holding his breath until, out of oxygen, he gasped.

It was Earl who finished the story for her. "The doctor told her she'd be fine," he said. "That she'd go on to have other children, that she could forget it even happened, but he was a quack and something went wrong. We were never able to have them, and it was his fault." Earl took her hand. "She'd come to terms with it . . . I'd come to terms with it. But then . . ."

"You learned about Jenny on Friday night," Warren said. Belle nodded. "When did you find out he was coming to the club?"

"I didn't know he was coming until a couple days before. Mr.

Packingham said I was to make up an extra room because Mr. Moulton was coming. I was nervous, but it would have been okay. If . . . when I heard the men talking and I realized . . . about Delana and Jenny . . . I just, I saw white, Detective. I don't remember what I did. I tried to get Jenny out of there. I didn't want her to hear that kind of talk. But then I went back to the kitchen and I just stood there, and then Delana came in and I couldn't tell if she'd heard or not. The men were still fighting. I . . . it was like I was in a dream. I did what I had to do in the kitchen. I cleaned up. But I didn't sleep at all that night. The anger, it was like a poison. All morning I tried to put it aside. After lunch I went into the kitchen and saw that Delana had been cutting up the pork roast. She'd left the knife on the counter and taken off the apron she was wearing, and I just wanted something to do. I was so upset. I put the apron on and started working on the roast. But I couldn't settle. Earlier, I'd heard Mr. Packingham come in and say that Mr. Moulton was going to go hunting by himself in the afternoon, over on the eastern edge of the woods. I knew where he was going. It was a place he told me to meet him sometimes. It was a place he liked." She closed her eyes for a moment before picking up her story again.

"I decided to follow him, to confront him. I wasn't thinking straight. Like I said, I had the knife and I guess I just . . . took it with me and I went out. I put boots on but I don't think I even wore a coat. I found him in the clearing. He was waiting for someone, I think, and I guess I walked after him and I was still holding the knife. And then he heard me and he turned around and . . . he was confused. I said, 'Why did you make me get rid of it and you didn't make her? Why couldn't I have had the baby? Why did you take me to that doctor?'

"He said, 'Belle, I don't know what you're talking about.' He was confused. He'd forgotten. I could see that he'd forgotten that he'd ever . . . with me. That was what did it. He didn't even remember me!

"Before I knew it, I was looking down at him and the knife was in his heart, and there was blood on my apron and he was dead. I didn't know what to do. The apron was . . . covered in blood. I came back to reality. That's the only way I can say it. I realized what would happen if someone saw me, so I came out here, and I threw the apron in the basement so I could get it later and ran back to the lodge. I was worried I'd be missed, but it was very quiet when I got back. Skip was sitting by the fire, looking depressed."

"But then when did you shoot—" Warren started to say before realizing. "You shot him," he said, looking to Earl. "You shot him and took the knife away from the scene to make it look like it was someone other than Belle? You knew we'd know from the knife. Her knife. A kitchen knife. You found him the next morning and instead of reporting it, you took the knife out and you shot him with the Winchester rifle you'd brought along."

"I knew it was Belle," Earl said. "I recognized the knife, and she'd been very upset Friday night, almost catatonic, but she wouldn't tell me why. So I took the knife, and I knew I needed to make it look like an accident, so I shot him with the rifle, brought the casing with me so you wouldn't trace it to the Winchester, and then I went back to the club to tell them I hadn't found him. I didn't have time to put the Winchester back—I shouldn't have taken it but it was the first one to hand and I knew I might need to fire some distress shots if Mr. Moulton was injured—so I left it in the woods and got it later to replace it. I guess I put it back in the wrong place, though, because Jack noticed. I was going to wash the knife and put it back in the kitchen and hope no one realized, but Delana was coming down the hall, so I dropped it into the pocket of Jenny's coat. I thought I could get it later, but then I realized it . . . directed attention away from us, from Belle and me.

"You know the rest. Jack and Skip found him and . . . you showed up later that day. I knew there was a chance that the autopsy would show he'd been stabbed, but there was a chance it wouldn't too."

"Which one of you killed Jack?" Warren asked them, though he knew the answer. "You, Earl?"

Belle started to say something, but Earl put a hand out and patted her knee. He nodded at Warren, his head hanging, his expression grim.

"But why? Had he figured it out?"

"Not quite, but I knew he'd get there in the end. I came back after I'd shoveled the path out to our cottage because Belle was worried she'd left a candle burning in the kitchen. I have extra keys of course, loads of them. I saw a flashlight in the gun room, and I heard you and Pinky talking. I was worried you were getting close to figuring out that Belle had killed Bill Moulton, and I figured I'd better stay at the lodge for a bit in case you put two and two together. I hid in the supply closet next to the gun room, and then when you went up to bed, I went into the gun room to think about what to do."

"Jack had been thinking too," Warren said.

Earl smiled wryly. "Yes, unfortunately. He came in and just stood there for a bit, staring at the wall. He'd noticed that the Winchester wasn't where he thought it should have been, and it got him thinking, I guess. I showed myself then. He was afraid of me. He knew it was wrong that I was hiding there. He said he'd realized it wasn't there on Sunday when we collected all the firearms and ammunition for you, and he asked me if I'd taken it with me when I went searching for Bill. I could see him trying to figure it out and put it together. The knife, he said. The knife had gotten him thinking, and he just wanted to know if I'd taken it or . . . I had my old stiletto from my service days. Just in case. And, well, he didn't see it coming."

"Earl," Belle said quietly.

Warren turned to look at her face as she gazed at her husband, as she realized the enormity of what he'd done for her, out of love for her. He felt a sudden revulsion for what he was about to do. He would arrest them. They would both go to prison, likely for the rest of their lives. If it had been just the initial crime, Belle might have done a few years and then been released. But the cover-up, the subsequent homicide, the concealing of evidence—it was more than enough for Earl, at least, to die in prison.

Warren had made a choice that night in Sylvie Weber's kitchen. It had felt like the compassionate choice, even if it had been wrong in the eyes of the law.

He could not make that choice again. Warren was a sworn officer. He had a responsibility to make sure that crimes like these did not go unpunished. But that didn't mean he didn't wish it could be different.

"We're not getting out of this, Belle," Earl said.

"I know," she answered softly.

"What gun did you use to wake us all up?" Warren asked. He was so close to understanding.

"This one," Belle said. "Earl took it after he killed Jack. Once he was back at our house, he waited a while and then went out into the woods and fired it toward the ridge." She raised the Winchester and pointed it at Warren.

"You don't want to do that," Warren said. "I'll have to shoot you, Belle. I don't want to shoot you."

"No, Belle," Earl said. "Not you. We'll say something happened, an accident. It should be me." He gave Warren an apologetic smile. He didn't want to do it, Warren realized. But he would do anything to protect the woman he loved.

For many, many months after Maria's death, Warren had wondered what he would have done if he had come home during the attack. He had wondered if he would have had the courage to kill a man to protect his wife and unborn child. Now, looking at Earl Canfield's determined face, he knew he would have done it. He knew he wouldn't have hesitated.

"I'm sorry," Warren said. The place where the bullet had grazed his upper arm had started to throb. "Belle Canfield, Earl Canfield, I'm placing you under arrest for the murders of William Moulton and Jack Packingham."

"No!" Earl said, getting to his feet and taking the rifle from Belle and pointing it at Warren. "You're not going to—"

And then, in a rush of cold air and noise, the door slammed open and Pinky came in, his revolver out in front of him. Warren leapt forward, kicking the rifle out of Earl's hands and pulling his arms behind him.

"Earl," Warren said again, "I am taking you into custody for the murder of Jack Packingham."

"Where's Jenny?" Pinky asked, his eyes wide and anxious. "Is she okay? Where is she?"

Warren nodded to the basement but said, "Belle said she's down there, but I don't know if she's hurt or . . ."

Pinky ran to the door and flung it open. "Jenny?" he called down into the darkness.

The voice that came up the stairs and reached them was loud and strong and rang all around the small house.

"I'm here. I'm fine, and I'm down here. *Oh, Walter!*"

Forty-one

When she got home, Alice shut off the lights in the kitchen and climbed the stairs to the second floor. She was so tired she skipped her usual cold-cream routine and changed into her nightgown, then fell into bed, sure she'd fall asleep in seconds.

But she didn't.

Instead, she lay there, a bit of moonlight reflecting off the snow and filtering in through the window, and found that the memories she'd been holding back for so long had started to trickle past the dam she'd built. It was as though witnessing the birth had moved the bad memories forward, the pain and anguish and guilt. But the good memories were there too now.

And so, for the first time in a long time, she let her mind wander to the garden at the house outside of Cairo where she and Ernie had been invited for dinner one night in 1940, as Rommel made his way across France.

"Alice is a gardener," Ernie had told the hostess, a French woman who had decorated the Belle Epoque mansion as though she were still in Paris. "Absolutely crazy about it. You should see our place in Washington."

"You'll have to come see the garden, then," the hostess had said, and she had showed Alice the traditional Islamic garden in the courtyard of the house. Alice had felt something she'd never felt, standing there in the warm, dry air of the Egyptian spring—a sense of peace, of the design of the garden centering her and making her a part of its infinite shapes. "Did you design it?" she asked the French woman. "It's absolutely beautiful."

The woman had laughed. "Oh, no. There is a man who does it. My husband, he said he ought to have an Egyptian garden since we're in Egypt, but I like English gardens more." She had a cigarette between her fingers, and raised it to her lips and inhaled. The smoke rose above her head in ribbons, floating above the walls of the garden. "The designer, he's quite famous. He brings men to take care of it sometimes and he likes to walk around and check everything. I can let you know when he is coming if you want to talk to him."

Alice said she'd like that. They went in to dinner, and home again the next day, she was sure the woman would forget, but a few weeks later, there was a message at the apartment where she and Ernie lived. *Designer will be here on Wednesday at 3. You are welcome for tea.*

Alice was driven out to the house. In daylight, it was not quite as romantic as it had seemed at night. The furnishings were shabby and faded. The woman, whom Alice did not like, had seemed almost mad with worry about what was happening in her homeland.

But the garden, now that Alice could see all of the plantings and designs, was even more amazing than she remembered. She had stood in the shade of a palm tree and looked around her at the repeated shapes that somehow calmed her brain before she raised her head to find the woman—Mrs. Marchand—and another person coming across the gravel courtyard. The sun was very strong, high in the sky, and Alice could barely see them. She had raised a hand to her eyes, to shield them from the bright glare.

"Mrs. Bellows," Mrs. Marchand had said. "I'd like you to meet Mr. Ahmed Osman, the garden designer."

She'd looked up into the eyes of a man about her age, a slender man in a brown suit and hat, with dark eyes behind small glasses. He took her hand, and she could feel the calluses on it. He might have a team of men to tend to the garden, but he did at least some of the work himself.

"Hello," he'd said. She had been conscious that the palm trees were not moving; they had been still and frozen in the warm midday air. She could hear water running somewhere and it soothed her. He had kind eyes, she'd thought to herself. Soft eyes. He'd smiled at her. "I'm very pleased to make your acquaintance."

Forty-two

The hospital was busy. Lying in his bed, bandages covering his upper bicep, Warren listened to the sounds of conversation out in the hallway. They had told him he could go home whenever he wanted, once he'd eaten something, and he had dressed in his regular trousers and the nurse had helped him to put on a shirt. He stood up carefully, still a little lightheaded from lying down, and waited until he had his bearings to stand up completely. Then he walked down the hallway and into the maternity ward.

"Where is Mrs. Weber?" he asked the nurse at the desk, and she pointed to a room down at the end of the corridor. Warren found the room number on the door and hesitated for a moment, then poked his head in. She was asleep, her eyes closed and one hand resting on her chest. Her hair was loose, one piece lying across her forehead in the shape of a cat's curled tail.

She looked very pale, except for two broad, bright spots of color on her cheeks, and Warren was watching her when her eyes fluttered open and she said, "Oh, Mr. Warren. I heard you were injured. Are you okay?"

"I'm fine," he said. "Just a flesh wound. I'm on my way home now."

"Isaac told me about what happened at the Ridge Club. It's awful. I met Belle Canfield once. I liked her."

"It is awful," he said. "They're good people, I think. Sometimes passion . . . Well, sometimes people do things they don't mean to do." He could feel himself blush. Why had he said that?

"Where's the baby?" she asked, suddenly panicked. "She was here."

"I suspect the nurse took her so you could rest," he said. "I heard you had a bad go of it."

She nodded. "I think Mrs. Bellows saved my life," she said. "And Isaac too. Isn't it funny to think of it, Mr. Warren? Isaac coming to Bethany and me helping him, and then, well, him helping me? Would you like to meet the baby? I'll have the nurse bring her."

"I'll tell her," Warren said. He poked his head out into the hallway and told the nurse that Mrs. Weber wanted to see her child, and a few minutes later, the nurse brought a small, yellow-wrapped bundle into the room.

"Here she is," Sylvie said, holding the baby in her arms and pulling the blanket away from the baby's face. Warren looked down at her. She had black hair and blue eyes. Her nose was tiny and pink. She was sleeping, but she must have smelled her mother, because she started to shake her head gently from side to side and then pursed her little lips. She was so small! How could something so small become a person, become Sylvie, become her boys, become him?

"She's beautiful," he said. "How do the boys like their sister?"

Sylvie smiled. "Louis is quite suspicious, but the other boys seem very happy with her."

"Are they all right?"

"Yes. Isaac went to help Scott out. Mrs. Falconer has been there too and brought some food. Isaac said he can stay with them tonight, and Margot and I can go home tomorrow. Isaac brought the boys for a visit this afternoon, and oh, you'll never believe it, Mr. Warren!" She smiled, full of the story she wanted to tell. "The boys were raising turkeys. They were quite excited because they were going to use the money they earned to buy a television. But when they checked them in the snowstorm, the turkeys were all gone. They thought something had gotten to them, but when Isaac returned from plowing so Mrs. Bellows could take me to the hospital, he heard Bounder barking and went around to the side of the barn. What do you think? The turkeys had gone inside through a hole in the siding when it started to snow. They'd been hiding inside the barn!"

Her joy was infectious. He grinned back at her and looked down at the baby again. "I like her name."

Sylvie looked away and flushed a little, and then she said, "Her name is Margot *Frances*. You see . . . I didn't think I could get away with Franklin, her being a girl, but I wanted to . . . I am grateful to you, Mr. Warren. I wanted to put your name—or part of your name—in there." She looked toward the hallway, where anyone could be listening. "Her name is Margot Frances because we owe our lives to you, Scott and I, and . . . and I wanted you to know."

Warren turned suddenly away because the baby's face and the name and her voice had cracked something open in him, and he felt tears rushing to his eyes, and he didn't want her to see. But then there was no way around it. After a moment, he turned and let the tears spill and he let her see and she smiled, and then he took a deep breath and gathered himself and said, "Well, she's beautiful, and I'm glad you're both well. I should let you get some more rest. Besides, there's a nurse who is looking for me. They won't let me go home until I eat something. Is there anything on the menu you recommend?"

Sylvie's face glowed as she looked down at the baby. "The cottage cheese isn't too bad," she said. "If you like pineapple, that is. Thank you, Mr. Warren."

"I don't think you should call me Mr. Warren," he said after a moment. "Everyone else calls me just Warren."

"But it's not your name," she said, raising her eyes to meet his. "I'll call you Franklin. But you have to call me Sylvie."

"Okay, Sylvie," he said.

"Goodbye, Franklin," she said. He waved goodbye at the door. The baby was sleeping. Sylvie smiled and waved back.

Once he'd eaten the cottage cheese and taken the extra bandages from the nurses, he stepped outside to wait for his ride. Plow trucks had cleared the parking lot, and he watched for the state police cruiser. Eventually it came, and as Tommy Johnson pulled up and parked and then jumped out to come around and open the door for Warren, he said, "Here he is, the hero detective. Well done, Frankie!"

Warren settled into the passenger seat. He didn't bother with the belt. Tommy got back in and pulled the car out, turning onto Main Street. "What a mess, huh?"

Warren looked at the winter wonderland outside the windows. "I like it," he said. "Snow always makes me feel like a little kid."

"I know what you mean," Tommy said. "When it's all clean and white like this, it's like a fresh start, in a way. I sometimes think the new year should start on the day after the first snow."

"You're right," Warren said. He laughed, surprising Tommy and himself. "You're absolutely right, Tommy. It really should." Tommy took it slow around the green, and Warren gazed out at the transformed world, every bit of it glittering in the afternoon sun.

Forty-three

Collers' Store was busy on Thursday morning, a week after Thanksgiving, and Jenny had to wait for nearly ten minutes with her bag of sugar and the applesauce that her father liked with his pork dinner. The pork dinner was going to be a surprise for him when he got home from the hardware store, and on Jenny's way downstairs to walk over to Collers', her mother had said, "Oh, and Jenny, get some sugar too. I'll make a cake!"

Jenny wasn't sure exactly what it was they were celebrating, but she had the feeling it had something to do with the murders at the Ridge Club. Jenny's mother had been quiet for most of the week since they'd gotten home, barely wanting to go out because she said everyone was going to ask about it and want to know if she'd suspected Earl and Belle. Jenny still didn't understand exactly why Belle had gone temporarily insane and killed Mr. Moulton. Her mother said that Belle had been angry about something Mr. Moulton had done and that it had been a kind of accident, her killing him, but then Earl had tried to cover it up because he wanted to protect Belle, and that's how Mr. Packingham got killed. Strangely, this explanation made sense to Jenny. She had seen Earl put his hand on Belle's back once when he was walking past her in the kitchen, just the tiniest, smallest little thing, and yet Jenny had been able to tell how much he loved her. And in the way she turned to smile at him, Jenny had been able to tell how much Belle loved him.

Her own parents weren't like that very often, but just last night, after her mother got off the phone with Mr. Warren, who had called to tell her that Earl and Belle were going to plead guilty so there wouldn't be a trial and he wouldn't need to talk to her and Jenny about it anymore, Jenny's mother got up and went over to Jenny's dad and sat right down in his lap, hugging him and leaning her head against his chest. He was surprised, but he let his newspaper drop and he put his arms around her, and Jenny went to find something in her room because it was nice, but it was also embarrassing, like she'd seen something she shouldn't have seen.

Jenny had the sense that there was something her mother wasn't telling her, and she knew it was probably about what she'd heard the men say, the gossip about her mother and Mr. Moulton. Jenny usually liked to know everything, but somehow she thought of the truth, whatever it was, about Mr. Moulton and her mother as a rotten potato. If she were to dig it up, it might ruin all the other ones. Better to leave it in the ground, she thought. Better to let it rot there.

"Hello, Jenny," Lizzie Coller said to her when it was Jenny's turn. "How are you feeling?" Lizzie, who was usually a bit short with everyone, actually looked at Jenny and seemed to be sincere in her inquiry. Jenny had noticed this over the past week. People were just more interested in her since the news had gotten out about her being in the basement when there was shooting going on and just before Walter broke down the door and saved everyone.

"I'm fine, thank you, Lizzie," Jenny said, putting her items on the counter. Jenny could feel that everyone in the store was listening and watching.

She was a celebrity, Jenny realized. She, Jenny Breedlove, was a celebrity.

Lizzie rang her up and Jenny was handing over the money when the bell on the door jingled and Jenny looked up to see Walter coming into the store. He didn't see her at first, and for just a moment, she watched him wave to someone at the back of the dairy section and smile at someone else, and she thought about what a nice person Walter was and how he always had a kind word for anyone who needed one.

And then he saw her. Jenny raised a hand and waved at him, conscious of the huge grin that seemed to be spreading across her face. "Here's your change," Lizzie said, but Jenny, flustered now, didn't put out her hand for it.

"Hi . . . uh, Jenny," Walter said, stammering a little and then putting his head down and suddenly walking quickly toward the back of the store. Jenny realized that Lizzie was still holding out the money, and she apologized and took it, and when Lizzie put the sugar and the applesauce in a bag and handed it over, Jenny started to say, "Thank you, Lizzie," and then suddenly, Walter was there, standing next to the counter and looking at Jenny.

"Walter?" she said.

"Jenny." He seemed to be somehow frozen, like he had gotten himself to the counter but he did not know what to do now. And so he said again, "Jenny."

"Yes?" Jenny said. She was conscious of Lizzie watching them and everyone else in the store watching too, though they were trying to pretend that they weren't. "Walter?"

And then she realized something. Walter, though he seemed to be quite nervous, wasn't blushing. In fact, he was quite pale, his usually ruddy face drained of its customary color.

"Would . . . would you like to see something at the Lyric on Saturday night?" he said in a strangely aggressive voice that confused her at first until she realized that he was gathering up his courage to say it, that he had to spit it out or he wasn't going to say it at all.

And for once, Jenny Breedlove did not know what to say. So she nodded and smiled, and that seemed to be enough for Walter because he said, "Good," and walked off, leaving Jenny staring at Lizzie Coller, who raised her eyebrows the tiniest bit, which for Lizzie was quite a lot, really.

Acknowledgments

I am incredibly grateful to the Vermont Digital Newspaper Project, the Vermont State Archives and Records Administration, the Vermont Department of Libraries, and the Vermont Historical Society for making archives of Vermont newspapers available to researchers. The Vermont Historical Society and Vermont Humanities provided many resources I have found invaluable in writing this novel.

Once again, I am indebted to the many people who shared with me stories of this period in Vermont and New England history. Keep them coming!

Big, huge thanks go to the whole team at Aevitas Creative Management and to everyone at Minotaur Books—I am so lucky to have you all behind me! Thank you to my editor, Kelley Ragland, and to Katie Holt, Sarah Melnyk, Allison Ziegler, Kristin Nappier, and David Rotstein. You are the best.

I want to send out a gigantic thank-you to the absolute heroes who own and staff the independent bookstores that have so championed this series. You do amazing work and the world wouldn't be the same without you!

To my author friends, thank you for cheering, commiserating, and writing amazing books! Thank you to Tessa Wegert, Carol Goodman, Sharon Short, Lucy Burdette, Hank Phillippi Ryan, Paul Doiron, my fellow national board members of Mystery Writers of America, and all my other writer friends who toured with me and provided community!

As always, I am overwhelmed by the love and support of my family and friends. Thank you to Sarah Piel and Douglas McAlinden for the cozy writing spot and for your friendship! Thanks to the best book group ever for everything. Thank you to Sue, David, Tom, Otis, and Edie Taylor, Vicki Kuskowski, and of course, to Matt, Judson, Abe, and Cora Dunne. I love you so much.

Finally, I am absolutely heartbroken at the loss of my beloved agent of seventeen years, Esmond Harmsworth. Esmond was brilliant, funny, kind, and an absolute original. He passed away after the completion of this novel but before its publication and his wise advice and feedback made it so much better. I will miss him so much and I am so grateful to him for all he did for me—and for his friendship. Thank you for everything, Esmond.

About the Author

Sarah Stewart Taylor is the author of the Sweeney St. George series, set in New England, the Maggie D'arcy mysteries, set in Ireland and on Long Island, and *Agony Hill,* the first in a new series set in rural Vermont in the 1960s. Taylor has been nominated for an Agatha Award and for the Dashiell Hammett Prize, and her mysteries have appeared on numerous Best of the Year lists. A former journalist and teacher, she writes and lives with her family on a farm in Vermont where they raise sheep and grow blueberries. You can visit her online at SarahStewartTaylor.com.